The Rise of Io

"It's like *Blade Runner* and *Men in Black* had a baby and took over the world."

Dan Wells, author of the Partials series and I am Not a Serial Killer

"With rich world-building, twisty politics and plot, plus some kickass leading ladies, *The Rise of Io* had everything I look for in sci-fi – and more. I loved this book!"

Susan Dennard, author of Truthwitch

"Wes Chu's meteoric rise to popularity isn't the least bit surprising. He's the freshest voice in science fiction since John Scalzi and James SA Corey, and is leading the charge to revitalize the genre."

Myke Cole, author of the Shadow Ops series

"Ella is a strong protagonist, scrappy & determined. You're going to love her!"

Laura Lam, author of False Hearts

"*The Rise of Io* is the perfect SF adventure! A scrappy young heroine, an alien civil war, and intrigue aplenty highlight this terrific beginning to Wesley Chu's epic new series. Fans of Pierce Brown's *Red Rising* take note… Ella is the new SF underdog to root for!"

Christopher Golden, New York Times bestselling author of Snowblind *and* Tin Men

"*The Rise of Io* is a great ride, and I desperately want a Quasing. The idea of a cosmic cheering section in my own head sounds delightful. Not to mention, my Quasing would make me totally boss. Anoth

Melinda S

ALSO BY WESLEY CHU

The Lives of Tao
The Deaths of Tao
The Rebirths of Tao
The Days of Tao (novella)

Time Salvager
Time Siege

WESLEY CHU

The Rise of Io

ANGRY ROBOT
An imprint of Watkins Media Ltd

Lace Market House,
54-56 High Pavement,
Nottingham,
NG1 1HW
UK

angryrobotbooks.com
twitter.com/angryrobotbooks
Io, let's go

An Angry Robot paperback original 2016
1

Copyright © Wesley Chu 2016

Wesley Chu asserts the moral right to be identified as the author of this work.

A catalogue record for this book is available from the British Library.

ISBN 978 0 85766 581 2
EBook ISBN 978 0 85766 583 6

Set in Meridien by Epub Services.
Printed and bound in the UK by 4edge Limited.

All rights reserved. No part of this publication may be reproduced, stored in a retrieval system, or transmitted, in any form or by any means, electronic, mechanical, photocopying, recording or otherwise, without the prior permission of the publishers.

This book is sold subject to the condition that it shall not, by way of trade or otherwise, be lent, re-sold, hired out or otherwise circulated without the publisher's prior consent in any form of binding or cover other than that in which it is published and without a similar condition including this condition being imposed on the subsequent purchaser.

This novel is entirely a work of fiction. The names, characters and incidents portrayed in it are the work of the author's imagination. Any resemblance to actual persons, living or dead, events or localities is entirely coincidental.

Angry Robot and the Angry Robot icon are registered trademarks of Watkins Media Ltd.

To Paula and Hunter

CHAPTER ONE
The Con Job

They call every major world war "the war to end all wars." The day we actually get a war that deserves the title is the day the world ends.

Baji, Prophus Keeper, two days before the Alien World War, the war that almost ended all wars

Ella Patel loved metal briefcases. When she was a little girl, her appa used to take her to the cinema, and anything that was shiny and expensive and worth stealing was always kept in metal briefcases. She had learned that obtaining these sleek, silver boxes was the key to success, riches and good-looking, tall Australian men with muscular arms and etched cheeks.

Today, Ella's dreams had come true. In bunches. The Australian men part was the notable exception.

Purple smoke drifted into the air out of the many cracks and rust holes of the Cage, a local bar welded together from twenty-three shipping containers stacked across three levels. The smoke was followed by a string of loud bangs from a fool blindly shooting his assault rifle in a small metal-enclosed room. The results weren't pretty. Dazed bar patrons, eyes burning and ears concussed, stumbled out, some rushing away while others collapsed onto the muddy ground, too disoriented to walk.

Ella, a generous head shorter than the shortest patron, hid herself within the crowd as it spilled into the streets. She wore a set of swimming goggles she had permanently borrowed from an unsuspecting tourist and lime earmuffs bartered for with a pack of cigarettes. In her hands, she half-dragged two metal briefcases, each nearly as heavy as she was.

She waddled down to the bottom of the ramp leading to the bar's entrance and dropped the briefcases. She raised the goggles to her forehead, hung the earmuffs around her neck, and looked back at the Cage. People were still streaming out, and she could hear curses coming from inside. Just for good measure, she took out another canister, pulled the pin, and lobbed it into the entrance. This time, the smoke was yellow. So pretty. Satisfied, she picked up the two briefcases, grimacing as she plodded down the busy street.

By now, she had revised her opinion of metal briefcases. Like that mythical fat man who was supposed to give her presents every year, this particular childhood fantasy fell far short of the painful reality. Metal briefcases sucked. They were big, unwieldy, and their sharp corners kept scraping against her legs.

Ella passed a vendor pushing a cart filled with scrap. The two made eye contact, just briefly, and then she continued waddling, one small step at a time, down the street. She was about to turn the corner when four men in military fatigues ran out of the Cage. One of them carried an assault rifle. He must have been the idiot who thought it was a good idea to open fire blind in a cramped smoke-filled room with metal walls.

They saw the big, shiny, sun-reflecting metal briefcases right away and gave chase. Just as they reached the bottom of the ramp, the vendor pushing the cart plowed into them, knocking all four into the mud. Ella suppressed a grin; she wasn't out of danger yet. She continued down the side street and made four more quick turns, moving deeper into the

Rubber Market near the center of the slum.

By now, word had spread that someone had discharged a gun. Several in the crowd eyed her as she passed, first staring at those blasted shiny briefcases, then at her. A few glanced at the commotion behind her. Violence was just an unwanted neighbor who always lingered close by. Most of the residents ignored the ruckus and continued their day.

Ella could hear the gangsters behind her, yelling at people to clear out of their way as they barreled through the streets like raging oxen. She looked back and saw the lead man waving his assault rifle in the air as if it were a magical stick that would part the people before them. She grinned; that was the exact thing not to do in Crate Town. The good inhabitants of this large slum on the far southwestern edge of Surat didn't take kindly to being bullied. In fact, she watched as the main street suddenly became more crowded as the people – vendors, children and passersby – all went out of their way to block these outsiders.

By all indications, Crate Town's name was as appropriate as it was appealing. Located at the front line between Pakistan and India during the Alien World War, it had grown from the shattered remnants of several broken countries' armies. Without governments to serve or enemies they cared to kill, and no means of returning home, the soldiers became more concerned with feeding their bellies and finding roofs over their heads than fighting. The thousands of cargo containers at the now-abandoned military port proved the perfect solution for their infrastructure woes.

Four years later, Crate Town was a blight of poverty on the western edge of India as the shattered country struggled to rebuild after a decade of devastation. Ella wouldn't have it any other way. She called this hellhole home, and she loved it.

She grinned from ear to ear as she turned another corner, confident that she had lost the gangsters. She carried the briefcases another three blocks and walked into Fab's Art Gallery, halfway down a narrow street on the border between the Rubber Market and Twine Alley.

Fab's Art Gallery was the only one of its kind in all of Crate Town. There wasn't much need for commercial art when most of the residents lived in poverty. The gallery was long and thin, with perhaps nine or ten hideous paintings. A person didn't have to be an art critic to think that the owner of this gallery had awful, awful taste. One of the pieces was actually painted by Fab's six year-old son. It showed three stick figure hunters throwing pink spears at a stick figure elephant or giraffe or something. Ella didn't have the heart to ask Tiny Fab what the creature actually was. Big Fab, the owner, likely wouldn't have been offended by this, because the whole hideous art gallery front was his idea.

Ella walked behind the counter in the gallery and dropped the briefcases onto the floor. She collapsed, huffing and puffing. A pair of eyes blinked through a beaded curtain off to the side, and she saw the ends of a machete poking through it slowly retract.

"Was it everything you hoped it would be?" the crackly voice asked from behind the curtain.

"These things suck," she snapped, kicking one of the briefcases. That was a bad idea, since hard steel easily beat toes in rubber sandals. "I was a stupid kid."

A yellow-stained smile appeared beneath the eyes, and the machete pointed at the back door. Ella picked herself up and grabbed several strips of sweet salmon, ignoring the blade shaking at her threateningly as she passed by the beaded curtain. She wolfed down the strips as she entered a narrow alleyway and turned toward home.

Those gangsters would need the gods' own luck to find her during early evening at the market in Crate Town. They might as well try to pick a kernel of rice from a pile of pebbles. All she had to do was wait out the day and keep an ear to the ground. Eventually, the foreigners would learn why the slum she called home was nicknamed the dirty black hole. Not only was it admittedly and almost proudly filthy, once you lost something in Crate Town, you weren't going to find it.

That included people.

Once the coast was clear, she would fence the goods she had conned from the Pakistani gangsters, and she'd be living good and easy for at least the next few months, if not the rest of the year. It all depended on how many people were going to get sick this season, but from what she could gather from Bogna the Polish midwife, it was a great market right now for those with medical supplies.

Whistling, Ella rounded the corner and cursed the gods, all three hundred and thirty million of them. There, standing just out of arm's reach, with their backs turned to her, were three of the gangsters, including the one with the rifle. She froze and slowly took a step back. And then another. One more step would have cleared her from the intersection, but today one of the three hundred and thirty million gods hadn't taken kindly to being cursed at.

Just as she was about to retreat around the corner, something hard bumped into her from behind and, with a loud squawk, she found herself flying headfirst into the middle of the intersection then face down halfway in the soft ground. Sputtering, she looked up out of the mud. All three gangsters were staring directly at her. She froze. With just a little luck, they wouldn't recognize her covered in all this grime.

"Is that the translator who just robbed us?" one of the big ugly guys asked.

So much for luck.

"Grab her!"

Ella slipped trying to get to her feet and one of the other gangsters, even bigger and uglier than the one who had spoken, got hold of her. Rough hands grabbed her by the shirt and easily picked up her scrawny body. Ella flailed in the air as the man squinted at her face.

He turned back to the others. "I think this is the right bit–"

One of the few advantages Ella had as a small girl was that no one ever thought her dangerous. That was a mistake. She grabbed a shank strapped to the back of her pants, and right as the uglier guy looked away, jammed it into his armpit. The man stiffened and looked down at her, and then both of them went crashing into the ground. Ella scrambled to her feet and ran for dear life.

There were several loud cracks and the ground nearby spit up mud in a straight line. She careened to the left and barged into a stall, and then bounced off it, overturning a passing wagon. She turned down a side street, then another, hoping to throw off her pursuers. Unfortunately, once they had caught sight of her, it was easy for the bigger men with their longer legs to stay on her tail.

Crate Town was Ella's home though, her playground. She knew all the nooks and crannies like she knew her knuckles. She veered onto a narrow path between two rows of tents facing outward and sprinted as hard as her short legs could drive her down the divide, hurdling over the crisscrossing tent lines as if she were in one of those track and field races. Behind her, the tents began to collapse one after another as the two gangsters giving chase uprooted the stakes tying the lines down. Eventually, one of the men tripped and fell in a heap of tangled rope.

That was Ella's cue. She cut to the right and made her way into a refuse dump at the end of an alley behind a warehouse. This wasn't her favorite part of the plan, but one that almost always succeeded in emergencies. She found a small opening in the garbage heap and burrowed until there was only a small gap, just large enough for her to see the evening sky. Ella pursed her lips so tight her teeth cut into her flesh, and then she listened, and waited, breathing as shallowly as she could, both to avoid moving the garbage and to avoid smelling it.

Footsteps grew louder and faded. Men shouted nearby, and then they too were gone. Far away, a foghorn from a ship docked at the port blew, and then nothing. Few people came by this part of Crate Town except to dump their garbage, and most did so early in the morning. Once she thought the coast was finally clear, she stretched her hand out of the heap until it touched the air, and began to claw her way to the surface.

Just as she was about to poke her head out, she heard footsteps again. This time, it sounded like an army, far too many for it to be those gangsters. Ella pulled her arm back into the trash heap and waited.

Two figures ran by. There was something strange about the way they were dressed, as if they had thrown on their clothes hastily in the wrong way. The first figure, a man, reached the end of the alley and beat a fist on the brick wall. He was covered with a long dark jacket that seemed far too warm for Crate Town's early summer weather. He went to the adjacent wall and tried the doorknob.

"It's locked." His eyes darted around the alley. "We're trapped."

He was speaking English, not like the mushy version she'd seen in American movies, but more like how Ella had learned the language when she first attended school in Singapore. Her knowledge of the language had come mostly from cinema though. The man turned to his companion, giving Ella a clear look at his face. He was a tall Caucasian with a receding hairline, high cheekbones, and a face so white, light seemed to reflect off it. His eyes were huge, but that seemed more from terror than genes.

The other figure, a woman by the looks of it, pulled back her headscarf, and a mass of long blonde hair fell out. A quick appraisal of the woman's plain but finely-woven dark anarkali salwar told Ella she was well off. There were easily a dozen items on her person that Ella could fence.

The woman scanned her surroundings and Ella saw the glint of something shiny appear in her hand. "I guess we do it my way after all," she said.

Ella immediately liked her. There was something about the way she composed herself. She held her hands in front of her and leaned in a way that suggested she were about to pounce on something, or someone. Her posture felt confident, intimidating.

Most of all, there was something attractive about her face. Ella couldn't stop staring at it. It wasn't really a pretty face or anything out of the ordinary; Ella had seen much better in the magazines. Nor was it scarred or ugly. It had no unique features. It was just how the woman wore it. There was something so determined and confident about her. It was the way she set her jaw and that aggressive, determined look in her eye.

New footsteps approached, and then Ella saw shadows, two hands' worth at least. They surrounded the man and woman. Someone barked out words. There were sounds of machetes sliding out of their scabbards, and then the night became silent as all the players in that small alleyway froze.

And then chaos erupted.

Ella pitied the two. Two versus what looked like eight was terribly unfair. In the slums, numbers were all that mattered in a fight. She kept her eyes trained on the woman as the group of dark figures converged.

The woman attacked, swinging what looked like a metal stick in her hand. Her movements were a blur as she danced through them, flashes of silver slicing the air in the dim light. There was a beautiful violence to her, lyrical, fluid, deadly. Every time it seemed the shadows were about to envelop her, she would dance to safety, leaving a trail of falling bodies in her wake.

Ella had never seen anything like that outside of the movies, and she knew those kinds of fights were fake. This, however, was the real thing. In Crate Town, men got their way by being the biggest, strongest or meanest. There were few women here who could stand up to them. Maybe Wiry Madras by way of sheer meanness, but few others. Most resorted to cunning, cajoling or subterfuge. But this woman – this woman was something else.

Ella was so mesmerized, she forgot to keep her lips squeezed together. Her jaw dropped, and she took in a mouthful of garbage. She gagged and spit, then went back to staring at the woman.

Every so often, a random blow or cut would nick her, and she'd retaliate. A few more blows began to wear the woman down. She slowed, and the enemy attacks got closer, and soon she was getting struck more and more.

Ella held her breath, badly wanting to do something, to help, to fight alongside her. However, living on the streets, she knew the rules of Crate Town. She should not get involved. To her left, she noticed the man pressed against the wall. He had a silver stick in his hand, but he didn't fight. He just stood there, frozen, wearing a look of indecisive panic on his face.

This guy was leaving her to fight all these thugs by herself. This hit Ella right in the gut. He should be doing something! It was so unfair. Being smaller and scrawnier than most kids, she had often been bullied as a little girl. A righteous rage twisted and burned inside her.

She looked back at the woman. By now, more than half of her attackers were lying unmoving on the ground. However, the remaining three or four were beating her up pretty badly. Her movements were no longer beautiful; she was staggering from each blow. One of the men took a bat and jammed it into her stomach, doubling her over. Another punched her in the face, and she crashed into the pile of garbage not far from where Ella was hiding. The woman's eyes were glazed over and unfocused. Yet she continued fighting, struggling to her feet.

One of the men approached from the side, wielding a stick with two hands, ready to bash in her head. Ella watched the end of the stick hover in the air, about to end the woman's life. She looked down at the woman's face, and saw the determination still around her cheeks and mouth, even as the life in her eyes faded. Ella noticed the trinket around her neck and the expensive-looking watch around her wrist.

Something in Ella snapped. In a split second, she calculated the possible reward to risk for doing something. The woman was wealthy and there were only a few of those men left. Ella bet there would be a massive reward for saving her life. That, and honestly, it felt like the right thing to do, since that ass of a friend of hers was just standing there letting her die.

Ella jumped out of the garbage heap, shank in hand, and stabbed the guy behind the knee. He screamed and toppled over, and then the woman finished him off with a knife that magically appeared in her hand. She struggled to her feet and limped toward the remaining three thugs. She glanced over at Ella once, and then, without a word, focused on her assailants.

The three attackers weren't taking Ella lightly. They were clearly puzzled by this scrawny little girl holding a bloody object in her hand, and they maneuvered accordingly, trying to stay in front of both Ella and the other woman.

The woman attacked, baton in one hand and knife in the other. She swung them in wide arcs, and the sounds of clashing metal hung in the evening air. She ducked under a swing and jammed the knife into the sternum of one of the attackers. Another thug got behind her and was about to strike when Ella jumped on his back and jammed her shank into the side of his neck.

The woman turned to face him just as blood spewed from his mouth. She shot a side kick to his chest that sent both him and Ella crashing to the ground. Ella just managed to jump clear and roll away to avoid getting crushed. The woman nodded at her and, for an instant, smiled.

"Look out!" Ella cried.

The woman stiffened as the point of a blade suddenly appeared through her abdomen. She lashed out in a circle with her baton and struck the side of her attacker's head. Both bodies crumpled to the ground. Ella was on the man in an instant, her shank stabbing him in the chest over and over. She didn't know how many times she thrust downward but when sanity returned, she realized that her hands were covered in blood, and his eyes were staring off into nothing.

Ella looked at her hands and fell onto her back. She had never killed anyone before. At least, none she was aware of. She had stabbed dozens of people in her short nineteen years. Most of them had even deserved it. It was one of the occupational hazards of living on the streets, but she had never actually stuck around long enough to see someone die from injuries she had inflicted. Until now.

The woman next to her coughed, and her labored breathing snapped Ella back from her daze. She crawled over to the woman and checked her wounds. There was blood everywhere, and Ella could sense her life slipping from her body with every second. Ella hovered over the woman, frantic. She looked up at the man, still frozen in place near the back wall.

"Help me!" she screamed. "Do something! Save her!" She picked up a rock as big as her fist and chucked it at him.

It brought him out of his stupor and he rushed over. He checked her wounds and paled. He turned to Ella. "Where's the nearest hospital?"

"There's no hospital in Crate Town."

The two of them tried to lift the woman but the instant they moved her, blood gushed from the wound in her stomach. Her eyes rolled back and she grasped the man's arm. "Make sure," she gasped. "The news... Seth... reaches..."

And then she was gone.

Ella had seen enough death in her life for it not to affect her any more. Growing up during a war and then in the slums, she had seen terrible things. People beaten and robbed, their bodies left on the streets. The ravages of sickness and famine and starvation.

But for this death, Ella felt a terrible sadness. The feeling aggravated her. She lashed out at the closest person. She stood up and scowled at the man. "I saw you stand there doing nothing. Coward!" She was about to give him a swift kick to vent her frustration when she stopped.

The woman was glowing. A strange fog with sparkling lights was slinking out of her body until it formed a cloud hovering in the air. The tiny lights, thousands of them, blinked as if alive. The cloud began to float toward the man. And then it stopped, and then it moved toward Ella.

Ella yelped and retreated, taking several steps backward and tripping over one of the bodies. She fell onto her butt and began to crawl on all fours, trying to get away from this weird, supernatural demon stalking her.

The light floated directly above her and hovered. At first, Ella shielded her face, but then she peeked. First, one eye between her fingers, then both. Up close, the cloud with its thousands of swirling lights was beautiful. If this was a demon, it was an awfully pretty one. She reached an arm out toward it.

"You want her to be your host? You can't be serious," the man said. "You, get away from the Quasing."

Quasing? Ella had heard that name mentioned before in passing every once in a while. They had something to do with the war that had raged across the world for most of the past ten years. Is this what everyone was fighting over?

"She doesn't deserve you."

Ella had no idea who the man was talking to. However, being told she didn't deserve something grated on her. She had already experienced a lifetime of ridicule, of being denied and demeaned. She didn't need this feeble man to pile onto it.

"Shut it, coward," she snapped.

She reached for the living cloud, and then tiny bursts of light moved directly into her. Ella felt a jolt and a hard jab in the back of her skull. Her entire body clenched. She thought she heard a strange gravelly voice in her head that definitely wasn't her own.

This is probably a mistake.

Blinding pain punched her in the brain and Ella felt her stomach crawl up her throat. She opened her mouth to scream, but all that came out were the regurgitated chewed up strips of sweet salmon. The last thing Ella felt was the sensation of flying, or falling, or the world being pulled from beneath her feet as she hit the ground.

CHAPTER TWO
Ella Patel

Ella woke up to a blinding headache, like someone had driven an ice pick into her skull. She groaned and opened her eyes to hazy blobs melting into each other. A piercing yellow light in the distance poked at her brain, and a strange fleshy object hovered uncomfortably close to her face. Something muffled was rustling off to the side, and in the distance, she heard a low ringing, as if someone was banging a gong.

Slowly, her vision cleared, and the mushy blobs unmelted from each other and took form. The fuzzy object to her right came into focus as it coalesced into the face of the coward hovering over her. He was looking off to the side, talking to himself.

Slowly, the words became coherent. "…obtaining supplies and logistic support since we're off-book, and especially with our low clearance. As for our current bind, I'll see what I can do about locating a nearby training facility, although who knows, maybe she'll jump at the chance to escape her current predicament. That would be best. Just in case, though, I'll run a search…"

Ella did the first thing any woman who lived in the slum would do in this situation. She threw a left cross and smashed the man in the face. The blow snapped Coward's head back and he fell onto the floor. Ella jumped to her feet a little quicker than she probably should have, and the room swayed. She found herself standing on a bed wearing only her underwear. Coward groaned as his hands massaged the nose she had just broken.

She saw her ragged and dirty clothes folded neatly on a dresser, grabbed them, and hastily threw them on. She eyed the door and then looked down at Coward. She'd have to pass him in order to escape. She clenched her teeth and made a break for it. He sat up and tried to block her exit, and she rewarded him with a kick that hopefully broke his nose even more.

"Get away from me, you pervert," she screamed, making a mad dash for the door.

"Wait," he said, reaching out and catching her ankle.

She kicked out over and over until he let go, and then she fled the bedroom. She ran down a narrow hallway and stopped in an open area overlooking an upstairs landing. Where was the door? How did you get out of this place? She paused. This was a really nice apartment.

Relax. Calm down, and take a breath.

What was that raspy weird voice? Who was that? Probably just her brain trying to keep her from hyperventilating. Thinking about breathing made her breathe even faster, and she frantically looked for a way out. She found a spiral staircase in the corner of the landing and took it downstairs. She ran down another hallway and swung open a door at the far end, only to walk out onto a balcony thirty stories up in the air. Cursing, she ran back down the hallway and came face-to-face with Coward in what she could only assume was his living room.

He held a hand out cautiously. "You need to calm down."

Why was everyone telling her to calm down? That was the wrong thing to say to her, or to any woman for that matter. Ella tried to run past him and he shuffled to the side and blocked her escape. She tried to go left, and he shifted to block her again.

"Seems you didn't learn your lesson the first time," she growled, and threw a punch at his face.

To her surprise, she hit air. Ella tried to punch, kick, claw, and anything else she could muster, but Coward, now ready for her onslaught, was able to block or dodge all of her attacks, and with relative ease, it seemed. Finally, he caught her wrist in one hand, and held tight.

"You're going to hurt yourself," he said, and then swung around and put her in a headlock. "If you just calm down for a second, I can explain everything."

Ella stomped down with her heel on his feet several times and then elbowed him in the stomach. He loosened his grip on her just enough that she turned around and struck him open-palm on his already busted-up nose. She hit him square in the face and he stumbled backward.

"Let me go!" she yelled.

"Can you just calm down for a second?"

Listen to him. Take a deep breath.

There it was again. Roaring, Ella charged, flailing her arms and trying to overwhelm Coward with sheer aggression. She failed. Coward knocked her to the ground with a well-timed shove. Ella landed and skidded to a stop against the wall. She picked herself off the ground, rubbing her bruised butt. Coward wasn't just some guy off the streets. He obviously had some sort of training. If that was the case, why hadn't he helped the woman? Why had he just stood there like a relatively large shit and forced her to fight all those thugs by herself? The memory of the fight set Ella off again.

"You're starting to annoy me," he growled. "If you just give me a chance to explain…"

She scowled, grabbed a book off the dining table, and chucked it at Coward. He knocked it out of the air. She grabbed a cup, and threw that. He dodged. Ella began hurling everything within arm's reach. Coward continued to dodge and block until a glass ashtray smacked him square in the eye.

He dropped like a sack. Ella grabbed a lamp and, wielding it like a club, ran over to finish him off.

Stop!

Ella was in mid-swing when the loud word in her head startled her. She let go of the lamp and it went careening through the air. It hit the kitchen counter and shattered. Ella glanced at Coward, then scanned the room. There was no one else here. She looked in the mirror and stared at her own reflection. She looked perfectly sane; at least, she thought she did.

Coward raised his head off the floor.

"You stay put!" she hissed, shaking her fist. "In fact, if I ever see you again, I'm going to cut off your balls." She made a motion of stomping down on him, and he cringed.

Ella fled wherever this was, but not before robbing the place, swiping several trinkets and a bag of snacks off the counter. Finally locating the door, she left the apartment and took the stairs, not having trusted elevators since once being trapped in one for nine hours. Of course, she had never been on a floor in a building this high off the ground. After twenty flights, she was starting to rethink her hatred for elevators. By the time she reached ground level, her legs felt like rubber.

She exited the building and furrowed her brow at the stoplights hanging in the air above the nearest intersection. Where had Coward taken her? Crate Town didn't have stoplights at intersections, or tall buildings, for that matter. It took her a few minutes of sleuthing to realize she was near downtown Surat, a good distance from home. A taxi was too expensive, and the thought of spending money on a bus or a tuk-tuk aggravated her. She patted her pants and realized that neither of them were options anyway. She didn't have enough coins for the bus fare, let alone a tuk-tuk. That left walking or hitching a ride in the back of a truck heading in the general direction of Crate Town.

Ella scowled. Night had fallen, and most of the streets

would be unlit, which was dangerous for someone who didn't know the area. There was not much she could do now except start walking. It took over an hour on foot, and she cursed Coward with each step.

Luckily, she wasn't harassed too much. Some guys had ideas when it came to lone women walking the streets late at night. She received a couple of catcalls, and a few propositions from those who thought she could be had for cheap. Nothing she wasn't used to. One rancid man living on the street grabbed at her as she passed. Ella had reached for her shank only to realize she no longer had it. Lucky for him, she guessed.

It was well into the night by the time she finally reached her container cluster. Home was a top floor double-container of a five-stack. She had purchased the first container from Old Nagu, her next door neighbor, after two hard years of scrounging and living on the streets. She had earned the second after spending the last two years of Nagu's life stealing medicine for him. He died anyway, but on his death bed, he gave his container to her instead of to his son.

The son, a businessman who didn't even live in Crate Town and only visited his father twice a year, objected. In fact, the man said that since Nagu never signed over the deeds to either property, he technically owned both and tried to evict her. She sent him on his way with a ruined shirt, a pint less blood and the need to see a doctor to get his leg stitched up.

Ella's footsteps clanged against the rusty catwalk stairs attached to the side of the cluster. The sound was soon joined by a low husky barking, and the two sounds alternated in the night. "Hello, Burglar Alarm," she chirped, as the dog met her at the top of the stairs. The stray bitch lived at the side of the catwalk near the end of the stairway around the corner from her container. She had lived there ever since Ella first moved in. Ella would feel like something was wrong if she didn't hear the ugly mutt's greeting every time she came home.

"That's far enough," she said, as the dog followed her to her container. Their relationship only went so far. Burglar Alarm probably had more fleas than the kindergarten down the street. Ella dug a scrap of food she had stolen from Coward and tossed it into the dog's nest. The mangy black-and-brown mutt scarfed it down and wagged her tail. Ella tossed her another piece, then went inside.

She closed her front door with a hollow *thunk* followed by the lighter-sounding click of the lock. She took a deep breath, and slowly let the air leave her weary body. It had been a much longer day than she had anticipated, and she couldn't wait to go to bed.

First though, she scanned the inside of her home. Everything seemed in place, nothing was moved or stolen. She had forgotten to lock her door one morning, and some drunk had tried to rob her. The guy had broken into her container and made a mess of the place. Fortunately, Burglar Alarm prevented him from leaving, trapping the man inside. Unfortunately, that meant there was someone trying to club her over the head when she came home. Luckily, drunks weren't too quick or accurate, and she had sent him off tumbling down the stairs.

She had wondered why the dog was acting so crazy when she returned. Now, Ella always took Burglar Alarm's warnings seriously, and she checked every nook and cranny every time she returned to the container.

Ella's two containers were welded together and connected by an opening in the middle. Ella had to hire welders to cut that for her after she took possession of the container from Old Nagu. The left side was the living room and kitchen, containing a lumpy sofa, a cardboard box, a small television, a portable burner and a mini-fridge.

The other room was her bedroom. It was smaller, since she had converted the last fifth of the container into a hidden room behind the closet that held her valuables. It was also a place to hide if things got rough. She had learned her lesson after she had scared off the drunk and found almost everything she owned that was worth selling stuffed into a pillowcase.

Thank goodness for Burglar Alarm and her ugly face and that mean-sounding bark.

After Ella did a pass of her rooms and double-checked the locks, she took off her clothes and tossed them into a basket. They would need washing soon. There was some blood on them. She wasn't sure if it was hers or belonged to one of the several men she had scuffled with tonight. Bodily fluids were where she drew the line when it came to laundry. Besides, she had hidden in a pile of garbage.

Ella frowned. For the first time, she noticed a bandage on her side. She touched it gingerly and grimaced. That stung. She looked in her cracked mirror and raised an arm. Her fingers pawed at the edge of the wrap and she peeled it back. There was a long red gash held together by some sort of glue. Whoever patched her up had done a neat job. It was probably Coward. She grudgingly felt bad for beating him up.

Oh well, she would apologize next time she saw him. No wait, she had promised to cut off his balls. If Ella had one weakness, it was keeping her word. That was one of the reasons she was so popular in Crate Town. It was an oxymoron, but she was one of the few con artists the people here trusted.

Then again, no one said she couldn't cut off his balls *and* apologize.

Ella twisted her waist to make sure she wasn't going to bleed out while she slept, and then, satisfied and impressed at Coward's medical skills, slumped to her bed to finally get some sleep.

CHAPTER THREE
Io

Io was second-guessing herself right about now. That in itself wasn't an unusual occurrence, any more so than the need to transfer to a new host. Io had needed to make the move often over the centuries. Her transfer rate was higher than the average Quasing's, but that was more a product of the dangers of this day and age than of her inability to keep her humans alive.

At least that's what she told herself.

No matter the frequency, Io had made a judgment call tonight that was either going to allow her carefully-laid plans to come to fruition, or set her back a few years. But she didn't have much of a choice. Joining with Hamilton was not an option. He would have definitely wanted to abort and leave India on the first plane out, and that was something Io could not allow. That and the fact that Emily's auxiliary had proven to be disappointingly unreliable on his first mission. So much for high test scores at Prophus Training Academy in Sydney. The truth comes out when people start playing with live bullets.

Io checked the girl's state. She could already tell her new host was a light sleeper, which meant Io would have to be more delicate than usual. She waited half an hour more until Ella's breathing slowed and her consciousness moved into a deeper stage of sleep before taking control and sitting her up.

This human was so small, so light, so frail. Her limbs were like twigs. The girl had suffered dozens of small injuries and broken bones over her years of living on the streets. Many of them hadn't mended quite right. Fortunately, there was no major damage, although her nose really should be reset, with the way it obstructed her breathing.

Io took a step and stumbled, nearly tipping the girl forward onto her face. Controlling the body of an unconscious human was difficult, and Io was poorer than most Quasing when it came to this skill. She took baby steps and moved the body past the beaded curtain out into the next room.

Io found the girl's phone and unplugged it from its charger attached to a solar battery. After rummaging through Ella's memory for a few minutes, she was able to locate the passcode. She checked the contacts. Everything was coded. Clever, cautious girl.

Io dialed a number.

"Twenty-four hour wake-up service. We wake up to wake you up. Can I help you?"

"Identification Io."

"Voice recognition does not match Emily Curran."

Io pursed her lips. The six years they had spent together had been contentious, but also far too short. Emily deserved better, and Io owed it to Colin, Emily's father and Io's previous host, to have given her better. What had happened was unfortunate. However, Io had played this particular game long enough. It was time for something different.

"Host has passed."

"Base Binary code required."

"Binary code one, one, one, zero, one, zero, zero, one, zero, zero, one, zero."

Silence.

"Analyst Wyatt Smith here. You're off-book in India, Io. What the hell are you doing there?"

Io pulled the phone away from her ear and stared at the screen. Analyst? What the hell indeed. She put the phone back to her ear. "Excuse me, Analyst Wyatt Smith, there has been a host transfer. Why am I speaking to you and not to the Keeper?"

"New protocol," Wyatt replied. "Keeper is too busy these days to deal with every single host transition. Now, all lower-tier hosts and Quasing go through the call center."

Lower-tier.

Io wanted to tell Analyst Wyatt Smith exactly what she thought of him, his stupid call center, and being considered lower-tier. No matter what, she was a Quasing and she outranked all the humans who worked for the Prophus. She didn't outrank any other Quasing – well, a few, maybe – but she didn't have to take this insolence from a human.

"I demand to speak with the Keeper."

"Sorry, Io," said Wyatt. "Just following orders. You can talk to me now or call back later and talk to someone else. It makes no difference to me."

Io swallowed her pride and began to dictate her report. "Previous host Emily Curran expired during an ambush by Genjix agents. New host is named Ella Patel: 54 kilograms, height 1.65 meters, black hair just above the shoulders, light-skinned, of Eastern Asian and Indian descent. No distinguishable markings except for a rash on her upper back and right cheek."

"Medical issue?"

"Worse," Io sighed. "More like puberty."

"Can you confirm those measurements again?" Wyatt asked. "They all seem a little light."

Io looked into the cracked mirror in the living room, and raised one of the host's spindly arms. "Confirmed."

"Is there another identification regarding your new host, a UIDAI number or something?"

Io looked around and saw a wallet lying on the table next

to the stove. She checked the contents. There was nothing inside except for a few punch cards from restaurants, a train pass, and illiterate scribbles on scraps of paper. She found a crumpled state card in the back and recited the information.

"Stand by." After a brief pause, Wyatt began to tell Io everything about her new host. "Ella Patel, age nineteen, carrying dual Indian and Singaporean citizenship. Nice little arrest record she has there. All relatively minor crimes. Nothing to worry about.

"No education past primary school. Current residence: unknown. Mother, Ada Patel, formerly Ada Siong, Major in the Republic of Singapore Air Force, based at Vadsar Air Base, now deceased. Died operating for the South Asian Mutual Defense Coalition during the Genjix Third Wave blitzkrieg from Pakistan in the first year of the war." Wyatt paused. "At least Mom fought for our side. Hooray." It was a very lukewarm cheer.

"And the father?"

"Anu Patel. Formerly a havildar with the Indian Army. Went missing after the fall of Gujurat. Current occupation: unknown. Current residence: unknown. Last known residence: Dharavi Slums, Mumbai."

Io continued to listen a while longer. These were all things she could scrape from Ella's mind in time. Obtaining this information from the Prophus's database was much easier than probing the girl's brain, though. She would have had to update Command sooner or later anyway. None of it was going to matter in a while. None of it mattered now.

"All her relevant information is now scrubbed," Wyatt said cheerfully. "Her records – including her extensive criminal one – have been purged; her identifications, fingerprints, and visual markers have been removed; and she now even has a great credit score. She is a complete ghost in the world systems, save for our records within the Prophus Command repository. Congratulations, Io, you are now the proud owner of a tiny teenage delinquent. Put her to good use against the Genjix, or, at the very least, steal their stuff."

"Thank you, Analyst," Io said. "The new host will require training. What resources do we have in the vicinity?" Io doubted the girl's chances at a long life; not that it mattered, but she might as well go through the motions of a transition, lest she arouse any suspicion.

"You're on your own in that region. The Prophus were pushed out of India during the war. Truthfully, we never had a strong presence there to begin with."

Humanity had only discovered the Quasing's existence a quarter century ago with the invention of the Penetra scanners – the devices that could detect Quasing residing within hosts. It had been the turning point for their kind, and forever transformed their relationship with this planet's residents. For eons, the Quasing had manipulated the living things on Earth to further their goal of returning home: first the dinosaurs, and then the mammals, and finally the humans. They, however, always did so from the shadows. The veil had been lifted, and they became hunted by the very creatures they used to control.

The countries of the world eventually allied with either Prophus or Genjix factions. Hundreds of covert conflicts, coups, political manipulations, and one world war later, the two sides had settled into a cold war of sorts with both sides maneuvering in the shadows to gain the advantage over the other. All of this mattered absolutely not at all to Io right now, since the Prophus had no resources on the ground while she was here with a new untrained host.

"Wait." Wyatt interrupted her thoughts. "I have something that may or may not be useful. There's a retired combat operative living in your area. He used to be part of the Prophus Underground Railroad smuggling hosts from Russian to Australia. He also ran a training facility and safe house during the war. He's still drawing a stipend, so give it a shot."

Io grimaced. "That's it? No access to cash, weapons, logistical or support personnel?"

"Sorry," Wyatt said, not sounding sorry at all. "We have operated there occasionally, but to be honest, that region is a bit of a wasteland and has been tipping toward the Genjix for years. There are no priority targets, facilities, or resources. Speaking of which, why was Agent Emily Curran there at all? She's supposed to be in Chiang Mai overseeing the northern DMZ. And what about that possible Genjix site she found?"

Io ignored that line of inquiry. There were things she wasn't ready to explain yet, or ever. The longer she kept her plans secret, the more easily the pieces would fall into place. "I am going to make first contact with the host soon. I am not sure how long it will take before I can be up and running again."

"Wait, do you have possession of Agent Curran's body–"

Io hung up the phone. Hopefully, Hamilton took care of Emily's body. It was the least the Prophus could do for her family. Io looked in the mirror and stared at her new home for the foreseeable future.

She shrugged. Shit happens. It was time to get to work.

CHAPTER FOUR
The Assassin

The young sheik was an ass. A rich ass, sure, but an ass nevertheless. Shura noticed the way he undressed her with his stare and whispered to his bodyguard. She kept her eyes focused on the floor, submissive, tamed, innocent. She crossed the main floor walking perpendicular to the prince, making sure he could see her figure, the curves of her body showing through her tight dress.

It was conservative and not at the same time. It was lavender, and covered all of her body to the top of her neck. Her sleeves and gloves exposed no flesh, nor did the rest of the tapered dress that fell to her ankles.

Shura's blonde hair was pulled to one side. She was stylish yet demure, innocent yet curious. Her makeup and the long, reflective silver earrings she wore made her face glow in the light, and seemed to illuminate the room as she passed. That was a welcome byproduct of the special electrified polymer that helped mask what she really was. Advancements in Quasing detection prevention had improved by leaps and bounds during the war.

She still had to be careful. The polymer technology in her dress made her undetectable even if she was touched, but close contact from another vessel to her face would give her away. However, if it ever came to that, she should already be near enough.

Stop now.

Shura paused mid-step, looked back to where she had come from and scanned the room. Her eyes hesitated, just briefly, when she saw him, and a nearly undetectable smile appeared on her face. It was gone just as quickly as it came, and she continued searching the room for some imaginary friend.

The hook is in. Make yourself scarce.

The prince no longer bothered hiding his stare. Shura turned her back to him, and gave him a full view of what he wanted, or desired, and then she walked off, out of his view, away from the rest of the room that he fully controlled. This was what men like him did. This was why they sat on elevated platforms and balconies. These little men and their tiny kingdoms.

She stayed out of his way for the rest of the party, only making brief entrances into the prince's line of sight. Each time they were in the same room, she made a point of not looking at him, except for the briefest of moments, and always with an ever-so-slight nervous smile, and then she was busy meeting someone else.

The rest was predictable.

Near the end of the party, while chatting with a businessman from Frankfurt, Shura noticed two of the prince's bodyguards move in from either side. She ignored them even as the businessman became nervous at the sudden proximity of armed men in suits. She kept her eyes on the businessman as he excused himself and beat a hasty retreat.

Shura turned and came face-to-face with the prince. She gave him a slight bow. "Your Royal Highness."

"Thank you for attending my gathering." He reached for her hand and kissed her glove.

I feel nothing.

That means the prince felt nothing. Shura smiled. "Your home is beautiful, and congratulations again on your return.

Your presence has been missed in the city."

"I fear you have me at a disadvantage."

No, she didn't. No one within a hundred meters of someone in the royal family would have him at a disadvantage.

"Dominika Yumashev." She recited a version of her credentials in a way that reflected familiarity and then proceeded to probe him with the questions that swayed their conversation toward his interests. The sheik might be rich, and he might be guided by an infinitely wise eternal being, but he was still a young man.

Nicely done. I counted two personal bodyguards and eight more on the grounds.

"Confirmed, Tabs. This job will be easier than anticipated."

Shura suffered through the pretense of being charmed. He wasn't bad looking, and he was smooth. In another time, with his wealth and influence, she would consider him a possible ally, or even a consort. But it was too late now. Sides had been chosen. Destinies had been made, and all that nonsense.

As with many parties thrown by the royal family, the party grew larger the higher the moon climbed across the night sky. A few dozen guests had mushroomed into a few hundred. Eventually, this forced the two of them to seek a quieter place to continue their conversation.

Shura let him lead her upstairs, past his security perimeter at the party, into a private living area adjacent to his bedroom. She noted the two bodyguards trailing several paces behind. To her right was a set of double-doors opening to a balcony. To her left, an immaculately clean fireplace, unsurprising considering the heat in this region. Cords of wood were stacked off to the side. A leather couch faced the fireplace in the center of the room.

His Highness had good taste, at least. Shura made a slow circle around the room, pretending to admire the paintings and sculptures. The sheik went straight to the table next to the sofa and slipped off his blazer. He hung his jacket on the chair and undid his cuff links. Shura stopped at the liquor cabinet and examined each bottle, settling for an Alize, waving it above her head merrily. "Let's have a good time."

Rein it in a little. Your drama coach would be ashamed.

The sheik moved around to the couch and patted the seat next to him. "Come join me, my dear."

Shura pointed at the fireplace. "Can you light it? I find fires relaxing. It reminds me of winters at home."

The sheik waved a finger, and one of his bodyguards threw some cords into the fireplace. A few moments later, Shura could hear the crackle of wood and the heat of the flames on her back. She turned from the Chagall she was admiring and sauntered toward the sheik.

Shura stopped at the edge of the couch and slipped off her heels. She took her time taking off her long silver earrings and placed them on the sofa table. She shook her head and then sat down on the opposite end of the couch. "I'm glad to take those off. Now I feel relaxed. Why are you so far away?"

The sheik slid next to her. "I have been anticipating this all night."

She cupped his cheeks with her gloved hands. His face was flushed, and his breath smelled of mint and tobacco. He leaned in to kiss her. She met him halfway. Their lips touched.

The sheik's eyes widened.

Shura grabbed a fistful of hair on the back of his head with her right hand and yanked him off to the side, sending him tumbling to the floor. With her left, she grabbed one of the silver earrings on the sofa table and flung it across the room, striking a bodyguard standing at the door in the eye. He screamed as he pawed his face and fell to his knees.

The second earring streaked closely behind the first. The other guard managed to duck just in time, and the sharp point of the needle stuck into the wall. Shura leaped from the couch, jumping over the sheik, and closed the distance between her and the guard.

She trapped his wrist to his body as he drew his pistol. Shura's fingers contorted into claws and she jammed her hand into his throat. She squeezed, cutting through flesh and muscle until she felt his windpipe, and then she twisted her arm.

Shura had already forgotten him by the time his body hit the floor. She turned toward the sheik. The man, paralyzed with shock or fear, unused to violence, simply stared as she stalked him.

"Your Royal Highness Sheik Ahmed Al Nahyan of Abu Dhabi, sixteenth in line for the crown," she said, slinking forward with measured steps. "And hello to you as well, Khat."

Ahmed charged her. Shura barely had to shift her weight to trip him. He fell roughly, his back striking the marble corner of the fireplace. He groaned and writhed as she circled his body.

"Wha- Wha…" he stammered, as he tried to kick at her.

She shook her head. "Throughout the entire war, the emirates have stayed mostly on the sidelines, disdaining both Prophus and Genjix, and making it illegal to even become a vessel for a Quasing. The Genjix allowed you this neutrality out of respect."

Ahmed scrambled to his feet and tried to flee the room. Shura stepped on his ankle, and pressed down. He kicked at her with his other foot, but she applied harder pressure, until the ankle snapped. He screamed. She stepped forward and came down with her foot on his other knee. She pressed again, grinding her heel until the bones in his knee cracked as well. He tried to scream, and she stepped forward once more, kicking him in the mouth.

She knelt down next to his face and brushed the hair from his forehead. "So why, Your Highness, did you choose to become a vessel for the betrayers? What did the Prophus and their human friends offer you?"

"Please." The words came out of his mouth all mushed together. "This is all a misunderstanding, an accident."

"I don't believe so. Most of the emirates have strictly enforced Quasing detection. Penetra scanners dot every airport and road in and out of Abu Dhabi, and every royal palace. However, you made sure to have all yours disabled before your recent trip to Belgium." She leaned in and cupped his chin with her hand. "Is being a vessel everything you hoped it would be?"

You are wasting time. Finish this.

"Yes, Tabs."

"You can't kill me," the sheik whined. "My family will not allow it. You will be giftwrapping all of the emirates to the Prophus if my blood is on your hands."

Shura smiled. "I don't think so. You are far down the line of succession, low enough that you have little to lose and much to gain. Is that why you risked having a Quasing? Were you hoping to forge an alliance that raised your standing? Did the Prophus promise you the crown one day?"

Realization came to Ahmed, and the terror that was painted on his face melted away. He actually chuckled. "Is that what you think, you bitch? No, I don't want the crown. Being the king is a burden. I did it because it was the right thing to do, because I want my nephews and nieces to have a future. I want this planet to survive. Because…"

"Bitch? That's misogynist." Shura snapped his neck.

About time. I thought he would never shut up.

Shura leaned into the fireplace and grabbed a piece of burning wood. She walked over to the bottle of expensive vodka, flicked the top off with one hand, and took a large swig. She came back to Ahmed's body just as a cloud filled with hundreds of sparkling lights rose from the corpse.

Shura held the burning cord in front of her and spit the alcohol out of her mouth, spewing a jet of flames. Khat tried to avoid the fire, but the slow-moving Quasing was quickly engulfed. Shura took another swig and repeated the process several more times, until the last of the lights that was once a Holy One was gone.

Until the Eternal Sea.

"Until the Eternal Sea," she murmured. "Forty-seven and counting."

Indeed.

Shura could still hear the revelry downstairs and the house-shaking rumbles of the electronic music. She looked at the three dead bodies in the room and shook her head. She had predicted more of a challenge. It was far too easy to kill royals. Not like the old days.

Do not be too proud of this accomplishment. Back in the old days, they didn't have succession lists this long. Seems everyone is in line for a crown these days. However, an alliance between the Prophus and the emirates would have been problematic. Your standing has been raised.

Shura listened at the front door, and then walked out onto the balcony. She was five stories up with a hundred and fifty meter courtyard to the outer perimeter where a four meter wall with spikes on top awaited her. She scanned the grounds below and saw at least a dozen guards with dogs on patrol.

She reached down to the hem of her dress and began to unravel it. Within seconds, she had enough of the specialized rope to tie onto the balcony railing and rappel down.

Wait for the man with that dog to turn the corner. There will be a group of two guards following in forty-five second intervals.

Shura mapped out her escape and waited, watching as the man and the canine disappeared around the corner. She would much rather face two armed guards than a dog. She loved animals.

Now.

Shura leaped over the side and swung down, letting the rope slip loosely in her hands as she descended. Only when she neared the ground did she tighten her gloved hands around the rope to slow her fall. She landed in mid-step and sprinted barefoot to the wall.

Two man patrol on your left.

Instead of trying to avoid the men crossing her path, Shura charged them. No need to be target practice, after all. She stayed low and out of their line of sight, keeping a row of shrubs between her and them as she closed the distance. Once she was nearly within melee range, she leaped on top of one before he realized what hit him. A downward strike knocked the submachine gun out of his hands, and then she grabbed the barrel and pulled at an angle. The strap around his shoulder twisted and tightened against his neck and armpit, trapping his head and shoulder together. Shura held on to the carbine and lurched the man off his feet as she swung around and went low at the second guard. Her right heel swung in a wide arc and cracked the side of his knee, and, before his body hit the ground, a downward chop collapsed his trachea. He gurgled hoarsely for a few seconds before going limp.

Shura turned to the first guard, still pawing at the strap digging into his flesh. She tilted her head and studied his purple face, her hands turning the rifle in a slow circle, squeezing his upper body just a little more with each twist.

Stop playing around and finish him.

Shura placed her bare feet on the side of his neck and jerked the rifle upward.

Another patrol coming forty meters off. Avoid this one.

She took off again, dashing from cover to cover. Shura reached the stone wall and crept along its edge toward the gatehouse. She stayed in the shadows and counted. One guard house, two men, one canine, and two alternating cameras on each side. A half-moon of spikes on the gate decorated the four meter high fence.

This one was going to be tricky. She could take the guard standing outside easily enough, but would be hard pressed to kill the one in the guard house before he pulled the alarm.

With two cameras, each panning at different intervals, staying out of sight would be difficult as well. There was also the matter of the dog.

Take out the one in the guard house first. Shoot the one on the road. Open the gates. It is the most direct way.

"No, Tabs. That still leaves the dog and puts me in direct view of at least one camera."

Just kill the dog and shoot out the cameras. Be quick about it. It will catch your scent soon.

Shura bristled. That German Shepherd was a beautiful animal. She inched forward, her eyes tracking the near camera at the top corner of the gate. The guard with the dog had just turned and was pacing away. The near camera panned to the left, and began to return on its arc.

Shura took off, angling away from the wall and then veering back toward the gate. Her bare feet touched the hard iron bar, and she swung her body upward. She ran up the gate with her feet and reached to palm the camera. With a simultaneous push and pull of her body against different parts of the gate, she swung just over the iron spikes and was off, sprinting into the black night before any of those souls were any the wiser.

Shura had reached the end of the street and turned the corner before the sounds of the dog barking broke the otherwise quiet night.

CHAPTER FIVE
A Day in the Life

Ella woke up late the next morning, feeling drained, exhausted, and with a dull pain throbbing all over her body. She glanced up at the container ceiling. Light poked through the small holes, just enough for her to see her bedroom.

She vaguely recalled having the weirdest dream. She remembered the con job with the briefcases and hiding in the trash heap, and then there was that woman and the sparkling lights. Was that real? She remembered the fight, uncharacteristically jumping out and stabbing one of the men.

"What got into you, girl?" she muttered.

How many people did she stab yesterday, anyway? It felt like a lot, at least more than average. More than enough to fill her stabbing quota for the entire month.

After that, things got fuzzy and a little weird. She remembered the strange pretty lights, the puking and the passing out. Wait, did she actually remember passing out? Was that even possible? No, that man, that coward, she didn't know his name, had abducted her and taken her home and removed her clothes. Was that all a dream? Her hand wandered down her side and she felt the bandages. It seemed not.

Grumbling, Ella yawned and forced herself to get up.

Staying in bed wasn't an option. In her life, staying in bed meant not making any scratch and not eating, and there was always some punk who wanted to take her place. No, Crate Town was hers, and hers to lose. A samrājñī – a queen – must present herself to her subjects every day, lest any of them develop any funny ideas about trying to squeeze in on her turf.

She poured a bowl of water over her head, wiped her face with a wet rag, and dumped the dirty water down a small drainage pipe that ran down the side of the container cluster. She was about to get dressed when she saw her old clothes in the hamper. She could smell last night all the way from here. Ella sniffed her shoulder. No amount of hand and face washing was going to get rid of this stench. It was time to visit Wiry Madras. She sighed and grabbed a fresh towel, some clean clothes, and her dirty laundry.

Ella checked herself in the mirror on the way out. She bared her teeth and curled her hands into claws. "Rawr." She had survived to prowl another day.

She looked like a stray cat that someone had dunked into the river. Black Cat was her nickname among some of the older residents in Crate Town. When she had first heard it, she had thought it was because she was sleek and brought bad luck upon her foes. She found out much later on that they called her that because she was small, sneaky and pissed on everyone.

Today, something was a little different, a little off; she couldn't quite put her finger on it. Ella looked and felt the same, but she had always been pretty in tune with her body. A person had to be to survive on the streets from an early age. She twirled in front of the mirror once more, checking her back for anything out of the ordinary, and then, resigned to the fact she'd never look like those women she saw in magazines, left her container home.

Ella double-checked the locks on her front door and tossed

Burglar Alarm a snack on her way down. Crate Town at noon was a kaleidoscope of color that splashed the otherwise dreary and washed-out landscape. The crowds were thick with men, women, and children, many wearing brightly patterned sari and panche, painted the backdrop of rust and dirt and steel, adding much needed life. Lines of clothing – in yellows and pinks and purples – hung in the air on wires over the streets in between the riot of brown, red and green container cluster buildings. Blue and orange canvases draped over makeshift balconies and alleyways, providing a little shade against the suffocating heat.

Ella joined the crowds as the people went about their day. There was a rhythm to the slum, a heartbeat as the sharp sounds of dogs barking, horns blaring, and people shouting filled the air. Trucks honked as they tried to bully their way against the river of people, hauling lumber, aluminum and scraps.

Men pushed by her, sacks strapped to their backs or balanced on their heads. Women chattered while washing clothes, herding little ones, cooking delicious aromatic food that almost covered the constant acrid smell of rust, unwashed bodies and concealed sewage. Groups of the young and the old picked through mounds of refuse, looking for anything of value to sell, recycle, or repurpose. Crate Town was alive.

The first thing Ella did was head to the center of the slum, to the bath house. Wiry Madras ran this particular establishment, and it was easily the most expensive public bath house in all of Crate Town. That was fine by Ella. If there was one thing she allowed herself to splurge on, it was baths and laundry.

Wiry Madras, an ex-madam from Little Dhavari in the east, did a lot of good for the community here by employing and protecting many of the orphaned girls who otherwise would be on the streets. Ella had spent some time as one of those girls when she had first made Crate Town home, so she now considered the few extra rupees for washing services a way of paying it forward as well as repaying Wiry Madras.

Wiry Madras took her load of laundry and sniffed it. Her wrinkled face became even more prune-like. "Stupid girl playing in shit again. It'll cost you double, you filthy cat."

Ella stuck her tongue out and paid the premium. It didn't mean Ella liked the old woman. She had been on the receiving end of Wiry Madras's broom far too many times for the two of them to ever be on friendly terms.

The bath was exquisite, if only because of the state she was in when she first arrived. Otherwise, the water was murky and lukewarm, and the tub dirty. At least she had her own bath – Wiry Madras had been forced to give her a private tub when the other women complained about her. In the end, she came out clean and feeling refreshed, and finally ready to start her day, or what was left of it. Half the day had gone by the time she was dried and dressed.

The first thing she did was head back to the scene of the crime. Even though she had made away with two metal briefcases worth of goods, it wasn't a one-person operation. It took a small army of people – affiliates, as she liked to call them – to have pulled that caper off.

Tawny the Jerk, the lookout, saw her approach and broke into a grin. Ella reared back when he stuck his outstretched hand too close to her body. "What did I say about touching me, Tawny? I know what you do with those fingers." Ella tossed him a carton of cigarettes.

The corner beggar caught the pack deftly and his eyes skimmed the small opening on the top of the paper package. "Hey, there's only fifteen here. You're short."

Ella shook her head. "No way. That's the penalty for the watch you missed last week. Damn Omar nearly got the jump on me."

"It was right when I told you. Not my fault he changed his mind last minute."

"There's no right when it's wrong. Get it straight or next timc or I take back half."

Tawny made a rude gesture as she walked away. Ella skirted the narrow and crooked path down the wide street, her eyes alert for speeding motorists, beggars reaching for alms, little street rats running underfoot, or anyone else for that matter. Every single one of them was probably trying to rob, kill or con her, especially the damn kids. That was the thing with the kids. No sense of respect for the hierarchy, but that was the way of the streets. It wasn't that long since Ella had been one of them.

She gave several square meters of netting to Ghanash, the corner fruit vendor, for being her lead lookout. Three thousand rupees to Jango and his cart for the little diversion yesterday. Twenty thousand to Farg to give to Congee the barkeep for messing up his bar. Five thousand to Olle for the initial lead. The list went on until Ella had covered all of the players involved in her little heist.

On top of that, she gave an old coloring book to Hansy the nurse for the stitch-up last month. A sack of dried meats to Ando the leatherworker for her shank's new sheath. A needle and a ball of red yarn to Oldie Meen just because Ella liked the elderly lady. A handful of candies to the Mud Specks kids' gang, more for retainer and a future favor, but also a friendly gesture to not mess with her. If Big Mud decided to make her life miserable, it wouldn't take much for it to happen.

After finishing her rounds, Ella scanned the sky to see how much of the day she had left. For most, the day ended when the sun set. Things always got a little dicey once darkness fell in Crate Town.

She continued her way back to Fab's Art Gallery, making sure to put in some face-time among the people, greeting all the players and introducing herself to the newcomers who might need her services one day, or who might try to compete. Keeping an ear close to the ground was always the best way to stay on top of the goings-on here in the slum.

Her words eased stern scowls. Ella had put nine good years' worth of sweat and equity into this slum, and she had brought in enough stock to earn the people's respect. Now she was known, and that made her someone, which in this dangerous place meant everything.

The current worried gossip was a new rat gang that had popped up over the weekend. They were kids, ages ranging from seven to sixteen. They were dangerous because they were brutal, undisciplined, and didn't respect the way things ran in Crate Town. What they lacked in size, they made up for by swarming their victims like, well, rats. Another piece of interesting news was that the government had once again expanded the area of the construction site near the docks, already doubling their original plan and cutting into large chunks of the Dumas neighborhood in the west. There was a lot of grumbling from many residences and businesses about being forced to sell their properties to accommodate the construction of some secret government project.

Ella also got word that those Pakistani gangsters were looking for her. They had even put a reward out, dead or alive: one hundred Euros. She had preened a little when she heard that. Not bad. She was moving up in life, and in a foreign currency to boot. She didn't worry too much about the bounty. Crate Town was a big place with thousands of people. The chances of them finding her were slim..

The hot political topic on the streets was that Minister Kapoor, the newly appointed Deputy Minister of Gujurat, had taken an interest in Surat and had moved his office there from Gandhinagar, the capital. In his speech to the Surat Chamber of Commerce, he was quoted as saying that the battered city, still devastated from the war, was the key to revitalizing the entire region.

The young up-and-comer made a point of singling out cleaning up Crate Town and cited the construction on the docks as an example of India's need to rebuild and ally with their post-war neighbors. It was the same politician spiel Ella had heard hundreds of times before. Usually nothing came of it, and it rarely affected the dregs of society like her. However, people were saying this Kapoor was different, and that he might be a future prime minister of India.

Ella saw a picture of him. He was good looking, the son of a Bollywood star, and it seemed he had an unusual amount of political backing from several powerful places. In any case, his world was so far away from hers it might as well have been the moon.

Ella crossed the muddy path and reached the art gallery. She waved at Little Fab working behind the counter and nodded at Big Fab hiding behind the beaded curtains.

Little Fab waved back. "You leading to trouble today?"

Ella shrugged. "Is there any other day here in Crate Town?"

She leaned against the counter and chatted with the third and youngest Fab who was easily twice her age. Fab had named both of his sons after himself. He called himself Big Fab even though he was now a spindly stooped old man while Little Fab was the size of a cart. The older son just went by Fab. The Fab family was as much a staple in Crate Town as the mud, the stench, and the constant banging of the metal walls. More importantly, they were the most reliable fence for stolen goods.

Originally, they were one of thousands of refugees moved to camps during the war and told that these accommodations were temporary until the region stabilized. They were one of the first families to move to Crate Town when the containers were repurposed for housing. Now, a decade later, the same people were still living in their temporary homes.

Ella hopped on a stool and took a piece of gum from the pack Little Fab had so carelessly left on the counter. She popped it in her mouth before he could stop her. "Did you sneak a peek at my lovelies in those briefcases?"

He nodded. "A nice haul of tetanus and hepatitis doses. Short supply around here, especially with the rust getting worse."

"Will help a good amount of folks around here," she said.

"The ones that can pay."

Both chuckled.

"With supplies low," she said, "how much for the entire haul?"

He wrote a number on a piece of paper and slid it along the counter. Ella glanced at it and raised an eyebrow. She looked over toward the beaded curtains. "Your youngest isn't doing me right, Big Fab." The old man glanced up from his book, then went back to reading.

"It's a lot of money for us to tie up. We risk opportunity cost for months selling this," Little Fab shrugged. "Not like you can take this anywhere else, Ella. Besides, you brought some heat near us yesterday. Those punks are still prowling around looking for you. Take the offer or leave it."

Ella clenched her teeth and balled her tiny hands into fists. For all the work she had put in, she wanted double what he was offering. This was the biggest haul she had scored all year, and it was supposed to keep her afloat for months. She was the one who had scoped the job and done the legwork. She was the one who had risked her neck. More importantly, it set a poor precedence with the Fabs the next time she brought a score in. She knew she had quite a bit of haggling to do before Little Fab came up with something reasonable.

Little Fab was wrong about one thing: Ella could take it somewhere else. She could take her inventory to Puab, another fence in Little Dharavi, the next slum over, though she had hoped at least to keep the medicine in Crate Town. Sure, it was great to make some scratch, but helping the community along the way was a nice bonus.

She could sell it herself, but that was such a pain in the ass. She hated retail, especially when it came to selling medicine to neighbors. She had a hard ass image to maintain, but her resolve weakened when it came to those in need.

The two of them haggled for another fifteen minutes. Ella hollered, threatened, and screamed, pushing Little Fab far enough up that she no longer felt insulted. He knew she had limited options with such specialized inventory and held his ground. In the end, as much about pride and anger as it was unwilling to get ripped off, Ella slammed the two briefcases shut, intent on striking off on her own.

Take the deal.

She froze. What was that? Who was that? Was that her? She stared at the two metal containers on the counter, doubt suddenly flooding her head. She considered herself to have good instincts, and her gut was telling her to walk. Now, she wasn't so sure.

Little Fab noticed the hesitation. "All right, I'll give you five points on sales. Take it or leave it."

Five points was hardly enough, but it pushed Ella over the edge. She let go of the two briefcases and burned a little inside as Little Fab, all smiles, paid her out. Ella scrunched her face at the final tally.

"Great doing business with you," Little Fab said.

Ella swallowed the scorching words begging to escape her lips and stomped outside. She hated being on the short end, but the Fabs were the only decent fences around. If she pissed them off and they stopped doing business with her, she'd have to haul all the way to Little Dharavi to get any product moved. That was not only inconvenient, but dangerous.

In the end, she could only be mad at herself. She took the deal. No one twisted her arm. She could have held on to those two briefcases and walked out, and figured out how to offload them elsewhere.

These thoughts stewed inside Ella's head as she walked down the street. She replayed the scenario over and over, and wondered how she could have shook it out differently, but it all came down to her second-guessing herself, something she rarely did. This decision was going to haunt her for a few days.

Stop!

Ella was so surprised by the shout in her head that she tripped and nearly knocked a stall over. She put her hands together apologetically to the vendor and bowed. Rattled, she tried to continue on her way.

Stop. In front on the left. Someone coming right for you.

Confused, Ella looked to the left at the crowded market. At first, nothing looked out of the ordinary. It was a busy street with shops and steady foot traffic going both ways. Then she saw him: Uncle Manu. Their eyes locked and he began to run toward her.

"Oh crap."

Stupid careless girl. Usually, she was much more aware of her surroundings. She had been so deep in thought she would have plowed directly into him. Fortunately, he was still half a block away, and Manu didn't exactly move quick.

Ella slipped behind a tent and crossed a narrow alley between two container clusters. She turned the corner and took off in a sprint.

Head west.

Ella was about to follow the order blindly when she realized for certain that this voice definitely did not come from her. She had planned on circling east and grabbing some food before dusk.

This voice, where was it coming from? She looked around the narrow alley. "What the gods is going on? Is someone playing a prank on me? Some candid camera crap? I will knock your head off."

West toward the docks. The other way.

"I know where the docks are!" Nobody ordered Ella around, not even herself. She planted her feet and crossed her arms. "I'm not doing anything until you tell me who you are and what's going on. You're not the boss of me."

I just saved you from that policeman. He is still close by.

"I don't care."

Fine. I will make you a deal. Get to safety, and I will explain everything. I recommend the docks. Once there, I will explain.

Ella grudgingly nodded. The docks made sense. Few people other than fishermen, dockworkers and construction crews hung out around there. "Fine," she grumbled. "But you spill everything, yeah?"

I will. Get moving.

CHAPTER SIX
First Contact

Ella left the market area and grudgingly made her way west, traveling along narrow less-traveled back streets, cutting across the Rubber Market, then through the warehouse district and finally past the construction site.

The list of people after Ella seemed to be growing longer and longer with each passing day. Manu had been chasing her for months now, and it seemed she had misjudged the Pakistani gangsters' tenacity, thinking they wouldn't stick around after she had robbed them.

When she had signed on to be their translator, they had claimed they were heading back across the border that very day. A few of the gangsters must have stayed behind, which was surprising. She had only taken a tenth of the merchandise, and none of it cash. Ella had thought it wouldn't be worth their while to hunt her down. It seemed she had thought incorrectly.

She should probably keep a low profile until things blew over. After all, the longer they hung around Crate Town, the likelier someone was to sell her out. No matter how tight the community was here when it came to outsiders, everyone had a price.

She reached the docks just as the sun was sinking into the ocean, and sat down near the ocean's edge to watch the water lap the jagged broken concrete blocks. The air smelled of fish and brine and garbage, and the constant buzz of horns and people shouting was replaced by the honking of seagulls, slopping waves and construction machinery. Ella lay down against a cracked slab smoothed over by the elements and stared at the fast-moving clouds.

"OK, talk, you crazy intruder in my head. Who the gods are you?"

Do you know what a Quasing is, child?

Ella did not appreciate being called a child. She had, however, heard of Quasing. "It's those weird aliens that the world just fought that war over. What about them?"

I am one of those Quasing aliens, and I have chosen you to become my next host. You should feel honored.

"Is that so?" Ella said. "My amma fought in that war. She died for those stupid aliens. If you're one of those, then it's your fault she's gone."

I am sorry about your mother. Who did she fight for?

Ella's eyes watered. "She was a fighter pilot for the RSAF."

I am with the Prophus. It is the Genjix who are responsible for her death.

"If you weren't fighting at all, she'd still be alive!"

The Prophus and the Genjix have been fighting through our hosts for hundreds of years. However, we are getting ahead of ourselves. As I said, I have chosen you to be my next host.

"What does that mean?"

It means I have chosen to inhabit you. I will offer you my wisdom and knowledge. In return, you will offer your body. Together, we will do many great things.

Ella frowned. Offering her body to anyone didn't sound very attractive. "That sounds like a lousy deal. Feels like I have to do all the work. You just sit in my head and order me around. What do I get out of this?"

You get the benefit of my eons of experience and wisdom. I will train you to become an agent, and you will enjoy the many benefits of the Prophus network. You will no longer need to live on the streets.

"And all I have to do is let you tell me what to do?"

Of course. Think of it more as–

Ella sat up. "Yeah, well, no deal. I'm my own president. No one tells me what to do, and I don't want to share my body. You can leave now."

Unfortunately, that is no longer an option. I cannot leave until your death. We are bonded and must learn to work together as one.

It took several moments for that news to sink in. She was trapped with this... this thing. "What are you anyway?"

The Quasing hail from a planet far away from your solar system. We crashed millions of years ago, and have inhabited and guided some of the greatest people in history.

"Yeah, like who? Who have you been in?"

Rolf Andreasson the Berserker?

"A what?"

Captain Wilbur James Forrestor?

"Who?"

Well, it is not my fault you are uneducated.

Ella pulled out her phone and swiped a few keystrokes, and then she held it up in the air as if she were showing it to a ghost. "Well, alien invader thing, the Internet doesn't know who these guys are either, and the Internet even knows who the stray dog living next to my house is, so your guys couldn't have been that great."

There was a long pause.

Io.

"What?"

My name. I am called Io.

That gave Ella pause. For some reason, it never occurred to her this alien – this thing – had a name. Somehow, that made it more human, or at least more of a person than just some nebulous thing or virus in her head. She shrugged. Well, if Burglar Alarm had a name, why couldn't this stupid alien in her head?

All right. Let me deconstruct your thoughts for a second. First of all, I am not a thing. I am a living being just like you. Being from the planet Quasar, my physiology is different from the creatures of Earth and it offers advantages and limitations when compared to humans. We self-reproduce constantly, which allows us to move our memories, experience, and vast knowledge over millions of years, but we are physically limited while on your planet since we cannot survive in your atmosphere. That is why we must inhabit the living beings on Earth.

Second of all, having a name does not make me more human. The Quasing are far superior and more advanced than the dominant species on this planet.

Lastly, do not compare me with your mangy pet.

"Well, if you're so superior," Ella wiggled her fingers and pretended to quiver, "then why do you even need us lowly humans?"

What? I just told you. Are you even listening?

"Actually, I think you're boring," Ella snapped. "I've had enough of you and this dumb talk."

Well, that is too bad because you are stuck with me unless you want to jump into the ocean.

"Your Hindi sounds awful. Why do you talk so strange?"

It has been a long time since I have had to speak the language. I originally learned Braj Bhasha Sanskrit hundreds of years ago. It will take some adjustment to acclimate speaking in modern Hindi.

"Don't bother. I don't need you and I would appreciate it if you just stop talking as long as I'm alive," huffed Ella. "I'm going home." She stood up and stomped across the beach.

That will not happen and you do need me. A criminal gang is actively hunting you in your own neighborhood, it seems the police are looking for you as well, and the Genjix will now come after you.

Ella balled her hands into fists and tried unsuccessfully to push the voice out of her head. She felt like a cornered animal and, to make matters worse, she had forgotten to eat today, so she was starving. That was a bad combination for her.

Why are you risking your life stealing from low-level criminals for such small payouts, anyway? Is this how you want to waste your life?

"You don't know me," Ella seethed. "You don't know what I've been through. Who are you to judge how I live my life?"

I know a lot about you, more than I want actually. I probably made a mistake inhabiting you.

"I obviously made one saving that woman's life and getting you inflicted on myself!" Ella became aware that she had just practically screamed in the middle of a busy street. Fortunately, most of the people around ignored her. The citizens of Crate Town were good at minding their own business. Getting involved in other people's problems tended to lead to bad things. Even showing that you noticed could get someone in trouble.

However, there was a big difference between getting involved in something and paying attention. Everyone paid attention, and everyone gossiped. Ella was pretty sure that half the slum would know that she was talking to herself and screaming at nothing by evening.

Watch–

"Shut up, shut up, shut up. I don't want to talk to you anymore." Ella was so frustrated she was on the brink of tears. However, she would rather have died than had people on the street see her cry. That would just ruin everything.

No. Listen! One of the gangsters is eating at that curry stand to your left.

Instinctively, Ella slipped behind a stall and glanced over the side. She saw the patrons eating at the counter at the curry stand, and scrunched her face. "Are you sure? I don't recognize any of them."

The third one from the left facing the street. He was the muscle standing in the corner next to the door when the deal went down.

"How do you know this? I don't remember him at all."

An image flashed briefly into Ella's head. She was pulled back into the dark smoky room where the trade deal between the Pakistani gangsters and the Indian smugglers was happening. There were nearly twenty men and two women in that cramped room.

Ella had been hired to serve as the translator between the two groups. She remembered thinking how bad ass and cool those two women were. More images flashed in her head until one came from the time Ella had to look away because of the thick cigar smoke. That was when she saw the man standing in the back with his arms crossed. It was the same man stuffing his face, just meters away.

She pulled away from the street and took a different route. "How did you do that?"

I am in your head, girl. I can dig through your memories. I retrieved that con you pulled off yesterday to study how you operate. You are not a bad thief; a lucky one, perhaps. I found some problems with your plan. I also caught a few things you missed, like that man I just warned you about, or that you could have grabbed that satchel of cash instead of one of the briefcases.

"For your information, I didn't go for the money intentionally. If I had, both gangs would be on my ass. Right now, I only have a couple from one. I don't appreciate your poking in my thoughts like this."

I am not sorry you feel this way, because I have saved your life twice in the past hour.

Ella couldn't argue with that logic. "Fine," she sputtered. "Although I think you should ask for permission first next time. It's only civil."

Would it make you feel better if I do?

"Damn right it would."

As you wish.

"You're just humoring me, aren't you?"

Yes.

Ella couldn't help but crack a smile. At least this stupid alien had a sense of humor. Maybe she could make use of this situation, somehow use this thing to her advantage. After all, these aliens had to be rare, and rare things were expensive. Maybe Ella could leverage this alien in her head for some profit. She could worry about excising this Quasing from her head later on.

You know I can hear your thoughts, right?

"Damn it!"

Go get some food. We are hungry. Can we agree on that at least?

The mention of food made the gnawing pain in her belly worse. Ella nodded. "A truce then, at least until after I eat."

Very well, a truce. Now go get your noodles.

"You know way too much about me. I don't like it."

All right. Go get mushroom soup.

"I hate mushrooms."

I know.

"Cut it out!"

CHAPTER SEVEN
Shura

Shura the Scalpel stepped onto the commercial liner heading back to Moscow. She had stayed in Abu Dhabi one extra day, first to gauge the emirate's response to the assassination of someone in their line of succession – the reaction was muted, the news quiet – and second, to do some shopping and play a few rounds of golf. She had a weakness for both, and at one point in her youth had considered joining the LPGA and becoming a cultural operative for the Genjix in that capacity.

That, however, was not the path Tabs had chosen for her. She had always displayed a stronger talent for this type of work, and it suited her Holy One's skill-set. That was fine with Shura; she had never had the patience to master the art of putting anyway. Still, the enjoyment of the sport never left her, so she spent much of her free time on the greens. In fact, she had even played a full eighteen holes within earshot of her assignment the previous night.

What if someone recognized you? I did not raise you to be so bold or careless. One day, it will catch up with you.

"Please, Tabs, the country club next to the scene of the crime is probably the last place their security will look for an assassin."

There cannot be that many striking blondes running around.

Shura glanced at the rest of the first-class cabin. "In the

emirates? More than you think." She turned her attention out the port window as the airliner climbed toward the blue sky. "Besides, I'm just maintaining my cover. I would look positively guilty holed up in my hotel room all day. I need to keep my alibi intact for the next time Dominika Yumashev visits."

For more shopping?

"Among other things. The Prophus are fast running out of neutral parties to recruit now that they've hitched themselves to world governments and the red tape and oversight that comes with them."

The stewardess brought over a Moscow Mule and placed it next to her seat. Shura kept looking out the window as the view changed from shimmering sands to blue skies to, finally, the floor of white clouds. She would never admit it to anyone, not even Tabs, but she was feeling skittish right about now, more so than at any time in recent memory.

It was finally time to go home.

The sheik had been the last assignment on her slate. After that, as promised by the Council, she was allowed to finally return to Russia to attempt to reclaim her family's place and standing within the Genjix hierarchy.

Shura had been born into the Genjix. Both her parents were vessels, and her father had been a major rainmaker, a political and financial operative. Unfortunately, her parents had lost their standing and all that went with it when they chose the wrong side in a Council power struggle.

Fortunately, their sins had not been passed to her. Shura had inherited her mother's Holy One, Tabs, and had been raised by the Hatchery, the Genjix eugenics program that nurtured and trained Adonis vessels.

Since then, she had become a rolling operative, a fixer sent to solve problems. However, she had never been allowed to return to Russia and claim her birthright. That was her penance. Until now. After this last mission, her family's sins had finally been absolved.

Shura sipped her Moscow Mule and paused as she saw a small marking hand-drawn on the napkin. It was a Seal of Shamash followed by what looked like rough scribbles.

It is Akkadian. Council priority. Single hard line encryption. Two-two-two-two. Forty minute window from three minutes ago.

The timing for this communication was suspect. Shura drained the rest of her drink and ordered another, and waited until the stewardess brought it before getting out of her seat and heading upstairs to the business area. She went to the second row of private offices, entered room two, and clicked over to the second line of the video communicator. Her finger paused over the encryption double-tone as it changed levels. Perhaps her apprehension was misguided, and she was just being cynical. However, she doubted that. Shura punched in her code and waited.

And waited.

Finally, after twenty-five minutes, ten before the line encryption expired, a young Korean man in his early twenties appeared on the screen. He was thin but well-muscled, and carried an air of confidence that bordered on arrogant. No, he had long crossed that line. Like most other Adonis vessels, he was beautiful; perhaps more than most. Of course, that was to be expected from the leader of the Genjix.

"High Father." She bowed and kept her eyes low on the ground. Weston was several years her junior, but the human's age was irrelevant when it came to Genjix standing. His Holy One, Zoras, was the head of the Council and one of the most influential Quasing in all of history.

"Your work in the emirates was successful, I see. Who was the Prophus?"

"Khat, High Father. I sent him to the Eternal Sea."

"Until the Eternal Sea," Weston bowed his head and murmured. "Zoras remembers Khat as one of the first of us to explore much of the ocean depths, and one of the first to settle in Scandinavia with the Vikings."

Shura responded with respectful silence. The moment of reminiscing passed as quickly as it came. Weston looked up at her. "Your next assignment is to head to the Bio Comm Array site and take over the project's construction until instructed otherwise."

So much for her being cynical.

If I did not raise you to be cynical, then I have failed.

"Your will, High Father. However, I was on my way back to Moscow. Perhaps–"

"Your return has been rescinded."

Just like that, all her plans to reclaim her birthright and family honor were gone. Shura felt a ripple through her body.

Watch your words carefully.

"High Father." Her words were exact. One word from Weston and she could be commanded to slit her own throat. "I was promised after my last assignment to be given the opportunity to return to Russia to reclaim my family's standing within the hierarchy."

"And now you are being ordered elsewhere."

"I have served loyally…"

"And you will continue to do so."

"This is the third time I have been denied what was promised."

"This is not a request–"

Shura decided to take a calculated risk. She cut off the leader of the Genjix mid-sentence. "Speak plainly, Weston. At the very least, I am owed an explanation."

A long silence passed between them. She wouldn't be surprised if he ordered her to take a cyanide pill right now. However, raising one's standing required risk, and this was as much a show of force as it was finding answers from someone she considered an ally.

Finally, Weston spoke. "I'll be frank, Shura. You will never regain your standing in Russia. In fact, you will never step foot in your motherland ever again. Your family has a long history with deep ties there. They and Tabs opposed Zoras in their lust for power, and lost. For that treachery, you endure their punishment. The past holds nothing for you, not anymore."

Shura clenched her fist. "Weston, I have proven my loyalty many times over. The sacrifices I made–"

"– are the only reason you and Tabs were not sent to the Eternal Sea," said Weston. "The sins of the past cannot be wiped clean in one human's lifetime."

I had hoped that your loyalty and exemplary performance would offer you a fresh slate, but Zoras has always had a long and vindictive memory.

"Weston, I was raised in the Hatchery with you. I've saved your life more than once – in combat, from assassinations, sometimes even from yourself. I have been nothing but loyal. What is the real reason?"

"Because it is politically strategic," Weston shrugged. "China and Russia are by far our two greatest core strongholds and the most powerful seats on the council. It is advantageous for me to keep the Russian region unsettled and the council seat weak. None of the current players maneuvering for standing to occupy that seat have real substance. I won't allow a strong opponent to hold it.

"You are strong and resourceful, and have the potential to become a power if given the opportunity. Forge a new path for yourself, Shura. When the time comes, you'll have my support – if the circumstances are advantageous to my interests." Weston looked away, letting her know that this conversation was over. "You have your new orders."

The Bio Comm Array project is an important initiative. If we cannot rebuild a base of power in Russia, see if we can claim an advantage from the current situation.

"High Father," she asked quickly. "Am I being given ownership of the project?"

Weston shook his head. "The array falls under Rurik's

jurisdiction. He inherited it from his family's holdings." He paused. "In fact, he was the one who first suggested making your exile permanent. He made several concessions to me to see it happen." A small smile appeared on Weston's face. "I believe Rurik sees you as a threat."

I should have let you drown him that one time back at the Hatchery.

Shura's face stayed neutral, but inside she seethed. Rurik Melnichenko, another Adonis vessel from the Hatchery whose family controlled a powerful Russian mining company, was considered a leading contender to unite the Russian faction and claim the vacant council seat.

The two had met when she first joined the Hatchery. Her training had been delayed when her father pulled her out of the Hatchery during the Genjix Power Struggle, in which he had sided with the losing faction.

That reputation followed her throughout her tenure and put her at a severe disadvantage when it came to the cutthroat politics of the Hatchery. Even though she was more skilled, more intelligent, and had accomplished more than most of her class, she had fallen behind in standing. It was almost un-Genjix-like, all things considered.

"I see," she said. "So now I am to fix his failing operation?"

"You are to fix a troubled but vital Genjix project," Weston corrected. "One that is critical to our global enterprises over the next hundred years. The current delays are unacceptable. Fix it, and whatever standing or advantage you achieve from it, I will remember. Now, if there is nothing else, you have your orders. And Shura?"

"Yes?"

"I remember our time back at the Hatchery fondly. You were often the only one to stand by my side when it wasn't strategically prudent to do so. You were a great ally then and a loyal servant now. Because of this, I allowed your insubordination on the account of our past friendship. You have used that card. You do not have another."

She bowed. "Your will, High Father."

Shura kept her eyes focused on the ground long after the screen went blank. For as long as she could remember, she had planned to return to Russia to reclaim her birthright and her family's standing, and possibly lay the groundwork to fill the still-vacant Russian council seat. Now, the path before her was dark, her future unknown. Achieving standing was never easy or simple among the Genjix, and it was doubly difficult for someone in her position. She had thought her work sufficient to placate the Council, but that no longer seemed the case.

I warned you before. Standing is never given. It must be taken. You could not expect the Council to offer it just for doing as you were told.

Tabs was right. It was time she stopped trying to earn her standing and seize it. Something Weston said gave her pause. He had never been an ally of Rurik back at the Hatchery. Perhaps in denying her heritage, he was offering her something else. In any case, there was only one path forward now. She had to follow the Council's command and take control of this floundering project, even though it meant reporting directly to Rurik.

Unless you can somehow claim the Bio Comm Array as your own. Only someone on the Council will have the authority to take that from Rurik.

There was always that. Conflict bred innovation. That was their creed, even among their own. However, it was always a delicate balancing act to fight other Genjix for standing as opposed to acquiring it by defeating their enemies. Injuring a Holy One or disrupting faction goals were the only things forbidden. In this particular case, Shura would have to work within the confines of managing the Bio Comm Array construction while undermining Rurik's standing and acquiring ownership of it at the same time.

First things first, she was flying in the wrong direction.

The captain's voice came over the intercom. "Ladies and gentlemen, this is your captain speaking. Due to a mechanical malfunction and poor weather ahead, we are rerouting our flight plan to make an emergency landing in Surat, India. We apologize for the delay and will do everything in our power get you back on schedule as soon as possible."

The Genjix's influence ran deep.

At least that was one problem she didn't have to worry about. Shura remotely accessed a secured terminal and pulled up all the details, reports, and files of the Bio Comm Array project. She had a job to do. It was time to get to work.

CHAPTER EIGHT
Day After

Dinner was one of the most annoying experiences Ella had had to endure in a long time. Even though she was treating herself to her favorite food in the world – Singapore noodles, or half-her noodles as she called them – she couldn't enjoy herself.

The annoying voice in her head wouldn't stop talking. Every five minutes Io had to open her non-existent mouth and dole her wisdom out upon Ella. In the short span of one bowl of noodles, the Quasing had felt the need to educate her on where noodles came from, when stir-fry became a popular method of cooking, and why a human body burped. That last bit came, incidentally, right after Ella burped. Everything she did or saw, Io had something to say about it.

"I really don't care," Ella ended up repeating over and over again.

Well, you should. Your education is lacking.

The fragile truce the two had forged from Io saving Ella's life twice that night was on shaky grounds by the time she got home. She resorted to going for the nuclear option and drinking. She wasn't sure what the alcohol was, just some nasty gag-inducing yellow liquid that made her eyes water every time she took a swig. Ella didn't care. If it shut up the dumb voice in her head, it was worth it. She ended up drinking half the bottle before passing out on the floor of her bedroom.

The next morning, she decided that the pounding headache was worse than the jabbering Quasing. She woke up at dawn with the sun poking through one of the container wall holes and boring directly into her skull. She picked herself off the floor and staggered to the water basin. She tried to pry her eyes wider to look in the mirror and experienced fresh waves of pain right behind her eyeballs. A groan akin to that of a dying sheep escaped her lips.

Good morning.

"Damn, you're not a bad dream," she moaned. "You talk too loud."

Was all that drinking everything you hoped it would be?

She buried her face in her hands. "And you talk too much too. I remember you talking all night. Incessantly. How many hours did we argue before I finally passed out?"

Is that what you remember? Because I stopped talking ten minutes after you took that first drink. You spent the entire night arguing with yourself thinking you were talking to me.

Ella raised her head. "What?"

Yes. You were that drunk.

Now that she thought about it, she did kind of remember having some rather strange discussions about… about…

At one point, you went outside and asked Burglar Alarm when she was going to settle down and have puppies.

"You're lying," Ella said, her face turning red.

Io replayed the entire scene for Ella. It was actually a little worse than Io had described. Not only did Ella try to give Burglar Alarm marriage counseling, she ended up hugging the mangy dog and crying big fat tears about how she was Ella's only friend.

Ella felt some vomit crawl up her throat. "Do I have any of that drink left? I think I need to throw that devil juice away."

It is called tequila, and I agree.

That morning became the second in a row that Ella had wasted. She was in no condition to leave her home, and ended up reading comics in bed and drinking her entire water supply, which had been meant to last until the end of the month. It wasn't until midafternoon that the debilitating headache had receded somewhat and she felt well enough to leave the house without feeling as though the sun's rays were poking needles into her eyes. That and she was hungry again.

You are always hungry.

"Being poor does that to a person."

Ella spent the rest of the afternoon running errands, first grabbing more noodles for lunch, and then picking up her laundry from Wiry Madras's. On the way, she stopped by the art gallery to see if the medicine was selling. After all, points on sales wasn't nothing. She was surprised when she found out that Little Fab had already sold half of the haul in a day. She was even more shocked when she found out the prices he was asking. The fence was practically robbing the people here. She could have sold the medicine herself at half the price and made a complete killing.

Ella gritted her teeth. If she had only listened to her gut instead of the stupid voice in her head.

Like I was supposed to know demand was this high.

"Then why say anything at all? Why not just be quiet and let me do my thing?"

You are now my host. I did not want to waste the next month with you selling drugs on the streets.

"Month? He sold half of it in a day, at twenty times the markup." Ella shook her fists in the air. "I would have been rich."

No use crying over a bad deal. One cannot predict the future. Just move on.

"You shut up, you… you alien."

Ella stomped out of the Fabs more depressed than ever. She knew that, at the end of the day, she was the one who made the deal; Io hadn't forced her. Feeling sorry for herself, she decided to cheer herself up by either seeing the most recent American robot movie or playing dice at the Cage.

As she stood at the intersection trying to decide between the two, a boy from the Terrible Gandhis, one of the street rat gangs she had worked with in the past, ran up to her.

"Hey Ella," he said. "We're a man short to go fishing. Promise you're not the worm or the hook, and we'll cut you in full share. Want to come?"

She thought about it for a second. The ache of handing that huge score over to the Fabs was still fresh in her head. She felt the need to recoup some of that lost profit. She shrugged. "Sure, why not?"

Fishing in Crate Town had nothing to do with the water or fish. It was one of the first cons Ella ever learned. There was a truck route that passed underneath a low-hanging bridge from the docks, heading northeast up the highway toward downtown Surat. The street rats would tie a kid to several ropes and wait on top of the bridge. As a truck passed underneath, they would send another kid in front of the truck, forcing it to stop. They were the worm. Then the first kid would be lowered down onto the truck bed. They were the hook. The kid would then tie as many of the containers as possible to all the ropes, and they would haul it up.

There were several ways for the worm and the hook to get injured. The trucks could be too slow to stop. The hook could get pulled too late and left dangling in midair, or get pulled off balance and bounce on the hard steel bridge.

In the early days, the street rats used to just run up to the trucks and grab the loot, but then the drivers came out with clubs and beat them away. Some genius kid realized that there wasn't an easy way for the drivers to get to the bridge, so they began using ropes. It was a dangerous game, but was way better than starving.

As long as she wasn't the one dangling off a bridge or

running in front of the truck, it was a pretty solid gig. Ella followed the boy west to the docks and they made their way north toward the overpass. If she could nab a decent haul today on top of the big score yesterday, this might end up being the best week she'd ever had. Maybe she could finally afford some new clothes, or even a motorcycle. Her heart quickened at that idea. She had wanted one ever since she was a little girl and saw this American movie about these super-agent girls who rode motorcycles by day and ninjaed by night.

Or you could put those funds toward leaving this slum.

"I like it here."

What if I could offer you something more? Something better than what you have now?

"If it means I have to listen to you prattle on all day, the price is too high."

You will better yourself as a person. Listen to me: let me lead you, or you will never make anything of yourself.

"I like me, alien, and if you don't, you can kiss my ass."

So you are content being a conwoman for the rest of your life?

"It's a respectable living."

It is anything but respectable. Also, I do not think your instincts are wrong. There is something strange about this fishing job.

Ella stopped following the boy. Something had been nagging her. She looked up at the sky and checked the time. The best time for fishing was earlier in the day after the trucks were loaded. By late afternoon, the traffic leaving the docks was light. That meant there would be fewer targets, and the trucks that were passing through would drive by faster. She brought it up with the boy.

He pulled her along. "Late shipment from a container barge. It's packed right now. There're at least six crews working non-stop fishing. Hurry before it's too late."

Ella was dubious, but she didn't have much else to do today. Besides, she had already wasted most of the day. In

Crate Town, a person always had to be on the move. Move or die, sell or die, steal or die. One always had to be doing something, or be dying. She saw the rest of the crew of Terrible Gandhis loafing at the foot of the bridge. They waved at her to come over. Ella peered over the side of the street to the road below and frowned. There were hardly any trucks passing through.

Just as the boy led Ella around the corner, rough hands grabbed her from behind. In an instant, she was surrounded by several hard-looking men. The Pakistani gangsters had found her.

She scowled as one of the gangsters gave the boys a few thousand rupees. The Terrible Gandhis had sold her out for nothing. "You little shits," she snarled. "You'll pay for this when word hits the streets."

The gangster standing next to her backhanded her face, swiveling her neck violently. The right side of her face went numb and her legs gave out. The only reason she was still upright was because of the thug wrapping his arm around her neck.

"You're not telling anyone anything," the man who struck her grinned. He cupped her chin and lifted it to his face. "Tell us where our merchandise is or we'll drown your scrawny ass in the ocean."

Ella squirmed, but the thug's thick arms holding her in place were like a vice. She thought quickly in her head. "Hey hey, Io, help me get out of this. Please! I promise I'll listen. Use some alien magic powers or something."

There are five Terrible Gandhis and six large men. The ledge is to your left and there are containers to your right. There are no crowds or places to hide. Your only option is to surrender. We may be able to find a more opportune time to escape later.

"What? That's your stinking advice? Give up? I thought you were some military genius or something."

Sometimes, the best strategy is to surrender.

"Was that what you told all your soldiers when you were in charge?"

The last time I led soldiers in battle, we rode horses, and were butchered by an army of American Indians.

Ella wanted to grab her hair in frustration, but she couldn't reach it. Of all the aliens in the world who could possess her, she got the incompetent one. Well, *she* wasn't going to give up. She was as good as dead if she did.

She had to think of something. She clasped the massive forearm with her hands and tried to pry the gangster's fingers loose from her neck. She swung her feet back and forth, and tried to wiggle free. It was all to no avail. The grip around her neck tightened, and the thug smacked her with his free hand.

"Stop squirming before I just decide to choke you to death here on the spot."

Ella got a mouthful of his arm hair, and spat. Then she glanced at the brown flesh pressed against her chin, and decided on a different tactic. She opened her mouth, leaned in, and bit down as hard as she could.

The man screamed. He smacked her again. He shook her like a rag doll. Still, Ella clamped her teeth down on his flesh, biting down even harder until she tasted blood. The vice around her neck loosened, and the arm tore out of Ella's mouth as she felt herself fly through the air.

The left side of her body bounced off the metal wall of the container, but she was ready for it. No sooner did her feet touch the ground than she was off running. Large hands grabbed at her, but she squirmed away, scrambling on all fours, squeezing between bodies until she found an open path. One of the Terrible Gandhis tried to block her escape, and she pushed him so hard, he flipped over onto his belly. Then the way before her was clear.

Ella took off, taking advantage of her smaller stature and staying low to the ground, and made a beeline toward the busy crowds in the distance. She glanced back only once, and saw all of them – gangsters and Gandhis – giving chase. A low guttural growl came from the recess of her throat. She expected the gangsters to come after her, but these street rats were Crate Town. There was a code that the denizens here lived by. Damn kids had no respect for custom.

Watch out!

She nearly smacked into the ass of an old man and decided to focus on where she was going. She was pretty sure she could outrun the larger men since she knew this area, but the street rats posed a problem. Some of the older Terrible Gandhis were stronger, larger and probably faster than her, and they knew this area just as well as she did.

Turn left at that intersection.

"Like I'm going to listen to you, Ms Surrender."

Ella kept going straight, skirting around people and carts and vehicles as if she were racing an obstacle course. To both sides of her, just a few steps behind, swarmed the street rats. Behind them, the gangsters were having a harder time keeping up as they bowled into the crowds and knocked people off bikes.

To your left!

Ella looked and saw the tips of fingers grabbing at her shirt. She threw out an arm and sent a boy a head taller than her falling head over heels into the mud.

Turn right here. Those are narrower streets.

"No, that's stupid. That goes straight into Terrible Gandhi territory. I'll just get more of them on my tail." She turned left and ran up a ramp leading to the third level of a neighborhood stacked four containers high. She hurdled over railings and oil drums and ran across bridges made from wooden planks.

She looked back and saw two of the Terrible Gandhis close behind her. She crossed one particular loosely-assembled bridge, and when she got to the other side, knocked a board off while the boy was still crossing, sending him down to ground level, his panicked screams music to her ears.

Unfortunately, she had reached the end of the block. The gap between the container she was on and the next was too wide for a bridge, so she was forced to go inside. She entered what looked like a karaoke room and was about to head downstairs when the door slammed open and one of the gangsters appeared.

Ella was trapped.

She backed up until she bumped against the balcony railing. She could jump down, but that was a long fall. If she stayed up here though, she was as good as dead.

Use your hands to grab the clothing line and cross to the next building.

Ella stared at the rope. "I can't do that. I'm not a monkey."

Would you rather be dead?

She looked over at the advancing gangster and then back at the rope. She wasn't sure what was worse. Falling to her death or getting beaten to it.

That is your only choice.

"Fine, I can be a monkey."

Grimacing, Ella climbed onto the railing and jumped, grabbing the rope a meter away from the balcony. The gangster lunged forward and swiped at her, narrowly missing her feet. Ella, slowly moving one hand in front of the other, made it a few meters down the line safely out of his reach. She looked back at the gangster and stuck her tongue out.

And then she lost her grip on the rope and fell.

Fortunately, she hit the half dozen clothing lines crisscrossed in between the buildings on her way down. They didn't break her fall, but bounced her around enough that, coupled with the soft mud, she didn't crack anything open when she finally hit the ground.

Unfortunately, it dazed her long enough that by the time her head had cleared again, three of the gangsters were bearing down on her. She stood on unsteady feet and flinched as her right ankle screamed in pain. She limped five steps and nearly collapsed. They were going to catch her.

To your left are two uniformed policemen. Run to them.

Ella made a face. "That's not a good option either. The police and I have history."

Damn it, dumb girl. You have to trust me right now.

"Oh, this is a huge mistake, but fine." She looked back one more time at the advancing gangsters, and with a sinking feeling in the pit of her stomach, hobbled to the two policemen leaning against their car. She waved. "Hey, Sanchit. Hey, Dhruv, nice matching mustaches. You guys call each other in the morning to coordinate?"

The one named Dhruv squinted. "What the hell?" He reached over and yanked Ella by the collar and pulled her off her feet. He then picked her up and slammed her into the patrol car.

What are they doing?

Ella's face was pressed against the trunk. "I told you I have history with the uncles."

Uncles?

"What we call the police around here."

She looked to the other side and saw the three gangsters on the other side of the street, scowling. She pulled an arm free and gave them the middle finger.

The uncle named Sanchit grabbed her wrist and forced it behind her back. He leaned in close. "The inspector is looking forward to having a few words with you." The last thing Ella remembered was Sanchit grabbing the back of her head and slamming it toward the car trunk.

CHAPTER NINE
Surrett

Surrett Kapoor, Deputy Minister of Gujurat, was mid-sentence when he caught a glimpse of his reflection as he passed the hallway mirror. He stopped, squinted at his tie, and adjusted it so it perfectly aligned with how his suit hung off his shoulders and how his lapel balanced the blue of the right half of his tie with the handkerchief tucked into his breast pocket.

He turned to Amita. "Next time, tell me if I'm disheveled."

His assistant looked confused. "I'm sorry, Minister, but you look great."

"Public presentation is just as important as public policy in this line of business, do you not know that? What if I need to speak with the press?"

She checked her tablet. "You don't have anything on your schedule."

"That's not the point." He shook his finger at her. "A group of reporters could happen upon us in the hallway at any moment. Moving on. Where was I?"

"You were dictating your message. Friday evening."

"Ah yes," Surrett said. "I will be away this Friday and over water from six to nine, so depending on how far away from the coast I am, I may have limited access to email and messages. I will be hard at work in the office Saturday morning from seven until five, but will be spending the evening with a dear friend and will only respond to emergency calls. Please note that on Sunday, I will be the guest of honor at the Vapi Country Club and will be unavailable except through my assistant, Amita, who may be reached at her office or through the operating dispatch." He stopped just outside his office. "That will be all."

Amita tapped a few buttons on the tablet. "Your weekend out-of-office message is now saved, Minister. Is there anything else?"

Surrett shook his head. "Have a good weekend. Please keep your phone charged this time." He watched his assistant leave the reception room, and then proceeded into his office. He closed the door behind him, took off his blazer, and carefully placed it on a hanger, making sure there were no creases around the shoulders. Humming, he went to his tea cart and poured himself a cup. He looked up at the wall mirror and saw a pair of crossed legs in front of his corner couch.

Casually, and still humming, he strolled behind his desk and reached for the loaded handgun hidden inside a hollowed-out statue of Ganesh. He pawed around for a few seconds and came up empty. Shrugging, and now whistling, he reached for the phone on his desk.

"You don't want to do that."

Surrett froze. The woman spoke perfect Hindi with only a slight tinge of an accent. There was a sharpness to her enunciation that was too staccato in its delivery. He kept his hands up and slowly pivoted. "Oh, I did not realize I had company. Do you have an appointment?"

The woman flicked on the lamp on the console table next to her and her face appeared out of the shadows. The first thing Surrett noticed was her blonde hair. Next, her pale face – nearly sheet-white. Then he realized how beautiful she was and his heart skipped a few beats. He caught himself staring.

Slowly, the catch in his throat sank into his belly. Surrett was not an ugly man, with decent genes from his actress mother, but he definitely was not good-looking, powerful, or rich enough to have someone like her wander into his office. A terrifying realization hit him.

"Praise to the Holy Ones?" The words came out with less gusto than usual when he was standing before a high-ranking Genjix. If Surrett had one reliable quality, he was always properly simpering to the right people.

"Praise to the Holy Ones," the woman replied. Interestingly, her words were equally limp. She sounded almost bored, which was surprising for someone blessed as a vessel.

Surrett approached her and bent to one knee. He extended a hand. "I apologize, but may I confirm you?"

The woman sighed and held her hand out. Surrett flashed a mark scanner across her palm, and pulled up her bio. His eyes widened. She was a fixer, and a high-ranking one. That could only mean one thing. His eyes scrolled down to the name and the standing. The blood drained from his face, and Surrett found himself fiddling with his tie once more.

"Satisfied?" she said, pulling her hand away and wiping it with a handkerchief.

"It is an honor to receive someone of your standing, Adonis. How may I serve you?"

"How about you sit down in the chair?" she said. "You're not my lapdog. But while you think you are, fetch me a drink."

Surrett stood up and bowed. "Apologies, Adonis, but alcohol is frowned upon for those serving my administration. May I offer you something else? Coffee, tea?"

Shura rolled her eyes. "Tea this time. A Moscow Mule the next, understood? Now sit."

Surrett went to his intercom and buzzed Amita to bring in a fresh pot of tea. He took his time instructing her how he wanted it brewed, ordering her to use the finest they had available. He took that time to reach under his desk and palm the panel to begin surveillance in this room.

Surrett was loyal to the Genjix, but the battle for standing, especially among the Adonis vessels and those aspiring to the Council, could be brutal. An unblessed such as him often became collateral damage in their power struggles.

Besides, he owed his loyalty to Rurik, so it was almost his duty to spy on a competing Adonis vessel. This was a dangerous game, but one Surrett could take advantage of if the opportunity presented itself. If he could offer Rurik an advantage over one of his adversaries, it would dramatically help his chances.

"You can stop tapping that keypad under your desk now." Shura leaned back into the couch. "I disabled the console when I came in. Don't worry; if you do not see tomorrow, it won't be by my hand."

Surrett froze. He came around and took a seat in front of her abashedly. "If I may inquire, Adonis, how did you break into my office? The security to the administration building, and my wing in particular, is very tight. I have been in my office most of the day as well, yet you were able to bypass my security and come in right when I stepped away."

"Simple," Shura said. "Your security detail is amateur. It wasn't hard for anyone with a modicum of skill to slip past the sleeping fools at the gates, the moron at the garage, the incompetents wandering the hallways, the lech at the stairwell, and the old man in front who pisses every ten minutes. As for you stepping away–" she seemed amused, " –your voicemail and out-of-office email is bafflingly detailed. I'm surprised you haven't been assassinated yet."

"Those are strictly reserved for internal voicemails," Surrett said stiffly. "The public has no access to them."

The Adonis shrugged, just slightly. "Your mail server security isn't exactly top-grade either. That took all of fifteen minutes to access."

Amita walked in with a fresh tray of tea. His assistant

frowned when she saw the tall, beautiful white lady, no doubt wondering how she had gotten into the office. Surrett was willing to bet Amita was going to spend a few hours the next couple of days searching for a hidden entrance. Also, with the Adonis's striking looks, Amita might consider her something more unsavory and gossip with others in the building. He decided to nip that in the bud.

He gestured to Shura first. "How do you prefer your tea, Adonis?"

Amita's eyes widened and she gawked. She was low enough in standing to have never even met a vessel, let alone one of the Adonises. It was one thing to see an Adonis vessel in a video, it was another entirely to stand meters away. They were physically near-perfect humans.

"I am so blessed and honored–" Amita said, falling to one knee.

"Put the tea down and get out." Shura cut her off with a lazy wave of her hand. She shook her head as Amita beat a hasty retreat. "If I had to sit through this sort of ceremony every day, nothing would get done." She picked up a cup, blew on it and sipped. "No poison. We're starting off on the right foot, Minister.

"I would never, Adonis," Surrett stammered. "I serve–"

"Seriously, cut it out," Shura snapped. "My approval does not give you license to grovel more. Now, before we get down to business, soundproof this room. I'm sure there's probably another recording device I may have missed."

Surrett hesitated. There was indeed a backup. How did she know? He went back to his cabinet and took out a small gray machine. He placed it on the coffee table between them and turned it on. A low hum laid over the stillness, its resonance filling his ears. The pitch grew higher and higher until it became imperceptible to the human ear. He looked up at the Adonis and nodded. "The room is secure from all listening devices."

She placed the cup on the table in front of her. "Your primary responsibilities are to push India toward joining the Genjix and to oversee the construction of the Bio Comm Array project. One is progressing as planned. How is the other?"

"The Bio Comm Array construction goes as well as can be expected for a project of this magnitude," he replied. "However, I am confident–"

Shura took out a tablet and dropped it on the table with a loud slapping sound. She stabbed a finger on the screen, and several lists of blue numbers began floating in the air above it. "The Bio Comm Array was scheduled for its first test run a month ago. Facility construction is three months behind schedule, you're two hundred million Euros over budget, and the project has missed six of its last nine milestones. On top of that, you haven't even acquired all of the land stipulated in the blueprints."

"The build site is in a residential area," Surrett replied. "Land acquisition by law requires–"

"That is why the Genjix made you the Deputy Minister of Gujurat," she snapped. "So you can work around these bothersome laws."

Surrett bowed, the tie suddenly feeling very tight around his neck. "Since India has not yet officially joined the Genjix, there are obstacles that must be overcome. I apologize for the delays and will redouble my efforts."

Shura leaned forward. "I report directly to High Father Weston, and we both agree that this project is far too important to the Genjix for politics, so from this point on, I am taking over. You report directly to me, not Rurik. Is that clear?"

Surrett kept his eyes on the ground. His faith told him he should follow a direct order from an Adonis vessel. His loyalty told him he should at least pass this information along to Rurik, the owner of this project and the man who put him in charge. His ambition, though, told him to see how things unfolded. "Your will, Adonis."

Shura leaned back in the couch and crossed her legs again. "I see you have lobbied to be raised to a vessel."

Surrett choked on his tea. "Yes, Adonis, but..."

"Of course, given the rising output of the hatcheries from both Costa Rica and Moscow, as well as the new hatchery in Chengdu, attracting a Holy One may prove difficult for those climbing up the standings. One would almost need a sponsor. Has Rurik been supportive of your efforts?"

"I hope, in time, Father Rurik–"

"Perhaps you need a new sponsor." She smiled.

Sensing an opportunity, he bowed hastily. "It would be an honor, Mother."

"Good. Serve me well and I will personally see to it. I do not care if you report my presence to Rurik since I am here by the Council's request, but Rurik will make life tiresome for us both. If you do report to him, then I know where you stand, understood?"

"Yes, Adonis."

Shura smiled. "Good." She tapped the tablet and slid a finger to the right. Surrett's entire project plan appeared in the air. "I've identified the two most pressing issues: the supply chains are ineffective, and that is affecting the critical paths of the observatory structure." She pointed at a parcel of land on the northern edge of the site. "Why do we not already own from here to the river? It is absolutely vital we acquire and develop the area all the way to the docks. I don't care if it's residential. But I'm getting ahead of myself. Let's start with finances. What is the current status of your budget?"

Surrett experienced that sinking sensation in the pit of his stomach. The Adonis wasn't here to address the project's problems; she was here to take it over. His eyes flickered to the tiny camera hidden in the chandelier. It wouldn't be able to pick up audio because of the resonance disrupter she had him turn on, but it could still record video. He had to find a way to obey the Adonis, serve the Genjix, and yet still raise his standing. At the very least, he couldn't let her take the project away from him.

He was left with little choice. The key would be to find the wedge between Shura and Rurik and be the factor that influenced the winning side. Playing two Adonis vessels against each other was usually suicide, but standing had to be taken, seized, and Surrett intended to do just that. He glanced in the mirror and adjusted his tie until it was perfectly straight.

Conflict bred innovation. This was his chance.

CHAPTER TEN
Jail Time

For the second time that day, Ella woke up with a terrible headache. The first thing she felt was the cold, hard concrete on her cheek. She inhaled and gagged at the smell, and knew exactly where she was. Indian jail cells in the slums had their own unique, terrible stench, and this was by the measure of someone who had hidden in a pile of garbage the other day.

She sat up and stared at the rusty metal bars. On the other side, sitting at a desk facing the wall, was the man she dreaded seeing. She rose onto wobbly feet and grasped the bars with her hands. "Hey Uncle Manu, what does a girl have to do to get a drink of water around here?"

Manu, the inspector in charge of the Crate Town precinct, looked up from his work and smirked. "Well, hello, Black Cat. When Dhruv and Sanchit told me they had a present for me, I thought they were kissing my ass with more sandesh. Never in a hundred years did I think those two idiots were smart enough to catch you. They told me you practically walked up to them. I can only assume then that you wanted to see me so you could pay back that money you stole from me."

Why did you not tell me you conned the police?

"You didn't ask."

"Now, now," Ella replied to Manu. "It was an investment, and not all investments go our way."

"Is that so?" Manu said. He took a plastic cup and filled it with water. He walked up to her cell and held it out. When Ella reached for it, he pulled it back and took a sip. "I have an investment for you then. You get me back all the money I invested, with that fabulous return you promised, or you get to stay in this cell. You have until you die of thirst to pay me back, with interest." Manu took another sip and dumped the rest of the water on the floor, then walked back to his desk.

"How am I going to get your money back stuck here in this cell?" she yelled.

He began working again. "You're resourceful. Figure it out."

Ella sunk down to her knees and stared at the puddle of water on the other side of the bars. She reached between the bars with her hands and wetted her fingers, and then let a few drops fall into her mouth. She couldn't recall a worse situation than the one she was in right now. There was literally no one in the world she could think of who would be willing to give her money to get out of here, even if her life depended on it. That was a little depressing.

How much did you steal from him?

"I didn't steal. It was a bad investment. It happens."

Did you withhold vital information regarding the investment?

"Of course. He was the silent partner."

Did you fully intend on giving him the returns he expected?

"No, but who does?"

You stole from him. Dumb decision stealing from the police.

"Whose side are you on, anyway? Can you stop patronizing me and help me figure out how to get out of here?"

Already on it. Just relax.

It wasn't as if Ella had anything else to do in the cell. She lay down and stared at the ceiling, and traced the cracks running along it with her fingers. Much like how she used to see animals and faces and objects in cloud formations, she imagined shapes within the spiderweb-like lines that cut the ceiling.

She pretended that two dark, nearly parallel lines formed a mighty river and the small bumps on either side were hills. The pointy grooves became trees and the small circles transformed into animals. Before she knew it, she was staring at a lovely forest. Then she imagined that the water stains slowly spreading across the surface of the ceiling were waves of lava flowing over the land, burning everything in their path.

That went down a dark train of thought.

Ella sighed, and erased that image from her head. She reformed the lines again, this time imagining the two edges of a tower. The bumps on the sides were clouds, the grooves became planes, and the circles were bombs. The water stain became the smoke that choked the air.

You grew up during the war?

Ella nodded. "The day the Vadsar Air Base was attacked, I was in school down the street with all the other army brats. Teacher took us away on the bus and we fled south. I thought I saw Amma's plane get shot down."

I am sorry.

"I've been in Crate Town ever since. A kid doesn't have a lot of happy thoughts growing up in that world."

What about your father?

"He's an asshole. Appa and Amma got into a big fight a few weeks before the attack. The next day, he was gone. I haven't heard from him since. I hope he's dead."

Ella kept staring at the water stains, wondering if any of it was going to form a drip. At least she'd get a drink that way. Probably dysentery too, but it wasn't like she was going to live much longer anyhow. Maybe Manu was bluffing. She raised her head and looked over at the uncle still working at his desk. No, probably not. She was just lucky that bastard was too lazy to torture. Otherwise – she looked over at the car battery on the floor attached to clamps – things could really get unpleasant.

You have never seen the forest, have you?

"Nope. Army bases and Crate Town."

One day, I will show you.

"Like we're ever getting out of here alive. Didn't you say you were working to get us out?"

I am. Hang tight.

"It's already been three hours. How much more hanging do we have to do?"

There was a long pause.

"Hey, Io?"

Yes?

"That famous general you used to possess, the one that died to a bunch of American Indians, his name wasn't Custer, was it?"

As a matter of fact, it was.

"Go figure," Ella sighed. "Of all the aliens I get in my head... Wait, you weren't at that Alamo place, were you?"

No. Why do you only know those historical events and not the important battles I led, like Brownstown during the War of 1812 or Kemmel Ridge during the Great War?

Ella shrugged. "I get my education from television and cinema. If they didn't make a movie about it, it couldn't have been that important."

Rescue came later that evening. To Ella's shock, it came in the form of Coward, the man who had kidnapped her and brought her back to his apartment. The tall thin Englishman, looking decidedly uncomfortable, arrived with a suitcase of money and offered to bail her out. Manu was almost as surprised as she was and began to tack on demands to the final bill. Not only did Coward have to pay for bail, he also had to repay the money Ella had supposedly conned from Manu, as well as an additional fee for services rendered. To Ella, it was an astronomical amount, but Coward didn't even bat an eye as he counted the money and pushed the pile across the table.

"Pleasure doing business," Manu purred. He turned to Ella.

"And you stay out of business, you hear?"

Ella filed out of the police station and took a deep breath. It still smelled like garbage right outside the precinct, but not nearly as bad as her cell. She had only been there a few hours, but she felt as if she had done hard time. She looked over at Coward walking beside her, and stuck out her hand. "I guess I should thank you, Coward."

"I guess you should," he replied, shaking it. "My name is Hamilton, not Coward. Hamilton Breckenridge."

"Ham, Hameel... Feck..." Ella struggled over the name. She often had trouble with English words with too many syllables. "Can I just call you Coward?"

"Absolutely not."

"All right, Hammy. How did you find me anyway?"

"It's Hamilton. I've been monitoring you ever since you joined with Io. As her auxiliary, it's my duty to assist her in any way possible. It's important these days for all hosts to have backups."

Ella pretended not to notice Hamilton's face darken at that last sentence. "Well, does that mean you're backing me up now?"

"All hosts are ranked as commanders. I am here to assist you in any way possible." There it was again.

Ella had a pretty sharp eye when it came to tells. Being observant came with the territory in her line of work. She could learn a lot just from watching someone walking down the street, much more if they opened their mouths. From the cadence of their footsteps to the inflection on certain words, or even the way they hung their hands at their sides, everyone had tells.

It was also in the way their face scrunched or the way they spoke with gritted teeth. The biggest tells were always in the eyes, and right now, Hamilton's eyes were telling her he was unhappy with her, or this situation, or perhaps with Io, but he was doing his best not to show that he was surly.

"Hey Io, what's his deal?"

Hamilton was with my previous host for only a few months. He is sensitive.

"Sensitive about what? The guy is barely hiding the fact he hates my guts. Is he mad because I kicked his ass when he was creeping all over me?"

He was not creeping over you. He was tending to your wounds, and I believe he would disagree with you on who won that fight.

"Whatever. Whoever comes out of a fight prettier wins. If he's not mad that a girl half his size showed him who the bigger man was, then what is he angry about?"

Probably because you are my host, and not him. Both sides lost Quasing in staggering numbers during the war. Auxiliary ranks were created and assigned to assist hosts, and to serve as a backup for a Quasing in the event the primary host passes.

"You guys can die?"

Yes, if we are exposed too long to your environment without finding a host.

"So he's a backup body for you to inhabit if something happens to me?"

If you wish to put it that way.

"So why didn't you enter him instead of me when that woman died?"

I have my reasons. And her name was Emily, Emily Curran. You should respect those who came before you.

"Emma... Emily Curran, Emily Curran." Ella repeated that name in her head.

"Pardon?" Hamilton asked. "You say something?"

"Never mind."

The two walked in silence for most of the way to her container cluster. Ella wasn't sure what to make of this new tall, thin, pasty-white man. First of all, there was no way he could hang out with her regularly. He stood out like a sore thumb. It wasn't that white people were rare in the slums. Crate Town was a melting pot with people from all over the world. Indians lived in harmony next to Pakistanis, Koreans next to Japanese, Saudis next to Iranians. All people here cared about was survival and profit, not ethnicity.

Hamilton stood out because he did not look like he belonged in Crate Town. His clothes were too clean, his walk was too polite and timid, without the swagger that signaled to others not to mess with him. Frankly, she was surprised he hadn't been beaten up and robbed a couple of times already. It would totally ruin Ella's reputation on the streets to have this gangly foreigner following her around wherever she went. It would probably spell the end of her career as a conwoman.

Not necessarily a bad thing.

"Says you. I love my job."

Being a con artist is not a profession.

Hamilton escorted her all the way to her front door, and for a second, Ella was horrified and embarrassed that he might try to come inside. Very few people in her life had seen the inside of her home and she preferred it that way. This guy might be her new assistant or auxiliary or whatever they called it, but he was still a complete stranger.

To her surprise, Burglar Alarm greeted them without her trademark loud barking. The mutt went up to the man, tail wagging, and sniffed his hand and sat down. Hamilton even went as far as to scratch the dog's ear. Ella couldn't recall any time the dog was that friendly to anybody else. She wasn't sure how she felt about that.

"This is my home," she said. "You can't come in."

He nodded. "We have a lot of work to do. As a new host, your safety and training is of utmost importance. Since India is considered an unfriendly territory, I'd like you to consider leaving for a more Prophus-friendly country, possibly Australia or the United States or even Britain."

Tell him no.

Ella crossed her arms. "Not a chance. This is my home. I'm not abandoning it just because you say so."

Hamilton sighed. "I assumed that would be your position.

In that case, Prophus command has identified a dormant operative who can at least begin training you. Be ready at seven first thing tomorrow morning."

That was news to her. Ella crossed her arms and dug in. "Is that so? Nobody asked me what I thought about that."

"It's for your own good," Hamilton said. "You are in possession of a Quasing. It's your responsibility to protect Io."

I am very valuable, after all.

"You're not valuable if I can't see you."

"Besides," Hamilton continued. "I just paid a lot of money to free you from jail. Consider that payment enough for your training."

The man had a point.

"Fine," she said. "But if I don't like it, I can quit anytime."

"Of course."

"And I never have to pay you back that money you gave Manu."

"The thought didn't even cross my mind." Hamilton tipped an imaginary hat and then walked down the stairs.

Ella waited until he was out of sight, and watched as Burglar Alarm went to the top of the stairs to watch him leave. In all the time that the dog had lived on her front steps, Burglar Alarm had never seen Ella off like that. Ella stared curiously as the dog whined, and then went back to her nest.

There was more to this Ham, Hammy... Hamilton Booger... Bookerwidge – whatever – than met the eye. He was not only a coward, but a dog savant as well.

She went into her house and gave herself a good sniff. It seemed she had brought much of that rancid jail with her on her clothing. For some reason, ever since she got this alien in her, she'd been dirtying up faster than usual. At this rate, she'd need to visit Wiry Madras again soon. She stripped off all her clothes, treated herself to a fizz drink from the mini-fridge, and plopped down on her sofa.

The life that you know is over. Change is coming. Be ready.

"I really am stuck with you, aren't I? Until death do us part?"

Well, technically, until your death. I am then free to find a new host.

"Typical man."

We technically do not have genders. However, on this planet, most Quasing identify with the gender of our hosts.

"So you're female then."

Currently, yes.

She raised her drink again. "Girl power." She took a sip and paused. "This could be the most serious relationship I've ever had."

And it has only been two days.

"I guess if we're stuck together for life, I should know more about you, like where you came from and what you do and what you want and all that stuff? More importantly, I want to know what I get out of it."

I can do better than tell you. I can show you. Did you notice those flashes of images? That was me projecting my memories to you, or more specifically, my memory of your memory.

"Yeah, I wish you'd cut it out. It gives me headaches."

That is an unfortunate effect of active projection. Most humans can only tolerate it for a few seconds at a time while awake. While you sleep though, I can project for longer, and show you my history.

"Like watching a movie?"

In a way. You may not grasp all the details this way, but you will wake knowing more about who I am and where I came from. It will become your past as well.

Ella yawned. She went to the next room and jumped on the bed. "Sounds like fun. It better be fascinating. I get bored and fall asleep easily."

Well then, it is a good thing I have a captive audience. Hope you like nightmares.

"Wait, what?"

Good night.

CHAPTER ELEVEN
The Coach

The beginning is as good a place to start as any. The Quasing come from a planet known as Quasar at the other end of the galaxy. Wait, before we go any further, a quasar in human scientific terms has nothing to do with the name of our planet. The scientist who coined the term "quasar" was a host and breathtakingly uncreative. As you learn about us, you will discover that our influence has touched many aspects of humanity's history and evolution.

Time to get up. Hamilton will be here soon.

For the third day in a row, Ella woke up exhausted. She remembered some of what Io showed her the night before, but she couldn't quite nail down the details. It was more vague sensations, shadows, sudden streaks of light, warmth. She heard thousands of voices that spoke as one, felt a calmness as if she were floating in the middle of the ocean.

She couldn't quite wrap her head around all the imagery and needed Io to fill in the descriptions on what she had sensed or felt or whatever. To be honest, she wasn't impressed. She had thought being on an alien planet would be a more exotic and cinematic experience.

She stayed in bed longer than intended, chatting with Io about this first weird alien-induced dream until Burglar

Alarm announced someone coming up the stairs. There was a polite knock on the door. Ella scowled when she saw Coward's – no, Hamilton's – face. She checked the time. The guy was on the dot.

"Give me a few minutes," Ella said, slamming the door in his face.

There was still no way she'd allow the man inside. She took her time to wash and dress, and then fifteen minutes more to cook breakfast. She admitted she was acting surly and childish but if both Hamilton and Io were going to make her do something, then as far as she was concerned, she had no reason to hurry. Ella finally came out some thirty minutes later.

Hamilton was playing with Burglar Alarm, and if he was upset by being forced to wait, he didn't show it. "Good morning," he said, a little too cheerfully. "I brought you some tea, but I'm afraid it's gotten a bit cold."

Ella stared at the cup. She would have loved hot tea this morning. "No, lukewarm is just the way I like it." She took it from him and sipped. "Where are we going?"

"You'll find out soon enough. Come along."

The two of them left her cluster and walked toward the nearest main intersection, where Hamilton signaled for a tuk-tuk. Ella climbed in and didn't think anything of it until they left the boundaries of Crate Town. She began to fidget. As long as they stayed in Crate Town, Ella was comfortable enough letting him lead her somewhere. Once they left the safety of her home turf, she got worried. Hamilton was still a stranger. With every passing kilometer, she shrank deeper and deeper into her seat.

Stop acting so skittish. You must learn to trust Hamilton and me. We are here for your good.

"That works both ways, alien. I'm the one sitting here not knowing where you're taking me. If you want me to trust you, you need to start cluing me in on what you're up to.

Wait, why are we coming here?"

The tuk-tuk had just turned left into Little Dharavi, which, while not as poor as Crate Town, was much more seedy and known for prostitution and gambling rings. Little Dharavi was notorious for kidnapping children for the sex trade and was the home to much of the organized crime in the city. For all she knew, Hamilton could be selling her into slavery. Panic seized Ella and, for a moment, she almost leaped out of the moving vehicle.

Hamilton must have noticed the alarm in her eyes and grabbed her arm before she could jump. Ella pulled back with her elbow and reached for her shank.

Do not stab your auxiliary.

"I'm not going to let him sell me into–"

"We're here," he said, pointing at a small storefront off one of the main streets.

Ella frowned. "That's a boxing gym."

"Quite observant. What gave it away, the ring or the punching bags?"

"No, smart ass. I mean, what are we doing here?"

Hamilton stepped off the tuk-tuk and offered her a hand. "Where else do you think you were going to train?"

Now you know why we did not tell you.

"Damn right. I can't decide what's worse. Bringing me to this cesspool or taking me to a gym."

This is important, Ella. The people coming after you next time will be much more dangerous than those amateur gangsters.

"I've handled them fine on my own."

The police will not always be there to bail you out of trouble by arresting you. My enemies, and yours now, will just as likely kill policemen to get to me.

"Gods, fine, anything to get you to stop talking."

Ella felt intimidated the moment she stepped foot into Murugan's Mitts. The gym was on a busy side street nestled between an eyebrow-threading booth and an incense store.

The front entrance was a metal door currently rolled up with a faded sign hanging crooked from the wall. Several punching bags of assorted sizes hung from the ceiling in the front, followed by a boxing ring near the back.

There were maybe two dozen people of different ages and sizes inside. Some looked as young as seven or eight, others looked so weathered they could be her grandparents. Every single one of them stopped what they were doing as she and Hamilton passed.

Ella held her breath. The deeper they got into this gym, the worse it stunk of sweat and dirt. Everyone inside was shirtless save for a large young man sitting behind a desk in the back. He looked nothing like the others working out. He was a giant of a man, tall with beefy arms and an extended gut on a round body that looked like it had its own gravitational pull. His head was smooth and hairless, and oval-shaped like an overripe melon. Ella was willing to bet every coin in her pocket that was Murugan.

Murugan is the Hindi god of war.

"Oops."

Your education on your own religion has been lacking as well.

"I believe in all the Hindi gods. I just don't have all day to talk to them individually. I also fear an even higher power: hunger."

The melon-headed man stopped what he was doing and eyed them curiously. A tall white man and a tiny brown girl. The two of them must have made for an interesting sight. Finally, Melonhead spat to the side and went back to whatever he was doing. "The hourly rooms are a block over."

Hamilton cleared his throat and stepped forward. "Let come what comes, let go what goes."

Melonhead tilted his head and stared Hamilton down, then looked over at Ella, and then back at Hamilton. He pointed toward the exit. "Like I said, the hotel for the hourly rooms is one over."

Hamilton looked at a loss. "Well, this is Murugan's Mitts, the school of boxing and chiropractic, correct?"

"And we teach mallakhamba at nights," Melonhead added. He looked at Ella. "All classes are filled until late summer. You can sign up in the fall when children's classes begin."

Ella wanted to punch him right in his melon head.

"Are you Manish, the proprietor?" asked Hamilton.

Melonhead looked toward a small back room. "Uncle, some white pervert is here to see you."

"I'm not…"

An older Indian man appeared. He was obviously related to Melonhead, albeit a much less round and more pruned version. His physique showed remnants of a man who was once in really good shape.

He eyed Hamilton up and down. "Legs too skinny, needs to fill out his frame, but good reach. I can work with him." He looked at Ella. "You I can't, even for the other stuff."

"Are you Manish?" Hamilton asked again.

The man nodded. "Welcome to the finest boxing gym and mallakhamba school in all of India. I've taught the best. You here for some training, white man? I can make you a champion."

"Let come what comes, let go what goes," Hamilton said once more.

Any eagerness Manish had in acquiring a new student filled with potential morphed into a look of disgust. "Oh, you're one of those. After all these years…"

"Excuse me, Mr Manish, the passphrase."

"Fine, fine," the older Indian man said. "See what remains. You happy now? I haven't had anyone from the Prophus contact me for so long I thought you had all forgotten about me."

"Yet you have been more than happy to collect your stipend from us all these years," Hamilton said.

Manish shrugged. "Only a fool turns down free money.

Besides, I never said I wouldn't honor the agreement. So you need some training? You a new host?"

"It's not for me," Hamilton replied. He looked down at Ella.

Manish frowned, and walked a slow circle around Ella, eying her physique and pinching her arm. She felt like a piece of meat being appraised for market. "Fire in her belly. Small belly, small fire." She felt a hand press on her back and tug her shoulders. "Don't slouch, girl." He grabbed her wrist and raised her arm. "Like a toothpick."

Ella yanked her arm back and reached for her shank. "I'll show you a toothpick." The shank was gone. She patted the empty hidden sheath. "What...?"

Manish lazily twirled the shank in his hand. "Looking for this?"

Ella swiped at it, only to grab air as Manish flicked it back. Growling, she lunged at him and was sent tumbling off-balance. She would have fallen if he hadn't grabbed her by the collar and held her up.

"Give me my shank back, you old bastard."

"I see we have a lot of work to do. Let's start with your body and worry about weapons later." In one fluid motion, Manish flung the shank to the side, sheathing it in a wooden beam halfway across the room. "And from this point on, it's Coach Bastard to you."

Ella crossed her arms and took a step back. Not only did she dislike this guy, he was also bossing her around, although she was a little curious about how he was able to steal her shank without her noticing. Now that was something she wanted to learn.

Your education as an operative must start somewhere. Manish was an accomplished agent and has trained others over the years.

"Oh, fine, but you Prophus better be compensating me for all this effort."

We Prophus. You are one of us now.

"That remains to be seen."

"All right," Manish said, leading her to a row of weights on the side. He pointed at a workout bench. "Let's establish a baseline, shall we?"

What transpired over the next thirty minutes was a battery of tests that thoroughly betrayed her embarrassing lack of physical fitness. Hamilton and Manish, and probably Io as well, watched and judged her every move, or lack of. She did exercises to test her strength, flexibility, reaction and coordination.

At the end of the torture, she recorded a grand total of zero pull-ups, twelve push-ups, nineteen sit-ups, but she could touch her toes. When she hit the punching bag, it moved her more than she moved it, and she was rewarded with a sprained wrist for her efforts.

Things only went further downhill when they had her try to bench press. At one point, she wobbled so badly she almost dropped the bar on her head. Through all of these pitiful attempts, she grunted and growled as if she were giving birth. What she gave birth to was complete failure. She finished up the test feeling more than a little beaten up, downtrodden, and thoroughly humiliated.

That was bad. We really have our work cut out for us.

Ella's lone bright spot was when she ran through agility drills. She was abysmal jumping rope, but when it came to quick twitch movements and changes of directions, she impressed even the old coach. When Manish had some of his students try to catch her in a game of tag, she was able to easily evade every single one of them. That was the one skill from surviving in Crate Town that translated to these dumb drills.

By the end of the tests, everyone's spirits were down. Manish lounged on a bench off to the side, looking as if he had already lost interest. Melonhead was leaning against the wall, smirking the entire time. Hamilton was slouched forward, resting his head on his hand, his elbow on his knee.

He looked resigned, almost a little angry and not a little smug as well.

Manish slapped his lap and stood up. “All right. Let’s see how you handle yourself in the ring.”

“Wait, what?” Ella exclaimed. “Is your brain not working, old man? You want one of your gorillas to box my face?”

“It would be an improvement, and that’s Coach Old Man to you, you little stray.”

“That’s samrãjñ⊠ of Crate Town to you, raisin head.”

“Samrãjñ⊠? Hah.” Manish tossed her a set of boxing gloves. “My nine year-old grandson uses these. They might still be too big for you, but that’s all I have.”

“I’m surprised a man of your qualities managed to find a woman to produce an offspring.”

“For every ugly and desperate man, there is an equally ugly and desperate woman. Then there is you.”

As Ella approached him to get into the boxing ring, he leaned in and sniffed. “I smell the gutter.”

She sniffed him back. “I smell death.”

The two flung more insults back and forth, and by the time they had completed a dozen exchanges, both were grinning openly. Manish reached out and tussled Ella’s head as if she were a pet. He then raised one of the boxing ropes and pushed her inside. “Now get in there and show me what you got, and try not to get too much of your blood on my floor.” He looked over to the side. “Aarav, come box this runt.”

Melonhead came forward. She turned to the old coach. “Aren’t there supposed to be weight classes or something? I can’t fight this plump ox.”

“This is just a test to see how you move,” Manish said. “I’ll have the boy go easy on you.”

Melonhead, or Aarav, looked down at her in disgust. “You want me to beat this ragged stick?”

“Seems I’m the only one between us who has one,” she shot back. She regretted the words as soon as they left her mouth. Maybe antagonizing this large brutish man wasn't the smartest idea. Sometimes, Ella just had no control over what she said.

That is something we are going to have to work on.

Melonhead scowled and reached for a set of boxing gloves. He slipped them on and slammed them together with a loud whack. "We'll see what we can do about that big mouth of yours."

Ella's eyes widened as Melonhead climbed in and lumbered toward her. He looked much bigger up close. He kind of smelled like dirty undergarments too, but that was the least of her worries right now.

Melonhead slapped his gloves together twice more and opened his arms. "Give me your best shot, little weed."

Ella figured she only had one chance, which was to take him by surprise. She charged forward and nailed him as hard as she could in the stomach. Her fist made a small indentation in his belly and she bounced backward, tumbling onto the mat. Melonhead and the few curious spectators standing around the ring laughed uproariously.

His body is too thick and well padded. Your only option is to tire him out. You are quick and nimble. Avoid him.

Ella got to her feet and snarled at his stupid grin. "Screw that."

"You want more?" Melonhead said. He patted his belly and opened his arms again. "I'll give you one more try, and then I'm going to clobber–"

Before he could finish his sentence, Ella stomped up to him, pulled an arm back as if she were going to throw a punch, and then kicked him in the groin as hard as she could. Melonhead squeaked and fell to his knees. It made him just the right height for her to take another swing at his face. She connected to his chubby cheeks and sprained her thumb badly. Fortunately, it didn't take much more to knock him down as Melonhead tipped over to his side, sniveling and moaning in pain.

You do know that boxing uses only hands, right?

"There are no rules where I come from."

There was a brief moment of shocked silence, and then all the spectators began muttering amongst themselves. Several shot dark looks at her. The mood in the gym got ugly.

Ella hurried out of the ring and shook her gloves at Hamilton. "Take these off and let's get out of here before they lynch me."

Hamilton scanned the room and hastened to unlace her gloves. "That was probably unwise. We may need to fight our way out of here after all."

The low chatter grew louder, and before she knew it, Ella found herself surrounded by a small mob. She reached for her shank which, of course, wasn't there.

"Damn that sneaky old man." She had never missed her shank so badly in her life. "We're in trouble now."

Manish stepped in front of them and waved everybody back. He glanced over at Melonhead still writhing in the boxing ring. He yelled at the angry group. "What's the lesson here?"

"Don't box with cheaters," someone shouted.

"Don't box with a girl."

"Don't let a girl in the gym next time."

The comments only got uglier. Ella balled her fists and raged, but she was outnumbered twenty to one. She looked over at Hamilton, who actually managed to appear even angrier. At that moment, she decided to forgive him for being a coward.

"No, you idiots," Manish said. "The lesson to learn is to shut your mouth, stop showboating, and get your punch off first. It doesn't matter who your opponent is. Aarav's head is too big, he opened his mouth too many times, and he got his lund kicked." He looked over at Ella. "You two have wasted enough of my day. Get out of here."

Ella and Hamilton beat a hasty retreat toward the front.

"We'll find someone else to train you, I promise," said Hamilton.

"I don't want anyone to train me at all," she grumbled.

Manish called after them. "Tomorrow morning, be here at seven, got it? There'll be less of my kids around. We can get to work then."

Both Ella and Hamilton turned around and looked back at the coach. Ella was reluctant to say yes, but she also didn't want to say no. "OK."

"That's 'OK, coach,' to you, girl."

CHAPTER TWELVE
The Carrot

At first, the Quasing simply existed inside the dense liquid on the surface of Quasar that we call the Eternal Sea. Like most intelligent life, we became self-aware. We bred and evolved, and eventually discovered that we could join with each other, combining to transform into something greater.

Over time, the Eternal Sea became one giant living being, integrating all the Quasing together. We shared our collective memories, knowledge, and experiences. We were able to mature our young quickly through osmosis and drastically increased our reproduction cycle. We grew, evolved, and became ambitious.

The route to the build site took Shura through some colorful and seedy parts of Surat. For some reason, the minister had tried to shield her from the more impoverished and blighted areas of the city, as if she were some porcelain noble who had never seen abject poverty.

Having been on the front lines for most of the war, Shura had not only witnessed some of the most destitute places in the world, she had had front row seats to their creation, which was a much stranger and more moving experience. It was one thing to witness a slum, it was another thing entirely to see a beautiful city reduced to one right in front of your eyes.

Vienna still troubles you.

"I spent many wonderful years there. It will always be my favorite city."

I remember your delight at being stationed there when the war broke out.

"For my personal knowledge of the city. Only to see it shattered and reduced to rubble in the ensuing months." Shura couldn't keep the bitterness out of her thoughts.

Shura had endured some of the worst miseries humanity had to offer at that front. She had razed entire villages – the elderly, women, children – when it was discovered that they had poisoned her division's food supply. She had slept in blood-soaked clothes for months on end during the attack on Austria, when their supply lines had been cut off, and the enemy dominated the skies. She had eaten horses and dogs alongside her troops during the retreat east through Warsaw. She had cradled the blank-staring heads of her soldiers in her hands as she put them out of their pain.

She looked out the window as the car took her from the uneven and sagging neighborhood to one that all of a sudden looked completely symmetrical and orderly, as if the builders had decided to erect a city from LEGO blocks. Gone was her view of bent and misshapen buildings, awkward patchwork walls, and chaotic kaleidoscope of broken structures. Now, the buildings were stacked together with straight lines and perfect corners. Although the area was still a wretched slum, Shura approved of this novel use of old shipping containers.

"We're here." Surrett, sitting next to her, pointed to the side as the car turned off a main street. "Please wait inside while I have the police detail clear out the riffraff."

Right away, Shura could tell why the Genjix chose this area for the build site. It was embedded within a heavy residential area, limiting the enemy's options of bombing it. The Gulf of Khambhat also made the region easily defensible. The Tapi

River provided a natural breakpoint to regulate the water flow for cooling the bio generators while at the same time allowing supplies to be easily brought in by ocean.

Not only that, Surat is in an optimal geographical position relative to the moon's trajectory. This is the ideal location to build the Bio Comm Array facility. Now if only they can complete the project.

"That's what we're here for. To save the day."

Shura studied the fortified perimeter gates as they passed through the entrance. Many of the Bio Comm Array structures on the inside were pushing up against the fence while the slums on the outside were threatening to break in. A person could almost jump between roofs. Something had to be done about that.

The site needs another four thousand square meters, conservatively, as well as straight access to the ocean. That strip of residential land between the site and the docks is unacceptable.

"Among other things."

She looked back at the hundreds of miserable people milling about the streets outside the fence. The number of people in that kilometer of land, called the Dumas neighborhood, could be in the thousands.

The car came to a halt, and for the next hour, Surrett showed her, a little too proudly perhaps, the mostly-finished construction site. The work was good for the most part. The site was clean and orderly. Right away, Shura understood what sort of manager Surrett was. The man was a born organizer. He was meticulous to a fault, to the point where he didn't seem to know when to leave the extraneous details.

The minister painstakingly went over every single location of the site, leading her through the primary Array facility, walking her down the desalination pipes, and even taking her to the proposed Quasing housing facilities where the thousands of newborns were to be kept.

Shura stared at the patch of empty earth. "What am I supposed to be looking at?"

I can see why no other Quasing would choose him as a vessel. I am irritated just listening to him. If he were my vessel, I would order him to commit suicide by the end of the first day.

"You are rather fortunate to have my charming company then, Tabs."

Fortunate for you, perhaps. Else I would just have you drowned. Tell this human to move on past these frivolous details and to the important matters.

"I can read the blueprints later. Let's get to the problems at hand," said Shura, cutting Surrett off.

The minister nodded and signaled for the inspector of the police guarding them. "Inspector Manu, please clear a path for us to the street."

Shura watched as the police officers waded into the crowds with sticks in their hands. The people obviously knew who Surrett was, the looks on their faces clear as he walked among them. Everywhere they had gone so far today required the dozen burly uniformed men to constantly push back the crowds. These were people with little love or respect for the police. No matter how brutal these uniformed men were with their sticks, the rabble didn't seem to learn and kept filling in the spaces.

Every once in a while, a child would break through, only to get cuffed to the ground before reaching them. Shura wasn't sure how long this tension had gone on between the minister and the community, but it felt like a familiar thing.

Surrett looked at her apologetically. "As you can see, the local community has resisted us every step of the way. We need to clear approximately six city blocks for the build site to reach the docks. That's roughly two hundred structures, maybe eighteen hundred containers. We've offered them more than fair reimbursement, but most have turned us down. They are making things difficult."

A few beggars cannot stand in the way of an important Genjix project. Is this man feckless?

"Send these twelve police in with their bats and just root them out," Shura shrugged. "It's not like any of this will be missed."

"A few poor people are no problem," Surrett said hastily. "However, to clear the space for the site will require us relocating thousands of people living in those containers. This particular slum, known as Crate Town, is also notoriously tribal and insular when it comes to outsiders. Three of the community leaders who own stakes in this disputed area have been particularly vocal against the proposal and have turned the community against their own government. Now, we face opposition not only from those we need to move, but from the entire slum. That numbers in the hundreds of thousands."

Cut off the head and the snake will fall.

"Who are these three leaders?" Shura asked.

"Faiz the trader, Indu the monk, and Mogg the gangster."

The merchant, the priest, and the criminal. What sort of bad joke is this?

"Seems the joke is on us since we have to deal with it."

Shura said aloud to Surrett, "Why single out those three?"

"Faiz owns large swathes of the Dumas properties. Mogg is head of the dockworkers' union and also runs a large racketeering ring on the west side of Crate Town. Indu heads the temple in the heart of that neighborhood. They're the ones with the most to lose if we pave over it and turn it into a giant military facility."

"Can't you just arrest them for sedition?"

"Using force in this wasteland is like striking sand," Surrett said. "No matter how hard and how many times you hit them, little happens."

Shura sighed. "Very well. Let's go see one of them."

"Now?"

"Right this moment. I don't have time to waste, and neither does this project."

Shura followed Surrett and Manu as they carved a path

through the crowded street. She masked her irritation, but inside she raged a little. This all seemed so petty. She was used to dealing with world leaders and princes and presidents, not poor community leaders and business owners wallowing in dirt. The fact that the minister had not simply paved over these slums by now was just another indication that he didn't have the right mental makeup to climb any higher.

Do not judge so quickly. The young man is looking out for his future. Evicting thousands of residents makes for a poor public relations headline when one aspires to be prime minister.

"Genjix goals should trump personal ambition."

One could argue that elevating one of ours to become the leader of India aligns with our goals.

"Not if it delays a project as important as the Bio Comm Array. Besides, we need someone in charge who can establish permanent Genjix authority in this country, not compromise and get voted out in the next election cycle."

They entered a building much larger than the ones surrounding it, measuring nine containers wide and stacked four tall – a veritable mansion. It was also one of the few buildings on the block that had a yard and was not designed as shared housing. They entered a spacious and surprisingly well-decorated home with furnishings Shura would have expected from someone living in upper-middle class homes in Moscow. The well-kept and clean interior starkly contrasted with the rusted raw industrial container walls outside.

The hair on the back of Shura's neck pricked up. The home had air conditioning, running water, electricity, and – she checked the frequency signals on her watch – a strong network connection. This was hardly something she thought she'd see here in the slum. She revised her thoughts of Crate Town. She had assumed the homes here were temporary camps or shacks, but these were actually modular residences and would be much more difficult to uproot than originally thought.

This Faiz may be a difficult and expensive person to buy off.

"He is still a businessman, and in the end, he will only care about how much he can profit from this transaction. Let's go feed him a carrot."

Faiz was reputed to be one of the wealthiest men in the area. The people around him surely weren't living quite so richly. However, no matter how wealthy a man he was in Crate Town, he was still only a man living in a slum. He couldn't be that well off.

Tabs wasn't wrong though. The cost of buying wealth was an exponential equation. It wasn't that Shura didn't have the funds; she could easily buy off one man with Genjix money, but it would reflect poorly upon her to be so wasteful.

The Genjix prided themselves on efficiency, to accomplish as much as possible with the least amount of resources. It was also one thing to buy off one man, it would be another to buy off thousands, and once everyone else saw how much it cost to buy one, the price would only go up from there.

Shura noted the liveried servants, armed with machetes, doubling as bodyguards. One of the servants, more ornately dressed than the others, led them upstairs to the fourth floor.

There is not a firearm in sight.

"Guns shouldn't be hard to procure in this area. We are not too far from the front lines of a recently fought war, after all."

A taboo or some local custom, perhaps.

The servant escorted them to the end of the hallway where two guards stood watch in front of an elegantly carved wooden door. One of the guards swung the door open and they entered an office that Shura had to admit seemed positively rich. A handsome, well-dressed man with a head of gray hair and a neatly-trimmed beard sat behind an expansive wooden table that was far too large to have fit through the door. The top of the table was barren, except for an ashtray with a cigar burning inside.

Four lights from each corner of the ceiling covered every

centimeter of the table. Faiz was making a point. The entire room was set up to accentuate the table and to point out that he was wealthy enough to either build a room around it or that he had cut out part of the house to crane the table in.

"Master Faiz," the servant bowed nearly to his knees, "your guests are here."

Faiz stood up. "Welcome, Minister Kapoor, my friend. So good of you to come see me so soon after our last discussion. I hope you're not wasting your time again. Every week you come to speak with me as if you were asking for my daughter's hand in marriage, and every week I send you off disappointed. May I offer you tea, coffee?"

Surrett shook the man's hand. "Thank you for seeing me on such short notice." He sat down in the chair opposite Faiz while Shura leaned against the wall next to the door. She was content to let the minister take the lead. It afforded her more opportunities to study the negotiations and probe for an opening.

Faiz looked past Surrett's shoulder at her and leered. "Who is your friend? She is quite a knockout."

Shura decided to play along. She had noticed the half dozen Hindu idols and paintings dotting the walls on the way up here. She clasped her palms together and bowed. "*Namaskaara. Kaise hain aap*?"

Faiz brightened and barked out forceful sharp laughs. He turned to Surrett. "I like her. Where did you find her?"

Shura kept her smile painted on her face. She was happy to let the man continue to dig his grave.

Surrett coughed uncomfortably. "The government sent my associate here to observe, and possibly to find a way to break through our stalemate. My superiors within the administration have great need for this land. It's for the good of India. She is assisting me in these talks. The military speaks of this as a matter of national security."

That was a mistake.

Shura agreed. Surrett was trying to emphasize the inevitable nationalization of the contested area by their Land Acquisition Law, but in reality, he sounded desperate. To litigate through those channels could tie up the land for years. Failure to close a deal would also paint him as the minister who couldn't close on his own deal without help from the central government.

"National security, eh?" Faiz chuckled. "You haven't used that one before."

"Of course," Surrett continued. "This is most definitely a matter of national urgency. It is vital to India's security and economic vitality that we continue construction in a timely manner. The Ministry of Planning has already blessed this expansion. The contractors have been–"

That was another mistake.

Faiz waved him off. "I looked into everything you've said, Minister. You are not telling me the whole truth. The ministry has indeed approved construction permits, but that is simply paying off the right officials to sign pieces of paper. You're doing this for a foreign company. You're in their pockets." He wagged a finger at Surrett. "I looked into you, Minister. What was your stupid campaign slogan? 'Fair and honest Kapoor, we know what he stands for'? Hah. By the way, you used two words that mean the same thing."

"I'm sure we can come to a working accommodation," Surrett pressed. "We can pay you fairly for your properties or we can take them from you. Why not make a few rupees for your trouble? Otherwise, you'll just end up with nothing."

The two continued their negotiations, moving on to property value, trade, and relocation costs. After twenty minutes, they got nowhere and moved on to Faiz's business, which was being the largest slum lord in all of Crate Town. Faiz emphasized how unpopular this proposal was and how his reputation in the slums would plummet, and how he might even lose his seat on the Crate Town business council.

Surrett offered to move him out of the slums altogether and even offered a generous business incentive as well as assistance with a new tax-free base of operations.

Shura muttered under her breath. "Who does he think he is?"

He is a businessman who knows Surrett has to play by his rules.

"We'll see about that."

It became abundantly clear to Shura an hour into these negotiations that the only way Faiz would sell his substantial share of land near the river would be if the Genjix outright bought him out, at a valuation of roughly five times its worth. The man also made it clear that he was not willing to budge from anything less than that exorbitant price.

"After all," he said, "if you bulldoze all of the hundreds of units that I own, where will all the people live? All of Crate Town will blame me for allowing the government to take over. You must pay for my fallen reputation as well."

"You're asking five times the land value and you know it." Surrett stood up and waved his hands wildly. "Please, see reason."

Faiz took out another cigar, made an exaggerated show of sniffing it, and then cut one end. He lit it and took several puffs. "Supply and demand, my friend. You want prime real estate and ask me to give up everything. First rule of business is that something is always worth what someone else is willing to pay. Otherwise, feel free to find a way to work around my neighborhood."

We can afford that number, but it will set a poor precedent for all the other businesses. Impossible, actually.

Shura had had enough. She walked around to Faiz's side of the table and looked at the large collection of framed photographs hanging on the wall. The slumlord had a big family. Most were probably extended, which was a normal practice in this part of the world. Still, there were several pictures of him, his wife, and what looked like six kids.

"Excuse me, woman," Faiz said. "What do you think you are doing?"

"I'm looking at your beautiful family." She pointed at the youngest. "How old is this precious one?"

Faiz preened. "Little Tripti just turned three. She is the delight of my life." He turned to Surrett. "That is why I am fighting so hard for my family. I have my darling children to look out–"

Shura plucked the cigar out of his mouth and jammed the burning end into his neck. Faiz's scream was bloodcurdling. He batted her arms as she grabbed his collar and slammed his head once into the table and then backward into the steel wall.

She cupped his chin with her hand and then held the burning end of the cigar so close to his eye it burned his eyelashes. "Listen here, Faiz, you're going to take our more than fair deal, and you will sign and vacate all these premises by the end of next week. Do you understand?"

"What are you doing?" he cried. "Please, please, don't. Surrett, stop this crazy bitch!"

Shura jammed the burning cigar into his cheek just beneath the eye. "Oops, I missed. What did you call me?"

The door burst open and his two guards ran in. One charged, sliding over the table and swinging his machete. Shura grabbed Faiz's wrist and juked to the side at the very last moment, extending his arm. The machete sank into his bicep and he screamed even louder than before.

Shura speared the soft underbelly of the guard's chin, cocking his head back. She then grabbed his belt and pulled, sliding him off the table onto the floor. She gave him a swift kick to the temple and turned to engage the second guard who was charging from the other side.

The second machete flashed horizontally at her neck. Shura stepped into the swing, past the weapon arc, and spun. The blade stuck harmlessly into the wall, and Shura and the guard traded positions. She wrestled the machete from his hand as he tried to unstick the blade, and stabbed it downward straight through his shoe and into the floor. His scream joined Faiz's until a blow to the temple knocked him unconscious. She took a step over the two bodies toward the merchant, who had crawled into the corner, and seemed to be desperately trying to tunnel through the wall with his bare hands.

"Please, please, don't kill me," Faiz cried. "I'll take the deal. I'll take the deal."

She knelt down next to him. "You're going to take that deal we offered you, plus five percent, because you are a shrewd businessman. And if all your tenants don't move out by the end of next week, I'll dock twenty percent. Do you understand?"

He squeezed his eyes shut and nodded vigorously. "Yes, yes, that sounds fair. Very fair."

"And you're not going to cause any more trouble. Do you know why?"

"You'll take another twenty percent?"

Shura had long mastered the wicked smile. "No, I want you to be paid a fair value for your property. If you complain to the authorities or file a lawsuit or do something to cause me any more annoyance, I will take your beautiful three year-old Tripti and I will butcher her, and I will continue to do so with each of your lovely children until our agreement is made whole. And if that isn't enough, I'll move to your mother, father, and then your wife. The only person I will leave behind is your mother-in-law. Do you understand?"

He nodded again. "Whatever you want. I'll leave Crate Town. Just leave my family alone."

"Good." She stood up and turned to Surrett. "Have the papers drawn up. Our friend Faiz is eager to complete this sale and collect five percent profit from this transaction. He is a shrewd businessman."

CHAPTER THIRTEEN
Training

My people thrived for billions of years in peace, until one day, one of us dared to wonder what was beyond the Eternal Sea, on the surface of the planet or even further out in space.

To be honest, part of me wishes I could find that bold Quasing and smother him. If we had never reached for the stars, then perhaps I would have never been stranded on Earth.

Hamilton picked Ella up every morning at six for the next two weeks to bus her over to Murugan's Mitts. The first few days were hell. She was constantly forced to do strange things like swing hammers at tires, push sleds and drag heavy pieces of iron across the room as if she were some pack animal. The worst of those exercises was when he made her swing these vicious little torture devices up and down a few million times. It was all so stupid. And hard. What was the point of lifting something up and down all the time? She could just get a job at the grocery store and stock shelves all day if she wanted dumb, boring, menial labor.

First of all, the torture devices are called kettlebells. And second, it was not a few million times. It was three sets of ten, which equals thirty. Math is not your strong suit.

"You shut your dirty mouth, alien."

Io was less than useful. Instead of helping her train, she just harped on at her constantly. The damn Quasing was more annoying than Wiry Madras back when Ella worked as a cleaning girl.

Coach Manish was equally unhelpful. The hateful old man was an asshole, brutal and relentless. When she would struggle to lift something, he would yell at her and call her lazy and worthless, and then make her try again, but with a lighter weight. If she managed that, he would make her try the heavy weight again.

Ella cried every day for the first week, which was something she hadn't done since Amma died. She would take a tuk-tuk home and collapse onto her mattress, too exhausted and beaten up to do much else. Hamilton didn't bother escorting her home. As far as he was concerned, it didn't matter how she got home, as long as she was at the gym early in the morning.

For most of the second week, she plotted her revenge. Manish had refused to return her shank, so she set out to make a new one to plunge into that old man's back when he wasn't looking. She spent half a night searching the construction yard for a jagged metal piece and then wrapped cloth around the wide end to form a handle. She spent the other half of that night sharpening it against a rock, imagining punching it into the coach the next time he ordered her to swing one of those dumb kettlebells again.

You are not stabbing Manish. He is the only resource we have here. Besides, you are being compensated for your time.

That much was true. One of Ella's stipulations for going to that hellhole in Little Dharavi every day was payment for her time and efforts. She and Io had sat down the first evening to negotiate a stipend to cover her living expenses. She was spending most of her days in the gym; how was she supposed to support herself if she wasn't hustling?

At first, Ella thought it would be tough to hammer out

terms that would allow her to maintain the high standard of living she was accustomed to. However, Io's opening salvo was an amount more than twice what she usually earned on a daily basis out in the streets. Either these Prophus were stinking rich or Io sucked at negotiating. Or Ella was just poor. Probably the latter. In the end she was able to get Io to up her stipend to nearly four times what she made running cons and working odd jobs.

When she told Hamilton to pay her the agreed upon amount, the man actually furrowed his brow and asked if that was enough. Ella spent the next few hours after that kicking herself for not being more aggressive. She hated leaving money on the table.

You really need to stop thinking with the mindset that being a host is a source of income.

"What, you mean I should treat this less as a job and more like a lifestyle change?"

One that will be very short if you do not get up to speed.

No matter how good the money was, it was almost not worth it. Ella had always run cons for money and survival, but part of what she also loved about her work was the thrill. Seeing a carefully planned job come to fruition made her feel alive. Getting away scot-free with a nice haul felt like Christmas or Diwali. She likened it to having a birthday every month.

This wasn't the case with exercising at stupid Manish's stupid gym. There was no joy in getting beaten to a pulp every day. There was no sense of victory or that feeling she got after she had outsmarted an opponent. It was just pain, pain, Manish making fun of her all day, and more pain.

Surprisingly, the old coach gave up on this arrangement before she did at the end of the third week. It also strangely came at the moment when she finally achieved a breakthrough. It involved a lot of calluses and ripped skin, and her grunting and squealing like a pig being gutted, but Ella finally managed to do one pull-up. She promptly dropped onto her ass and lay in a heap on the ground huffing and puffing.

Melonhead actually cheered. He had spent most of the past two weeks standing off to the side making snide remarks and laughing at her weak efforts. For some reason, the more she suffered, the louder she could hear his voice echo across the gym.

This time though, as soon as her chin rose above the bar, he actually leaped off his stool to congratulate her. He picked her up by the armpits and swung her in a circle, seemingly generally enthusiastic about this minuscule achievement.

In many ways, overcoming this little hurdle was the small confidence boost she needed to think she wasn't a total lost cause. For the first time, she felt like she had accomplished something here, and it made her feel great; as if she had just pulled off some elaborate con that had come together beautifully. It was a tiny feat in the grand scheme of things – she had seen one of Manish's guys do thirty pull-ups without breaking a sweat – but this was a step in the right direction.

"All right," Manish, sitting on a stool off to the side, barked out. "Stop dancing around like fools. Let's see you do another!"

And just like that, the joy was gone.

Her next five attempts at pull-ups weren't even close. It seemed she had put everything she had into that one lift and now her body was spent. Manish, ever the grumpy, cruel taskmaster, shook his head and ordered her to move onto the dreaded kettlebells.

Ella scrunched her face as she stomped toward her round black tormentors. She stole a glance at the boxing ring. At least he hadn't made her try to box today. Every day he put her in the ring was the worst day of her life. Yesterday, the coach had had her box a fourteen year-old. It hadn't ended well for either of them. After the boy knocked her down for the third time, she threw a stool at him, and then he chased her around the gym for five minutes. Luckily for her, running away and evading bigger people was what she did best.

You know, eventually you are going to have to go in there and learn how to fight.

"You're the alien. Can't you just order him to teach me to fight in a way where I don't mess up my face?"

I am pretty sure all types of fighting involve getting your face messed up.

"Damn it!"

Ella was struggling through a set of kettlebell swings when Manish stood up abruptly and tossed his stick near her feet. "Stop it. This is a waste of time. We're not getting anywhere here."

His sudden outburst surprised Ella so much she let go of the kettlebell on the upswing. Fortunately, she couldn't swing a heavy weight. Unfortunately, it was still an eight-kilogram piece of solid iron. The kettlebell flew through the air and bounced off the wall, narrowly missing Melonhead's big melon head.

"Oh my gods!" the big man yelled.

Manish jabbed her small twig arms with his gnarled finger. "This is not working."

"I did a stinking pull-up today!"

"And in two years, you will be a very strong tiny girl who can beat up other tiny people. The first time you fight a Genjix who is normal size will be your last."

"I'm doing the best I can."

Manish sighed. "I know, girl, but like they say, you can't teach size." He looked across the room at where she had tossed the kettlebell. There was a small indentation in the wall from the impact. Melonhead sat there, frozen, eyes wide like full moons from his near-death experience. The coach went over to the desk and picked up a cricket ball, and tossed it to Ella. "Hit Aarav with this."

Ella caught the ball and hefted it in her hand. "What?"

"Go ahead. Hit him."

"Wait, what?" Melonhead looked up, confused. "Don't hit me."

"I don't think I should–" she began.

"I'll buy you lunch if you hit him on the head," said Manish.

Ella wound her arm up and chucked the cricket ball at Melonhead, albeit not throwing it very hard. It would have hit him square between the eyes had he not covered up and blocked it with his arms.

"Stop throwing things at me!" Melonhead roared.

"That's what you get for not getting out of the way," Manish shouted back. He took out the shank he had confiscated from her and tossed it at her feet. "Here, hit him with that."

She picked it up. "It's sharp. I'll kill him."

"You can't kill him. You don't throw hard enough."

"Oh yeah?" Ella flipped the shank in her hand.

"No, don't," Melonhead stammered.

I do not suppose I need to tell you that actually killing him is probably a bad idea, do I?

"You had better move out of the way, or I guess I'm giving the gym to your brother," Manish called out.

"Don't get out of the way, Aarav," one of the younger students piped up.

Ella held her hands a shoulder-width apart. "This wide." Grinning, she made a show of winding up, and then flung the shank so hard she fell off balance. Fortunately for him, Melonhead had a bad moment of analysis paralysis and didn't budge from where he stood. Ella also had pretty good aim. The shank blurred in the air and sunk several centimeters into the plaster, approximately a shoulder-width away from his head. She turned to Manish and shrugged. "More or less."

"More or less," the coach nodded. "I think we've found your niche, runt. There's still some work we can do. You throw like someone who never learned how to throw a ball, but we can fix that. First things first, we need to get you the proper tools. Wait here."

He went to the back and rummaged through several boxes in the corner, appearing a few minutes later with a jar of rusty blades. He plucked out a fat-looking knife with rubber edges, examined it, and then tossed it to her. "Try this one. Its blade-heavy, so it's good for a beginner, and you can't accidentally cut a finger off with it. We'll start with your throwing motion. Your technique is awful."

Ella felt a surge of excitement bubble up in her chest as she hefted the practice knife and imitated Manish's stance. For the first time, she looked forward to being told what to do.

CHAPTER FOURTEEN
Status Report

In the Eternal Sea, our potential was limitless. We were trillions in number, one and many, each with a purpose that served the collective whole, not unlike the many trillions of cells that make up the human body.

Slowly, the Quasing explored our home world, first claiming every inch covered by the Eternal Sea, and then millions of years later, finding a way to consume the entire planet, so that it truly became our world.

Ella left the gym later than usual after working on a few of the new exercises Manish had added to her training regimen. She was surprised to see Hamilton waiting for her. He had never bothered to pick her up after training before.

"Hey," she said. "What do you want?"

He held up a small purse. "Thought I would deliver your stipend personally and take you out to dinner to see how things are going," he replied.

Ella never said no to a free dinner. However, it had been her experience that few dinners were ever truly free. She crossed her arms. "No strings attached?"

"I'd like an update on how things are progressing, and I need some time with Io."

Ella wasn't sure what Hamilton meant by needing time

with Io, but the thought of having dinner with Hamilton to talk about her progress almost made the price of the meal too high to bear.

The update is needed one way or another. Do you actually think we are going to pay you without expecting results? You might as well do it over dinner.

"Fine," she said. "My choice."

Hamilton shrugged. "Just nothing too expensive or spicy, please. My palate hasn't been adapting too well to the local cuisine."

Ella picked one of the nicest and spiciest restaurants she knew. To be fair, it was one of the only restaurants she knew of outside Crate Town. Hamilton didn't bat an eye at the prices, but his face began to turn red shortly after they delivered the paratha samosas.

"So how are things?" he coughed, after draining his third glass of milk.

"Fine." The words came out muffled as she crammed the food in her mouth. This was the best food she'd ever eaten, low as that bar might be.

"Adapting well to becoming a host?"

"It's the best thing in the world." Ella noticed his face darken, and decided not to press her luck. No need to rub it in. "Io's kind of a jerk."

Hey!

"Emily used to say that all the time," Hamilton said. "It seems you two are getting along as well as expected, considering Io's reputation."

You can, you know, defend me a little.

"Did Emily ever tell you how much Io whines?"

Hamilton nodded. "The two bickered like teenagers, especially during long flights. It was the most annoying thing. Emily would verbalize the arguments out loud to me sort of as a tiebreaker."

The two of them laughed.

You are my host. You should be on my side.

Hamilton's voice trailed off as he shook his head. "Emily was gone from this world too soon. To fallen comrades." He raised his glass of milk. They clinked, and then he downed it in one gulp. Ella had never before seen a man so white turn so red from food. She actually had never seen a man so white, period.

"What about your training?" he asked. "How is that coming along?"

Ella picked at her lamb vindaloo. "Fine." The word came out barely more than a mumble.

"Are you making any progress?"

"It's none of your business," she snapped.

You are going to have to do better than that. We are paying you for each day.

With a sigh, Ella started from the beginning and detailed her month of painful workout regimens. Hamilton's face melted a little as she talked about push-ups and lifting weights and other rudimentary calisthenics. He asked her about how much weight she was lifting and how many sit-ups she could do in a minute and all these other strange metrics that, frankly, Ella didn't see any reason he needed to know. Halfway through describing her kettlebell routine, he stopped taking notes and just sat there. His mood did not seem to improve even when she talked about her transition to knives.

She finished going over everything right about the time the waitress brought over her sixth lassi, and something like Hamilton's fifteenth glass of milk. The two sat there for a few moments with neither saying a word. For a second, Ella thought she had said or done something wrong.

You did fine. Hamilton is probably concerned about your progress.

"It's barely been a month! What did he expect me to become in such a short time?"

It is not you. You did your best. Kind of.

"This is not going to work," Hamilton finally said, breaking the silence. "It will take far too long to get you up to speed. We may need to move you to a safer location for proper training."

Ella frowned. "Move me?"

"We have a training academy in Sydney or possibly the training grounds in Arusha."

"Wait, the Sydney in Australia?"

"Is there another? I'll see to arrangements–"

"I don't want to go."

"Nonsense. I guarantee it'll be much better accommodation than where you live now."

"I like where I live."

Hamilton leaned forward and laid a patronizing hand on her arm. "Trust me, it's for the best."

Ella was about to tell him where he could stick his stupid advice when she realized: this had nothing to do with her. Coward was desperate to leave Surat, and he couldn't do so unless she, or Io specifically, left as well. He wasn't looking out for her at all. That selfish bastard. Ella's grip on the glass of lassi tightened. She raised it up to fling it at him.

Do not hit him. Tell him I agree with you and that, as the Quasing, I am ordering you to stay here.

"Can you do that, Io?"

I am his superior. You are too, technically. A host is automatically ranked as commander in the Prophus hierarchy.

"Good, I hate the idea of wasting lassi."

She crossed her arms and puffed her chest out. "As the ranking Prophus person, I order me to stay here in Surat." She tried to come across as authoritarian, but was pretty sure she just looked slightly constipated.

"Sorry," Hamilton replied, shaking his head. "That would be Io's call. If she orders–"

"These are Io's wishes."

Hamilton furrowed a brow. "Is that so? Well, she'll have to tell me herself for me to believe that."

"How can she do that?"

Never mind.

"Never mind," said Hamilton at the same time.

The conversation on her training mercifully died, but it only got worse. Hamilton began trying to impress on both Ella and Io what a good idea it was for her to pick up and leave everything she had ever known. He became some sort of slimy travel salesman as he painted the training facility as if it were some sort of beach resort.

"I spent three months there myself during host training tactics. It's three square meals, a gorgeous view of the ocean you would not believe, and a clean room and bed."

"By myself?"

"Well, no, all trainees share quarters. At least I did when I attended."

Ella couldn't even imagine living in the same container with someone, let alone in the same room. Heck, it felt like Burglar Alarm was sometimes too up in her business, and the dog lived outside.

"The splendid thing in particular after your first year–"

"I have to stay for a whole year?"

"Three technically. As I was saying, after your first year, you'll be given weekends off to be on your own. That way, you can explore all of what the exotic land of Australia has to offer–"

"Wait, what? What do you mean, weekends?"

First year operative trainees are required to stay on the premise for ten months, save for family emergencies.

For some reason, her fool auxiliary thought free food, housing and schooling was worth being locked up in a foreign prison.

The schooling part of the offer was enticing. Having little education had always been a slight embarrassment, but no amount of free schooling was worth her freedom. Ella valued doing what she wanted to do when she wanted to do it. No one was going to tell her when to eat or go to bed.

"No deal," she said.

"You really need–"

"Dinner is over. I would like to go home now." She stood up and stormed out of the restaurant before Hamilton could utter another word.

The two rode a tuk-tuk back in silence. By now, darkness had fallen and thick clouds had rolled in. The scattered lights on random buildings and street lamps – the few that were working – flitted by as they sped down one of the main streets leading into Crate Town.

The tuk-tuk dropped them off a few blocks from her cluster, and they walked the rest of the way. She had offered to go home on her own, but Hamilton was adamant on escorting her all the way to her front door. She appreciated the gesture, but was pretty sure he would be screwed trying to find his way out of the slum by himself after he dropped her off. That was why most of Crate Town shut down after sunset. Only the rats – the rodent variety and the people who were up to no good – walked the streets and alleys at night.

Burglar Alarm greeted them, her tail wagging. Again, the dog seemed friendlier to Hamilton than she did to Ella. "Traitor," she grumbled, as she unlocked her door and went inside. She turned toward the doorway and saw Hamilton still standing there, waiting expectantly. For something.

You could always offer your place for him to stay overnight.

"No way."

"Goodnight." She slammed the door in his face with a very solid *thunk* of metal hitting metal, followed by the additional low click of the lock turning. She turned around and leaned her back to the door. "Weirdo."

She smacked her lips and reminisced about the wonderful lamb vindaloo, and with a cheerful hum, got ready for bed.

•••

An hour later, Io sat up from her bed and swung her legs over the side. She stood up and fell over. Luckily, she fell backward onto the bed again and spared Ella's body a possible head injury that would have been difficult to explain the next morning. She managed to get back onto her feet and moved – waddled really – out of her bedroom to the living room. She unlocked the front door and swung it open.

Hamilton sat on the front steps, leaning against the railing. He was scratching Burglar Alarm behind the ear, and holding a piece of leftover meat with his free hand. He looked up. "Io?"

"Come in."

Her auxiliary stood up, flipped the treat to Burglar Alarm, and strolled in. He closed the door behind him, and looked around Ella's home. "I can't believe people live in conditions like this."

"Speak softly." Io sat on the couch. "The girl is a light sleeper."

Hamilton grabbed a chair and sat down opposite her. "First of all, as a precaution, please verify your binary code."

Io gave it and then held out her hand. "Did you get what I asked?"

Hamilton dug through his bag and pulled out several pieces of electronic gear. He held up a small phone battery. "One crypto key that is compatible with Ms Patel's phone. I programmed the contacts you requested. You can authenticate from her phone to the encrypted OS with the verbal passphrase 'The vilayati own the mountain of light' or punch in code *8400#."

"Of course you do. Your people think you own everything."

Hamilton took out a small plastic case and popped it open, revealing a fat reinforced laptop with a handle on one end. "Standard protocol caused Emily's laptop to self-destruct within minutes of confirmation of her death. I begged desktop support to just transfer ownership to your new host, but they wouldn't hear it. Bloody tech nerds. Instead, I had them format mine for the girl to use. It's an older model, but you wanted to reconnect to the network right away, so this is the best I can do."

Io closed the lid to the case. "What are you going to use for now?"

Hamilton grinned. "I'm getting a new one. It will take a week or so and I'll have to head to Ahmedabad to pick it up."

"You give me your old junk and get a new one. I see. Thanks, auxiliary."

"At your service. One more thing," said Hamilton. "Your security level is unchanged and has been transferred. However, Wyatt made it clear your new host is not to have any access until she has been properly vetted. She is too much of an unknown at this point."

"Understood." Io closed the lid to the case. She'd have to find a hiding place in Ella's home. Otherwise, the girl might try to fence it at the market. "The sooner I get back online, the sooner we can get back to work."

"By the way, Command wants more information about the site Emily uncovered and has authorized additional surveillance. However, I'm on record saying we are not in position to carry out the assignment with your new host. We should move you to safety and bring in another team."

"Emily is dead. She died investigating that construction site. I will not let her death go to waste. I will see this through personally."

Hamilton paused. "It was you who told the girl she could stay in this slum, wasn't it?"

Io nodded. "I have my reasons, Hamilton. Our work here is important, and we are the only ones on the ground. I am not leaving until we discover what this site is for. Besides, I doubt we could force the girl to leave even if we wanted to."

Hamilton pursed his lips and then leaned in. He spoke in a whisper. "I have to ask. With all due respect, this is a bloody joke, right? What the hell are we still doing here, Io? First, Emily comes here rogue and gets herself killed. Instead of entering me, your auxiliary, you join with a street urchin. Now you have a new host who is not only unfit for duty, but uneducated and incompetent. And instead of moving to a safe and secure location, you allow this host to run roughshod and stay in this slum."

"It is not right to just intrude on her life and then whisk her away. A host is partners with her Quasing, not a slave."

"But your safety–"

"My safety is not a worry for now. We will revisit this if it is ever compromised. Besides, I am more than able to handle things on my own."

"Do you need help with that?"

Io was trying to put the crypto key battery into Ella's phone, but her clumsy control over her host's fingers made it look as if she were trying to pry off the back of the phone wearing mittens. Frustrated, she handed it to Hamilton, who popped the back effortless and placed the crypto key inside.

Io took Ella's phone and accessed the hidden menu with her passphrase. Satisfied, she nodded. "Any word from Command about your status?"

"My auxiliary captain is demanding an update and is threatening to recall me."

"That may not be a bad idea. I am off-books as it is. No need to risk your career on my account."

Hamilton harrumphed, raising his chin. "What sort of auxiliary would I be if I abandon my assigned Quasing in a vulnerable state? However, I do wish you would explain your logic behind inhabiting this…" he gestured at Ella "… individual instead of myself. Is it because of what happened during the ambush? I assure you," – he looked away, ashamed – "it was just a moment of weakness. I have been sick over my inaction and swear it will not happen again."

Io studied Hamilton's set jaw and clenched fists, and let

it go. Telling him to leave her was for his own good, but she couldn't push him too hard. It would just arouse suspicion. Io shook her head. "We will stay until the host wishes to leave of her own accord."

Hamilton pursed his lips. "What is our mission in the meantime?"

Io pointed west. "The Genjix are building something big over there. Emily died trying to discover the site's purpose. I want to pick up where she left off."

Her auxiliary shook his head. "Not in your host's current state of preparedness. I'll call in a field scout."

"That will not be necessary."

Hamilton crossed his arms. "I've given you a lot of rope so far with your new host. I won't allow her to willfully put you in danger. I'm calling in a scout. Let them do the legwork and present Command with actionable items. This is not negotiable, Io."

Her auxiliary was probably right. It was stupid to even pretend to use Ella in any sort of field capacity. Io nodded. "Fine. Call one in."

"Very well. If there's nothing else…" Hamilton stood up and saluted.

Io got up, stretched with the girl's body, feeling each joint twist and pop. The broken arm Ella had suffered two, maybe three years ago would need to be broken again if it was ever to heal properly. She also badly needed a massage. Some of her muscles were incredibly knotted. And this wasn't even scratching the surface of her poor diet, or her heart condition…

Io walked Hamilton to the door and out to the deck. She waited until the sounds of the footsteps on metal stairs disappeared. She took a deep breath, patted the mangy dog eying her expectantly, and then went back inside, locking the door behind her.

Hamilton was right about one thing. Command was

already unhappy with Io inhabiting a new host and choosing to stay in a hostile country. She was given some leeway only because the Prophus respected a new host's considerations. To a degree. For how long would depend on if the girl ever became satisfactorily trained. Io was sure both Hamilton and Manish were reporting the girl's progress to Wyatt. The analyst would make the call to extract her if he deemed it necessary. At the rate her training was coming along, Command might feel the need to intervene sooner rather than later, with or without Ella's consent.

Io sat back down on the couch and logged into the laptop. Within minutes, she was in the Prophus network, gathering information on the region and catching up on personal messages. Most were condolences regarding Emily. News of her death had spread quickly. The woman, while low-ranking, was popular among many in the organization. It was very touching. Io wondered how many of the other Quasing blamed her for Emily's death.

She looked in the mirror. "What a mess," she muttered. No matter what, she had to stay in India until she accomplished her goal. Everything would be all right after that. First things first, Io had to begin making amends for the mistake that had resulted in Emily's death and forced Io to extend her mission.

She picked up a phone and dialed a number. "This is Io. Something is coming down the pipe."

CHAPTER FIFTEEN
Bijan

After Quasar was claimed, we set our sights on space. We experimented with our potential, forming structures that rose up past the Eternal Sea and toward the stars. We bred massive ships that could withstand the difficulties of space travel, and quickly colonized Quasar's fourteen moons, bringing our Eternal Sea to those once-barren worlds.

We sought to expand even further, looking past our solar system to the beyond. This was the birth of our empire and how we arrived on Earth.

Ella had to admit she immediately took a liking to the man who appeared one morning at her front door. It was something that rarely happened for someone who lived on the streets. He had a gentle and kind face, and reminded her of what she thought her grandfather would be like if she had ever had a grandfather. Of course, some jerk out there had to have been the father of her father, but whatever. She had never met the man, so she might as well assume he didn't exist. But, if she had met him, she'd like to think he would look like this friendly old man.

Still, this was Crate Town, and she was a woman, so she greeted him in the appropriate manner. She brandished her shank and sicced Burglar Alarm on him as he clanged his way up her stairs. "Who are you? What do you want?"

The man, slightly stooped, thin-armed, with a long flowing beard, did not look threatened. If anything, he seemed amused. "Your dog is very pretty. Is your mother home?"

"My amma is dead."

The man looked taken aback, and then she saw the sympathy in his eyes. "Then you must be the person I'm here to see."

He walked up another step. Burglar Alarm was barking bloody murder. Ella stepped forward and waved the shank near his face. "One more step and you won't be able to see at all."

The man held up his hands and spoke in a soft voice. "There is a reality so subtle."

It took Command their sweet time to send someone.

"What? What crazy are you saying, Io?"

Repeat after me. That it becomes more real than reality.

Ella wasn't paying that close attention so she gave it her best shot. "It's more real than real?"

The man frowned. "You're new, aren't you?"

"New to what?"

"The Prophus. The job. Being an operative."

It was Ella's turn to make a face. "I didn't know I was one."

The man smiled. "Well, if you're working for us, then welcome to the family."

"Am I, Io?"

Yes, you are. Congratulations, you are now officially logistical support for the Prophus in this region.

"What does that mean?"

It means when agents run operations here, you are here to provide support: food, housing, equipment, and expert knowledge on the local area.

"Sounds an awful lot like I'm running a hotel."

Logistical support sounds more official.

"How much does it pay?"

Is this all you think about?

"Yes."

The man standing at the doorway interrupted her negotiations with Io by sticking out his hand. "I'm Bijan. Bijan Baraghani."

Ella shook it. "Ella. This is Burglar Alarm."

Bijan scanned the area and then looked at her half-opened container door. "Can we go inside?"

Ella became suspicious again. "Why do you want to come into my home?"

Let him in. He is a Prophus scout here to conduct surveillance on the construction site at Command's request. Your job is to assist him.

"Why can't I do that survey thing? I know Crate Town like the back of my hand."

Because you have no idea how to survey. However, you know Crate Town like the back of your hand, so show him around. He will probably use your home as his base of operations.

"Since when are you renting my home out and booking me as a tour guide?"

Since you got on our payroll.

Greed overcame outrage. Ella made a face like she had just smelled something foul. "Fine." This free money she was getting from the Prophus was getting less and less free by the day.

Fifteen minutes later, Bijan had settled into her couch, and she had laid out the ground rules. The man was allowed to stay in the living room side of her home, but her bedroom was off limits. This also wasn't a hotel, so she wasn't cleaning up after him, nor was she going to feed him. Also, the bathroom was hers, so he would have to shower and relieve himself outside.

Your hospitality skills could use some work.

Bijan seemed to take her many rules seriously and in his stride. He even jotted down notes and asked her questions about some of the particulars, specifically the use of her toilet, which really was nothing more than a hole outside in the corner of the catwalk next to Burglar Alarm's nest. He sat down on her lumpy couch, which was doubling as his bed for the next week – he had assured her his mission wasn't going to last longer than that – and looked around. "Now that I'm settled, I'm hungry."

"I told you," she snapped. "This isn't a hotel. There's no room service."

He smiled. "Can I take you out to lunch, Ella? As a thank you for putting up with an old man?"

That shut Ella up, and she stared at the ground, slightly ashamed. She spoke in a small voice. "Well, all right if you're paying."

Can you take realizing you are an asshole a little more gracefully?

"You're the asshole, Io."

Ella…

"It'll give me a chance to show you around," she said gruffly.

"Excellent," said Bijan. "And thank you again for your hospitality."

"Shut up," she muttered under her breath. People acting too nice weirded her out.

The two spent the next half hour wandering the narrow streets of Crate Town. Ella showed Bijan the safer main streets to use and the alleys to avoid where some of the meaner street rat gangs holed up. She walked him through the shortcut along the canal leading back to her container, and pointed out the tall cluster stacks he could use as landmarks in case he got turned around. She familiarized him with Wiry Madras's bathhouse and laundry, pointed out the decent restaurants, and took him to Twine Alley when he asked where to buy changes of clothing.

They settled on a restaurant she had never been to before to try some American food. This was a first for her, so she let Bijan, who claimed to have been to the States at least twice, order for them. He got her what they called a lamb cheeseburger. After being such a big fan of their film and culture, Ella was completely underwhelmed by her first taste of supposed American cuisine. She took one bite and gagged. "There's no seasoning, and it tastes undercooked."

"That's how they do it in the Americas, I think."

Certain types of raw meat are a delicacy in many countries.

"Raw anything is disgusting!"

During their disappointing lunch, Ella got to know Bijan. She was surprised to learn that he had grandchildren. Shouldn't he be bouncing toddlers off his knees and chasing them in the yard as opposed to, well, whatever it was he did for the Prophus? She realized she still had not grasped all the nuances of this war between the alien sides.

Bijan chuckled. "I suppose I should be playing with young Omid and Jaleh back in Tehran. However, this sort of work is all I've ever known, and the Prophus have a horrible retirement package. Also, my dearest wife, Leila, may Allah cherish her forever, loves me more than life, but can only put up with me in small doses. If I never leave the house, she really will be the cause of my death."

After lunch, Ella took him to the marketplaces for things he could buy legally, and introduced him to Little Fab for things he couldn't. She berated Little Fab until he offered the Prophus agent a good discount on a pair of military thermal binoculars the fence had had in his possession for years. Bijan's own pair had cracked during his trip here.

It was early evening by the time they parted ways. Bijan walked Ella back to her cluster and then hoisted his pack over his shoulder. "Don't wait up for me. I'll probably be gone all night. When I return, how do I get inside?"

"Just knock," she said. "I'm a light sleeper. If I don't hear it, Burglar Alarm will wake me."

Bijan nodded. "Thank you for showing me around, Ella. I'll see you in a few hours."

She felt a strange tightening in her gut. She called out to Bijan as he turned to leave. "Be careful. If any of the street rat gangs try anything, you give them my name and tell them I will beat them into the mud if they bother you."

He grinned. "Don't you worry about me, girl. I've been doing this job for a long time, and this one is as by the books as they come. Tomorrow, why don't we try sushi for lunch? Can you find a restaurant that's not too far away?"

"Sure," Ella beamed.

"Io, what's sushi?"

You will absolutely hate it.

Before going to bed that night, Ella looked up what sushi was, and then went to sleep wishing she hadn't. The lone restaurant in Surat that served Japanese cuisine was on the opposite side of the city in an upper-class neighborhood that she never had reason to step foot in. The very thought of eating fish raw made her want to puke. Still, if someone else was buying, who was she to turn it down? Ella fell asleep looking forward to spending time with her new friend.

The next morning, she woke up alone. Bijan's things were untouched. He had not returned that night. Ella waited until late afternoon before finally leaving her home. She went to the markets and to Wiry Madras's and Fab's Art Gallery to see if the kind old man had stopped by. He hadn't, and Ella never saw or heard from him again.

CHAPTER SIXTEEN
The Stick

We were one, but we were not equals. Some became the building blocks of our kind, becoming parts of ships and infrastructure. Others transformed into different forms of energy or matter. Many of us with talents and skills and knowledge coalesced to occupy positions of power.

While the collective was the combined thoughts of trillions of Quasing, each of us had our own roles and purposes within the whole. The ones who morphed into energy were known as the Catalysts. The Foundations formed the basic structures of our civilization. The Keepers held our history and our future direction. The Carryalls bred to become giant ships to take us across the galaxy. The Minds were the brightest who existed solely to process thoughts, ideas and data.

I was a high-standing Receiver, one who facilitates the communication between worlds in our burgeoning empire. The other Receivers and I were tasked with the great responsibility of keeping the many as one even across the galaxy.

Contrary to what Shura had told Faiz about shutting up and being happy with the deal she forced upon him, word of what happened had spread like a fire across Dumas, the contested area of Crate Town between the construction site and the docks. Perhaps it was the burn marks on Faiz's face or the injuries to his guards or the mass eviction notices to his tenants that he sent out the very next day, but soon everyone knew that the white foreigner who accompanied the minister was not to be trifled with.

When Surrett asked if she was going to punish Faiz for leaking the events of that night, Shura said no. This news had the exact effect she intended. If she was willing to be heavy-handed to a powerful businessman, what chance would anyone else have?

In a few days, half the businesses and land owners in Dumas had sold their properties to her at slightly depressed values. Most were just happy to walk away from the transaction in one piece and with some sort of return. The remaining half were still holding out, but Shura was confident they would fall in line soon enough. They just needed a little more of the right sort of encouragement.

"Why even pay a fair value if we're just going to bully them into selling?" Surrett had asked.

Shura shook her head. "It's one thing to give them a bad deal they can live with, it's another to steal from them. If they feel robbed, they'll seek to address that injustice, either through the court or through violent uprising. If they get a raw deal but feel it's not worth the trouble, they will just walk away."

I have taught you well.

"My Holy One deserves only the best vessel."

Shura walked along a street on the north end of the construction site. The last of the properties outside the perimeter had just been sold this morning, and the tenants vacated. At this rate, they could begin demolition of the container structures immediately and expand the site perimeter by the end of the week.

This was already a promising start to her new reign as the head of the Bio Comm Array project. This was the exact sort of news the Council needed. She would wait a little while longer until she had enough positive updates that the Council would have no choice but to consider passing her permanent ownership of this project, and possibly India.

Right now, she was on her way to the docks to deal with a more serious problem. While the businesses and residents of this neighborhood were easy to intimidate, the dock union had dug in and made it clear they intended to fight her every step of the way. Shura was going to speak with their leader, who not only was the head of the dockworkers' union, but incidentally one of the more powerful gangsters in the slum.

The headquarters of the union – a squat, ugly building three containers tall by fifteen wide – looked like any other warehouse on the beach, except for the fifty or so orange-garbed dirty roughs milling in front. Some wielded machetes, others two-by-fours and metal rods. None wore a smile as Shura, Surrett, and their escort of policemen approached.

I count at least forty outside. Probably more inside.

"Uh," Surrett stammered. "Perhaps we should return another time."

"And show weakness?" Shura said. "You don't think there won't be even more the next time we come?"

"We can come back later with more police."

Shura looked at the half dozen officers guarding them. "Two or twelve, it probably won't make a difference."

Not true. If the situation escalates, the humans around you will provide proper fodder and buy you time to escape. I will not lose a vessel to these vermin. I do not see any firearms.

"That seems to be the case around here for some reason."

In fact, Shura hadn't seen anyone else with a gun since she had arrived. No one within the slum was ever packing. Even Inspector Manu's men escorting her were only armed with batons.

The crowd parted before them and then closed in behind them as they made their way up the rusty planked path leading to the front entrance. Her guards squirmed nervously as the smelly, scowling dockworkers came within arm's length and herded them through the wide open warehouse. Instead of containers and cargo, it was filled with even more dockworkers. A rumbling of mutters and the banging of sticks and blades on the metal floor grew as they ventured deeper into the building.

"Seems they've rolled out the welcome mat."

There are hundreds here. They knew you were coming.

"I wasn't particularly hiding this item on my itinerary."

This is a show of force. The crime boss is letting you know he will not be pushed around like Faiz.

"That, or we just have more bodies we'll need to wade through."

Shura, staying relaxed, scanned the perimeter. There was the small double-door they walked through, three sets of large garage bays on the far right, and a set of smaller windows a little too far out of reach on the left. Several round staircases dotting the ground level led upstairs to a catwalk that crisscrossed the ceiling above them.

You will never make the bay doors. Go up.

"That will depend on how close I am to the stairs."

See that stack of containers at the side? If something happens, head in that direction. Abandon the minister if necessary.

Near the center of the back wall, a group of men huddled together under the shine of a low-hanging ceiling light. One of the hunched-over men noticed the rabble of dockworkers herding her group toward them, tapped the man next to him, and then one by one, like lemmings, they looked her way. The cluster of people between her and the table parted like the Red Sea, revealing a cluttered round table with piles of paper, several bottles of booze, batons, metal rods, and enough bats to start a cricket league. Only one person at the far end of the table was sitting down, just outside the edge of the spotlight.

Their escort stopped at the end of the table and took several steps back. The muttering crescendoed and several began to bang the ends of their shovels and sticks in unison on the metal floor until the noise became deafening.

Surrett was about to say something when Shura held a hand up. "We are in Mogg's territory. We wait." The entire room stood around a few more minutes until Mogg finished writing something in a ledger, then slammed the book shut with a slap. The rumbling in the room died immediately.

Mogg leaned forward into the light. "So you're the one who prettied up Faiz and poked holes in his boys. I always told him he should have hired union."

To Shura's mild surprise, Mogg, the reputed crime boss, union leader, and most feared gangster in Crate Town, was a woman.

"Shrimati Mogg," said Surrett, bowing lower than he did for Shura when they met. "I wish–"

"Keep your mouth closed, Minister," Mogg snapped. "I'm talking to the pretty lady."

Shura stepped up to the end of the table and studied the strange Indian woman. She appeared middle-aged, stoutly built, and had her hair chopped short. It was faint, but the left half of her face was scarred; acid perhaps? An old gash on the right side, climbing all the way from her chin to her scalp, was definitely caused by a blade. Mogg had seen some rough business in her day.

The woman was, in turn, studying her as well, her eyes lingering on Shura's face and her body-fitting suit. Mogg's head dipped under the table, and then reappeared a few seconds later. She grinned. "Flats. Practical. Almost the ensemble, but you drew the line somewhere."

"Some compromises are too costly."

"You have the bearing of a soldier, girl."

"And you the absolute ruler of a very small kingdom."

"Yet one you wish to own."

"A small kingdom here can be worth a larger kingdom elsewhere."

Mogg chuckled. "The empty suit over there already tried that on me. He wants to move me an hour inland. I run a dock union." She threw a thumb at the men surrounding them. "How are we supposed to do our jobs landlocked at the other end of Crate Town?"

Shura shrugged. "Be a union doing something else."

"You hear that, boys," Mogg barked. "Should we rename ourselves the plumbing union? Or how about trucking?"

"Actually," said Surrett. "The BMS labor union–"

Shura turned to Surrett. "You heard Mogg. Be quiet."

The banging of staves and shovels and sticks on the floor began again, shaking the entire building as their echoes bounced around the metal walls. Mogg threw a hand up and they quieted instantly once more. Her jovial expression took a serious turn. "I think we like being the dock union. Now, get out before someone gets hurt."

Did you notice that? Near precision. These are not normal dockworkers. Half are probably ex-military.

Shura scanned the rough-looking men and saw the small signs everywhere: battle scars, bullet wounds, aggressive stances. A good number of them had seen war before. She was in a more precarious position than she had anticipated.

Mogg must have noticed Shura eying her men. "Are you really as tough as Faiz painted you to be, or is he just trying to save a little face?"

At that moment, Shura decided she needed to gamble and give this room something to think about. She grabbed the wrist of the nearest goon, pulled him off balance, and then bent his arm at an unnatural angle. He screamed, and then she let go before she broke his arm. Another of the workers pawed at her. She slapped his hand away and, with a kick to the midsection, sent him bowling over several more of his friends.

To your left!

The end of a shovel swung lazily near her head. Shura

caught it with one hand, and then pushed, jabbing the handle into the gut of her assailant. The mob closed in on her small group, knocking the policemen over as a riot sparked in this small enclosed space. Just as it teetered out of control, Shura shut it down. She drew her pistol and swung it in a wide circular arc. Mogg's men cried out in alarm and stampeded backward, some running over their friends as they retreated.

The muzzle of her gun came to a rest pointing at Mogg, and then Shura placed the pistol on the table. "I could fight you, Shrimati Mogg, but I'd rather work with you."

"I can't be threatened or bought off," Mogg snapped. If Shura's little display of force fazed her, she didn't show it.

"I don't want to do either. I want to work with you. Name a price."

Mogg studied her, and then broke into a grin. "I like your spunk, girl. I'll play." She glanced around the room and made a show of adding up all the assets. Shura would bet her life that the woman knew exactly how much she wanted. "To buy all union property and to have us no longer be dockworkers? Let's see, in rupees or dollars or euros…" The price she named was astronomical, almost an insult. It would have made Mogg a very wealthy woman.

Surrett guffawed and began to protest. Shura held up a hand. He shut up. Looking Mogg straight in the eye, Shura nodded. "I'll double your number, under one condition."

"Wait, what?" Surrett choked.

"You'll… You'll double my demand?" That threw Mogg off her game. She looked just as shocked as Surrett. She became suspicious. "What's the condition?"

"I've doubled your asking price because now you work for me – you all do now – and the first thing you're going to do is help me convince the rest of the Dumas residents that selling the land to me is in everyone's best interests. And if they disagree, you make them agree. I give you half now, and half when the entire Dumas neighborhood is fully requisitioned to the site." She raised her voice so everyone in the room could hear. "I require extra workers for construction, security to maintain peace, around the clock dock work, and hundreds of other positions filled. I will gladly pay all of Mogg's people double the standard rate."

Might as well triple. Their daily wages are so pitiful it would matter little. The rupee has been particularly weak since the war.

"I'll keep that card in my back pocket to play when the time comes."

Right away, she could see the greed in their eyes. Their fierce loyalty to Mogg and to this slum was shattered by her generosity. In the end, loyalty was simply a matter of price. Shura suppressed her smile; no need to gloat. Human nature was so predictable.

Surrett leaned in and whispered. "Adonis, that is drastically overpaying for labor and for the land. We can hire men off the streets for much cheaper. I have government connections–"

"You don't understand," said Shura. "I'm not hiring them to work for me. I'm hiring them to break Crate Town."

CHAPTER SEVENTEEN
The Game

It was a bold and exciting time for my kind. As part of our great expansion, I was assigned to a scout Carryall to explore this quadrant of the galaxy. My position on-board, as Receiver, was high in standing. I numbered the thirty-fourth out of over six million Quasing on board. Our purpose was to discover new suitable worlds, and to set up beacons to guide settlement Carryalls for colonization.

Ella spent the first few days waiting for Bijan to return, or at least come back for his stuff. When he didn't, she began to ask around and came up empty. Word came down from Big Fab a few days later that a water rat, one of the many scavengers who lived on the beach and always smelled like fish, had tried to sell him back the same binoculars he had sold to Bijan, among other items. A quick follow-up and a bribe to the water rat revealed that he had acquired the binoculars from a fisherman who had dredged up an unrecognizable body floating at the mouth of Tapi River.

Ella tried to be tough about it and shrug off the news. This was a fact of life in Crate Town. In any slum actually. People died; bodies turned up. Nobody ever cared. You moved on. Besides, she justified, Bijan was a complete stranger. She had only known him for a day. Who was he to her, besides a friendly face?

For the next week, Ella was in a foul mood. When she wasn't at the gym, she was constantly in a malaise, and moped around the streets when forced to go out for food. She found herself waspish and short-tempered, and quick to draw her shank, at least quicker than usual.

Io wasn't much help either. The stupid Quasing's feeble attempts to make her feel better, telling her this was a cost of war, that people came and went, that she had better just get used to it, only made her feel worse. Ella thought this new normal Io was trying to sell her sounded like complete rubbish, even if it was true.

That infuriated Ella even though she knew Io was probably right. She had thought her Quasing would be more sympathetic about it, Bijan being one of them and everything. But then, Io wasn't even the same species, so why would she? The alien probably looked at her the same way she looked at Burglar Alarm.

Ella spent those nights sitting on the catwalk with the dog, leaning against the railing and staring at the stars and that pretty white band that stretched across the sky. She just didn't feel like being alone in her container. She even let Burglar Alarm nuzzle up next to her as she scratched behind the mutt's ears.

That is the Milky Way.

"I didn't ask you."

Well, it is.

It had become all of a sudden too quiet in there. Loneliness had never bothered her that much, until now. Ella stared at Burglar Alarm and pretended the dog had died, and very nearly burst into tears. She looked away and berated herself. What was wrong with her? It was only a dog. Not even really hers. Just some stupid mutt that adopted the small space next to her home.

No, Burglar Alarm was her only friend, and the only living

being in her life who had never abandoned her. Not like her mother, Old Nagu, Bijan, or her stupid good-for-nothing worthless asshole father.

I will always be with you too, Ella.

"Oh gods, that's even worse!" she wailed.

The only thing that helped keep her mind off Bijan was her training at Murugan's Mitts. Manish's retooling of her training had made all the difference, and Ella experienced a complete turnaround from the horror that her first few weeks there had been. Now, she was actually enjoying learning how to become an agent.

For one thing, lifting weights and punching bags was only a small part of her regimen. There were days where she didn't even have to lay eyes on a kettlebell. Instead, the coach had her throw things: baseballs, cricket balls, American footballs, chopsticks, knives and basically anything else she could get her hands on.

Ella loved it, and was fascinated by the degree of skill and diverse techniques required to throw things properly. From a full windup baseball throw to flicks of the wrists, there were so many different ways she could hit people.

Manish had called her a natural from the get-go, and she improved every day. By the end of the second month, she could pull a 250-gram throwing knife and hit a target ten meters away pretty reliably eight out of ten tries. By the end of the third, she could pull it from a sheath strapped to her wrist and hit a target within half a second.

"Release at the top of the arc," Manish scolded, as he ran her through a series of exercises where she had to hit several targets in succession. She stood in the middle of the boxing ring while Melon and several other students tossed things up into the air for her to hit. Every once in a while, Manish would throw a tennis ball at her that she would have to dodge. For every time he pegged her, she'd have to wipe down one of the wrestling poles before the evening class.

Since these lessons began, Ella had had to wipe down every pole every day save one. That was fine with her, though. She was learning more now, and having more fun every single day than the first few weeks combined. More importantly, she was growing more confident of her own abilities to defend herself.

"Remember, it's easier to loop your momentum than to stop," Manish called out. "Spin, girl, spin!"

A ball bounced off the side of her head. She twisted to the side and let loose a throwing knife no longer than her hand. It just missed a Frisbee Manish had lobbed into the air. Ella looked to her left and flung another knife at an old boxing glove hanging on a rope from the ceiling. This time, her aim was dead on, and the knife sank into the glove. Another tennis ball plunked her in the shoulder.

"Getting careless," Manish called out.

Growling, Ella made a big show of aiming a knife at Manish. She saw his eyes dare her to follow through with it, as she winded up her throwing motion, and then spun in a circular arc and hit a target behind her.

She looked back at the coach and grinned. "How'd you like that spin, old m–"

He bounced a tennis ball right between her eyes. Her eyes watered and she fell onto her ass ungracefully. She pinched the sting in her nose and felt blood trickle down to her mouth.

"I thought you executed it well," he said matter-of-factly. "Now, get cleaning. The evening class is coming soon."

At the end of the day, after wiping down poles and spacing them throughout the gym, Ella and Melonhead shared a meager dinner of lentils, mong and toor, and watched the advanced mallakhamba class from the back. Melonhead leaned in and nudged her. "You know, maybe you should give it a try."

"Why should I?" She punched him in the shoulder. "So you can laugh at me?"

If her punch registered with him, he didn't show it. Melonhead shrugged. "It's good for coordination, hand strength, and balance. And face it, it's a lot more fun than swinging kettlebells."

That was probably true. As much as she vocally disdained the monkeying around, she was honest enough with herself to know that it was mainly because she was too self-conscious to even try. She was also shocked to see how amazing Manish was at it as well.

According to his files, he was a champion mallakhamba competitor before he became a Prophus agent. That was how he was discovered. In fact, many of our agents operating in India over the past two hundred years were former mallakhamba competitors, since the Genjix had control of the military.

Melonhead nudged her and pointed toward the entrance. "Is that your friend over there?"

Ella followed his finger and saw Manish and Hamilton huddled together near the front of the gym. Then she saw the old boxing coach pass a brown paper bag to him. Or it was more like Manish subtly and smoothly passed something to Hamilton and the tall lanky Brit muffed the hand-off.

"What do you think Manish gave him? Secret agent documents? Cash? A frozen liver?"

Why are you so suspicious and think the worst of everything? It could be a packed lunch for all you know, or diarrhea medicine. Hamilton has a sensitive stomach, you know that. Definitely a higher likelihood of either of those than secret documents or a black market liver. Besides, this is not the 1960s. Nobody passes around paper documents anymore.

"Then why is he being so secretive?"

Would you like the world to know if you had bowel problems?

Ella didn't buy it. She decided to put some of her stealth skills to the test and sneak up on them – more for fun and curiosity than anything else. She slipped past the men and women trying to stay up on the poles and skulked behind the rickety boxing ring on the opposite side of the room until she was almost within earshot.

Unfortunately, Melonhead decided to see what she was up to and followed. Creeping was not one of his talents, and he attracted the attention of Manish when he slinked directly into Ella and knocked her off balance out of her hiding spot. She landed on all fours with a squawk.

"Oh hello, Ella," Hamilton said. The brown paper bag disappeared from sight. "I was just talking to Manish. He says you've made leaps and bounds in your training."

"Enough that I think I deserve a raise," Manish said.

Hamilton laughed. Ella couldn't tell if he was laughing sarcastically or if he was just a bad actor. In any case, the Brit pretended he didn't hear the coach and walked up to her. "Come on, I'll give you a ride home."

The man was acting funny; Ella didn't like it. He was either lying to her or trying to trick her, or something else untrustworthy. He was definitely hiding something.

"We're not done here yet," she said.

"Go home, girl," Manish said. "Class was over three hours ago. You've been staying later and later because you want to eat my food. Stop loitering."

The truth was Ella actually enjoyed watching the mallakhamba class. The girls and two boys in the class were all so graceful. They seemed to be defying gravity. The more she studied their movements, the more she admired and appreciated the skill, strength and technique they needed to accomplish some of these feats.

Maybe Aarav is right. You should join that class.

"Oh, I could never."

You will not know until you try.

"I'll think about it."

"You hungry?" Hamilton asked. "My treat."

Ella had eaten less than an hour ago, but a Crate Town kid never said no. "Sure. Anything but American food."

"All right," Hamilton replied. "I managed to locate an expat restaurant serving English food. I've been yearning for some fish and chips."

An hour later, while being served black pudding, Ella revised her opinion on the worst thing she had ever eaten.

"They caught him just before dawn," said Wyatt through the laptop's computer screen. "He had just moved from the eastern position and was heading north to take some shots of the river. He was streaming video to our relay the whole time. It caught the entire encounter. At least he got one before the feed went dead."

Io and Hamilton were huddled in Ella's living room as Wyatt debriefed them on Bijan's tragic death. The Brit, true to his word, had taken Ella to a local restaurant run by an expat who decided twenty years ago to retire in India and open a restaurant that served English food and played football on the television around the clock. The food was a little worse than average, by Hamilton's standards, but it was completely worth it for him to watch Ella gag for a change. After weeks of Hamilton struggling with the local cuisine, it was nice for him to have the tables turned.

As was their routine now, he escorted her home and waited outside until she was asleep, and then Io opened the door and let him in. They got to work trying to uncover what the Genjix were building in this region.

"He wasn't armed, Wyatt. We sent him out with hardly any protection." Hamilton shook his head. "Did Bijan die quick at least?"

"We don't know. The feed cut off during the struggle," Wyatt replied. "It wouldn't have made a difference. A field scout's defense is not weapons and armor. The real question is, how was he found out? Was it bad luck? Was Bijan being sloppy?"

"Did he find anything?" Io asked quietly.

"Not a lot, but something." Wyatt looked off-screen. "It's

a good thing Emily discovered this site. We would not have known of its existence otherwise. The Genjix are warping all satellite surveillance within a fifteen kilometer radius of the site with some sort of cloaking technology. Bijan had just started mapping out the blueprint of the site when he was caught."

"What happens next?" Hamilton asked.

"We need better intel," said Wyatt. "Can you two finish the work?"

Hamilton shook his head. Io nodded.

Wyatt looked confused. "Which is it?"

"I think the girl is ready," Io said. "She knows the area. Let her scout the site."

"The girl is absolutely not ready," Hamilton insisted. "Send someone else. A full recon team this time. Ella can be their local contact. She knows the area well and can find the supplies they need."

"I'll see what I can do," said Wyatt. "This region is becoming a hot issue in Command, and is escalating. For now, be careful, lay low.

"One more thing." The analyst stopped speaking as if he were trying to formulate the right words. Io could see the skin around his eyes tighten as he drummed his fingers on the desk. "I don't want to alarm you, but diplomatic channels indicate that India is going to fall to the Genjix soon."

Hamilton frowned. "How soon?"

"Probably a few months. Within the year. We do not have any operatives in their government, and the ruling party is leaning staunchly Genjix. We may need to pull you out at a moment's notice. Be ready."

After the screen went blank, Hamilton turned to her. "We're in a bad spot. We should get out of here as soon as possible."

"You are free to cut and run," Io snapped. "I am staying. You heard Wyatt. Command is escalating our findings here. For once, I am leading the charge on something big. I intend to stay and see it through."

Her auxiliary stiffened, and then finally sighed. He dug into his pack and brought out the brown paper bag that Manish had given him. "Here. At least take this."

Io took the crumpled bag and looked inside: a rusty handgun and four magazines. She took out the handgun, checked the sights, and then loaded one of the magazines. It was smaller than the military issues the agents used and looked to be about fifty years old. She frowned. "Russian made. Where did you get this?"

"From Manish. His basement is full of ancient weaponry from the many wars India fought with Pakistan. It's all about that old. This one here is one of the smaller ones."

"Ella does not know how to shoot."

Hamilton shrugged. "After what happened to Bijan, I didn't want the girl to not have any protection, and she can't knife her way through everything. I figure you can walk her through the basics. I'll talk to the coach about giving her formal training so she doesn't shoot her foot off. That is, unless you're concerned enough about her safety to pull her out of here for some real training."

"No."

Hamilton stood up, resigned. "So be it. I had better be off. I'll let you know what Command decides to do with the recon team. In the meanwhile, I'm going to start planning an extraction in case things go south. If what Wyatt says is true, and this is about to become Genjix country, we should have an exit strategy in place."

Io nodded and watched her auxiliary leave Ella's home. He was saying and doing all the right things, being loyal. However, Io had no doubt whatsoever that if she had entered the Brit instead of Ella, Hamilton would have fled India weeks ago. Io would be halfway around the world by now, most likely back in the United Kingdom.

That was one thing Io could not allow.

CHAPTER EIGHTEEN
Playing Safe House

Our ill-fated ship was injured by an asteroid and, as it was dying, detected an atmosphere that could support Quasing life. It set course for Earth and broke into fragments once it struck the planet's atmosphere. The destruction caused by our ship's impact ushered in a new Ice Age.

Quasing were scattered all over the planet. Without our Eternal Sea, the survivors of the crash were suddenly alone, unable to communicate and be one yet many with each other. What little atmosphere the ship had detected on Earth was not an expansive sea, but the many millions of living creatures that lived on its surface. We discovered that by entering the living creatures of this planet, we could survive.

This time around, Ella received word about her new guests a week before they were scheduled to arrive. For the first time since she moved in, Ella had her home cleaned. Not just an hour picking trash off the floor and putting stuff away, but really cleaned with a dust rag and mop and scented water.

She was now finally making a steady enough wage from the Prophus that she didn't have to go out on the streets every day. At first, she thought she would get bored with a regular routine, but soon saw the benefit of not having to hustle to eat, even if it did come with strings attached.

I am a string?

"With an anchor attached to the end."

One of the small advantages of having this regular income was she was able to plan ahead and splurge a little of her earnings. In this case, after some gentle nudging from Io, she capitulated and hired two of Wiry Madras's younger girls to help clean her home from top to bottom. The place was such a dump she needed help.

When Ella was a little girl, she lived in Vadsar Air Base, where the living quarters were so small, she wasn't allowed to have more than a duffel bag of belongings. Later on, when she was homeless, cleanliness wasn't a thing. If your spot was too clean, people took it. If it got too dirty, you moved on.

Even after she obtained her own container, she still lived as if she were homeless. Living on the streets was a harsh teacher and a cruel master. Once you learned its lessons, it was difficult to break old habits. Today, Ella was trying to unlearn them by getting on all fours and scrubbing the floors.

"This sucks," Ella grumbled. "I should just move."

You do live in a container. Have you considered just tilting it and have everything slide out?

"That's not possible. These containers are all welded together."

I was joking.

Ella stopped in mid-brush. "You aliens can joke?"

We probably have a better sense of humor than you do.

"I don't know about that. I'm pretty funny."

If you say so.

Ella spent the rest of the week stockpiling supplies for the team. Hamilton had provided her a list of things to acquire in preparation for their arrival. Most of it was in the form of food, blankets, sleeping bags, water, and various low-tech electronics. Her job was to assist the team in any way and serve as their local runner if necessary.

To be honest, Ella was excited about this job. Between this

and her training, she felt like somebody. She had a sense of purpose and wasn't just another vagrant scrounging a meager living on the streets.

For the first time in memory, she cared about the little details about herself that she had never considered before. She cared about how she looked and smelled, how clean her home was. She wanted these other Prophus – her peers now – to respect her.

On the day the team was scheduled to arrive, she paid for a solo tub at Wiry Madras, had her hair cut and eyebrows trimmed, and did a full load of laundry for fresh clothes. She even prepared snacks in case they were hungry.

Now you want to open a hotel?

"I just want to do things right this time."

Ella, what happened to Bijan was not your fault.

Ella's lower lip quivered. Io had told her the news about the field scout's fate earlier that morning. She had assumed that was what happened, but it still broke her a little inside when she heard it. She scoffed. "Of course it wasn't, you stupid alien. I wasn't there. Why would you even think that? That was a dumb thing to say." She tossed the rag in her hand across the room and dropped onto her freshly de-lumped couch. She crossed her arms and sulked.

I am sorry for saying that. It was not considerate of me. Of course it is not your fault.

"Maybe... Maybe if I was with him, he'd have been all right. I could have found him a better hiding spot or served as a lookout." Her hand drifted to the shank strapped to her back. "Maybe I could have helped him fight them off."

All you would have done is ended up dead like him.

Ella's eyes watered. She wiped her face with her arm before tears and snot could dribble onto the clean sheet she had just laid over the couch. Picking white cloth was probably a stupid idea. She could already see traces of rust and brown at the edges near the ground. No wonder it was the cheapest Lapi the merchant was offering.

I told you to pay a little extra for the brown wool.

"What? No, you didn't. You told me to get the white one to brighten up the place."

All right. Perhaps it was not the best choice. Anyway, the team is scheduled to arrive in the middle of the night. You should get some sleep in case you have to wait up for them.

That probably was a sound idea, but Ella wasn't ready to call her work done. She got up and paced the room, checking her shelves, now stocked with more food than she ever had here before. Her eyes rested on the generator in the corner.

"There are five on the recon team, right?"

On average only two to three in the room at any one time.

"This generator isn't going to cut it. It can barely keep all my stuff powered, let alone handle whatever stuff these secret agent guys are going to bring in." She stood up. "I'm going to stop by Chuy's and get a spare generator and some battery packs."

It is getting dark. Wait until tomorrow. There is no rush.

Ella looked through one of the peep holes. It was approaching no man's time. She had maybe an hour, possibly two, before the streets got dangerous. The best thing to do would be to just wait until morning. No, Chuy always offered the best deals at the end of the day, right before he closed shop, eager to get home to his family. Ella headed for the door.

Wait. If you insist on going outside, take some protection.

Ella touched her shank in its scabbard. "I'm never without it."

I mean real protection.

"You mean all the training I've been doing with Manish has been for fun?"

Look inside the hidden compartment in your bedroom.

Ella did as she was told and frowned, after prying back the hidden plate, at a brown paper bag next to her wad of

Euros and DVD collection of Raghu Dixit Project, Swarathma, and Duran Duran. She picked up the heavy bag and looked inside. She made a face and waved the bag violently in the air. "What is this? Why is it here?"

You put it there.

"Like hell I did. There are no guns in Crate Town."

A sequence played in Ella's head. She saw Hamilton pulling the brown bag out of his pack and placing it on the table. He patted the bag twice with his hands and said something she couldn't quite make out. Hamilton looked down at her and then headed for the front door. There was another flash and she saw her tiny brown hands carrying the bag and hiding it in her spot. When did this happen?

She distinctly remembered thinking that there was no way she was letting him in and shutting the door in his face. In fact, she recalled thinking about how she had left her laundry in the living room and how she'd rather die than let anyone see that. Yet, that image of him standing in her living room felt pretty real. Did she actually let him inside? She began to doubt herself.

You mean this?

Another scene flashed into her head, which seemed to pick up right after the previous one. In it, Ella followed Hamilton to the door. He stepped outside and then turned around to face her. The entire vision flickered, and then Ella slammed the door in his face. She turned toward the room. "Weirdo."

Ella's mouth dropped. "That's not how I remember it."

You have had long, stressful and tiring days. You sometimes forget details. It is normal.

"Like gods it is," she muttered. Or was it? "Oof, don't ever do that again, alien."

She had to sit down to clear her head. Those recent scenes Io had projected were longer than usual and it gave her a ringing headache, as if someone had placed a cowbell next to her ear and was banging it incessantly.

Apologies. Long sequences stress a host's brain. A conscious human can only endure these scenes for seconds at a time. That is why we tend to only flash snippets of memories.

"I still don't remember that happening. I would have remembered." If there was one rule that most residents of Crate Town believed in and enforced, it was that no guns were allowed, and this had nothing to do with curbing violence or crime. Any time a fool was seen packing in Crate Town, it was almost guaranteed to be an outsider. Not even the uncles in the slum were packing.

Regardless, I want you to take it with you when you leave the house, especially at this hour. Remember those gangsters?

For good measure, Io flashed an image of the three gangsters and those little asshole Terrible Gandhis. It still didn't convince her. She dropped the brown bag back in the hiding spot and began to put the plate back in place. "Forget it. It's not going to happen. I'm not carrying this."

Ella, for once, listen to me. This is for my protection as much as it is for yours. I insist you carry this whenever we leave the house.

"Oh fine, you big baby, happy?" With a snarl, Ella grabbed the bag and threw it into her backpack. She felt immediately weighed down by it.

Yes, although I would prefer you use the holster and strap it to your belt for quicker access. One thing at a time.

"I don't even know how to use the stupid thing."

It is already loaded with the safety on, and it is a low enough caliber so even someone like you should have no problem using it. Click the safety and fire. That is all. I will give you pointers along the way. You probably will not need it this time, but I want you to start getting used to carrying it.

That was the last thing Ella wanted to hear. For the next thirty minutes, Io droned on about gun use, safety, and technique. All of it went right over Ella's head. Without actually holding the gun in her hand, she had no idea what the Quasing was talking about. It didn't help that Ella was also busy navigating the darkening streets of Crate Town. Pretty soon, Ella just tuned the alien out.

You are not listening to me.

"Damn right. Like you said, the streets aren't safe at night. I need to pay more attention to what's going on than to you."

Listen, you silly human, I am a being who was on this planet when dinosaurs roamed the Earth. I am more intelligent and wiser than you will ever be. When I speak, you listen, understand?

Ella bit her lip. More stupid talk from the snobby Quasing. She was about to keep arguing when she almost missed an important turn and realized it was probably a waste of time. Until she was on equal footing with this overbearing alien, Io was going to keep bossing her around. Unless... Ella suddenly had an idea. She made a sharp turn and ran down a side street.

Wait, where are you going? Chuy's is the next block over.

A few seconds later, before Io could stop her, Ella sprinted into Fab's Art Gallery. "Hey Little Fab, you still open?"

The youngest Fab was with a customer inspecting a crate of tablets. He looked up. "Twenty-four hour service, cat. What's up?"

Ella took the brown bag out of her backpack and flourished the handgun. Both men jumped backward, arms raised. Off to the side, the Fabs' muscle, their great aunt Nitu, shifted to Ella's left. Ella slapped the handgun on the table with a heavy *thunk*. She upended the contents of the bag. "How much for the gun and all these bullet holder things?"

This is Prophus property. You are not allowed to sell this.

"Where did you come by that?" Little Fab asked.

"How much?"

Stop!

Little Fab scratched his chin full of stubble. "I don't know what you want me to do with this thing. There's no market for guns here in Crate Town. I guess if you just want to get rid of it, I can give you three thousand–"

"Deal."

Io made a sort of strangled noise in Ella's head. A few minutes later, she walked out of Fab's Art Gallery three thousand rupees richer. She skipped along the street whistling to herself. She knew Little Fab had ripped her off, yet again, but this time she didn't care. She had something more important to win from that exchange.

How dare you?

She stopped walking and sat down on the ground in the middle of the road. This probably wasn't the right time, and it was a little childish, but she had to draw the line somewhere. It was time the two of them had a heart-to-heart talk about their relationship. "Do you really want to force me to do something, alien? Do you want to see how far I'll dare?"

We will discuss this later. Now that you've sold the gun, it is best we finish your errand as quickly as possible.

Night had fallen upon Crate Town and the crowds in the streets had thinned to a trickle. That was when things became dangerous. Ella sprinted the rest of the way to Chuy's, rented a generator and three spare battery packs, and hurried home. Along the way, with the newly-earned money from her one and only time as an arms dealer, she also bought a bag of sweets.

Ella got home shortly before eleven and checked for any intruders. Once she was sure the coast was clear, she plugged in the spare battery packs, tossed some sweets to Burglar Alarm, and made herself comfortable as she waited for her five guests to arrive.

CHAPTER NINETEEN
Recon Team

I was one of the very last to leave and explore this planet. The piece of the ship I was in – one of the largest – had crashed in what is now known as the Yucatán Peninsula. I labored for eons with the few thousand survivors with me, trying to establish a communication link back to Quasar. Ultimately, there was too little of the Eternal Sea left for us to properly form the necessary array for the Receiver to contact the home world. However, I worked until the very last moment, until all hope was lost.

Captain Kim Kim Lee hated only two things in his life. After two grueling tours on the Finnish front, one in Mongolia, and three in Siberia during the Alien World War, he had experienced the worst of humanity, seen some truly vile things, and had had to perform some awful acts himself. Still, through all that death, destruction and evil, Lee held very little hate in his heart. He loved everyone, even the people he had to kill in combat. Especially the ones he had to kill in combat. That was his religion, as well as his method of coping with the otherwise cruel world.

There were two exceptions. The first was his father.

If anyone asked about his worst moments in life, he always went back to the time of his birth when his alcoholic father, drunk, used three surnames for his name. And then, after cursing him with a nonsensical name, disappeared from his life forever. God, Lee hated that man and painted his old man's face on the enemy every time he went to battle.

"Sorry, K2," Chuang, his second in command and current driver's side passenger, said as he twisted the knobs. "I think the air conditioning is busted. Want me to request a refund from the rental office?"

That was the second thing Lee hated more than anything in the world. There was a very specific and intentional reason why all the tours he had fought in all those years were north of forty degrees north latitude; Lee hated hot weather, and especially hated humidity. Hated it with a burning passion, right up there with how much he hated his old man.

Unfortunately, this was an emergency mission and his team was the only qualified recon group in the region available on short notice. So as fate would have it, here they were, here in hot-as-hell India, with the air conditioning busted. This was his worst nightmare.

"You're damn right I want you to," Lee growled, his hands gripping the steering wheel tightly.

No matter what he did, he couldn't get comfortable. Beads of sweat slithered down his cheek and dribbled off his chin. His lower back squelched from wetness anytime he shifted. His pants stuck to his legs as if he were wearing thermals. It was the one of the most disgusting feelings he had ever had to endure.

Chuang dabbed her forehead and fanned herself with a folded-up newspaper. A smirk grew on her face. "Look on the bright side, we only have to put up with this for the next few weeks."

Lee's knuckles on the steering wheel turned white.

Higgins leaned in from the back seat and patted both of them on the shoulders. He inhaled deeply through his nose and made an exaggerated contented sigh. "Ah, the smells, the sweats. It is making me homesick. Welcome to my world."

The rest of the recon team was very familiar with Lee's quirks. Higgins was the only one who dared openly complain about how their team always operated in the tundra. Lee allowed the Jamaican to mouth off and gave him a standing offer to transfer out of Lee's unit whenever he wanted. The offer had stood for seven years now.

"At least we're almost there," Lee grumbled.

He turned off Highway 228 onto the 196 and began the final stretch toward this place known as Crate Town. Lee hadn't told his people yet, but he had some concerns about the safe house as well. Or more like the lack of a safe house. The intel he got during the briefing sounded sketchy. All five of them were going to bunk with a new host who owned a shack in the slum? That hardly sounded promising.

"Who's our contact again?" he asked, to no one in particular.

Navah piped up from the back of the van. "The host's auxiliary, a Hamilton Breckenridge."

"Breckenridge?" Chuang said. "Does he have a title? Lord Hamilton Breckenridge."

"The third," Higgins added. "Defender of the uptight pants."

Thomas, their sniper, sniffed. "Auxiliaries. Glorified personal assistants with heads way too big for their rank."

"I was asked to join the host auxiliaries," said Navah.

"Why didn't you?" asked Chuang.

"And miss out on all the fun freezing my ass off holed up in some ditch with you guys? Never."

"You should have taken it," Lee said softly. "It's a good step up. Can't hang out with us bums forever."

"Watch me, K2."

"Turn here." Chuang pointed at an intersection leading to a cluster of warehouses. "Our contact is meeting us in the one marked C3."

Lee pulled the van into the shadow of one of the large buildings. It was past midnight, but the sky was clear and the moon lit up the ground like a giant theater stage spotlight. Lee sent Thomas out first while the rest of his team took position near the van.

The sniper reported ten minutes later. "All clear. Found Warehouse C3. Two hundred meters west. Water on two sides. Only road from the east. There's something that looks like a junkyard just to the south."

"Let's go."

"What is this place?" Thomas asked.

"Former drydock from the war converted to grain storage facilities," Navah said.

Lee led his team west on foot, walking along the south side of the street. Even though the odds of being seen were low, they hugged the shadows and moved at a measured and quiet pace. Thomas joined them halfway to C3. Lee held a fist up and took a moment to listen to the background noise.

Nothing. He took a deep, labored breath.

"Like soup, eh?" Higgins grinned. "Just like home."

"Hell is a jungle," Lee replied.

"Then I must be the devil, yeah?"

The recon team reached Warehouse C3, and after a few seconds of walking the perimeter, found the unlocked west door, as instructed. The door creaked open and they filed inside one by one. Moonlight shone through a row of windows near the ceiling of the cavernous room, creating shadows and depth in the otherwise completely dark space.

A large object hovered in the air in the center of the room. It took the shape of a fishing boat as they neared. One of the shadows on the boat moved. Lee threw a fist into the air and his team scattered behind cover.

The shadow spoke in clear Korean. "Be not afraid of growing slowly."

"Be afraid only of standing still." Lee butchered his Mandarin, but it was passable for the job. "Well met, Auxiliary Breckenridge?"

The shadow approached the bow. "Captain Kim Kim Lee, welcome to Surat."

Lee signaled for the others to stand down. Funny, Hamilton Breckenridge didn't have much of an accent. In fact, he sounded almost…

The lights to Warehouse C3 turned on, revealing a tall Indian in a sharp suit standing on the boat. Before Lee could bark out a warning, armed men flooded into the room. Before his team could react, Lee was faced with two dozen muzzles pointing at them.

"K2?" Chuang asked. She and Navah stood back to back as they swung their rifles back and forth. They were completely surrounded.

"Drop your weapons, Prophus, and you'll live," the Indian man said.

Lee assessed the situation. His team was outnumbered and clustered together, and the enemy held the higher ground. There were no options here.

"Stand down," he barked. Lee knelt down and put the rifle on the ground, and then he stood with his hands up. One by one, his team followed his lead.

"All right," Lee said. "We're surrendering. Honor your word and guarantee the safety of my soldiers."

The Indian man watched in silence as his soldiers disarmed the team and cuffed them. His gaze swept across each of them one by one. Finally, he limply waved a finger at Navah.

"Save the captain and that one for interrogation. Kill the rest."

"Yes, Minister," one of the soldiers barked, and then they closed in.

The hard banging on the front door reverberated across the walls of Ella's entire container. She woke with a start and nearly fell off the couch. She blinked away the sleep as the ringing thundered in her ears.

Ella sat up and felt a tweak in her back, either from one of her many workout bruises or from this uncomfortable couch. She must have dozed off waiting for the recon team. This thing made for an awful bed. It almost made her feel bad that she was making others sleep on it. She checked the time: eight in the morning.

Their flight was probably just delayed, or perhaps traffic was heavy coming down from Ahmadabad.

"In the middle of the night?"

Well, what did she know? Ella didn't have a car. In fact, she couldn't even drive. The incessant banging continued, and was soon joined by Burglar Alarm's barking. Ella pawed the shank off the coffee table and crept to the front door. She held the shank near the gap with one hand and grabbed the handle with the other. "Who is it? What do you want?"

"It's Hamilton."

Ella yanked the door open. "About time you got here. And why were you banging so hard? You scared the crap..." She peered behind him. "Where's everybody else?"

He stormed past her. "They never came. I waited at the train station until six."

Was their flight delayed?

Ella relayed Io's question.

Hamilton shook his head. "Flight landed on time. I called the rental company. They picked up the van at eleven."

"They're only a few hours late," said Ella. "Maybe they stopped for breakfast somewhere or were sidetracked with shopping or..." Her words trailed off when Hamilton gave her a look as if she was talking nonsense. "Did the van have GPS? Is there a way to figure out where they are?"

The look he gave her grew worse. "They're a recon team."

"So?"

"So of course not. What kind of deep field recon team allows a tag hanging in the air so someone can follow their trail? But yes, the rental van had a GPS, and I'm pretty sure that's the first thing they disabled when they got in the damn vehicle."

Hamilton collapsed onto Ella's sofa, covered his face, and then ran his hands through his hair. Ella frowned at how familiar he seemed with her place, yet she still could not remember any time when he had come inside. For the life of her, she couldn't recall that scene Io had shown her earlier.

"Io, you're screwing with my head somehow. I'm not stupid."

I do not know what you are.

"Come clean with me. I know something's up. If you want our relationship to work, we have to be honest with each other."

Fine. I admit I may have some control over your body while you are unconscious. I have had to use it intermittently to do some work, and yes, that included having Hamilton in here.

"You lying bodysnatching bastard!"

It was with good cause. I did not want to overwhelm you. Your hands are full as it is with your training. It is for the best.

"I know what's best for me, not anyone else! You don't get to lie to me."

Hamilton stood up abruptly. "This is the second time it's happened. Something is wrong; possibly a leak. We should abort." He looked over at her. "For your and Io's safety, we should leave India as soon as possible."

"Like hell I'm leaving home," she snapped. "Wait, a leak?"

Ella, listen to me carefully. I know you and I have important things to hammer out, but we have a more pressing issue. Hamilton has been trying to get us to leave your home now for weeks. It makes me wonder; is there something here he does not want us to find out? He says there is a leak; maybe it is him.

The shank materialized in Ella's hand again. She thought about kind old Bijan and those people who were supposed to be staying here at her place. Was he responsible for their disappearance?

Put the shank down, Ella. Do not raise any suspicion. We have no proof, and even if we do, this is not the time. Act normal, calm him down, and we will plan our next course of action.

Io was probably right. For once. Ella placed the shank on the table and grabbed a cup. She filled it with water and brought it over to Hamilton. The Brit, sweating profusely, drank it.

"We should leave," he repeated.

She shook her head. "We're missing all these people now. Io says it's our duty to find out what happened to them. Besides, this is my home. I'm not going anywhere. You're free to run if you like."

Hamilton stiffened and his lips quivered. He placed the cup on the coffee table so hard she thought he might have cracked it. "I am not abandoning my post, even if the host and the Quasing refuse to see the wisdom of it. However, I am reporting all of this to Command."

I wonder who else he is reporting to. Do not trust him, Ella.

"I never liked him anyway."

She waved Hamilton off. "You tell whoever you feel like telling. I'm not going."

"Are you concerned that they'll come for you here?"

She shrugged. "I've been here all along. I figure if the Genjix can find people who have been here only a few hours, they should already know where I am. Maybe the leak is somewhere else."

That went right over Hamilton's head. He got up and walked over to the door. "I'm going to check the hospitals in the area, just in case they got into an accident." He paused. "You know, Command probably won't send anyone else to help. Not after losing a scout and an entire team. We don't have enough intel to have an actionable plan. We're just wasting–"

"I'll do it then," she said. "Show me how to use the gear and I'll get that information myself."

Hamilton stared. She could see the disdain in his eyes. "You have no idea what you're getting yourself into." He went outside and slammed the door shut.

Ella listened to the echo of metal ringing until it disappeared, leaving her standing in her living room in silence with only her thoughts.

Do not worry. I will help you become a great spy.

Well, almost only her thoughts.

She sighed. "Fine, let's get to work. By the way, how much of a raise am I getting if I do this?"

CHAPTER TWENTY
Rut

I did not give up on making contact until all options had been exhausted, and even then, I kept trying. Part of me was confident that I had the knowledge and skill to pull off some sort of miracle. Part of me just wanted to be the savior of my people.

However, the miracle never came. There was too much damage, we had too little of the Eternal Sea with us, and too few of us to form the necessary components. One by one, as what little supply of our Eternal Sea dissipated over time, the other Quasing left to explore this world.

In the end, I was alone.

Ella spent an entire day wallowing in bed. After she kicked Hamilton out of her home, she crawled under the sheets and moped. She wasn't sure what disturbed her more, learning that the recon team had disappeared, that Hamilton might be a double agent, or that Io had been messing with her body doing gods-know-what while she slept. It all left a bad taste in her mouth.

She stewed in her contempt of everyone, everything, and most of all, herself for caring. Every little thing that had gone wrong lately was starting to eat her up inside. Life was so much simpler when the only person Ella was involved with was herself, and she didn't have to care about anyone or anything else.

Her day of moping turned into three days. Io tried to talk to her a few times, but Ella didn't feel like listening. What else was the alien hiding, and what was Io doing with Ella's body while she was asleep? For all she knew, Io could be taking over her body and robbing banks or ninjaing around Crate Town at night murdering people or sucking blood out of children like some pasty-faced vampire. Actually, Ella wouldn't mind that.

Now you are just being ridiculous. As I have said repeatedly, a Quasing's control over an unconscious human is weak. I can barely walk your body upright, let alone kill someone.

Still, every night Ella tried something different to make sure she stayed in bed. The first night, she went to sleep hugging her bedpost, and was pleasantly surprised when she awoke in the same position. She did a careful walk around her living room, checking if anything was moved. Everything seemed untouched and in the right place until she checked the power generator. It was twenty percent lower than it should have been.

I had to update Command about the recon team. I had no choice.

That was when Ella began to take the more extreme measure of tying one arm to the bedpost with a rag. That seemed successful for the next couple days, although it could be that Io didn't need to use her body for anything. She also wasn't sure if the alien knew how to tie knots. Io said she didn't have the agility to do so, but it wasn't like Ella was going to believe what she said anyway.

On the morning of the fourth day of her self-imposed imprisonment, she received a visitor. Burglar Alarm began to bark, and then there was a furious banging at the door. Ella tried to ignore it, hoping whoever it was would go away, but the banging continued, as did the dog's barking. When she still didn't answer the door, the persistent jerk crawled onto her roof.

Footsteps clanged on the container and she saw an eye appear through one of the holes. The stomping continued for a few more minutes and then whoever it was began to bang on her front door again. Finally, after ten minutes of her walls ringing, Ella couldn't stand it anymore. She leaped out of bed, grabbed her shank and stomped toward the front door.

Maybe you should consider the possibility that whoever is outside is not friendly.

"That's why I have a shank in my hand."

What if he is armed with a gun? Too bad you sold the gun I gave you for a bag of treats.

"I told you, no one uses guns in Crate Town."

Famous last words.

Ella got a sense of where the asshole was standing, opened the door, and charged outside. She jabbed at where she thought the person's neck would be, and instead nearly stabbed the very large boob of a very tall man. Fortunately, she stopped just short of breaking skin.

Melonhead looked down at the tip puncturing his shirt and poking into his flesh. He pinched the tip and moved it to the side. "Hi, Ella."

The shank disappeared from view behind her waistband. "Hi, Melonhead. Sorry about your shirt."

He shrugged. "What's one more hole?" He looked her up and down. "You haven't been to the gym. Uncle Manish is worried about you."

She coughed. "Sorry, I've been sick."

"Are you feeling better now?"

She nodded.

"Good, he told me to bring you to the gym. Let's go."

Ella was about to refuse when she hesitated. She had run out of food last night and hadn't showered in days. Maybe stabbing someone at the gym would make her feel better. Besides, she could shower at Manish's gym instead of paying Wiry Madras. Maybe get a free meal from it too.

"Fine," she huffed. "Let me get my stuff."

Melonhead's ride was a post-apocalyptic dystopian tank. Actually, it was a Volkswagen cobbled together from the corpses of several other vans that he had patched with square plates wherever they didn't fit together properly.

"This is the magic carpet right here." He stroked the side of the van as if he were running his fingers through a woman's hair.

"It's very colorful," Ella said. That was the extent of the compliment she could muster for this ugly thing.

Wait, we are not riding in this contraption. It does not look safe.

"It took me two years to put together," he said, sliding the back door open for her.

Ella stopped. "What are you doing? I'm sitting in the front with you."

"The doors on the right side don't work."

She looked inside. There were no windows on that right side either. Ella went around to the other side of the van and gaped. It wasn't that the doors on that side wouldn't open, there weren't any doors at all. Instead of an actual side of a car, she found herself looking at what essentially was a steel wall welded into place. This thing was a container on wheels.

He came around next to her. "I ran out of money to buy the rest of the pieces, so I made do. Got it from Crate Town actually."

"At least it's bulletproof," she said.

"Well, if you ever want to rob a bank," he grinned, "you know who to ask to be getaway driver."

Ella went back around to the sliding door and crawled inside. There was a bunch of junk in the back, and it took a fair amount of navigating to shimmy her way to the front passenger side seat. Melonhead got into the driver's side, and after a few false starts, had them speeding toward the gym.

Speeding might have been a slight exaggeration. The tank's top speed was somewhere around forty kilometers per hour, probably due to its tiny four-cylinder engine and the several tons of metal strapped to its body. Ella gripped the railing on the door as the tank bounced and wobbled on the uneven road. This thing didn't have much of a suspension either, and she was pretty sure if it hit anything remotely like a dip in the ground, it wasn't ever going to be able to climb its way out. A couple of times, it looked as if it were about to tip over when it made a turn, and struggled mightily when it climbed uphill. Hell, it seemed to struggle when it went on flat terrain as well. Basically, it would have been the worst getaway vehicle in the history of bank robberies.

"I would have gotten there faster in a tuk-tuk," she grumbled.

You would have gotten there faster in a golf cart.

"What's golf?"

Never mind. The sport of kings.

Ella looked up the sport on her phone. "Wait, it's that boring thing where they hit that tiny ball with a skinny stick into a little hole?"

It is. One of my hosts was a professional golfer. It means he was one of the best to ever play.

"Yeah? What's his name?"

Alfred Scalzan.

Ella looked that up too. "Says here he was the 191st ranked golfer some fifty years ago. I didn't know they had ranks that high."

That is for the whole world!

"I'm not saying he's not good. It's just that being ranked 191st is kind of like getting a modak treat just for showing up. It's hardly the best to ever play."

What would you know? What have you ever done to distinguish yourself?

Ella looked out the window as they pulled into Little Dharavi. "I've lived in one of the largest slums in India on my own since I was ten. I survived, thrived even. I bought a home, and I didn't compromise my body or morals to do it."

By stealing and conning innocents. That does not compromise your morals?

"I was a scrawny girl whose mother had just died and whose father had abandoned her. I did what I had to do. Let's see your stupid golfer do that."

There was a long pause.

I apologize, Ella. I have only looked into parts of your past, and I know it was not easy. It was not right of me to judge you.

She shrugged. "It's all right. I'm used to being judged. It's all people do when they eye me walking by. Am I a thief, a prostitute, or something worse? I've had a lot of time to think about why life isn't fair."

How did you come about being named Ella? It is not very Singaporean or Indian.

"Music was Amma's first love, before she discovered flying." As always, when the topic switched to her mother, Ella had to keep it together. "She named me after her favorite jazz singer."

Tell me what happened with your mother. You said she was a fighter pilot for the Indian Air Force. Was she shot down?

Ella felt little stings in her eyes, but she blinked them back. She would never live it down to Melonhead if he saw her tear up for no reason. "The Chinese and Pakistani armies launched a surprise attack. Something happened where the emergency alert systems didn't get triggered, so our base didn't know it was coming." She bit her lip. "In any case, by the time we found out about the attack, they were already on us. Amma's plane was one of the few that made it off the ground. It became an evacuation instead of a battle."

I am sorry to hear that. Did you ever find out why the alert was never sent out?

Ella shook her head. She knew she didn't have to, because they were communicating inside her head, but it was a habit. "The government blamed human error and faulty systems, but someone at the base said it was sabotage."

Probably the Genjix.

"Doesn't matter anymore, I guess."

Melonhead pulled the tank in front of Murugan's Mitts and parked. Ella waited for him to get out first, since his side was the only door that worked. Instead, he turned to her and looked as if he had something to say. Ella waited. He said nothing. She began to fidget. He opened his mouth again. Again, no words came out.

"OK. Bye," she stammered out.

"Wait, Ella," Melonhead said, putting a hand on her arm. She resisted her natural reaction to pull away. "Do you want to grab coffee sometime?"

"Sure." The words came out of her mouth before she mentally checked the meaning behind his request. She cringed a little inside, but decided to hell with it. "Are you paying?"

You are such a cheap date. You really need to stop saying yes to anything for free food.

"Quiet, alien. We're just hanging out. Besides, coffee is a luxury I don't get to drink often, and it's definitely not a date."

"Sure." Melonhead broke into a grin. "The man always pays for a first date."

I told you so.

"Damn it."

"I'll let you know when I have some free time," she added quickly. Ella hurried out of the tank and walked briskly to the gym entrance. She should have thought things through a little more carefully before saying yes to Melonhead. Relationships around these parts were weird sometimes. For all she knew, Melonhead might come from one of those families where it was coffee date one day and an engagement the next. She shuddered.

She looked back as he did a twelve-point turn with the tank – he wasn't a bad guy. She could do much worse. Not to mention he was going to own the gym once Manish retired. That meant she and Melonhead could double up those payments from the Prophus, one for her agreed stipend and one for Manish's retainer as well.

I hope your aspirations in life rise above staying in the slum. Besides, an income should not be the primary reason to marry someone.

She sniffed. "Says the alien who probably never had to worry about starving to death."

You would be surprised at the things I have had to go through on this planet.

Ella stood in front of the gym and took a deep breath, soaking in the familiar scent of sweat and piss. The hairs on her arms pricked up at the humidity, and she welcomed the familiar sounds of gloves striking leather and the coach's growly voice barking from somewhere inside. She had to admit it, she missed this place.

Manish gave her the eye when she trotted inside. "Look who crawled back from the gutter. Back from your vacation, runt?"

"Ready to work out some aggression and draw some blood, coach."

"Good." He tossed her a set of boxing gloves. "Lace up."

CHAPTER TWENTY-ONE
A Hitch

The initial shock of the planet nearly consumed me. I was deep within the ocean, blind and desperate, being torn apart by the currents and the terrible pressure of the depths. With only seconds to live, I searched for the nearest eligible vessel.

I ended up joining with a sea creature that humans never discovered. It dwelt on the bottom of the ocean filtering sand and eating microorganisms. This creature became my new home. I do not know how long for because there was no sense of time in the blackness of the ocean floor.

It was eaten by a predator, who then became my new home. After that, it too was eaten by an even larger predator. And then another. It was a cruel cycle that continued for millions of years. This was my introduction to your world.

Shura put Mogg's people to work right away. Overnight, they transformed from a union of dockworkers who racketeered on the side to a full-blown terror group whose job was to force the remaining hold-outs of Dumas to sell their properties. They intimidated the businesses and harassed shoppers at the storefronts. They loitered on the streets and clogged major intersections, and they did all this with the police looking in the other direction.

Within a few weeks, most of the businesses were forced to

close. The residences soon followed. All that remained was one very influential Jain monk. This was the confrontation that concerned Shura the most.

She had visited Indu shortly after she completed their arrangements with Mogg. He had graciously invited her into his temple and offered her tea. His temple was little more than a container ziggurat, with sixteen containers on the ground level, twelve on the second, eight on the third, and so on until his little throne on the sixth floor.

At first, Surrett had tried to buy the man out, offering to relocate him to another part of the slum. When the monk refused, the minister tried to offer to build a real temple for him. When he refused again, Surrett actually offered him a position as head monk of the massive Hutcheesing Temple further north in Ahmedabad, one of the great Jain temples in India. However, the man held his ground, content just to sit in squalor with his herd. Surrett finally dropped all pretenses and tried to flat-out bribe the monk, offering a generous stipend.

Shura was impressed by the man's faith and steadfastness. "It is too bad we did not recruit him at an early age."

I disagree. Lack of ambition is a terrible weakness. A vessel who does not strive for standing will never reach their maximum potential.

After that, the Jain monk refused to see them at all the next two times they called. The problem with the man was the Genjix had nothing he wanted. He couldn't be bribed, he had no need for wealth, and he was perfectly content living this simple life until his last breath.

Unfortunately, his temple was in the heart of Dumas. Construction could not proceed without the monk agreeing to give up or relocate the temple. To make matters worse, Indu's flock numbered in the thousands. A forced removal would incite massive riots. This gave Shura few alternatives.

Shura sat at the desk in her office and grimaced. Frustrated, she pushed the piles of surveillance photos off to the side.

She had spent hours searching for a solution to this problem that wouldn't cause an avalanche of collateral damage. All indications were pointing toward one solution, and it wasn't one she relished.

You tried the carrot. The stick will make things worse. That leaves only one other option: the Eternal Sea.

Shura grimaced. She was pretty sure a beating wouldn't change the man's mind, and killing clergy was a sordid business, even if it was in the name of her own religion. Their followers tended to react to it poorly and illogically, and it generally caused a much larger mess than the original problem. Still, she had given the man every chance to accept what had to be done. It was up to him to make the right choice.

Make it look like an accident.

"Ugh. That's even worse."

Now you are just being lazy.

That was true. Staging an accident was a lot of work. It required a tremendous amount of planning and preparation, there were always so many unknown variables to deal with, and the chances of it all going to shit were pretty high. It was rarely worth the hassle. Shura would almost rather walk up to the monk and put a bullet between his eyes, and then just deal with the fallout. She sighed. Tabs was probably right; this was the best solution.

Shura made the call to Surrett to assign an around-the-clock tail on the monk. She would need to gather as much information as possible on his routine and habits before devising a plan, and her time was far too valuable to waste following the man herself. She didn't trust the minister's inexperienced operatives to pull off the assassination and make it appear an accident; she would need to carry that out herself. If word ever leaked that the Genjix had tried to kill a revered Jain monk, the consequences would be severe. It wouldn't be an overreaction for them to expel all Genjix from the country.

She was relaying final instructions when a light began to blink on her console. She saw the contact number and, at first, chose to ignore it. Let the man wait. Then she realized she was being petulant. In his shoes, she would have done the exact same thing, if not worse.

"Get to work," she instructed, and then tapped over to the other line. A picture of a good-looking blond with a strikingly square jaw appeared. "Hello Rurik."

"Shura, I believe you intended to acknowledge me as 'Father'."

Now is not the time, Shura. You are not ready to confront him yet.

The two locked eyes for several moments before she finally lowered her gaze. "Father."

He chuckled. "Shura, always the prideful one. You never did let go of that chip you have on your shoulder. Does the ghost of your father haunt you to this day?"

"All things considered, I do not expect him to haunt any other."

Rurik smirked. Shura wanted to reach her hand through the screen and sink her claws into his neck. However, she let it go. The memory didn't hurt, not anymore, but it still left her feeling numb.

"I see that High Father Weston has ordered you to oversee one of my projects."

"Someone has to," she said.

"I thank you, daughter. Don't get too comfortable. I expect you to keep the lights on until someone of proper standing can take the helm."

He is goading you. Give him nothing.

"I know what he is up to, Tabs."

"Give me a status report," Rurik said.

Shura was sure he had thoroughly investigated the situation here in India by way of the minister before contacting her. This was nothing more than a dog-and-pony show to humiliate her and put her in her place. Shura was obligated to report to Rurik how his program was doing. He was of higher standing than she was, at least at this moment.

As a small test to see how much Rurik actually knew about the project, she padded some of the dates. A slight raise of his eyebrow and a momentary hesitation in his movements informed her that he had received contradictory information.

At least now we know who Surrett is latching his wagon to. In truth, considering our two positions, it was probably the wisest path. Nevertheless, it is good to know where the minister stands.

Regardless, they were all here to strive to fulfill the will of the Holy Ones. All the maneuvering between them was just the Genjix way of making sure their vessels were operating at their best. Conflict bred innovation.

"Good, daughter," Rurik said. "I will finish consolidating my holdings in Russia by the end of the year. After that, I intend to visit and inspect my holdings. I expect the Bio Comm Array to be fully operational and signaling by then. Hold down the fort for me until then."

Shura stared at the screen long after it went blank. Rurik was five years her junior. He was also a mediocre vessel who only survived the Hatchery because of his family name and the billions that came with it. Fortunately for him, the man knew his limitations and was generous in leveraging the resources he was born with.

Unfortunately for everyone else, he overcompensated for his deficiencies with a vicious streak and a long, vindictive memory. Shura had suffered Rurik's insecurity and cruelty firsthand at the Hatchery when he had tried to lord his family name and wealth over her. Rurik and his gang had harassed and pushed her around for days upon her return, mocking and physically threatening her, saying children of traitors did not deserve to be at the Hatchery. Shura responded by catching him without his hangers-on and dunking him underwater until he passed out. Their relationship only went downhill from there. Taking the project from under him would be a sweet victory.

If we miss the target, you will make an enemy for life, not that you two were ever going to be friends anyway. It is one thing to earn the animosity of a spoiled child, it is another entirely to earn the wrath of a billionaire in control of one of our most powerful regions.

"Then I better make sure I don't miss."

Six months is not a lot of time. We will need to move our timetable up if we intend to take our claim to the Council for ownership of the project.

"There is still a lot to do, and we've sunk in more money than I prefer at this stage. The Council will raise an eyebrow when they see the bill."

That could not be helped. Fortunately, the payments to Faiz and the majority of the landowners have mostly been taken from the government and partially from the Bio Comm Array budget. The payments to Mogg and her hooligans, though, come directly from your requisition.

If we do not bring the array fully online and the project back on schedule before he arrives, you will not be able to make a case to take ownership of the project.

"That means I will have done nothing except help my enemy." She stood up abruptly and grabbed her coat. "No time to waste then."

Where are you going?

"I changed my mind. I will personally survey Indu's movements. It's time to kill a priest."

CHAPTER TWENTY-TWO
Trust

For millions of years, I moved from sea creature to sea creature, being nothing more than a listless passenger watching these aquatic animals survive and evolve. What do I remember? Not much. I was a ghost, barely conscious, having left all hope in that ship after I had failed as a Receiver.

There were many times I wondered why I even bothered. Why not venture out into the ocean vessel-less, get torn apart, and simply cease to exist? I thought myself the last of my kind on the planet. I was resigned to never bask in the warmth of the Eternal Sea ever again. I believed I was alone and forgotten in the universe.

Eight hours after Melonhead had dropped her off at the gym, Ella again regretted ever getting out of bed. She seemed to have forgotten all her training in three days. Her cardio was off, her muscles seemed to have melted into nothing, and her reflexes were so poor she felt like she was wading in the Gulf of Khambhat.

Finally, even Manish had had enough.

"You move like garbage and you look even worse."

He bounced a tennis ball off Ella's head. She even saw it hurdling lazily toward her, but was too slow or indifferent to duck. And this was after two rounds of Melonhead playing bongo drums on her forehead in a sparring match. Even the speed bag had gotten a lucky hit in and cracked her on the head.

Frustrated, she screeched and kicked at the closest thing within reach, which unfortunately was Melonhead. Luckily for him, he was used to her random outbursts by now and smoothly stepped out of reach of her short legs.

"What's wrong with you?" Manish asked, slipping through the ropes and walking toward her. He held out his hands.

"Nothing," she grumbled, holding her arms out so he could take the gloves off.

"You're done," Manish said. "Go wash up and help Aarav prepare dinner."

Ella quickly washed up and wiped herself with a damp rag, and then the three of them moved the table to the front of the gym and sat down to eat. That was the nice thing about working out here until the early evening. Melonhead's cooking was pretty mediocre, but free food was the best food in the world.

The three of them feasted on some deformed samosas and watered-down palak soup, and then people-watched as the families who lived in the neighborhood came out to play now that the day had cooled. The setting sun was retreating behind the one-story shacks that made up most of Little Dharavi. What little orange light was left blended with the rust that covered nearly every inch of the building walls.

Ella studied a couple nearby watching over their two young children, half-naked and barefoot, playing on the broken streets amidst a pile of blue plastic container drums next to a trash heap. She wondered if that's where she was going to be in a few years. Assuming she even wanted children. Ella was drawn to the little girl, wearing a brightly colored but worn out orange embroidered sari, one hand clutching a doll, the other playing in the mud. She hadn't grown up like that little girl.

Her upbringing had been middle-class, whatever that meant. Sure, they had to move all the time because her parents were in the military, but she really couldn't complain. There was always a roof and four good walls, and she never went to bed hungry. She had playmates, a good enough education and good enough grades. She played the bassoon, took gymnastics classes, and had many friends in grade school. So what happened? How did she end up all alone in the world living in Crate Town? What happened to that life that once held so much promise?

That war happened. That damn Quasing Alien World War. It ruined her life. The war that had consumed the world for eight years had devastated her country. India was one of the principal battlegrounds, and society had fallen apart within the first year. It had been a struggle to survive.

Ella didn't even know who had won. All she knew was that she had lost. Amma was gone, Appa disappeared, and now here she was, living off the streets and calling a post-war slum home. Ella didn't know if she should be sad or angry. She chose to seethe. She just wasn't sure who she should seethe at, so she latched on to the easiest target.

"Damn all you aliens."

Are we never going to get past this?

"Not in a million years."

It is a good thing I can live that long.

Ella tore her gaze away from the family. Any longer and she might start crying, and then she would never hear the end of it from Manish and Melonhead.

"Hey Aarav," Manish said. "Put these dishes away."

"Why don't you have Ella do it?" Aarav said. "I cooked the food."

"Because I want to talk to her, you lazy oaf. Now clean up before I bodyshot your kidney out of you and sell it as a replacement to drunks."

Melonhead looked as if he was going to retort, then

stomped off. Ella got up to help with the plates.

Manish put a hand on her arm. "Let him do it. I do want to talk to you."

"You're awfully mean to him," said Ella. "Why? He's your blood. You're nicer to everyone else."

Manish looked back at Aarav. "My nephew still has a lot of growing up to do. He and his brother and my grandson are all I have left in the world. I'm retiring after this year, and he convinced me to give him the gym instead of selling it. Says he'll give me a quarter of the profits until I die. I would rather he not lose the business and me end up a beggar on the streets." He turned back to Ella, and put his arms around her shoulders. "That's where you come in. Did I ever tell you I like you? I consider you the daughter I never had."

Ella wasn't born yesterday. She curved an eyebrow at Manish. "Really?"

"Like my own flesh and blood."

A tingle shot through her spine. "Coach, if you say the words I think you're going to say, I'm going to punch your nose. There's no way I'm going to marry that melonhead nephew–"

"Oh gods no," Manish choked. "I said I liked you. Why would I want to saddle you with that buffoon, even if he is my sister's son. What I'm saying is, the Prophus stipend has always been a good twenty percent of my earnings. Once I retire, the payments won't continue. If that's the case, I'm afraid Aarav won't be able to keep the doors open, and I won't get my steady retirement income. Unless, of course, you, as a Prophus agent, tell them you require this gym's services to complete your training."

That is not how it works, especially considering you are the only operative to train here in over five years. Manish has been taking advantage of an oversight. His days of free money are over.

Ella considered both Manish and Io's words. "You want to stay open. I can make it happen. What's my cut?"

"I think we can work something out," the old man grinned.

What? You are not allowed to embezzle from the Prophus.

"Hush, alien. I need some new clothes."

The old man was growing on her. Even if he did want to use her to scam the aliens. If anything, it just reinforced that Manish and her were like-minded people, and she found that endearing. It was nice to have someone looking out for her, to not feel like she was alone all the time.

What about me? I am here.

"You don't count, alien."

"Uncle," Aarav shouted from inside the gym. "The water heater is acting up."

Manish stood up and patted her on the shoulder. "We can discuss terms later."

Ella watched the old man go inside, and listened to the shouting match that erupted between him and his nephew. She leaned back in her chair, put her feet up on the table, and basked in the cool breeze. The wind brought with it a slightly foul stench, but it probably masked something worse. Ella couldn't remember the last time she had smelled something pleasant, unless it was the heavy scent of cologne on some slimy man, which again was just another stench masking something worse.

Her thoughts were interrupted by a group of young men passing by. One of them, unsteady on his feet, kicked a chair at the table and sent it tumbling down the sidewalk. They continued joking and staggering away.

"Hey!" Ella stood up. "Pick that back up."

"Pick it up yourself, whore," one of the men replied. The others laughed.

Let it go. It is not worth the trouble.

Ella looked down at the plate, the knife and the half-cup of lassi in front of her. She reached for the lassi, and then changed her mind. She wanted to finish it. Her hand moved over to the dull dinner knife. She hefted it in her hand and pulled her arm back.

No. Do not throw it. There are nine of them there. I am ordering you to put the knife down.

Ordering her, eh? She'd see about that. Ella aimed and then hurled the knife as hard as she could at one of the scrawny guys wearing a sleeveless T-shirt. She had aimed for the guy's head. Fortunately, she missed, instead nailing him square in the back. To her surprise, she had flung the knife hard enough that it actually stuck into his flesh. All that training had produced results.

First of all, your windup is still way too long. Second of all, you are an idiot.

The man screamed and hunched over, frantically grasping at the knife embedded in his back. The rest of them stopped and stared openmouthed at their injured friend. After the initial shock wore off, one of the braver ones pulled it out of his back. The group's attention turned toward Ella. Their faces darkened.

"Hmm. This could be a problem."

You think?! Get inside, quick.

Ella ducked as the knife flew past her head. The group approached and surrounded her. She planted her feet and glared back at them defiantly, daring one of them to hit her first. This wouldn't be the first time she got knocked around for standing her ground, but she wasn't going to let these jerks cow her. One of them gave her a hard shove. She almost fell over, but managed to stay on her feet.

Another to her right looked at the poles inside the gym. "Isn't this the school where they teach those strippers?"

The guy who pushed her chuckled. "Of course, that's why this whore is here."

"Who would pay you?" a man to her left sneered.

Ella's fingers contorted into claws and she lunged, scratching the face of one who was laughing. She stomped on the foot of another, and then tried to squeeze between two bodies to escape. Someone grabbed her by the shirt, and then a blow across her cheek sent her flying into the air. She landed with a thud, the wind knocked out of her. She groaned.

One of the men knelt down. "Next time, don't mess with your bett–"

Ella kicked up and hit his nose with her heel. A spray of blood splattered all over her as his head snapped backward.

"My nose is broken," he cried, holding it. Then they were all over her. Ella tried to cover her head with her arms as three men began punching and kicking her.

Just as quickly as it began, the beating ended.

There was a scream. Ella pried an eye open and saw one of her assailants on his backside begging for mercy. Towering in front of her was Melonhead, swinging his fists and punching another in the face over and over again. She looked to the other side, and her mouth dropped as she saw Manish pounce on three men at the same time.

She had never seen Manish move before, except when he flung himself around the poles. She was amazed at the sight. Where Melonhead was this bull of a man wrecking his way through two men, Manish ducked and dodged as if he were dancing. His movements flowed gracefully as he evaded the clumsy blows from those lumbering idiots, and then he would retaliate with a flurry of fists. Within seconds, half of the group was lying on the ground, while the other half fled down the street.

Aarav chased them for a few meters before stopping. He bent over and picked up two of the bodies and pushed them after their friends. "Don't come back," he yelled in a booming voice, "or I will beat you until your mother feels it in her womb."

What does that even mean?

"I don't know."

Manish came over and offered a hand. She accepted and groaned as he pulled her up. He held her face in his hands and felt a painful spot on her cheek. "Anything broken?"

She shook her head.

He made *tsk* sounds and kissed her forehead. "You're a brave one, girl. Stupid as an empty spit bucket, but brave." He pulled her in close and gave her a rough hug. He then guided her inside the gym. "Go wash up. Aarav will drive you home."

Ella gave him a puzzled look, but continued inside. Manish's worry for her felt strange and weirdly touching. She wasn't used to someone being concerned for her wellbeing. She never thought she missed having a father figure. It was kind of nice.

She went to the locker room and checked her reflection in the uneven mirror that made her face look like it was half the size of her body, and made her eyes perfectly circular. That was why she liked it. She had grown up looking at the pictures of the beautiful women on newsstands and in magazines, and they all had such round eyes. Hers were thin slits by comparison, and no amount of trying to pull her eyes wider as a little girl made them any larger.

You look awful.

She did look awful. One side of her face was a mess of red and purple while the other had a gash from her ear to her nose. Her right eye was puffy like that one time she ate lobster and almost died. She closed her left eye and strained to see.

You could not just let it go, could you?

"Well, I'm sorry if I'm not as big of a pushover as you are."

There was a knock on the door, and Melonhead came in. "Here." He handed her a bag of ice. "For your face. Uncle says I need to drive you home."

Ella stopped him before he closed the door. "Hey, Me... I mean, Aarav, thank you for helping me back there."

"No problem."

"If there's anything I can do, please just ask."

He paused. "It would be great if you don't kick me in the balls anymore."

"You got it."

He closed the door.

A man of few words, but he gets to the point.

"I do hit him there quite a bit. I just can't reach anywhere else that hurts him."

Ella spent another fifteen minutes in front of the mirror trying unsuccessfully to look a little less of a disaster. She didn't have any makeup to cover up the bruises. She wouldn't have known how to apply it anyway.

She left the locker room and walked into the mallakhamba class already in session, feeling very self-conscious. She kept her hair covering her face and her eyes glued to the ground. Manish, threading through the class, gave her a small pat on the back as she passed.

Aarav was waiting for her outside the gym. He looked at her face, puzzled. "What were you doing in there for so long? You look the same."

"None of your damn business," Ella snapped. Then she remembered she had promised to be nicer to him. "I mean, thanks for the ice. It helped the swelling."

"Not really. You still look pretty awful." Aarav grabbed a set of car keys from the table. "Come on, let's go."

CHAPTER TWENTY-THREE
Truce

By the time I ventured out into the terrifying world, tens of millions of years had already passed. The Quasing had scattered all over the planet and, unknown to me, many of them had rediscovered each other and had formed a kingdom of sorts in Africa among the primate tribes. Searchers were sent out to find other Quasing and bring them back into the fold. This was known as the Gathering. I was one of the last found.

A Quasing named Khat, who inhabited a Scandinavian hunter, caught my vessel – a minke whale – while hunting. By then, the world had changed. I had somehow slept through the entire birth and adolescence of humanity. In hindsight, it was probably the right call.

Sometimes, I wish I'd slept through all of it.

Even though exhausted and a little beaten up, Ella had trouble sleeping that night. By now, the bruises over her face and body had turned a ripe purple and were shooting pain up and down her nerves whenever she opened her mouth. She was also having some trouble lifting her left arm above her shoulder. She was plain miserable. Somehow, she'd managed to make leaving the house the wrong decision after spending three days not leaving the house.

Ella, I would like to apologize, and declare a truce.

She crossed her arms. "OK, alien, go ahead."

What?

"You want to apologize, so apologize then."

I just did.

"No, you didn't. You said you wanted to apologize."

Fine. I am sorry.

"For what?"

I am sorry for misleading you about a Quasing's ability to take over an unconscious host.

"And trying to cover it up when I caught you?"

Yes, that too. Technically, you did not catch me. I confessed.

"And you'll ask for permission next time you need to do this?"

Absolutely not.

Ella sat up in bed, and immediately regretted making that abrupt movement. "What's the point in apologizing if you're going to keep doing it?

That is just the way it has to be. I have been working tirelessly at night not only on your behalf, but for the Prophus as well. You do not want to be involved in this sort of grunt work.

"Try me."

Very well.

Io led Ella to the living room and showed her the laptop stashed under a pile of boxes in the corner. She logged in and watched as walls of numbers and letters scrolled across some colorful boxes.

"This is boring," she muttered after a few minutes.

I told you. Click Alt-tab to the next window. Open up the report from the network regarding the Iranian pipe line.

"How do I do that?"

The alt key.

"Which one is the alt key?"

That button left of the big one on the center bar and then the second down from the far left.

Their process slowed to a crawl, since Io had to tell her

where to click and what to type. Soon, another problem became apparent.

Ella, can you read any English at all?

She shook her head. "Some of the words. I know all the letters and numbers. It's putting them together that can get confusing."

I can switch the computer's language to Hindi if you prefer, but my Hindi reading comprehension is weak.

"I'm not great at that either, at least not anything harder than third grade."

How could your parents have been so delinquent in your education?

Ella shot back hotly. "Well, Io, we had a stupid war that bombed Singapore into the Stone Age and ravaged all of India. We were kind of too busy avoiding Chinese kill squads and searching for food to worry about reading stupid letters."

I am sorry. I never bothered to check.

Ella stayed silent, her face burning.

Would you like to learn?

"Learn what?"

I can teach you how to read. You are pretty adept at picking up and speaking languages, seeing how you can speak half a dozen.

"You can help?" she said, in a small voice. She had learned to read English and Mandarin as a child, and some Hindi living on the streets, but it was just enough to survive. She couldn't remember if she had ever cracked a book open before. It had always been a bit of an embarrassment for her.

You have to learn to read sometime. Might as well start here.

For the rest of the night, Io taught Ella English, walking her through the alphabet, punctuation, and keys, all while doing whatever work she was doing for the Prophus. It was at the same time hard and frustrating, yet energizing and hopeful.

To Ella's surprise, a lot of forgotten childhood lessons came flooding back to her. Before she knew it, she had a headache, was sweating, and was thoroughly enjoying herself.

It wasn't until the first rays of light began shining through the dozen small holes poking into the container wall that Ella realized she had stayed up all night. She stood up, stretched, and tilted her stiff neck from side to side, and then stared at the beads hanging in the entranceway to her bedroom rattling against the breeze.

She should sleep, but she was supposed to work out, but she hadn't slept all night, but she was supposed to work out, but her body was still beaten up from getting beaten up. Her tired thoughts ran in circles as she debated whether to get dressed or not.

Go to bed, Ella. Your body needs some time to recuperate anyway. I will send Manish a message once you are asleep letting him know you cannot make it. With your permission, of course.

Ella cracked a small smile. She yawned. "I'm going to sleep until tomorrow."

Actually, we have a job later this afternoon. The deputy minister of Gujurat is giving a speech about a project. Hamilton is going to record it for Command. I want to make sure he is doing his job. After he makes the recording, I want you to take possession of the video.

Ella perked up. "Are you putting me out in the field? Like, am I going to do real work?"

In a way. This should be a relatively safe way to get your feet wet and give you a taste of what an operative does.

Ella paused. "The speech this minister is giving, does it have anything to do with everything happening in Dumas? Everyone there is supposedly up in arms."

That is what we are going to find out. Because we lost both the field scout and the recon team, Command is not willing to commit any more resources. I told them you and I will gather this information. The truth is, I believe a native of Crate Town will have a better chance than the outsiders we brought in.

Ella stood a little taller. She felt important. She felt like she was making a difference.

You have not done anything yet.

"Stop ruining my moment."

All right, but the speech is in six hours. If you want to rest before then, go to bed. I will let Hamilton know to meet here first.

Ella hopped under the sheets, her body tingling with excitement. This whole spy thing was becoming more real every day. For the first time in her life, she dared think about life outside of Crate Town, about possibly being able to do more than just survive. For once, she looked forward to it.

"Hey, Io?"

Yes?

"You have my permission to use my body to do your work, but no funny business, OK?"

Thank you.

"And Io? I also accept your apology."

Go to sleep, Ella.

Hamilton did not look pleased when he arrived a few hours later. His entrance was precipitated by Burglar Alarm's barking, followed by his now-familiar polite and rhythmic knocking. She could literally tell it was him by how he banged on her front door. As she had done for the past few years, when Ella was woken by her entire container shaking, the first thing she did was reach for the shank on her nightstand. Then she remembered she had a job to do.

Ella jumped out of bed and gathered her things: her shank, two knives, pepper spray, and her best shoes.

Your job today is to observe the minister, not assassinate him. If things go according to plan, you are going to stand in a crowd, record the video, and then go home.

"What if Hamilton doesn't want to give up the recorder?"

Fine, then you can stab him.

Ella touched the sharp tip of her shank with a finger, and, with a wicked grin, slipped it into its sheath in her back waistband. Her thoughts wandered to Bijan and the recon team again, not to mention Emily. Was this all Hamilton's fault? Was their blood on his hands? She quivered with rage just thinking about it.

Keep it to yourself. We have no proof. Otherwise, if he is guilty, he may decide to just run, and then we will never get justice.

She swung the door open and looked at him coolly. "Stop knocking on my door so hard."

Hamilton's eyes widened. "What happened to your face?"

"None of your business."

His reply was just as curt. "I don't see why you need to come, but Io insisted, so let's go. No time to waste."

Ask him if he has the recorder.

Ella did so. Hamilton took out a pair of sunglasses and put them on. He tapped the side of the frame. "High resolution camera here on the right side. We'll need to be within fifty meters of the speaker to pick up audio."

She was impressed. "That is so cool. Can I try?"

Hamilton handed them to her, and the sunglasses slipped off her face as soon as she tried them on. She felt the tiny bridge of her nose between her eyes and then grimaced. She handed the glasses back to him. "They need to make these my size."

"Of course," he shrugged. "There's also the matter of us standing in the crowd. At your height, we may have some problems getting a good shot. The minister's speech is starting soon. By the way, this job shouldn't be difficult, but in case we run into any problems, I need you to follow my explicit instructions."

The two walked down the stairs of her cluster and made their way west to Dumas. On the way there, Hamilton bossed her around, telling her how to act, what to do if they got caught, and where to go if they were separated. It was almost as if he thought he was the host or something. The entire way, Ella kept her hand close to her shank.

CHAPTER TWENTY-FOUR
Riseevar

Sea creatures live pretty basic lives. They spend their days eating, sleeping, breeding, and then dying. Usually by being eaten. But then, is that not how all creatures on this planet live? That was what I thought until I occupied my first human.

Let me be perfectly clear: humans are nowhere as intelligent as Quasing, especially someone as formerly highly-regarded as myself. However, yes, you are all much, much more intelligent than even the smartest fish, and much, much more complicated and harder to influence.

Shura scanned the large crowd that had gathered in the field for Surrett's announcement. By now, most of the major businesses and residences in Dumas were gone, but hundreds of transients and beggars remained since they had nowhere else to go. They just ended up squatting in the now-empty containers and looting whatever was left behind. There were still too many for Mogg's people to run off, so she devised a way to flush them out all at once.

All it required was bait. She had the minister announce a major speech today, and with it, as a gesture of goodwill toward the people of Dumas, the government would feed all who attended the rally. Surrett arranged to truck in several tons of food and, after spending the entire morning showing his face and feeding the masses, he was going to give a speech about how this construction site marked a new era for Crate Town. He would tell them how it would bring jobs and economic stimulus and security to all of Gujurat. Some of it would even be true.

While the people were busy stuffing their faces and hearing empty promises, Mogg's people would sweep through Dumas, rounding up stragglers and anyone still left in these mostly-empty streets, and throw them into jail. By the time the rally was complete, the people would discover a new perimeter fence cordoning off the entire neighborhood. Then its demolition could begin.

Except for the center of the neighborhood, she remembered, as her gaze fell on a cluster of people sitting near the back. A squint of her eye and an upturn of her nose was the only thing that betrayed her irritation. One particular man, a spindly shirtless old man who looked to be almost more hair than person, drew her attention. Indu the Jain priest was surrounded by five hundred of his flock. At first, she was surprised that he had chosen to attend this speech, and then, the second he moved his flock up near the front, she knew exactly what he was going to do.

She had spent the past few days watching his building from across the street. Unfortunately, it seemed he rarely ever left his temple. In fact, today was the first time in a week, at least that she knew of, that he had ventured out of his ziggurat.

Shura watched as the minister walked onto the stage. She scanned the crowd of three thousand or so from Crate Town, who were probably here more for the free food than anything else. No matter the reason, the bait seemed to have worked. At the very worst, they should be able to clear enough sorely-needed land to keep them on schedule.

The chatter became louder, and the decibels climbed as Surrett appeared. He waved at the crowd and strode with confidence and purpose to the center of the stage. The temperature of the audience, numbering several thousand, was a mixture of anger and curiosity. Nobody was happy with Mogg's gangs running amok, and nobody wanted to have to sell properties, yet they weren't upset enough not to eat his food.

"Welcome, people of Crate Town, citizens of Gujurat," Surrett boomed through the loudspeaker. "I hope you have all had your fill of vada and jalebi, quenched your thirst with tasty lassi. First of all, I'd like to thank an honored and elder citizen and philanthropist of Crate Town, Mr Faiz Mustafa, for organizing this event and bringing all of us together, although I have to take some credit for today's success. Originally, he wanted to serve just murukku, but I told him, Mr Faiz, how can we..."

Shura tuned him out. To be fair, Surrett was pretty good at working the crowds. He was a gifted orator, had a natural presence, and a way of connecting with his audience. Pretty soon, the mood in the crowd changed. He had transformed their simmering anger to chuckles and smiles, and had melted the tension that hung heavy in the air. She could see why the Genjix had chosen him as their politician to prop up in India.

That, and we had a very limited candidate pool.

"You're just being critical, Tabs. It's not his fault our recruiting here is practically nonexistent. That will all change soon. For now, this man is an asset. He's actually not doing too badly. Most of the peasants here are eating up what he has to say."

"Adonis." One of her operatives hurried over and bowed. "The Penetra scanner picked up something during a security sweep of the crowd. We triangulated the target at my three o'clock, approximately a hundred and fifty meters."

She did a quick once-over on the crowd. "The tall white man with the sunglasses?"

"Or within two meters of his immediate proximity. We've verified he's not one of ours."

The crowd here was at least a quarter non-Indian, which was expected, since the remnants of half a dozen armies now called this area home. Even then, that man stood out. He was easily a head above most others and several shades lighter than those around him. The Prophus must really be hard up on operatives if they had to send someone like him into this region.

Because you blend in so well.

Shura harrumphed. "I'm different. In this situation, I'm supposed to stand out."

She turned to her operative. "Pick him up. We'll beat the truth out of him, or at the very least eliminate another Prophus."

"Your will, Adonis."

Shura stared at the tall white man. The Prophus shouldn't be operating in this region. India was a dead zone, a no man's land in terms of international affairs, and they'd had the entire region cloaked from satellite surveillance ever since the project kicked off. It would take another decade at the very least before the country got back on its feet, so what could they be doing here? Unless, of course, they had somehow gotten wind of the Bio Comm Array. That would be unfortunate, since the project was still so secret and new that a leak this early could be catastrophic.

A commotion erupted among the crowds. And there it was. Twenty minutes into Surrett's speech about the future of Dumas, Crate Town, Surat, Gujurat, and all of India, Indu's entire flock stood up in unison and began a deliberate march toward the back. Never mind that they were taking the long route. No, they parted the crowd to let all of Crate Town know what Indu thought of Surrett and his speech.

Shura glanced at the minister. To his credit, he didn't miss a beat. She could tell the sudden exodus rattled him, just a little, as the pace of his words increased by a tick. It was a very public display and would lay to rest any chance of the two sides reaching middle ground. Not that she was looking for it.

Shura had been trying to find a way to kill the man with an accident for a week now. She was running out of time. If she couldn't figure out a way to do it quietly, she'd have to just do it messily and deal with the fallout.

Find a way. A public execution is not an option. I guarantee you do not want to have to butcher the rest of his flock as well. It will undoubtedly draw the media's attention.

Shura would deal with him later. For now, she had this Prophus agent to contend with. She caught sight of the Genjix team closing in on the tall white man, pushing through the crowd toward him.

Within twenty meters, they dispersed into the crowd. A few seconds later, five spread out to surround him. The Prophus operative stood blissfully unaware, still staring straight at Surrett.

Amita came sprinting up to Shura. "Adonis! Adonis!"

"What is it, girl?"

"You gave orders to pick someone up in the crowd. You have to call them off. Please, Adonis!" She was stuttering so hard the words barely came out.

"Why? It's a Prophus spy. That's what we do when we find one. We pick them up, we pry off their fingernails for information, and then we cut off their heads. And if we're lucky, we take a flamethrower and fry the Holy One when he tries to escape."

"Not that one, Adonis." The words began to tumble quickly out of Amita's mouth, things that were likely classified that no one should know about. Shura's hands curled into claws in frustration even as she sensed an opportunity.

This is an interesting development.

"I can't believe that idiot Surrett didn't tell me about this earlier."

We never asked, and he is a Genjix agent with his own standing to consider. Would you if you were in his shoes? Regardless, it does not matter. We know now.

"I guess not."

We can take advantage of this new resource. In fact, it complements our plans rather well.

Shura pulled up the comm and reached the Genjix lead when he was less than five meters from their mark. "Stand down."

"Adonis?"

"Stand down. Leave one to tail."

The five operatives that were seconds away from apprehending the spy melted into the crowd immediately. Fortunately, the spy seemed none the wiser.

"Not a very observant man, is he? What is he doing here at the rally?"

Only one way to find out for sure.

Shura turned to Amita. "Tell your minister I want to see him right after this event. He has a lot of explaining to do."

Surrett came by her suite at the hotel later that evening. He must have come directly from the rally. He had the look of a man who had stood outside in the hot, humid day, and he smelled that way as well. His usually perfectly-pressed suit was a mess of wrinkles and stains. A day mingling with people living in slums would do that to a person. Shura watched in disapproval as he tracked faint prints of mud onto her carpet.

"Adonis, you summoned." He bowed and moved to sit in the chair opposite her.

"Stay standing." Shura looked down at Surrett Kapoor's bio on her tablet. "I've looked into you. You've been busy. You've risen from a low-ranked operative with little standing to a favored in this region. Rurik didn't even know you existed a year ago, and now the Genjix are pushing you as the next candidate for prime minister."

"Praise to the Holy Ones," he bowed.

"Your rise is primarily due to you uncovering several

Prophus operations in this region: the listening post in Nepal, the research facility near Kyoto, the Abelard Program, and the location of over a dozen safe houses in the north Thailand DMZ. Impressive. You state in your report you unearthed these Prophus operations by" – she traced the exact wording with her fingers on the tablet – "leading your handpicked expert team of investigators and counterintelligence agents."

"I am but a humble servant," Surrett bowed, a little higher this time. "Adonis, the information–"

Shura leaned forward. "Tell me, is your team still around? I'd love to meet them."

He stiffened. "Unfortunately, they've disbanded. They're needed elsewhere. It's unrealistic for me to consolidate so much talent in one place when they could do so much good–"

Shura held up a hand. "Speak truthfully, Minister. I know you're handling a Prophus double agent. Is he your 'handpicked expert team of investigators and counterintelligence agents'? Is this how you've uncovered all those operations? Are you being fed intel by a Prophus traitor?"

Surrett adjusted his tie, and coughed. "The Prophus's code name is Riseevar. I made contact with the double agent nine months ago."

"Really? Interesting. And you chose not to divulge this information in your reports?"

He shrugged. "Does it matter how I've come across my intel? My results speak for themselves. My team located the Prophus operative. I turned Riseevar, and the Genjix have completely leveled Prophus operations in this region."

He has a point there.

"This seems like a pretty important piece of information to exclude when I first demanded an account of all your resources."

"They are unrelated," Surrett said. "You are only here to oversee the completion of the Bio Comm Array construction. My other programs are my own."

We cannot fault him for that.

"According to the report you sent the Council, you uncovered operations scattered all over southeast Asia, but none in India." Shura held up her tablet, which displayed a photo she had taken earlier. "Why was Riseevar standing in the crowd at your speech today?"

"That's the arrangement," Surrett replied. "The Prophus recently acquired knowledge of the Bio Comm Array project. Riseevar is running interference and counterintelligence until India has officially turned Genjix."

"And what does Riseevar get for his dedication?"

"The traitor wishes to join the Genjix and be on the winning side. Riseevar specifically requested to be involved in the Bio Comm Array in a high-ranking capacity."

The pieces began to fit. She pulled up another of his reports. "The Prophus agent Emily Curran's death. That was part of the deal."

"That part was botched," Surrett admitted, "which is why Riseevar is still out there running interference. Curran was investigating another matter here in India and stumbled upon the Bio Comm Array project. She was the one who tipped the Prophus off. I decided that the best way forward was to have Riseevar participate and sabotage their investigation on the Bio Comm Array facility."

"The scout and the recon team was the traitor's doing." Shura couldn't find much fault in that. It was a sound plan and was paying dividends in spades for the Genjix. "Why am I only learning about this now after I nearly blew the asset's cover?"

He looked her straight in the face. "Would you if you were in my place? Would you offer up a personal valuable asset and sacrifice standing to another?"

He has a point there as well. However, we need this Riseevar.

"I suppose not," she said. "I won't fault you for keeping this source to yourself."

"Thank you, Adonis."

"But now that I am aware of it, hand over all of the information. I will oversee how to best proceed from this point on."

Surrett didn't reply. He set his jaw and his eyes darted around the room. She could see his thoughts run as he frantically tried to figure out a way not to lose such a powerful playing piece to her. He took a step backward.

It was time to pull rank. Shura stood up and stared the non-blessed Genjix operative down. "I am an Adonis vessel, Deputy Minister. Hand it over right now or I will gut you from throat to navel before you step out of this room. And before you die, you will reveal your source because it will be the only way I will stop your suffering."

Well, that escalated quickly.

Surrett's eyes widened and, for a second, he looked like he was going to run anyway. Then he bowed and took out his tablet, and punched a few keys.

Shura checked the file and then nodded. "You may leave."

"Adonis," Surrett begged. "You promised to sponsor a Holy One if I prove myself. Perhaps we can reach an agreement–"

"Get out."

That was inelegant, Shura. The minister has a right to be compensated for a valuable resource. You should have offered him assurances.

"The only thing the man desires is to become a vessel. In my estimation, he is not worthy and I refuse to lend my reputation to sponsor a Holy One for him."

This will come back to haunt you.

Shura had already forgotten about the deputy minister. She skimmed the dozen Prophus operations, safe houses, and spies that Surrett had uncovered. He had been very public and detailed on all of the victories in his reports.

The man really does seem to like writing them.

More interesting to her was how he had gone about

becoming the handler of this Riseevar. According to his own private admission, he had not discovered a Prophus double agent as he had claimed. Rather, this Riseevar had come to him because of a past indirect personal connection involving some event in Greece shortly before the start of the Alien World War.

Shura dug even deeper. Her eyes widened when she came across a ten year-old report. She smiled, a warm memory sweeping over her. She brushed her fingers over the name on the tablet. "Hello, love."

That is a name I have not seen in a while.

"I see it appear now and then in scattered reports. He's building quite a name for himself. I wonder how he is doing."

It is too bad we cannot use the double agent to get his attention.

She read the old report several more times, noting the relationship between Emily Curran and Surrett Kapoor. Her thoughts lingered on how the report ended and the list of casualties that followed. "That was why the Prophus agent Emily Curran was here in India," she muttered. "The woman was looking for closure. She was hunting for the person responsible for Greece. That was how Surrett got in touch with the double agent. She was lured."

Perhaps there is a way we can use this to our advantage. Listen carefully.

Tabs's plan was bold. It required certain assumptions and more than a bit of luck, but this was the leverage she was looking for. She pulled up her comm and made the call. It took a few jumps through operators to underlings to subordinates to direct reports – her standing was too low to call someone on the Council directly – but she eventually reached who she was looking for.

The face of a handsome young Korean man appeared in the air above the tablet. "How goes it, daughter? The regular updates from the minister in charge of the project went from annoyingly excessive before you got there to absolutely nothing. What is going on?"

"High Father Weston, I have a proposition for you."

Weston chuckled. "You forget your place, Shura, but I'm amused and a little intrigued. You have five minutes."

"I want you to officially title the Bio Comm Array facility under my control. In fact, I want you to give me India, the entire region."

"Why would I do that? There are half a dozen high-standing vessels with interests in that country, including my own. Until a Holy One has the strength to conquer and claim it, it stays unclaimed. It is the Genjix way. To just offer you a territory with as much potential as India makes little sense."

"Because I can get someone you want," Shura smiled. "Someone you, or your Holy One Zoras specifically, want badly. Give me India, and I will deliver him to you."

CHAPTER TWENTY-FIVE
The Bait

Moving from animals to humans was a very rough transition. With animals, I could simply nudge their instincts to get them to do what I wished. Humans possess immensely more independent thought than animals, yet at the same time, were so much more irrational. Your species is just really hard to deal with. They are so random, so erratic, so emotional. And do not even get me started on pubescent humans.

It took me a hundred years to get acclimated to your species. At first, I had a fair amount of trouble even keeping them alive. I went through my first four human vessels in a span of six weeks. The first lasted less than five minutes.

Ella had finally turned the corner in her training. She was already making quick progress with the knives, and now Manish had begun adding elements of Escrima knife fighting.

"After all," he had said, "what if you run out of knives?"

"Wouldn't they already be dead, or at least bleeding like pigs?" she had answered. He grunted, then proceeded to dodge six knife throws and box her head silly. Ella got the point. The old man was a slippery target. They spent most of their days now doing exercises that involved short vicious strikes with blades.

Pull from sheath, slice arm, slice thigh, stab chest. Pull from sheath, dodge, slice the side of the knee. Roll from harm, pull from sheath, stab downward into the top of feet. The emphasis was always on getting to safety, cutting the part of the body closest to her, be it a hand or leg or butt, and then escaping. Rarely did Manish want her to make a killing blow. The repetitions went on and on until Ella felt as if she could do them in her sleep, but they kept going.

"This is starting to bore me," she bellowed in exasperation after several weeks of twelve-hour days. "You're starting to bore me." As much fun as this was at first, Ella's attention could only be held for so long.

"Bored of knives already, eh?" A devious grin appeared on the coach's face. "Really, that's too bad." He disappeared into the back office and came back a few minutes later carrying a black tube of cloth. He placed it on the table and slowly unrolled it. Ella's breath caught with each unrolled segment as it revealed an assortment of shiny blades of all shapes and sizes. The last to come out of the black bag of goodies were two wicked-looking serrated black knives, each as long as her forearm. They were awfully pretty. She reached for one. Manish slapped her hand away. "Still bored?" He broke into a smile and handed her one of the long knives.

Ella handled the knife reverently and practiced some slashing motions. It felt wonderful in her hand. "It's lighter than it looks."

"High-grade carbon steel. Here." He handed her one of the smaller knives. "Balanced throwing knives. They're a little heavier than what you're used to, but they'll fly true."

Ella oohed as she took one and flung it across the room. It lodged in a wooden beam with a solid *thunk*. She took another knife and spun, throwing it in the other direction, puncturing the back of a plastic chair. "These are so nice."

Manish handed her another knife to play with. "Been sitting in my closet ever since I retired. Thinking maybe you'll put them to better use."

Ella's eyes widened. "Coach, I can't."

He waved her off. "It's all right, girl. They're all yours. I'll charge the Prophus a premium for them anyway. Just take care of my babies and promise to use them on the Genjix. That's all I ask."

Ella plucked two more knives out of their pockets and held them in each hand. She pretended to pull them out of an imaginary sheath strapped to her thigh. "I'm going to need to get Ando to make new sheaths for these knives." She broke into a wide smile. "I feel like a real badass, a real knife expert." She practiced more slashing motions.

"You think you're an expert with a knife?" Manish laughed. "At best, you are a good beginner. I've taught you enough that you won't cut your skinny toe off. Five more years and I maybe will admit you are my student."

"Five more years?" Her voice climbed an octave. "I've already been doing this forever."

"You've only been training for four months."

"But all day every day!"

"Maybe if you weren't so adamant about guns, you could switch it up a bit," a voice said from the door. Ella only knew one person with a British accent. Her face scrunched and she squeezed the knife in her hand tightly.

Remember. Give nothing away.

She turned to face Hamilton. "What are you doing here?"

What did I just say? Be nice.

"I can't help it."

Ella hadn't seen her auxiliary since they recorded the minister's speech. They had spent most of the day there, blending into the crowd as they snapped photos and recorded videos of the minister, and tailed him as he walked through the event.

After he left, they spent the rest of their time taking photos of anyone who looked important. Besides the minister, Io had Hamilton and Ella snap photos of all of the minister's assistants, personal bodyguards, and this out-of-place but pretty blonde woman.

She thought it was all a waste of time. After all, the minister was always on television and had his face on posters all over the city. Couldn't they see what he looked like on the Internet? Hamilton had explained it had something to do with facial recognition software or blah blah something something with their special secret equipment. He also explained the advanced electronics they used recorded much more than video and sound. Ella wasn't sure what that meant and assumed it was just some spy stuff.

What made Ella suspicious most of all was, after they were done, he had balked at handing the raw data to her, as Io requested. The man actually tried to disobey Io's orders and keep it all to himself. They got into a shouting match inside her home and it got so bad Ella had to bar her door and threaten him with her shank. Her auxiliary finally relented, but any trust she had for the man was shattered, and things had only deteriorated from there. After all, as Io had confirmed, the one common thread between all the recent bad things that had happened lately was the Brit. He was jealous of Ella having a Quasing and had the most to gain from betraying them.

"Hello to you too, Ella." Hamilton looked over at Manish. "Greetings, coach."

"Did you get me my raise?" Manish waved back. "I'm putting far too many hours into this ungrateful runt."

"You said you thought of me like a daughter," she shot back.

"I said that because I needed someone to help with the chores."

"Is she still refusing to learn how to use a gun?" Hamilton asked Manish.

The coach shook his head. "I've given up trying. You want her to shoot, you teach her."

"How utterly stubborn and foolish," Hamilton said.

Ella threw her knife and sunk it into the soft mud in between Hamilton's feet. "Don't talk to me like I'm not standing right here."

Hamilton approached Ella and leaned in. "Message from Command. Wyatt wants to know if we had any more raw data from our surveillance. He said it wasn't as useful as Command had hoped."

Tell him we sent everything.

"Are you sure?" Hamilton pressed when she replied.

"Of course I'm sure." Ella didn't actually know. She remembered plugging the thing into the laptop, punching a bunch of keys, and dragging and dropping files from one folder into another. She remembered watching some bar move until it hit one hundred, and then that was it.

Ella had taken to using the computer, and within a few short weeks under Io's tutelage, had picked up reading English rather quickly, but she still had a way to go. Her Quasing had said she was already reading at fourth-grade level, which honestly didn't sound so great. Still, it was better than nothing.

One step at a time. I am proud of you.

"Would you mind if I stopped by tonight to take a look at them?" he asked. "I thought we went over everything rather thoroughly. Just as a precaution."

Do not let him. He may be trying to delete something important.

Ella shook her head. "Sorry. I'm busy."

"Oh? With what, may I ask?"

"None of your business."

"I'm your auxiliary. If it's Prophus business..."

"It's not," Ella replied hastily. "It's personal." She looked across the room and blurted out the first thing that came to mind. "I am hanging out with Aarav." She began kicking herself immediately.

"Oh?" Hamilton looked over at Manish's nephew and smirked.

That only pissed Ella off more. "Hey Aarav," she yelled, so loud her voice carried across the room. "Where are we going tonight?"

Aarav, who was teaching a beginners boxing class, locked eyes with her. He looked confused. "Uh, what?"

Ella crossed her arms and stomped her feet. "Are you telling me you forgot?"

The big man looked crestfallen. "I must have forgotten."

That poor stupid guy. Ella felt awful for putting him in this position. She promised she'd make it up to him later. She turned to the Brit and shrugged. "Heart as big as a whale. Brain as big as one too."

Hamilton frowned.

I do not believe that metaphor works. A whale's brain is–

"Hush, alien. I get it."

"Well, I wouldn't dare interrupt your plans," said Hamilton "At least I know where your priorities are. However, this is important. We need to head back to the construction site and retake some shots."

Tell him you will do it yourself.

"Can I? I don't know how."

What are you talking about? You are Ella Patel, the samrãjñ⊠ of Crate Town. Of course you can. I will guide you if you need help.

Hamilton did not look pleased when she relayed Io's orders. He offered to come with her, and then when rebuffed, insisted. The man became insubordinate and came uncomfortably close to becoming aggressive. The spat between the two of them grew loud enough she noticed both Manish and Aarav inch closer.

Finally, Hamilton threw his hands up and stomped off. Ella didn't bother hiding her grin. Frustrating the snobby traitorous Brit was a new form of enjoyment for her. She nodded at Manish and Aarav in thanks and went back inside the gym.

One thing nagged at Ella as she began to eviscerate the

wooden practice dummy. What was Hamilton looking for? It was obvious he was looking for something specifically, but what? And what could he hope to accomplish going back for more surveillance?

Decoys. It has to be. He is trying to grab false intel to mislead us.

That had to be it. She stopped mid-slash. "So how do we know what's real and what's fake?"

Unfortunately, we will need to acquire detailed pictures of everything and compare its location with our satellite tracking, and then shoot it through analysis.

"I have no idea what you just said. You might as well have been speaking Korean, which, by the way, can you speak it? I've always wanted to learn. All the good Karaoke power ballads are in Korean."

Focus, Ella. It means we have a lot of work cut out for us. First thing tomorrow, the Prophus is putting you out in the field.

Ella grinned as she began another set of knife exercises. She was moving up in the world.

CHAPTER TWENTY-SIX
Promotion

I feel bad not bothering to remember the names of my first few vessels. Unlike some who remember every damn vessel they ever joined with, I went through mine as if they were disposable. Let me see.

My first human vessel was one of Khat's oarsmen shortly after he killed my whale vessel. That partnership lasted all of four minutes. His name was Torgeir or Torgo or something. We both kind of freaked out and he jumped into the ocean and drowned.

I managed to return to the boat and inhabit another human, I forget his name. This time, I stayed silent and watched and waited for an opportunity to communicate with him. When I finally did, he slit his own throat that very night. That was a poor omen of things to come.

The next morning, nearly five months since the day Io first joined with her, Ella ran her first solo job as an operative. She worked herself up to the point of hyperventilation as she readied her gear the prior evening, and ended up tossing and turning the entire night. In the morning, she threw up her breakfast five minutes after finishing it.

She left the house before dawn and made her way west across Crate Town toward the gulf. Ten minutes into her trek, she considered turning back. Not because she was too nervous or scared or had changed her mind, but because she had stashed so many knives on her person that they weighed her down. A few of the handles clanged together, making her sound like a busted wind chime whenever she took a step. It was also uncomfortable.

"I really need to go see Ando today to get some sheaths made," she grumbled. "I don't know if it's safe for me to sit down with all this crap on."

Who told you to pack every single knife you own? I told you to only bring three.

"I was worried I'd miss and run out."

They are knives. You can reuse them.

Ella looked back the way she had come. She could just see the tip of her cluster at the end of the block. Maybe she should...

"Oh, forget it," she sighed. "I've already gone too far."

What? You are four blocks away.

"I know."

Ella continued west, making good time while the streets were still mostly empty. She wouldn't be so lucky on the way back. Crate Town was already waking up: children carried pots on their heads to fetch water, women hung wet clothing over lines, men stoked fires in metal drums and fire pits, and vendors pulled wagonloads of vegetables and scraps toward the market.

Ella stayed alert, treating every sight and sound as a potential threat. Behind her, a rolling metal door clicked open. A woman yelled at her husband. A dog howled. A blue piece of tarp hanging loosely off a roof slapped the side of a container as it blew in the wind.

You are taking this a little too seriously. You are going to get tired out working yourself up like this.

"I'm a secret agent now. Isn't this what I'm supposed to do?"

Just relax. You being this jumpy is making me jumpy.

That only made Ella feel even more anxious. She reached the edge of the construction site within the hour and followed the outer fence southwest to the end near the water's edge. There, Io had her lie down near the tip of a mound of garbage and walked her through how to use the secret agent photo and video recorder. Twenty minutes later, she was done.

"Wait, what? That's it?" she exclaimed, feeling a little short-changed.

That is it. We can go home now.

"I got dressed for this? Gods, it took me longer to sheathe all my knives."

It is your fault for working yourself up into a tizzy. I do not know what you thought you were going to do your first time out.

"I strapped twenty knives on me!"

No one told you to prepare to invade Pakistan.

"I feel like this job is incomplete if I don't get to at least throw a knife at someone, or something."

Arm a girl and suddenly she thinks she is ready to take on the world. Come on, go home before a patrol catches you loitering and asks questions. You will get your chance to stab someone tomorrow.

"We're doing this again?"

Every day until further notice.

The next day, Io brought Ella to the same place and had her take the same photos, taking special notice of a truck bed that held several large curved dome-shaped panels. She did the same thing the day after that, and the next. For an entire week, Ella would come to this exact same spot near the top of a pile of refuse and record the types of machinery and materials parked under a wall-less building with a triangular A-frame roof.

By the end of the fourth day, any excitement and thrill she held for the job of being an operative was crushed by the sheer drudgery of the tasks. Io added a few more bits of information to acquire: snapshots of ships off the coast, the names of the supply companies on the sides of trucks and vans, and anyone going in and out of the buildings who didn't look like a nobody.

The construction crews started early each day. Ella even saw Deputy Minister Kapoor walking the grounds several times, and entering and exiting buildings, particularly a busier finished one in the back corner next to the really giant building that was still being built. Io was really big on getting shots of the minister, which felt weird to her because the man's mug was hanging off a giant poster on one of the construction billboards. Still, she did as instructed and clicked away at the minister as if he were a Bollywood star and she a paparazzo.

A couple of times, she caught a few shots of that strange-looking blonde woman touring the site with an entourage trailing close by. She grabbed a few shots before Io told her to move on and focus more on the minister. Something about the woman piqued her curiosity though. She seemed completely out of place. Who was she? What was she doing here?

For one thing, her hair was so blonde and shiny it glowed like a light bulb. Ella wished she had hair like that. She had never had long hair. It wasn't a good idea in her line of work with people always grabbing at her, not to mention it probably wouldn't be very hygienic in Crate Town. Who knew what bugs made their nests–

Can you focus on the task at hand and worry about hair later?

"Sorry."

Ella moved on, climbing down a mound of shattered appliances and furniture and up a hill spiced with rotten food. She moved onto the impressive pile of moldy clothing stacked two stories high and then was forced to wade through a lake of… she didn't even want to know what it was filled with.

Io's confidence in her grew by the day. By the second week, Ella was spending most of her days surveying the entire site, from the main complexes in the south to the current Dumas construction area all the way up to the docks. She enjoyed this process and almost felt like a real spy, except when the job was painfully, tediously boring. Soon, she had her favorite spots surrounding the entire construction site picked out, and every day she made her rounds, snapping at the work and documenting the daily changes.

In the first two weeks, she had come across a patrol three times. All three times, they were extraordinarily easy to avoid. Those teams of three guards, wearing mismatched clothes, looked more like dockworkers than soldiers, and they seemed more interested in talking and smoking and kicking cans than actually patrolling. Each time, she stayed hidden, took a couple of snaps of them with her camera, waited until they passed, and then moved onto her next position.

It made her wonder again how an old expert like Bijan got caught. Poor guy must have just not known the terrain. She began to beat herself up again for not accompanying him, at least for the first day.

If I beat myself up over every defeat, I would have time to do little else.

"Yeah, like what?"

I would rather not talk about it.

"Give me an example."

If you must know, I was one of the advisers to the chief architect for the Maginot Line.

"What's that? I don't remember this in your stories."

We are still working our way through the Dark Ages. The events involving the Maginot Line happened way later.

An image of several round concrete forts flashed into her head. They reminded Ella of a movie she once saw about little people who lived in homes buried underground. "They look cute. What were they for?"

It was a defensive line to repel a German invasion.

"What happened?"

Uh, the Germans just drove around them.

Ella laughed so loud she worried that the patrol that had disappeared over the next mound would hear. She covered her mouth and retreated into a refrigerator missing its door. She stayed there for fifteen minutes and waited for the coast to clear.

As the minutes ticked by, Io clarified some of the dreams of her glorious career inhabiting humans. If anything, it comforted Ella that the Quasing weren't all-knowing and powerful, that they were just as culpable and mistake-prone as any human.

"So, explain this thing with these first humans? How did you know their language if it was your first time?"

That was part of the problem. I could not speak with this man. Having been used to certain types of animals for so long, the transition was difficult.

"You couldn't just read his brain and pick it up?"

Assimilating human thought takes time. It is often like reading a book. That is why I did not know everything about you right when I joined with you.

"I get it. So what am I thinking now?"

Active thoughts are much easier to pick up. You are thinking about trying that new restaurant that opened just outside of Crate Town. I warn you, I do not think you will take well to fried chicken.

"Is chicken from Kentucky bad?"

It is not actually from Kentucky.

After the chatter from the patrols had died, Ella crawled out and made her way to Metal Mountain at the far northern end by the Tapi. There, on the south shore of the river mouth a ways from the docks was a giant mountain of broken containers piled five stories high.

This was where the docks discarded their unused containers. During the early days of the war, when any semblance of order had broken down, the docks and the ships that unloaded there began to dump empty containers at the northern refuse site. Eventually, a cone-shaped mountain of empty cargo containers grew, complete with tunnels and crevices and caves.

Back when Ella first became homeless after the Vadsar Air Base had fallen, she and hundreds of others had sought refuge in Metal Mountain. Unfortunately, the mountain also attracted the sort of people who found the complex tunnels useful to hide in. Now, most residents of Crate Town stayed away from Metal Mountain unless they were conducting shady business.

It gave Ella the perfect vantage point for her surveillance, and she spent the rest of the day hidden near the tip of the mountain taking dozens of photos of the construction site. Over the course of these day-long jaunts, she and Io finally fell into a rhythm. She soon learned that she could get a lot more accomplished and with less effort if they worked together instead of butting heads all the time. It was also a lot less exhausting.

Good communication is key. You will learn that we often share the same goals.

"Are your goals to eat and make money?"

Well, not directly, but–

"Then we really don't have the same goals."

What if I can guarantee that working together will lead to more food and money?

"Hmm, if you put it that way, sure. Seventy-thirty split?"

Whatever you say, Ella.

Working with others was new to her, and for the first time, Ella discovered she enjoyed having a partner, especially as her surveillance runs grew longer. It was nice having someone to talk to during those long boring stretches, and she had to admit, albeit reluctantly, that Io gave pretty solid advice. She began to trust the alien, which was a difficult thing to earn from someone who survived on the streets. As long as Io knew who the boss of her body was, Ella could see this partnership working out.

I am the brain, you are the muscle?

"Hah, fat chance, alien. More like I'm the muscle and the brain, and you have an advisory role."

How about you are the brain and the muscle, except when I have advice you need to follow, and then you follow it.

"All right, that sounds good. Wait, you're trying to trick me."

I would never do that.

Those thoughts lingered as she lay in bed and studied the moonbeams that poked through the small holes of the ceiling. It had been less than half a year since Io had come into her life and already, things felt so different. It was weird, but Ella could barely remember how she had lived before that fateful night. She murmured a blessing to Emily for bringing her Io.

For the first time since her mother died and her father abandoned her, someone had her back. Manish had become the father she always thought fathers were like. Aarav was the big brother she couldn't stand but knew she could lean on if she needed, and Io was the imaginary friend who wouldn't shut up but Ella knew she would miss if she ever disappeared.

Really? You see Manish as your dad, Aarav your brother, and I am a talking teddy bear?

"Hey, that's a step up from my previous opinion of you."

Fair enough.

"If it makes you feel better, you're also my teacher now too."

That does. Thank you.

"So what am I going to dream about tonight?"

Where did I leave off? Oh yes, my hosts were dropping like flies. By the way, I am not trying to be flippant about killing humans. Your kind is just really hard to keep alive…

CHAPTER TWENTY-SEVEN
New Management

Next was the midwife named Agata. Then the woodcutter with the long beard, and then the young human experiencing puberty. That last one was the worst. They all suffered tragic and quick deaths. It was a very confusing time for me. None of the creatures I inhabited before had ever tried to kill themselves.

That is a very distinctly human trait.

I asked Khat why I was not able to keep my humans alive while other Quasing could, and he explained that most Quasing with human vessels had thousands of years of experience within them, and in the Cro-Magnons, Neanderthals, and primates that came before them.

Coming in late, I had a much steeper learning curve.

Shura hit send on her tablet and watched as her instructions were wrapped with several layers of encryption and dispatched. It was time to put the wheels in motion. Her gaze lingered on the screen at the little graphic of the message being folded into a locked chest and disintegrating into the ether. Who said the Genjix did not have a sense of humor?

That graphic makes no sense. Whoever in Security created it is wasting time and resources and should be disciplined.

"I take that back. We really don't have a sense of humor."

Shura had been in constant contact with this Riseevar and

had negotiated her own deal, superseding the arrangement Surrett had made. Whereas the minister had dangled vague promises and strung the Prophus operative along, she didn't mess around and set firm deliverables. So far, Surrett had been squandering this resource and only using the double agent to run interference and counterintelligence on the Bio Comm Array project.

Shura needed and wanted to catch something larger and much more significant. If this Riseevar could deliver her that, then she would bring the defector into the Genjix fold with a guaranteed elevation to moderately high standing. That was the price of admission.

It was a very good deal for Riseevar and an even better one for Shura. It was, unfortunately, a bad one for Surrett, since she had effectively locked him out of the deal. Also, for Shura's plan to work, she needed bait, irresistible bait, bait that would overcome reason and logic and lure the target to her. The link between Surrett and the big fish was thin but strong.

The minister had, of course, protested being used in such a way. When she had revealed the plan to him, he paled and insisted on an alternative. When she informed him that catching the bigger fish was more important than his life, Surrett became desperate and came dangerously close to insubordination. Fortunately, he saw the light when he realized that his best chance of survival was to put his life in her hands in the service to the Holy Ones. She had assured him that she would do her best to ensure his safety.

You told him putting him in the line of fire was a minor detail in the plan. That is hardly a confidence booster.

"It *is* a minor detail. Who does he think he is? The minister will do as commanded when the time comes." Shura leaned back in her chair. Things were finally coming together. Not only was she about to catch a high-ranking Prophus, the production of the Bio Comm Array project was finally back on track. They might even begin the first trial by the end of the month. That would put the project three months ahead of schedule. If she could turn this troubled project around so quickly and make a statement with a successful test, then there was no chance the Council, especially with Weston's support, would refuse her all of India once it became a Genjix state.

The icing on the cake was, after weeks of searching for an opening, Shura had finally devised a plan to eliminate the Jain priest without raising suspicion. Through a combination of bribes, subtle and not-so-subtle intimidations, and research, she discovered that Indu had a weakness for freshly picked rambutans, and one of his disciples went to the market every day to buy some. It was one of the few patterns in his life and the only luxury the monk allowed himself.

Indu was a careful man and had a taste tester, having survived several assassination attempts over the years. It seemed Jain politics were every bit as vicious as the secular version. Small doses of hydrofluoric acid injected into the fruit over the course of a few weeks would do the trick. In the end, the good monk, in his ripe old age, would suffer a heart attack and experience a very natural-looking demise. After his tragic death, arrangements were already in place to promote his two assistants to become head monks at the temples in Mahudi and Vataman.

The assimilation of Dumas would then be complete. The majority of the demolition was already well under way. Several thousand tons of materials and supplies were sitting on the docks waiting to begin the build-out of the housing phase of the project. Everything depended on whether Indu died next week or next month.

This has not been the most direct of approaches, but definitely one of your more elegant ones. I approve. Not a moment too soon, either. News from Moscow is that Rurik is close to consolidating his hold on Russia. He just sent two of his rivals to the Eternal Sea and obtained the fealty of four others.

"If things go as planned, by the time Rurik ever gets around to focusing on the Bio Comm Array and India, it will be too late."

Shura pulled up a map of the construction site. Mogg's thugs were becoming problematic. They had spent most of the past month chasing away the residents and businesses in the area. Some she was able to integrate with the construction crews, but most were unskilled, wasted bodies that she relegated to guard duty. It was a waste of capital and manpower, but she had little choice. Mogg's union was just that, a union. Shura could not even fire these people unless she was willing to take on all of them. Eventually, she intended to replace all the workers with more reliable and loyal Genjix crews from China and Russia, but by then Mogg and her people would be accustomed to Shura's high wages, so the transition would likely turn violent. That was an inevitability, but at least six months down the road. She could arrange to have military moved in–

The door to her suite banged open so loudly, Shura whipped out her pistol with her finger on the trigger. Fortunately for Surrett, she never fired unless she was sure of her shot. The man was a sliver away from taking two slugs to the head. She glowered as he walked in unannounced. No, he was strutting.

Be careful. Something is wrong.

Shura lowered her pistol, but kept it at the ready. "How dare you? Something better be burning to the ground, Minister."

Is he making a play for me? Killing him may be the right move. Be ready.

Genjix history was littered with instances of the unblessed, desperate for a Holy One, assassinating a vessel and forcing the Holy One to use their body. However, that was not how the Genjix operated. Anyone could kill. That was the easy part. Being accepted by the Holy Ones was the true challenge. Unless an unblessed was accepted by a Holy One, it never ended well. How trustworthy could an operative be if they stooped to stealing a Quasing? Usually, at some later date, the Holy One always arranged to have that false vessel assassinated.

Shura wondered if this was one of those instances. Surrett was desperate to become a vessel, and they were alone in this room. However, he was a much bigger fool than she gave him credit for if he thought he could defeat her in a fight.

"I apologize for interrupting you, Adonis." His bow was hardly a nod. He stepped to the side of the entrance.

To Shura's credit, she masked the shock on her face when a handsome man in his late twenties with a long, muscular build, flanked by two bodyguards, walked in. His hair hung just past his chin and his eyes were sunken in just enough to smolder. If Shura didn't already know who he was, she would have guessed the man was the lead singer in a soft rock band.

There is a window behind you to your left. You are twelve stories up.

"I won't survive that jump."

Of course. I am referring to my survival if necessary. However, I do not believe it will come to that. Remember his standing.

Shura bowed just low enough to follow protocol and show respect. "A pleasant surprise, brother." She glanced at the smug look on Surrett's face. The man must have received a better deal of his own – which, to be honest, couldn't have been that hard, since she hadn't offered him much to begin with.

"We are no longer at the Hatchery, Shura," Rurik said. "You forget your place."

She kept her gaze on the table. "Apologies, Father."

"You are surprised to see me?"

"Notice would have been appreciated, so I could prepare for your arrival."

Rurik came to the other side of her desk and sat down. He

glanced at the stack of blueprints on the left side of the table and then at the map of the construction site on the right. Shura's mind raced. What did Rurik know of her plans? How much could she still salvage? If he was only stopping by to check in on the project's status, then all might not be lost.

Rurik tapped the map with his forefinger. "The minister has briefed me on recent developments. I am pleased with your work."

"I serve the Holy Ones."

"We are back on schedule?"

"Yes, except for one last property that requires a delicate touch."

"Ah yes, the temple. When will that be cleared?"

It wasn't a good sign if Rurik was informed of that specific detail. "A few weeks. A month at best."

"All that for one old monk," he muttered. Rurik pointed at the room's communication console. "Link me."

Shura had no option but to do as she was ordered. She waited while Rurik made a call on his tablet and then, with a brush of his hand, patched the communication into the room. Her throat caught when Weston's face appeared floating in the air.

They both bowed. "Praise to the Holy Ones."

They must have interrupted Weston during his workout. The young man's face was covered with sweat and a trickle of blood poured down the crown of his head. The rumors out of China were that the high father enjoyed training with live weaponry. They waited patiently as he toweled off. Finally, he addressed them. "Rurik, Shura. What is it?"

"High Father," Rurik said. "I'm informing you that I've come down to Gujurat to take command of the situation. Seeing how important the Bio Comm Array will be to the Genjix, I felt it was my duty to personally oversee its execution."

Weston shrugged. "I'm glad to hear you are finally giving it the attention it deserves. There's no need to interrupt me just to tell me what you should have been doing all along."

Rurik bowed. "I also want to assure you that the operation to use the defector Riseevar to capture the high-value Prophus operative is still in play. I will personally ensure its success."

Weston raised an eyebrow and his mouth curled up. "I see. Zoras values that objective dearly."

"Of course, High Father," Rurik said. "I assume that in taking ownership of this delicate task, the promised reward of controlling India still stands?"

"I see your game now, Rurik," Weston chuckled. "I don't care who owns the country, just get it done. If you are successful in capturing the target, India is yours."

Shura's heart sank. She had been betrayed and outmaneuvered. Rurik had slid in at the right moment to take credit for her work. Not only that, he now stood to reap the reward promised her.

I warned you. You pushed Surrett Kapoor too hard, and did not offer him enough incentive to stay loyal.

Shura stood next to Rurik, head bowed, humiliated, as he completed his conversation with Weston. The Russian had given her just enough credit to not make this appear like theft. Her standing from her work here would rise, but in the end it paled next to what she deserved. Especially now, with Rurik on the cusp of controlling both Russia and India, he would be more entrenched than ever, and should be able to successfully challenge for a seat on the Council.

Rurik stole a glance at Shura, a cruel smile growing on the edges of his lips. He looked back at Weston. "One more thing, High Father. Adonis Shura has done such a competent job with the project that I would like to keep her on board after I take control of India, for the sake of stability and continuity, and under my command, of course."

Shura's veins froze. She might have done too competent a job here. Rurik could justifiably argue that she was necessary to this project's success, and if he kept control of the project, he could keep her under his thumb indefinitely.

Weston studied Shura's face, and then Rurik's. "You don't control anything yet. Show me you can be entrusted with the success of this important Genjix initiative and you will have all the resources you need."

Weston's head blinked from view. Rurik smiled and went over to her cabinet to pick up a bottle of scotch. He held it toward Shura and then to Surrett. Both shook their head. Rurik looked at the empty glass in his hand and tossed it. He went over to the couch and drank directly from the bottle. The man was reveling in his victory.

He smiled at her and then looked over at Surrett. "Don't be too angry with the minister, Shura. He did what he thought best."

"What did you offer him?" she asked.

"I guaranteed him a Holy One. A salute to you, Surrett Kapoor." Rurik raised his drink as the minister bowed again. "The man deserves it after bringing so many victories to the Genjix."

"Well," Shura said. "I see you've made yourself comfortable. By all means, Father, my suite is yours. If that will be all, I'll leave you both–"

Rurik cut her off. "Actually, I have orders for you." He stood up and went over to her desk, placing the bottle on the table sloppily. He pointed at the Jain temple in the center of the map of Dumas. "I don't want to wait a month to begin construction. Clear out the temple. Tonight."

"Are you sure that's wise, Rurik?" Shura said. "It will only rile the local populace. I have a plan already in motion. It will only take–"

She never finished her sentence. Rurik walked up to her and punched her in the gut. The wind rushed out of her and she collapsed, falling to one knee and sucking in deep gulps of air.

"Don't *ever* question my orders again, Shura," he growled. He grabbed her by the collar and hauled her to her feet. "Don't think I didn't know what you were trying to do, and don't think I won't make you pay for it. Do you understand?"

Shura nodded. "Yes."

Rurik put his hand around her throat and squeezed. "Yes what?"

The room dimmed. Shura barely managed to utter the words. "Yes, Father."

"Good."

The iron grip on her throat loosened and Shura fell back to the floor, her hands shaking. This time, she wasn't shaking from pain or humiliation. The coward had attacked her unprovoked with his rank and a horde of bodyguards at his back. This was the only way he would have dared laid a hand on her. Well, she would show him how far she dared. Her hand drifted toward her waist.

No. This is not the time. Rurik has two guards here and half a dozen more outside the door. If you make a move, you will not survive the fight. Even if you do, your life will be forfeit. Bide your time. We will strike once we are covered, no sooner.

Shura's hand froze, and she stood up. She looked in the mirror and studied the angry red marks around her neck. She turned to Rurik, coolly. "Is there anything else, Father?"

Rurik walked over to the table and, with a swipe of his arms, cleared all the markers from the map onto the floor. "Call in the police. Get in there and arrest anyone who still trespasses by tonight. I want it all demolished by tomorrow."

Within two hours, Rurik's cadre of elite bodyguards, leading a group of a hundred policemen and three hundred of Mogg's thugs, swept over the Jain temple. A protest grew and was violently dispersed. Clashes broke out along the blocks near the streets bordering Dumas, spilling out into the surrounding neighborhoods. The conflict spread like a ravaging disease from street to street, cluster to cluster until it eventually consumed the entire western half of the slum.

By nightfall, Crate Town was in upheaval.

CHAPTER TWENTY-EIGHT
The Pickup

The sixth human was a man named Rolf who fancied himself a berserker. He accepted the voice in his head as that of Odin, one of their Norse gods. That context provided us an understanding to establish a strong bond. I learned a lot about humans through him.

Unfortunately, just because Rolf thought he was a berserker did not mean he actually was a great warrior. In his very first battle, during what is now known as the Battle of Fulford, he broke from his shield wall in a fit of excitement and charged the enemy on his own. Rolf took an arrow to the belly and lay on the battlefield writhing in pain for several days before finally getting run over by a cart.

Ella stayed away from the west side of Crate Town during the first four days of the riots. The fighting had spilled into the streets and spread block by block with each passing day. The majority of the chaos and violence were far enough away from her neighborhood that most days, the only thing she noticed was the heightened tension hanging in the air, and the worry that no one could conceal. By the end of the week, after the military had been called in, Crate Town had settled down into a simmering boil.

Usually, she stayed away from local and regional politics,

and was only vaguely aware of the cause of the conflict between the west-side residents and the government. It had something to do with the construction site and the Jain temple in Dumas, so all the devout were up in arms.

However, this particular situation hit a little closer to home. It felt personal. Maybe it was because she had been scouting the build site every day, maybe it was because she knew it had something to do with the Prophus and the Genjix, or maybe because it appeared as if this construction was eating up huge chunks of Crate Town. In any case, she found herself wanting to take sides and join the people. However, Io counseled hard against it, and Ella reluctantly stayed on the sidelines.

Do not get involved more than necessary. You have a job to do, an important one.

"But isn't everyone just fighting the Genjix? Isn't that something we should be supporting?"

The people of this slum have no chance. The more they fight, the more they will suffer. Do not join a losing cause. I have fought enough of those for both of us.

Ella spent most of the days indoors, learning her letters and helping Io get caught up with the digital paperwork. Due to the sensitive nature of her work, she had to filter the data sent to Command through a series of security measures, encrypting and jumping through clouds and translating through several different languages. She didn't know who she was sending the information to, nor could she replicate the instructions without guidance most of the time. She didn't really need to, anyhow. Io just told her what buttons to push, and she did it.

The secrecy was completely intentional. After the recent disasters with Bijan and the recon team, her alien was keeping her orders on a need-to-know basis. Ella didn't mind being kept in the dark when it came to stuff like this. It was actually kind of exciting.

For all we know, the leak could be your coach. What do you really know about him? Hamilton was the one who found him. And Emily had only worked with Hamilton for a few months. He is as much a stranger to me as the others.

On the eve of the fifth day after the initial violent clashes had calmed down, Io surprised Ella by telling her she was resuming her regularly scheduled surveillance the next morning. This time, Ella packed eight knives, up from the four she had taken to carrying.

The threat level should not dictate how many knives you carry. A pistol makes all of this irrelevant.

"No guns in Crate Town," she hissed.

Io surprised Ella again the next morning as she was about to head out. *Change of plans. Grab some cash. Head east and grab a tuk-tuk.*

Ella looked back toward her bedroom and squinted. "How much cash?" She had been saving the majority of her stipend and had built up quite a hoard. At this rate, she estimated she could actually move out of Crate Town and buy a home in Surat within a year. She had had to spend some of the money on Io's requests once in a while but every time, it was only after Io had pried that cash from her tightwad fists.

Just enough to take a tuk-tuk to the airport. You do not have to worry about taking one back.

"Am I going to get reimbursed?"

No.

"Then I don't want to go."

That is not an option. We are not paying you just so you can live in a nicer apartment. Consider these small expenses part of your generous salary.

Ella grumbled every step of the way, but eventually grabbed a wad of cash and stuffed it into her pants. She exited her cluster and followed Io's orders, hailing a tuk-tuk and wading upstream against tire-to-tire morning traffic until she reached the outside of the airport.

Instead of heading to the entrance, Io had her make her way to the southeast, toward a cluster of warehouses across a marshy field at the far edge of the airport. Along the way, Io gave her a quick update on the job.

Your recent work surveying the site has been invaluable. Command has escalated this Genjix operation's threat level, and we are now moving to the next phase of the project. They are sending in an elite black ops team to assess and take over operations. The recent upheaval in Crate Town has given us the perfect opportunity to destroy the site. You will be their local support. Your orders today will be to rendezvous with the team at the airport and take them directly to a safe house.

"Safe house? What safe house? Where is it? Did Hamilton set it up?"

I kept Hamilton out of the loop and we are going to keep it that way. Your place is not large enough to house the entire team. Besides, too many people know where you live. The team requires a more secure location for their base of operations.

Something about this mission felt different, more pressing. Ella wasn't sure if she should feel honored or terrified, but it made her feel important. She could almost sense Io's tension seeping into her. She was also grateful that the Prophus thought well enough of her work to send another team, especially after the unfortunate consequences to the last people they sent.

"Why can't they just head to the safe house on their own? Why can't I just meet them there?"

Because of the recent security issues, Command is not taking any chances. There will be no middle man. You will be their first contact when they land, and their last when they leave. There is only a handful in Command who knows they are even here.

She crept ankle-deep in water along the tall grass and waited as a plane sped by and took off. Then, staying low, she sprinted across the runway into the bog on the other side, and continued toward a group of warehouses. There was a dirt road from the north that led to the main body of the airport, but she had not seen any vehicles pass through yet.

Ella flattened against the slope and peered through the tall grass. A gray van rumbled from the far street and came to a stop inside the cluster of buildings. She waited for fifteen minutes until the van sped off again toward the airport. Ella stood up and grimaced at the mud caked to her clothing.

"I still wish you would tell me ahead of time though. What if this team needs to stop by my place during the middle of the day? It's a mess right now. I just got my laundry back from Wiry Madras and my underwear is all over the place. You have me running through sludge so often I have to wash clothes every other day."

If I tell you ahead of time, it defeats the purpose of something being clandestine. You should just keep your place prepared for visitors at all times. You are the only designated support in this region.

"I'm too busy. If you need to control me while I'm asleep, maybe you could also clean the house a little."

I do not take over your body to become your maid.

"I'm just saying. You should make yourself more useful. Pick up after me or do the dishes or something."

Do not hold your breath.

Once the coast was clear, Ella proceeded to the warehouse. The morning sun was now climbing up the sky, shrinking the shadows and exposing more with each passing minute. The tall grass she was passing through rustled, making her feel as if she were being watched or followed. The cluster of buildings grew more foreboding the closer she got. Worst of all, she wasn't on familiar turf, so wouldn't know where to run if things went south.

Ella felt tingling up and down her spine. She usually didn't get nervous running cons, even when she had robbed all those gangsters. When you had little to lose, you didn't fear losing it. Sure, being dead would suck, but life hadn't been that great to begin with. Now, she felt like jumping out of her skin.

Maybe it is because you have something valuable worth living for: me.

"More like the opposite. I don't remember being nagged this much since I was a kid."

Ella reached the first building in the cluster and pressed against the wall. She didn't know why she was lurking, but she felt the need to. She was used to the tight, cluttered spaces of Crate Town. This much open space creeped her out. A worker walked by and gave her a puzzled look. He shrugged and continued on.

Maybe you should try to stop sneaking around. You look guiltier than if you just walked normally. Go to the building marked 7B. It should be the one on the far end to the left.

"Are you sure? I feel like something bad is going to happen if I just walk around in the open."

Just act normal. Is that so hard?

"Fine. But if I get in trouble, it's going to be your fault."

Ella left the shadow of the building and made a straight beeline toward the warehouse at the other corner of the cluster. No sooner had she walked three meters than someone stopped her.

"Excuse me, miss. Can I help you?" a voice said from off to the side.

Ella jumped like a cat and came face to face with a short, dark-skinned man with a very round face. He was stocky, his body reminiscent of an oil drum, and he had crazy hair that stuck out in all directions. His eyebrows were so thick, they nearly covered his eyes.

"Nice job, Io. Stop sneaking around, Ella. You look guilty, Ella. Just walk in the open, Ella."

Like I knew this was going to happen.

"I was just, uh, passing through," she said aloud to the man.

"This is actually private property." He smiled. "I'll have to escort you."

Ella had no choice but to nod and do as he said. There was something about him that made her squirm. It wasn't that she felt threatened by him or that she sensed any danger. It was... his smile. She kind of liked it. He was actually sort of ugly, but there was something about the way he looked and spoke to her that made her feel a little funny inside.

You have strange taste.

"He's cute, in an unconventionally awkward kind of way. How do we get to the warehouse if he's going to lead me off the airport grounds?"

Just let him lead you outside and then double back once you lose him.

"I bet sneaking around sounds like a good idea right about now, doesn't it?

No need to be smug.

Ella tried to play it cool as she walked with the man. His name was Nabin and he was Nepalese, which surprised her. His accent was a little strange for someone from there, as if it had some British or Hong Kong to it. Nabin was an aerospace engineer who maintained the planes at the airport. He was relatively new to Surat, having only arrived a month ago on a six-month contract.

"Does that mean you're leaving after your contract is up?" she asked.

"Probably," he replied, "unless they extend it."

Ella successfully hid the disappointment on her face. "Well, if you need someone to show you around the city, I could be your tour guide." She quailed a little inside. That was a lot bolder than she had meant to be.

"Perhaps." Nabin's hesitation was only for a split second, but it was there.

Ella's heart cracked a little there too. She had had very few instant crushes in her life, and all of them were on movie stars. Anything remotely resembling a real relationship had led to nothing, and every single one of them had broken her heart. It was a good thing she was half-lizard and her organs always mended over a weekend.

Ella threw a sidelong glance at building 7B as they passed, and was surprised when Nabin turned toward it. She hesitated.

He looked back and waved at her to follow. "We have a crew digging a new drain pipe on the other side. If you're not careful, you'll end up falling into a ditch. It's safer if we make a detour. Come on."

An alarm began to ring in Ella's head. Her gut told her to run. She looked down the path he was leading her to. Nabin stood there and waited for her expectantly.

If you take off, he will definitely know something is amiss, and will probably alert security. It will be difficult to come back later on. It should be fine.

Ella reluctantly complied with Io's orders. Just in case, her hand drifted to her long knife. She was pretty sure she could handle him if something happened. Just as they passed the door leading into 7B, it opened. Before she could react, Nabin threw his arms around her and dragged her inside the building.

Ella squirmed but his grip was a vice, so she bit him. He cried out and loosened his hold. The knife appeared in her hand and she jammed it at Nabin's ugly face. To her surprise, he dodged it at the last possible second and grabbed at her again. The man was faster than he looked, but not fast enough. Ella twisted away before he could wrap his fingers around her wrist. She slashed once at his chest and again at his throat. Both times he just managed to stay out of her reach, if barely.

Nabin tried to close the distance and smother her, but she rewarded his efforts with a nick to the arm that sprayed blood into the air. He grunted and backpedaled. Sensing an opportunity, Ella charged, swinging the knife in short vicious arcs. Nabin managed to dodge her attempts to eviscerate him, but lost his balance and fell backward. Ella straddled his chest, knife coming down at his throat.

A hand grabbed her knife wrist and Ella felt cold metal

pressed against the side of her head.

"Drop it." She heard a click of metal near her left ear. "I will not say it again."

The knife fell from Ella's hand and clattered on the ground. She raised her other arm.

"Get up. Slowly."

This time, Ella understood his words. Those lessons with Io were paying off. She did as she was told. She glared. "I thought you were nice."

"I'm the one who's not nice? Look at this." He held up both arms. One had a set of teeth marks and the other was dripping blood. "Do you know how many germs are in the human mouth?"

"I hope your arm rots and falls off," she spat.

Ella became aware of several figures close by. The one to her left was still pressing a gun into her temple. The rage she had aimed at Nabin was replaced by a growing fear. She was in way over her head.

Make no sudden movements until we know who they are.

"Is this the host who the Penetra scanner was chirping about?" a woman said from the darkness.

"Yep," Nabin replied. "It was either her or the janitor. I checked him first."

An Asian woman in combat fatigues appeared. She held some contraption up to Ella and nodded back into the darkness. "This is the one. Get the Adonis."

Watch what you say carefully.

Io had told Ella enough about the Genjix breeding program and Hatcheries that she expected a swimsuit model.

A hooded figure appeared behind the woman and reached out to Ella. She pulled back, but that asshole Nabin prevented her from squirming away. The figure touched her arm. "It's Io. You can release her."

That is him. That is the person we are supposed to meet.

Nabin let go of her. He picked her knife off the floor and

handed it back to her handle first. "Sorry about the cloak and dagger, girl. We just had to be sure."

She shot lasers at him with her eyes as she rubbed her bruised wrist. She took back the knife and considered stabbing him with it. Instead, she slipped it back into her sheath.

"Asshole," she muttered, and turned her glare back to the hooded figure. "Who the gods are you, kidnapper?"

"A feisty one here," the woman chuckled.

The figure pulled the hood off his head. Ella gaped and couldn't recall a time in her life where she was more disappointed by the way a man looked. Being called an Adonis came with certain expectations. He wasn't good-looking or bad-looking, just... just plain.

The Adonis stuck out his hand. "You must be Io's new host. Welcome to the Prophus. My name is Cameron Tan."

CHAPTER TWENTY-NINE
Past and the Present

Over the next several hundred years, I moved from human vessel to human vessel, trying to find my bearings and understand humanity. I traveled across Europe, from Rolf the supposed berserker to a Saxon trader to a Frank monk and a Spanish peasant. None of my vessels ever made a mark in history and were quickly forgotten.

Unlike a few of my kind, I struggled to lift my vessels to become more than what they would be without a Quasing. Whereas Tao built an empire in Asia and Chiyva revolutionized warfare with the Roman Legions, I was barely able to coexist with my vessels, let alone influence them, let alone drive them to perform great deeds and rise above their place in life.

Ella stared at Cameron Tan's outstretched hand. Even though they were technically on the same side, she didn't know who these people were. Her natural reaction, honed by years of living on the street, kicked in. She kept her hands at her sides. "Ella. Just Ella. I'm here to take you guys to the safe house."

Cameron took being left hanging in stride. "We'll be ready in a few minutes." He turned to the rest of the people around them. "Secure the area. Three on the perimeter. Keep the Penetra working. Load up the van."

"Yes, Commander."

Two more figures appeared from the shadows. Ella counted six total bodies, including Cameron, Nabin, and the woman. The Nepalese and two others exited the building. Her first instinct was to search for a way out. One end of the hangar was the large bay doors. The only other exit was the one she had come through, which at the moment was being guarded by the woman and one other. Just a quick eyeball on both told her that these guys could take her in a fight without even trying.

"Walk with me," said Cameron. "I have a few questions."

There was something in his demeanor that made her wary. He wasn't cocky, just confident. This was a guy who was used to having his orders followed. She crossed her arms. "We should get going."

"Show the commander some respect," the woman said sharply.

Ella glared at the woman. "Mind your own business."

"No, no," Cameron said. "The girl is right. We should get to the safe house. We'll have plenty of time to talk later."

Ella turned her attention to Cameron. At first, he seemed unassuming. He was of medium height, medium build, and had a normal face. He had some Asian features, but his darkness came from the sun. He sported a beard that almost managed to connect at the sides. Not quite, though. He was maybe in his late twenties, early thirties. He carried himself much older than he appeared, and he somehow looked laid back and intense at the same time.

Even with her untrained eye, Ella could tell Cameron was a dangerous man. It wasn't just because he was muscular; he wasn't big, but she could see definition under his clothing. It was in the way he moved. The man was graceful; not like a dancer, but like a snake. He appeared relaxed, lazy even, but the tension around his eyes told another story.

Maybe he just likes tight clothing.

"Maybe he thinks he is a superhero."

Maybe he wears children's clothing.

Ella bit her lip and masked the grin growing on her face. She enjoyed making fun of these people. They all took themselves so seriously. She also appreciated the fact that Io had loosened up with her too. It made her Quasing so much more bearable.

Fifteen minutes later, the seven of them were in a van rumbling north up the road toward an industrial district next to Magadalla Port. At least that was where Ella assumed they were going. Io was only providing instructions at the turns. Three of Cameron's people sat up front while he, Ella, Nabin, and the woman sat in back with all the gear. Ella rolled her eyes at the metal cases stacked next to her. She was so over metal luggage.

She noticed Cameron staring, making uncomfortable googly eyes at her. Being noticed was almost always a bad thing in her line of work. Being stared at usually meant she had just got caught. She squirmed and instinctively looked for some shadow to disappear into. Then she noticed something else in Cameron's stare; he was sad, grieving almost. Was this guy feeling sorry for her? That pissed her off. She didn't take pity from anyone.

"What are you looking at?" she snapped.

"Seeing you sitting there with Io made me think of an old friend." He gestured at the rest of his team. "By the way, this is Dana, Nabin you've already met." The two waved. Cameron patted the driver on the shoulder. "That's Dubs driving. Lam's in the middle. She's my second in command. Jax's my rookie on the right." Dubs, eyes still on the road, raised a hand. Lam looked back and smiled. Jax gave them all the middle finger.

Cameron grinned. "Jax is actually a ten-year veteran, but he's new to my team. There are no actual rookies here. This is about as crack a group as you're going to find. We draw from the best."

"Damn right, sir," Dana said. "Everyone wants to work with Tao and the Adonis host."

Ella made a face. "Adonis, eh? You're not that good looking."

Cameron smiled. "A beautiful human is a Genjix requirement for an Adonis vessel. It is a term they apply to people trained since childhood at their hatcheries to become perfect vessels for their high-ranking Quasing. The Prophus don't have Adonises, but I guess I'm the closest thing our side has to one. My Quasing, Tao, joined with me when I was three and has trained me to be an agent almost since then."

"She's right about one thing, Cam," Jax said. "All those Adonises I've encountered were pretty hot. You got hit with the ugly stick compared to them."

"All those Adonises tried to kill you, too," Cameron replied.

The rookie shrugged. "Nobody's perfect."

"He looks good to me," added Dana. "Well, at least from the neck down. Maybe if we put a paper bag over his head."

Cameron grinned. "I'm going to remember this during your reviews. Insubordination, disrespecting a superior officer..."

"Don't forget she stole your dessert last night," Dubs added.

The van erupted in laughter as the rest of the team began calling out all the things they'd done to him, and then to each other. They must have been together for a long time, Ella mused. They acted like what Ella imagined a family acted like. It was weird. It was such a big difference when compared to Io and Hamilton, who seemed completely dysfunctional.

Hey!

"Well, you are. I'm just saying, Io, not being an asshole goes a long way. I couldn't stand either you or Hamilton for the first few weeks. I still kind of can't. I'm already liking this crew."

Cameron leaned into her. "We'll be working together for the next few weeks. You get used to this ragtag bunch. Look out for Nabin though. He's a charmer."

Ella pursed her lips and rolled her eyes exaggeratedly, but her cheeks burned. She caught herself throwing glances his way a few times, and she wasn't sure why. Nothing about him was that appealing individually, but the whole of him was kind of attractive to her in an ugly duckling way.

"We're here," Dubs said, as he pulled the van past a set of rusty gates and up a driveway.

"Hey Ella," Cameron asked. "How did Io acquire this safe house? Our records indicated it was decommissioned before the war."

Emily was using this before she passed.

Ella relayed Io's words, and it seemed a satisfactory answer for Cameron. With a hiss, the van stopped next to the factory adjacent to a loading dock. The little band got out and was still ribbing each other when Dana, holding some contraption in her hand and waving it back and forth, raised a fist in the air. "Penetra scanner momentarily grabbed two pings. Now they're gone. It could have been a ghost, maybe not. Some of the tracks and footprints look fresh. This building isn't abandoned."

Cameron scanned the grounds and looked at Ella. "Is anyone else here?"

Tell him this safe house is commonly used by operatives moving across the continent. Traffic is light but not uncommon.

Ella repeated Io's exact words.

"Better safe than sorry," he muttered. "Weapons out. I want a full sweep of the factory first. This place doesn't look too secure."

The tone in the team changed immediately. All the friendliness they exhibited was gone in an instant and she could see who these people truly were underneath. The joking stopped and they became all business. No mistake about it, they were killers.

"Io, is something wrong?"

The Adonis is just being overly cautious. Considering all the recent leaks, I do not blame him. I would not worry too much.

Ella found herself agreeing with Cameron. Her gut was telling her something was off as well. Those with bad instincts rarely survived on the streets. She drew a throwing knife in each hand.

"Need a rifle?" Nabin asked, pulling one out of his bag.

She shook her head. He looked puzzled and then shrugged. He slung his pack over his shoulder and then checked the magazine. Ella liked that he didn't ask for an explanation. When he was ready, he signaled to Lam and then they all filed out of the van.

As they walked toward the dock entrance, he leaned in close. "It's probably nothing, but on the off chance it gets hot, stay close to me. I'll keep you safe."

Ella's heart fluttered. That was the most chivalrous thing anyone had ever said to her. Few men had offered to protect her before. On the other hand, it also made her think he thought she couldn't take care of herself. She was going to have to set him straight about that.

"Just don't stand in my way," she said, "or you may end up getting a knife in the back."

He grinned. "I will trust that your desire to see me alive will keep me safe."

Oh brother. This guy is too much. He is so cheesy.

"I love cheese."

"Lead the way," Cameron said.

It took her a few seconds to realize he was speaking to her. Ella hesitantly walked to the front of the group. It was a good thing Io told her where to go, or she would have been completely lost. They entered the factory through the loading docks, down several dilapidated hallways, and into an office area cluttered with old desks, stacks of moldy cardboard, and chairs missing legs. The other end of the room was half-submerged in a pool of dark liquid. The room stank of shit.

The group spread out, flanking Ella and Cameron on both sides. Dana, standing next to Ella, pointed a handheld device up. "I thought I blipped again just now. To the right, one story up. It's gone now. Maybe another false positive. Possibly interference from something in the old factory?"

"Maybe not," said Dubs. "I don't believe in ghosts."

"Where is the safe house located?" Cameron asked. "Please tell me it's not underground."

Ignore that question. I will let you know when we get there. Make a right at the next door.

"Next room over," Ella said aloud and pointed at the large double-door to their right. Their progress slowed as the team crawled forward, clearing out each area as they passed. Their meticulousness began to make her feel anxious, and she tensed as Nabin and Dana positioned themselves on both sides of the door. Dana glanced through one of the circular window holes and nudged the door open just a sliver. Nabin, crouched, crept in, and Dana followed. A few seconds later, an arm appeared and waved for the rest to go on.

They entered an area lined with long tables and benches. The ceiling was three stories up with two rows of broken-windowed skylights. A catwalk overlooking the first floor hung in the air, crisscrossing the entire room. Mounds of garbage, broken furniture, machinery and crushed steel drums littered the floor.

Listen carefully, Ella. When I give the word, I want you to run forward as fast as you can. Do not stop until you reach the other end of the room.

"What? I don't understand."

Just do as I say when I tell you. Head straight into the middle of the room.

Ella followed Io's orders blindly, willing one foot to step in front of the other. Her skin crawled as her gut did backflips. Something was terribly off. She looked down; her hands were shaking so hard, she was in danger of cutting herself with her own knives. She looked back at Cameron and the rest of his team. Almost subconsciously, she reached out and pushed him on the chest. "Something is wrong. Go back."

Wait, no. What are you doing?

Cameron held up a fist and everyone froze. The room became

silent and time seemed to still, save for the wind whistling through the holes in the ceiling and an occasional piece of debris swirling like in miniature cyclones. His orders came low and quick. "Back to the van. Out the way we came in."

They nearly made it back to the double-doors when Jax swung his rifle to the side. "Movement left flank. Multiple contacts." The rest of the team ducked behind cover as a small army of uniformed figures flooded into the room from three directions.

"It's a trap!" Lam said.

Rough hands grabbed Ella by the collar and pulled her behind a column. "Get behind me," Nabin said.

"They have the high ground," Dubs added.

"I have two Quasing on the Penetra scanner," yelled Dana.

Ella peered over the side and saw more figures appearing on the catwalk overhead.

"Prophus, you are out of position and surrounded. Surrender!" a voice on the far side of the room shouted.

"Lay down your arms," another voice barked from up on the catwalk.

What have you done?

"What do you mean, what have I done? I didn't do anything!"

How difficult is it to follow simple directions?

"You're not making any sense!"

Everyone was shouting at once as they swiveled their rifles at the multiple targets that surrounded them. For another twenty seconds, each side dared the other to fire first.

Even having never been in a firefight before, Ella knew they were in deep trouble. There was a line of soldiers on the catwalk, and there seemed to be even more on the ground level. They were wearing police uniforms. Any hope Ella had had that this was just a big misunderstanding vanished.

Two figures appeared on the catwalk at the far end of the room. Ella recognized the woman. She was the stunning blonde Ella had occasionally seen touring the site. The man standing next to her was equally blond and beautiful, if not more so, though that could just be Ella's personal bias.

Ella caught herself staring. How did people like this exist? How could there be so many ridiculously gorgeous evil people in the world? She glanced over at Cameron and then back at those two perfect human specimens looking down at them. Why in gods' hell were the Genjix Adonises so good-looking while the Prophus ones weren't? Life was so unfair!

The woman walked up to the edge of the railing and leaned over. She didn't seem particularly worried about getting shot at. She smiled. "Hello, Cameron Tan. It's been a long time."

Cameron, who had taken cover behind a crate, stood up. His mouth dropped open. There was a long pause as the two locked gazes. Finally, he spoke. "Alex? Is that really you?"

"Alex is long gone. She died the night her father died, executed by the Genjix for treason. The name is Shura now."

"Executed by the Genjix? Is that what you call it?" Cameron's face had turned sheet white. He set his jaw. "You're the one they call the Scalpel."

The woman smiled. "I'm glad my reputation precedes me."

"Who is Alex?" Ella whispered to Nabin.

He frowned. "I don't know. The name sounds familiar though. The Scalpel I've heard of. She's a dangerous Genjix Adonis."

The beautiful guy looked impatient and snapped irritably. "This is adorable and boring. You will waste my time no longer." He nodded off to the side. "Keep vessels alive. Kill the rest."

There was a loud crack and Cameron's body convulsed. Lam came sprinting from the side and dragged him down.

Ella screamed.

Dubs rolled a canister across the floor and a cone of smoke shot into the air.

Both sides opened fire.

CHAPTER THIRTY
Discovery

In the period before what is now known as the Renaissance, I was of low standing, barely a small cog in the Quasing's plans for this world. During those days, there were no Prophus or Genjix. We were still united, one and many, and our goal on this planet was to develop humanity to the point that they could build ships to take us back to Quasar.

For thousands of years, hearkening back to when the Cro-Magnons warred with the Neanderthals to see which species was superior, the Quasing had believed the most efficient way to advance humanity was to drive them into a state of constant change. In order to do this, our purpose was to make sure there was never peace or stagnation within human society. The Quasing were the cause of many of the conflicts humanity waged with itself. This was based on the Conflict Doctrine, which stated that conflict bred innovation.

Things were not going as planned. But then, Ella had no clue what the plan actually was, except she was pretty sure this wasn't it. All she knew was a barrage of gunfire was peppering the floor and walls around their position. Chunks of cement, dust, and wood exploded, raining down upon her in such volume, she had trouble breathing and could hardly see through the smoke.

The thunderous reverberation from the constant gunfire in this large room shook her to her core. She was so terrified she couldn't do anything other than huddle behind the column with her arms wrapped around her head.

You should have run when I told you to.

"I don't understand!"

Stupid girl.

"You shut your fat alien mouth!"

Ella peeked around and saw the rest of Cameron's team firing from their defensive positions. Dubs took out another smoke grenade and lobbed it into the air. Lam barked out several orders, and then dragged Cameron over near Ella and Nabin. "Damn it, Cameron, are you all right?"

He groaned and clutched his chest. "That hurt like hell. Hang on, give me a second to catch my breath." He pulled his shirt back and pulled out the flattened slug embedded in his armor. He threw the hunk of metal off to the side and took a few deep breaths.

He got Lam's attention and made a bunch of hand gestures. His orders spread silently through the team and then, in unison, they got up and retreated. The sound of rifles spitting all at once was deafening. Nabin wrapped his arms around her and half-dragged, half-carried her back the way they had come.

As soon as half the team had passed through the doors, Nabin pushed her against the wall and then he and Dana took position on the sides. The pair guarded the rear while the rest of the team pressed on ahead. When a group of soldiers appeared, they opened fired and pinned the soldiers back around the corner. Even in the chaos, Ella could tell how organized and tactical their movements were. She didn't know how they all appeared so calm amidst this chaos. It was all she could do to not pee her pants.

"Back to the van," Cameron barked.

This team is drawing all the heat. Find a place to hide and wait this out. Do not get involved in the firefight. Stay alive.

"What? I don't..."

Ella saw a dark hallway off to the side. For a second, she almost broke from the group and followed Io's orders, but it just didn't feel like the right thing to do. And then it was too late as Nabin swept her up and dragged her along with them.

Damn it, girl!

"What happened back there?" she asked Nabin. "Why did Cameron looked so dazed when he saw that woman?"

"I don't know," he said. "I've never seen him like this."

The team burst through the door to the loading dock and was sprinting toward the van when a squad of the police or Genjix – Ella didn't know who was who anymore – blocked their path. There was a hail of bullets and the team scattered to the sides. Nabin dove on top of her and pushed her down to the ground. There was a fierce exchange of gunfire, and just like that, it was over. Ella smelled smoke and sweat as Nabin lay on top of her. She looked up and came close to the Nepalese's face.

"Are you all right?" he asked gruffly.

"You're really heavy," she replied. "And you have bad breath."

"Sorry," he muttered. "I've been in the air for the past thirty hours. I haven't brushed my teeth in two days."

"That's OK," she said.

Nabin got up and helped her to her feet. He looked to the side and spoke softly "Oh no. Dubs."

Ella followed his gaze and saw Nabin's teammate sprawled on his back. The two of them crept over to him. She saw his blank stare and gasped. Nabin tried to cover her eyes, but she batted his hands away.

"I've seen dead people before," she said.

Cameron rushed by and unslung his rifle. He handed it to her. "Take this. I'll take him. Come on buddy, stay with me."

"He's gone, commander," Nabin said.

"Shit, shit." Cameron picked up his fallen comrade and slung him over his shoulder.

"What are you doing?" she asked.

"We don't leave our own behind." He turned to Lam. "Buy us some time." He prodded Ella forward. "Come on, get to the van."

Lam ordered the others to stay back as Ella and Cameron sprinted halfway down the length of the building to their parked vehicle. She looked back and wondered who was going to die next. Living in the slums, death was a common occurrence, but it was usually because of starvation or disease. At worst, it was from a knifing in the dark or in alleys. Rarely did it happen with such violence.

The two of them just reached the back door of the van when they were ambushed. This group was dressed differently, in unmarked black attire rather than police uniforms. They spooked Ella and, to her embarrassment, she dropped her knives. Cameron, however, didn't miss a beat. Using Dubs's body as a shield, he charged all five men.

Any misgivings she had about him earlier faded in an instant. He rushed toward them head on and with such force that Ella couldn't help gasping. He reminded her of how Emily had moved when she had fought all those thugs, except he was even quicker, deadlier, like a devastating force of nature.

Just when it looked as if one of them was going to shoot him in the chest, Cameron somehow twisted and dodged the bullet at the last moment, and then he was on them. Cameron drew his handgun and shot one at point-blank range. He speared another in the throat, putting a round in him as the man fell, and then slipped to his right, dancing away from the muzzle of a rifle. He pistol-whipped a shooter when he got within arm's reach, and then popped another round in the man as he was falling down. The last soldier couldn't even spin toward him fast enough. Cameron grabbed him by the back of the neck, and with some elaborate throw that looked as if they were ballroom dancing, sent the man careening headfirst into the side of the van.

Ella just stood there, worthless, her mouth dropped open. "Oh my gods." This guy had taken all of them out in the time it took her to draw a breath.

An Adonis is not like others. They are trained from a young ag –

"Wait, there's five guys," Ella muttered. "Cameron, there's one mo–"

There was a crack of a gunshot and Cameron staggered and fell to one knee, clutching his lower back. His attacker stepped behind him and struck him in the back of the head with the butt of his rifle.

"You're lucky the Adonis wants you alive, betrayer," the man said.

Ella, no! Do not get involved.

Ella wasn't listening. A hundred hours of Manish's repetitive training kicked in. Her eyes scanned the man's body, and then her hands flashed to her thigh band. A throwing knife streaked out a quarter of second later and bounced harmlessly off the man's left shoulder.

"Crap."

She pulled out another knife and tried again. She missed by a hand span. Filled with adrenaline, her shaking hands just couldn't throw straight. This time, though, she had gotten the man's attention. He turned toward her, but Ella was already slipping away from his line of sight, her right hand going toward her back waistband while her left went to her right ribcage. Now she understood why Manish grilled her so relentlessly on knowing how to throw with both hands. The third throwing knife was flying out even as the combat knife appeared in her right hand. It, too, missed and bounced off the van with a loud clang.

"Why does my aim suck?"

You are not used to a live fire situation. Take a deep breath.

Having to think about breathing made her breathe even

faster and she began to hyperventilate. Fortunately, her last throw had forced the soldier to duck, buying Ella time to close in. She charged him, swinging her long serrated knife. She slashed him twice on the arm and once in the knee. The last slash buckled his legs, and then she jammed the knife into his chest.

Unfortunately, it didn't go in very far. Either the body armor he wore was too tough, or she wasn't strong enough. It was probably both, but her blade sunk only a few centimeters in and then stopped. The man threw an arm out and nearly took her head off. Ella ducked at the last second, but lost her balance and fell onto her butt. She scampered backward on all fours as the man, snarling, stood up and limped toward her.

"I'm going to rip your nose off," he growled.

He pulled out his own knife and suddenly pitched forward onto his face. Cameron had grabbed his legs from behind, and was on top of him moments later. Three brutal strikes to the back of his head, and the man stopped moving.

Cameron looked at her. "Are you all right?"

Ella exhaled and managed to nod. Cameron gritted his teeth and stood up. He stumbled and put a hand on his right lower back. "That's a busted rib."

The sound of pounding footsteps grew, and they turned to see the rest of the team sprinting toward them. Jax stayed next to the wall and continued his suppression fire at the loading dock. Lam took one look at the bodies around them and noticed one of their assailants picking himself off the ground. She raised her rifle and plugged him once in the chest.

She turned to Nabin. "Get the van started."

Ella helped Cameron climb into the van bed while Dana and Nabin picked up Dubs's body. The van was pulling away from the factory when Jax broke from his position and came sprinting after them. He managed to climb inside as they turned at the end of the driveway. Lam and Dana closed the double doors behind him and the group watched somberly as they sped away.

Ella, sitting next to Cameron, watched as more soldiers poured out of the factory. One of the last to come out had a shock of blonde hair. The woman walked to the middle of the street and stared as they pulled away. Ella heard a sharp intake of breath as Cameron looked on.

"I can't believe it's actually her," he muttered.

"How do you know her?" Ella asked.

He shook his head. "It's a long story. We had a thing when we were young, briefly."

Ella frowned. "Thing? Wait, you dated that coldblooded bitch?"

"It's complicated. Alex and I have history."

"Alex? She said her name is Shura."

Both Shura and Alex are nicknames for Alexandra.

"That's what I knew her by." Cameron grimaced and laid down on the van floor. He looked up at his worried team. "We're going to need to find a safe place to crash tonight. Dana, can you locate another safe house?"

"Sorry, Cameron, the Prophus have no active safe houses in this region. There are a few expired resources, but none have been verified since before the war."

"Can we book a hotel?" Lam asked.

"That's risky," said Cameron. "We don't know how much influence the Genjix have here. Five foreigners with our descriptions can't be hard to locate. And then there's the matter of Dubs's body, especially in this weather."

Ella saw the look on everyone's faces and felt the need to do something, to make herself useful. They were all strangers and she didn't owe them anything, but she felt responsible for what had happened. No, she *was* responsible for what happened. Everything was so messed up.

Your home is their only option. It will not be comfortable, but it is a roof over their head.

Ella nodded to no one in particular. It was the least she could do. After all, she was local support. It was her job to take care of them. All she had done was lead them into a trap. It seemed no matter what, all the Prophus who came here were somehow doomed.

She opened her mouth and was about to offer to let the team crash at her home when it hit her. She had everything backward all along. She was wrong and Hamilton was right. She was the double agent! Ella's world came crashing down inside her head. Her gasp was so loud everyone stared at her. She covered her mouth with her hand.

Ella…

She was Bijan's contact when he came to survey the site. She was the recon team's contact. Now, she was Cameron's team's contact. She had led Cameron's team into a trap and the Genjix were waiting. They were all nearly captured and one of their own died. Every time these Prophus had trusted and depended on her, she had failed them. Now, Io wanted her to bring these people to her home. What were the odds that the enemy was going to find them there?

"Io, it's you! You're the leak. You're the traitor."

"Are you all right, Ella?" Nabin asked. "Your face is white as Everest."

Listen to me carefully if you want to survive. There is more–

Ella turned to the side and threw up.

CHAPTER THIRTY-ONE
The Hunt

I was living an uneventful and peaceful life within a barmaid in Spain when the conflict within the Quasing erupted. Our kind split into two factions, the Prophus and the Genjix. The Genjix wished to escalate the Conflict Doctrine and push humanity in order to force rapid advancements in technology and culture. The Prophus felt the Quasing had already gone too far, that humanity could develop more quickly without being in a state of constant struggle. While the Genjix had always called humans their vessels, the Prophus saw them as hosts and felt their relationship should be more symbiotic than parasitic.

At the time, I declared for the Prophus partially because I believed in their philosophy, but also because constant war was dangerous for a Quasing. We are the most vulnerable when we change hosts. Also, in a shock to all, the Keeper, our leader, had chosen to side with the Prophus, the only one of the original Grand Council to do so.

In hindsight, my choice may have been a mistake.

Shura stepped onto the street and watched as their quarry escaped, leaving a trail of bodies in their wake. Most of the casualties had been the incompetent Indian police. She walked back up the driveway and knelt by the bodies in the parking lot. These were Genjix operatives. Cameron Tan was every bit as good as he was reputed to be.

Fluid. Natural instincts. Good use of space.

"He has grown," she murmured.

She had observed the Prophus's flight from the third-story roof as Cameron's team had fought off the police's overwhelming numbers as they retreated to the van. This was an elite unit, no doubt about it.

That is what happens when we contract with amateurs.

"We didn't have much choice. The country is still recovering from the war. Most of their veterans have been drafted into the military. The police are more used to kicking beggars around than dealing with a special ops team."

Shura could have gotten involved and possibly altered the outcome of the ambush. It wouldn't have been too difficult to rappel down and hit Cameron while he was occupied with the Genjix team. However, she would be without support. This wasn't her show anymore, so why should she put herself at risk?

For the glory of the Holy Ones?

"There are other ways to achieve that."

Rurik appeared a few minutes later, screaming at the policemen milling about. It seemed neither he nor Sabeen spoke Hindu. He turned to Shura, red-faced. "What happened? We had a hundred men. How did they escape?"

Shura kept her face neutral, but relished his manic inexperience. The ambush had been problematic from the start. Rurik had erred on the side of caution and held the units meant to cut off the enemy's escape for too long. By the time they were ordered in to contain the exits, the enemy was already moving. Now, they would be forced to hunt them down.

She watched her words carefully. "Perhaps if you had brought more operatives instead of your personal retinue, the circumstances might have been different. Or if you had ordered your security detail to participate–"

"My detail stays with me," he snarled. "I am the head of Russia, Shura. Never forget that. My protection is paramount. I am not expendable, like some lowly operative."

Sabeen is forever overcautious and trying to compensate for his lack of combat experience. I should tell you about his time in General McClellan. The general was already a decorated Genjix officer before Sabeen joined with him. Sabeen somehow took a savvy military veteran and made him incompetent. The man sat on his ass for months doing nothing with one of the biggest Union armies while General Lee maneuvered circles around him.

"Weren't both Lee and McClellan Genjix operatives?"

Yes.

Shura chuckled. "Conflict breeds innovation."

While Rurik had proven gifted in navigating the treacherous Russian political hierarchy, it came at a cost. Not all vessels and Quasing were experienced and skilled in all areas. Both he and his Holy One, Sabeen, severely lacked tactical experience. Outside his brief tenure during the American Civil War, the last time Sabeen had commanded a combat unit, it involved chariots.

In Rurik's case, he was too young to have fought in the Alien World War, so had spent the majority of the conflict financing the war and keeping the bombs dropping. It was an important role he excelled at, but hardly relevant to the ambush tonight. As an Adonis vessel, he had too much self-esteem to delegate the task to someone with more experience, especially someone who he considered a rival.

Shura turned to Surrett as he came running, huffing and puffing. "Station units with scanners at every airport, hospital, bus, and train station. Set up checkpoints on Highways 6, 228, and 170. Mobilize the coastguard and have them take position at the mouth of the gulf. Conduct a bed to bed search at every hospital. I know we hit at least one of them."

We need more scanners.

"And get us more Penetra scanners, Minister."

Local law enforcement is not equipped to deal with this situation.

"Get me real soldiers, not these fools," Shura snapped. "Call in the Indian special forces."

"But Adonis," said Surrett, "calling in the military will raise questions."

"You mean, get *me* real soldiers," Rurik said. "You forget your place, Shura."

Young Rurik is trying to make a name for himself on the operational and military side, so he is particularly sensitive to rank and protocol. It gives you no advantage to antagonize him on such small matters.

Shura looked deferentially to the young man. "Apologies. Your orders, Father?"

Rurik paused. "The airport and docks. Shut them down. Put out a warrant for their arrest. Five foreigners should not be too difficult to locate."

"Shutting the airport down is problematic," said Shura coolly. "A Penetra sweep should be sufficient. A coastal blockade is easier to enforce than searching through thousands of containers. A warrant will be ineffectual. There's no need to drag in the judicial system. Working through the minister should be sufficient. Other than that, your orders will be carried out."

No need for snark.

Rurik pulled up a map of the region. "Damn these incompetent Indian police. The Prophus could be anywhere."

"They're heading southwest toward Crate Town."

"How do you know?"

She held up her tablet. "I ordered one of our operatives to plant a tracer on the vehicle when they arrived. Just in case."

"Then why are you still standing here?" he raged.

Shura looked to the side as four police SUVs pulled up. "I took the liberty of calling them up as soon as the Prophus escaped into the van." She spoke to the nearest officer. "Inspector, you're with me." She turned to Surrett. "Gather the rest of the police. Follow as soon as possible."

Moments later, Shura led a train of police vehicles toward the slum. She had five Genjix agents and twenty police officers with her. She checked her tablet. The van had entered Crate Town and was heading toward the gulf. Did they have transportation awaiting them? How could they? According to Riseevar, the team had just arrived that day. Could they already have an escape plan in place?

The van was moving erratically once it entered the slum, making several odd turns and crisscrossing major streets as if it were trying to throw them off.

What are they doing?

She contacted Surrett. "Is the coastal blockade up yet?"

"Yes, Adonis," he replied. "Three boats already on patrol were rerouted. Two more are en route, and six more have been activated. I'm on my way to Crate Town now with sixty police."

That is not enough, but it will have to do for now. Send units to guard the south side of the Tupi River and a search party to Hazira Mangroves. If the Prophus evade the patrols northwest, then they are as good as lost.

The van came to a stop with Shura still five minutes behind. She instructed two of the vans to break off and head directly to the other main intersections. With a spot of luck, they could encircle the coverage of the Penetra scanners and pick up the vessels' trail.

"Sirens off. Go in quiet," she ordered.

Six minutes later, a swarm of police surrounded the abandoned van. It was too late, though. The Prophus were long gone, their tracks covered, and there wasn't a blip on the Penetra scanner.

"Any signals?" she asked the other squads positioned nearby.

The responses all came back negative. Shura swore. How had they moved away so quickly?

They knew they were being followed and must have dropped off the two vessels at one of their sharp turns. That is the only way they could have escaped.

Shura studied the pitch black buildings of the slum. Crate Town was too large and dense, with too many places to hide. She did not have enough resources on hand to conduct a door-to-door search, especially at this hour.

Depending on what materials many of these buildings were made from, the scanners might not even be powerful enough to penetrate some of these walls. The equipment the police used for the ambush tonight wasn't of the highest quality.

Cameron Tan had escaped. For now.

It is a safe bet they are hiding somewhere in this slum. Containment is now the priority.

"Where else could they be?" she murmured.

Check the home.

"Unlikely, but worth a shot."

Shura contacted the minister again. "Pull all forces back and set up checkpoints at every street leading in and out of Crate Town. When police reinforcements arrive, spread them out until they completely blockade the entire perimeter of the slum. None of them gets out. Take a squad and pay Ella Patel's home a visit. Perhaps Riseevar left some clues regarding their whereabouts. Stay there until morning in case they return. When is the military arriving?"

"I'm working on it," said Surrett. "Hopefully within a few days."

"A few days is too late. I don't care if you have to wake up the Chief of the Army Staff. Do it now. I want the military here by morning."

"Yes, Adonis."

Shura hung up the phone and signaled to the policeman wielding the scanner. "All right, pull back to the perimeter. We're locking them in."

CHAPTER THIRTY-TWO
Truths

The Genjix came down on the Prophus suddenly and mercilessly. History came to know the birth of our civil war as the Spanish Inquisition. Thousands of Prophus and their hosts were imprisoned, stripped of whatever rank and position they held.

Like most Prophus, I was not prepared for the onslaught. The Genjix leveraged their hosts' superior numbers, political positions and wealth to openly hunt us down. This public outbreak of violence was unheard-of at the time. Our kind had always operated in the shadows. Now both factions used humanity as their pawns as they openly waged a war that rages to this day.

Wiry Madras did not seem happy to see Ella when she walked into her establishment. But then Madras never seemed happy to see any of her patrons. That was the one advantage of owning the best bath house and laundry cleaning service in all of Crate Town; you could be as mean as you wanted to your customers, and they all happily put up with it.

She was especially mean to all the girls who used to work for her, since she always offered them a pretty steep discount when they used her services. That was the thing about Wiry Madras. The old woman had a heart as big as her tiny body, even if most of it was as dark as her soul.

She crossed her arms as Ella walked inside the front lobby. "You again, Black Cat? What are you doing that you have to wash every day? It's not healthy, especially since what I charge you barely covers the hot water. Also, your laundry isn't ready. I need to have Kaea wash it again. There's some stains in there that…" Her voice trailed off when she noticed the five additional obviously military-like bodies walk in after Ella. There was only the briefest of pauses before she went off on Ella again. "You stupid girl. What did I tell you about bringing trouble to my door?" Ella opened her mouth to reply, but Wiry Madras cut her off. She bowed to Nabin, the one brown person in the group who she must have assumed was the one in charge. "Officer, I don't know who this wretched girl is. I'm just a humble old merchant. Whatever she said–"

"They're with me," said Ella.

"Well then." Wiry Madras eyed the dangerous but exhausted looking crew up and down, probably trying to decide if they were worth the trouble. "Water is still boiling if you want it hot. Five hundred rupees. Cold baths only two hundred. If you have laundry, it's by the–"

"We need a place to stay."

Wiry Madras shook her head. "I take in homeless girls, not strapping big men in uniforms. These people are obviously trouble. I won't have that in my–"

"We'll pay you a hundred Euros a day." Cameron held up one finger. "One room, total privacy, and your silen–"

"Welcome, welcome, my friends, to Wiry Madras's." She opened her arms magnanimously and stepped to the side. "Right this way."

Wiry Madras shooed one of the girls to prepare a room and then gave them a guided tour of the four large communal pools and the dozen smaller individual tubs, past the laundry room where ten of Madras's girls were hand-washing clothes, to the back of the building.

It brought Ella back to her early days in Crate Town. After being run out of Metal Mountain by the gangs, she had survived on the street for a few weeks before Wiry Madras took her in. The old woman had put a roof over her head, given her a mattress, fed her two meals a day, and then put her to work for fifteen hours at a time.

It was hard, and Ella hated Wiry Madras for much of it, but she loved the old hag as well. The woman had protected her and the rest of the girls when they were most vulnerable, and had helped them move on with their lives when it was time for them to go. She still remembered the day she had left. Wiry Madras had given her a hug – the first that Ella could remember – and slipped five thousand rupees into her pocket. It had brought Ella to tears.

Wiry Madras slapped her on the back of the head. "Pay attention, Black Cat. Listen, you keep your thugs here in line. Walk in through the back door. I don't want them to spook my good customers."

"Yes, ma'am."

Wiry Madras turned to the others. "One more thing. The price does not include bath and laundry services. If you want a hot bath, it's ten Euros. For a cold one, it's five. Laundry is ten Euros per basket."

"What?" Nabin exclaimed. "Earlier, you said it was five hundred rupees."

"That's international business for you," Wiry Madras shrugged. "If there's nothing else..."

Ella exchanged glances with Cameron, and then gingerly raised a hand. "There's one more thing, ma'am."

"What is it, cat?"

"We have a dead body in the van. We need you to store it for us."

Wiry Madras looked as if they were all crazy. Negotiations went downhill from there.

•••

Ella found some time alone on the roof of Wiry Madras's four-story building later that day. By now, the team had settled in, taken baths, and eaten. Madras was pulling out all the stops and catering to them as if they were staying at the Taj Lake Palace. She was probably making a killing too, although it seemed money was no object to these Prophus foreigners, or at least they had no idea what things should cost in this part of the world.

When Wiry Madras had asked for a thousand Euros to store Dubs, Ella had gotten indignant on behalf of the Prophus, even though she felt a greater allegiance to Madras. It was outrageous, but Cameron had accepted her demands without a fuss. Even the old woman seemed surprised that he agreed to her initial offer. At the very least, he could have asked for some free baths or something.

You cannot ignore me forever. You will have to deal with this awkward situation sooner or later.

Ella might not be able to ignore that traitorous alien forever, but she was certainly going to try. At the very least, she was going to pretend that parasite wasn't living in her body right now.

The situation is a lot more complicated than you realize. I am doing what is best for both of us. Your life depends on it.

Why should she care what this stupid alien was thinking, anyway? All this time, Io had made Ella think she was her friend. Now, she knew this flaky two-faced liar had tricked her, had used her. She had only pretended to be Ella's friend. In fact, she could never trust Io again. That no-good traitorous backstabbing manipulating snitch had gotten good people killed.

I have my reasons. You are still young. I have been on this planet since before humans walked the Earth. There is much you do not understand about the way things are in this world.

Ella did her best to tune Io out as she sat on the roof with her legs dangling over the edge. Her view wasn't great.

Madras owned the entire building, but her four floors paled in comparison to the neighboring six- and seven-clusters nearby. All she ended up being able to see were the side walls of other clusters, save for the main street in front. Still, it was high enough that the noise on the ground felt distant.

This day has been trying and you are still in shock. Get some rest. Come back to me with an open mind tomorrow. I will explain everything. It will be for the best.

A little while later, she felt someone approach from behind. She tensed and reached for a knife near her thigh. No one knew she was up here. She had run away from the group at her earliest opportunity. Her nerves were on tilt from the day's violence, and she was having trouble processing her recent revelation.

"Hey Ella, mind if I join you?" Cameron said.

When Ella didn't answer, he invited himself and sat down next to her, kicking his legs up over the side. Neither said a word as they stared at the setting sun. She honestly would rather have been alone, partially because that was the company she usually kept, but mainly because she was afraid she might accidentally leak that her stupid stinking alien was a stupid stinking traitor. After all, it was all she could do right now not to blurt it out.

Listen to me very carefully. They cannot know what you think you know. Remember, the only way anyone can get to me is by getting through you. Hear me out first. In time, you will realize that our goals are aligned.

"Just shut up, alien! Can't you take the hint? I don't want to talk to you. The Genjix killed my amma, and you convinced me you were fighting them. And now I find out you're one of them!"

Ella might have been raging at Io in her head, but her anger must have been painted on her face. Cameron looked at her worriedly. "Are you sure you're all right?" he asked. "Did I or my team do something to offend you?"

Tell them everything is fine. Trust me, you do not want to give me away. You say anything and at the very least, they will cut off all support. That means no more stipend and no more training from Manish. Is that what you want?

Ella grimaced. She felt trapped either way. She was stuck in this predicament as long as Io inhabited her, and there was nothing she could do to rid herself of this blasted Quasing. It took today's harrowing events for her to realize how serious this alien war was. She couldn't just hide in her container here in Crate Town any longer. She was involved in something way over her head. Sooner or later, someone was going to catch her.

I can give you a way out. Let me explain everything once we are alone.

"Fine, but if I don't like your answer, I'm turning you in."

You do that and you will have signed your own death warrant.

"Don't threaten me, alien. I won't be blackmailed."

Just assure Cameron for now that you are fine.

Ella swallowed her anger and threw Cameron a weak smile. "I have a headache, and Io's being an asshole. That's all."

Cameron chuckled. "Emily always did say Io was more trouble than she was worth."

"For an alien that's supposed to be millions of years old, she makes a lot of dumb decisions," said Ella. "Is your alien like that too?"

Cameron shook his head. "Tao's usually on point. He used to be in the likes of Genghis Khan and Lafayette and other military geniuses. He invented Tai Chi."

Now he is just bragging.

"All Io has inhabited are a bunch of people I have never heard of. I must have a defective alien."

"Perhaps." Both Cameron and Ella laughed.

No need to be insulting.

"You deserve it."

"I just wanted to thank you personally," said Cameron. "Your warning at the factory bought my team the precious seconds we needed to escape."

"I led you to that trap," said Ella. "Mr Dubs died."

"If you hadn't warned us, we all would have. You saved our lives today, Ella Patel. My team and I owe you our gratitude." He held out his hand.

Ella shook it, but inside she quailed. It was eating her up. She was the one responsible for all this in the first place.

In this instance, you are innocent.

"I should have figured you out months ago."

You give me far too little credit.

"You also saved me when that last guy at the van got the jump on me," Cameron continued. "I personally owe you my thanks for that as well."

"You're welcome." The words came out hardly more than a whisper. Ella's face flushed, partially from how much of that fight was sheer luck and partially from all these excessive compliments. It was just too much, and she wasn't used to it. It felt weird.

"Is this a private party?" a voice piped up from behind. "Or can anyone crash?"

Both Ella and Cameron looked over as Nabin strolled up.

"Something up?" Cameron asked. "What's with your girlfriend there?"

Ella's face flamed until she realized he was referring to the rifle Nabin had strapped around his shoulder.

"Lam decided we should start a guard rotation. I drew the short straw." The Prophus agent sat on her other side and placed the rifle on the ground. He checked their hands. "Anyone have booze?"

Cameron shook his head. "I asked the madam for some earlier. She tried to charge me so much I thought we were back in South Korea."

Nabin laughed. "That one nightclub, man. Cameron, I

warned you. You just about popped a vein in your neck when you got that bill."

Cameron made a face. "Yeah, that didn't go over well back at base. Audit flagged it and escalated it to my mom. You believe that?"

"His amma?" Ella asked.

Nabin grinned and nudged her with his elbow. "Our glorious commander here has the additional great honor of being the son of Jill Tesser Tan, the Keeper and leader of the Prophus."

Ella's eyes widened. "You really are an important person."

Cameron blushed. "I prefer to keep that on the down low."

"Your amma runs the whole thing and she lets you come to places like this?"

He tapped the side of his head. "The host follows his Quasing's specialty. In my case, Tao is one of our best covert operatives."

The host follows the Quasing... Ella wondered what that made her. Did that mean she would be marked as a traitor as well?

Or you could just follow my lead next time.

"By the way," Nabin said, "Lam wants to talk to you. She and Dana are taking inventory. We need to source more supplies. We lost most of our gear when the shit hit the fan."

Cameron looked at Ella. "Can you help with that?"

She nodded. "I know people. Crate Town is mine."

"I kind of figured. I'll get you a list." Cameron patted her on the shoulder and stood up. He stretched and winced. A groan escaped his lips and he touched his lower back again. She couldn't help but notice the muscles rippling underneath his loose shirt. If only his face was as nice to look at as the ones on those people who were trying to kill them.

Nabin and Ella watched until Cameron disappeared down the stairwell. He leaned into her and Ella felt her heart beat faster. She still wasn't sure what she saw in him. Maybe it was the way he always smiled, maybe it was because he was her bodyguard during that firefight, or maybe it was just because she felt safe.

He shivered. "It's cool tonight."

"You should be used to it," she said.

"Nah, I like my heat."

"You don't sound like any Nepalese I've ever met," she said. "Where are you from?"

"My family moved to the States when I was four. Raised in Atlanta, actually, where it's sweltering. Actually, it's not too different from here."

"How did you get involved with the Prophus?"

"Crappy grades and an extensive shoplifting record closed some doors. Joined the army instead. Found out I was actually pretty good at playing soldier and got recruited by the Prophus. You?"

"Genjix killed my amma. Living on the streets ever since."

"And now you're my superior officer, Commander," he joked. "You're pretty good with a knife. You almost got me back at the airport."

"I would have if the rest of your folks didn't save you."

"Probably true. Where did you learn to fight?"

"Kung fu movies and a pole dancer."

He chuckled. "Is there a reason you don't use a gun?"

"There are no guns in Crate Town."

Nabin frowned. "That's not really a reason, but OK."

The two settled into a comfortable silence. By now, Crate Town had shut down, and the horizon to the west was nearly pitch-black except for occasional lights dotting the night. In the sky, she saw the blinking red light of a plane descending. A lone dog howled until someone yelled for it to shut up.

Ella thought about her home. Were the Genjix looking for her there? She thought about that stash behind the hidden plate and worried. Everything she had in the world was in there, and now she might not be able to go back. Or maybe she was just being paranoid. If the Genjix had known about her place all along, why wouldn't they have just picked her up long ago?

Then it hit her. The answer was staring her in the face. They hadn't picked her up all this time because they didn't want to. "Io, what game are you playing?"

All you had to do is ask. Of course they knew where you lived. You have to believe me when I say I hid my real plans from you for your own protection.

"You should get some sleep," Nabin said. "It's going to be a long day tomorrow."

The idea of sleeping after the adrenaline-filled day reminded Ella how exhausted she was. She was about to drag herself off to bed when she realized that Nabin was going to be on watch up here by himself for gods knew how long. She stifled her yawn. "How long are you stuck up here?"

He checked his watch. "Three hours thirty-nine minutes and forty-one seconds."

"I'm not tired yet. Mind if I keep you company?"

"Would be my pleasure."

Ella thought she heard Io make a strangled noise. She leaned into Nabin and looked up at the stars that were just beginning to pierce the black veil of night. "Tell me about this Atlantis place you're from."

"Atlanta."

"Isn't that what I said?"

"No, you said Atlantis. That's a mythical sunken city… never mind."

CHAPTER THIRTY-THREE
The Past

The Genjix wielded the Inquisition like a club. Though I did not inhabit a king or a warrior or any vessel in positions of power, they hunted me down just like they did any other Prophus. None of us, regardless of standing or position, were spared. This conflict between the two factions fell perfectly into the Genjix's plans, and into their Conflict Doctrine, and set the tone for the next three hundred years in Europe.

I decided to flee rather than fight my own kind. In the early sixteenth century, my host crewed one of Juan Ponce de León's expeditions to the New World, where he discovered the land now known as Florida.

Cameron Tan woke with a start and tried to sit up, stopping only when the pain in his chest reminded him of yesterday's events. He took a labored breath and forced himself up. He took a quick count. He was missing one.

It is 0600. Dana has third watch.

"Got it, Tao."

It was a good thing someone was on watch, if anything just for the space it freed up in this small room. It was so cramped, they wouldn't have been able to fit anyone else in here unless they started stacking bodies. Heck, he didn't know how they were squeezing five in now. He made a face at Jax's bare feet inches from his face.

Jax and Lam were sleeping next to the cot in the center of the room. Nabin and Ella were asleep on the other end, leaning against each other back to back. That did not look comfortable. A wave of guilt washed over Cameron for having hogged the only cot. The team had insisted though. He was the only one dumb enough to get shot.

Twice.

"Thanks for the reminder."

There was also Dubs. Cameron spent a few moments mourning his friend. No matter how many times it had happened to Cameron, the hurt never went away. Dubs was one of the first to sign up when Cameron had created this team. They had met in the early days of the war and had promptly gotten into a fist fight over a game of bridge on a C-130 transport flying to the front line. The guy had bloodied Cameron's lip. Cameron ended up separating Dubs's shoulder. Dubs was in a firefight that very next day and had scored the most Genjix kills. That was when Cameron knew he wanted him on his team.

The worst part was the team wasn't even supposed to be here. They were supposed to be on vacation, sitting on the beach in Whitehaven sipping Mai Tais and being obnoxious tourists. Cameron took out his phone and read the message:

URGENT. EMILY GONE. GREECE MYSTERY SOLVED. JUSTICE FOR SETH.

Attached to the message were coded rendezvous coordinates, and now they were here. Cameron had read that message a hundred times and analyzed it a thousand ways. His team had just completed an extended operation stabilizing Tanzania, and this was the first opportunity he could find to come. Unfortunately, Dana had caught wind of it and the rest of the team followed.

Now Dubs was gone.

Cameron took out a worn photo from his wallet and studied

the faded image. This had become a ritual for him every time he lost someone under his command. It was a photo of a bunch of college kids posing in front of the Parthenon in Athens on a perfect summer day. He was the lanky one on the left end. There was Emily with the guy she was dating at the time – what's his name – in the center. Next to her were Negin, Annelie, Marilyn, Surrett, Yang, and then Seth. Cameron's gaze lingered on the Chinese kid and then over to Seth. Emily and Seth were his best friends during university. The three of them, all children of Prophus operatives, had enrolled in a summer program in Greece the summer before the war had started.

And then the war had started.

That picture was taken the day before the first volleys. The next day, Greece declared for the Genjix. The three of them and the rest of their class suddenly found themselves behind enemy lines. Cameron was ordered to leave his friends behind and smuggle a Prophus operative with important intel out of the country. Cameron had taken it upon himself to lead his friends and several of the other students to safety as well. In the end, Seth and Yang hadn't made it. Those were the first two people to die under his command.

How many times do I have to tell you? It is not your fault. We were betrayed. One of the other students was a Genjix, or at least a sympathizer.

"I should have been able to get them all out."

The odds were stacked against you. You did your best.

Somehow, the Genjix were able to hound them every step of the way. At the time, Cameron was convinced it was Yang, the son of a powerful businessman in China with Genjix ties. He believed Yang was betraying them right up until Yang died saving his life. Cameron closed his eyes and replayed those scenes in his head.

Yang and Seth.

"I was suspicious of the guy who saved my life."

I thought it was Yang as well.

"That doesn't make me feel any less guilty."

One of these days, I am going to wipe those memories from your head.

"Can you actually do that?"

If I cannot, then I will make you drink a jug of tequila while you are asleep.

Cameron's gag reflex kicked in, remembering Emily's twentieth birthday. He brushed his finger along her face in the picture. It had been over five years since he had last seen Emily. The war had separated them by an ocean. The incidents in Greece had hit her hard. She had become a Prophus operative, she said, because she wanted to make a difference. Cameron knew it was also because it was her way of coming to terms with Seth's death. He wondered if she had ever found that peace.

Enough wallowing in the past. It is time for answers.

Cameron looked over at the sleeping Ella, and then stood up and tested his body. A little stiff here and there and definitely a busted rib, but nothing too serious. His range of motion was going to be limited for the next few weeks. That was his own fault anyway, freezing up like that when he saw Alex. What a rookie move.

You think?

"I don't need a lecture right now."

It has been far too long since your last one.

"What are you talking about? You harped at me for half an hour last month when I lost track of the supply convoy."

Like I said, far too long.

Cameron knelt down next to Ella and waited. Her eyes opened. "Cameron or Tao?"

"It's Cameron. Io?"

Io nodded. "Outside." She tried to stand. Cameron grabbed her arm to support her and together they tiptoed out of the room. Io's control over Ella's body wasn't great. She looked as if she might tip over a few times. He wasn't sure if that was because Io hadn't gotten used to her new body yet or if the Quasing just wasn't very good at controlling unconscious humans. In either case, walking up the stairs to the roof proved too much of a challenge, so Cameron just picked her up and carried her the rest of the way. Dana waved from her little perch as they walked onto the roof.

"I'll take over," he said to her as they joined her in the shade.

Dana frowned. "Sure, Cameron? I only started about fifteen minutes ago."

Cameron shrugged.

"Suit yourself." Dana gave him a nod and went inside.

Io sat down awkwardly on a cracked plastic chair while Cameron leaned against the railing. He scanned the expanse of Crate Town. "I'm sorry about Emily. You lost her and her father pretty close together. That must have been hard."

"Until the Eternal Sea," Io said. "She was a dear friend to you as well."

Until the Eternal Sea.

"What happened?" Cameron asked. "What was she doing here in India? I followed up on her assignment before I arrived. She's supposed to be in Thailand, but she went rogue."

"She found a lead, Cameron. They killed her for it."

"What lead?"

"Emily came across a financial statement from an Indonesian law firm while tracking Malaysian separatists. The Genjix were using the firm to funnel funds for political campaigns. She came across a small-time Indian politician that they were throwing their support behind." Io took out her phone and pulled up an article. She handed the phone to him.

Cameron read it aloud. "In a surprise to most pundits, the dark horse candidate won a landslide victory over incumbent Harrauj Bandi, making him the youngest ever to occupy the office in this region's history. The son of a Bollywood actress..."

His voice trailed off when he scrolled down to the picture of the deputy minister. Cameron took out the photo from his wallet and placed it next to the one on the phone. He looked older and had lost his awkward boyish grin, but it was the same man. There was no mistaking it. Cameron was staring at Surrett Kapoor, his childhood friend, now a Genjix-backed politician.

If that is not a smoking gun, then it is a hell of a coincidence.

He looked at Io, who nodded. "You and your friends were betrayed by a Genjix operative, which is what led to Seth's death."

Emily found Seth's killer. It had been Surrett all along.

"He was responsible for Yang's as well. I never found out who it was." Cameron's voice broke.

"That is why she went rogue," said Io. "She was tracking Surrett when we were attacked by the Genjix."

Cameron clenched his fists. "That bastard is going to pay for this. Pay for everything."

I understand your need to find justice for both Emily and Seth, but you have a more pressing problem. Alex is here as well. That is not a coincidence.

Tao was probably right. They had lost most of their supplies at the factory. They didn't have a real base of operations to work out of. They didn't even have a clear Prophus objective. His team was supposed to be enjoying three weeks of R&R in Australia before heading back to Tanzania to search and destroy a Genjix-backed arms manufacturing ring. Instead, he had led his people here on a personal vendetta.

"I'm a bad leader. I'm sucking them into my private crap."

Your team will follow you to hell, even to Florida.

Cameron turned to Io. "How is Alex involved in all this? It's been fifteen years since I last saw her. I can't believe she just happens to be here while I drop in."

Io shrugged. "I do not know anything about that. To be honest, I am surprised your paths did not cross earlier. You are arguably two of the top operatives in either organization. It is as if you have been avoiding each other."

"Hardly." His tone was harsher than he had intended. Cameron drummed the railing with his hands. "Let me get this straight. Emily tracks Surrett and uncovers a massive base under construction in western India that has been cloaked from satellite surveillance. The Genjix find and kill her, but not before she sends a warning off to the Prophus. Command sends two separate units to investigate, both are missing and presumed dead."

What does Io hope to accomplish here with a new host? She should have left as soon as Emily died, especially in a country as dangerous as India.

Cameron stopped drumming the railing. "What are you still doing here, Io? You had no actionable items once Emily passed."

"Is it not obvious? I am here to finish what she started. I owe that much to her. On top of that, the Genjix are building something big there. I gathered as much intel as I could with a new host and limited resources, and then once I could not proceed further, I sent for you."

"All off-book? Command says they've been trying to recall you for weeks."

"Command does not view revenge as a legitimate operational objective. Besides, the girl does not want to leave."

Cameron nodded. "I can see that. Ella comes across as stubborn. She's a little firecracker. How are things going between you two?"

"She is headstrong, untrained, and difficult." There was a pause. "Her loyalties are easily bought."

Cameron raised an eyebrow. "Really?"

That is not my read on her as well.

"She is a conwoman and a thief. She is unreliable."

Either I am mistaken or she is more skilled at her game than I give her credit for.

"I'll be careful around her then," said Cameron.

Io nodded. "All right. We had better head inside. I can feel my host rousing. Remember, Cameron, watch what you say around the girl. Ella Patel cannot be trusted."

CHAPTER THIRTY-FOUR
Uneasy Truce

Shortly after reaching Florida, my host died of dysentery. I ended up inhabiting the alligator that ate him. To be honest, I did not mind. In the five centuries since I had first inhabited Torgeir or Torgo or whatever his name was, changing hosts had become a regular occurrence. While other Quasing grieved over their lost hosts, I had become numb to the transfer.

I hid in the Florida swamps for the next several decades, content to once again live within the animals while history passed me by.

Io waited until Cameron settled in to take over Dana's watch before leaving. She went back downstairs to their room and checked who was still asleep; everyone was accounted for except for Dana. Io continued past the kitchen entrance and saw her eating breakfast at the corner. The woman gave her a lazy wave. Io waved back stiffly and noticed Dana frown quizzically and then focus again on her ragi idli.

Now was Io's chance. Moving as fast as she could in Ella's body, she walked to the front of the bath house and found Wiry Madras at the counter getting ready to open for business.

The old woman looked at Ella's awkward gait. "What's wrong with your leg, Black Cat? Are you hurt?"

"I need a tub, a private one."

Madras's eyes narrowed. "This early in the morning? Don't be up to no good in my place of business, girl. I don't allow–" Io plopped a stack of rupees on the counter. The money disappeared so quickly she didn't even see Madras move. "First two are being drained and cleaned. Take the third on the right."

Io hastened to the assigned room and closed the metal door behind her. She slid the lock over with a solid click, and then listened. Except for the dull gurgle of water in the pipes and Wiry Madras's sharp voice penetrating through the walls, she couldn't hear much else. Io moved to the tub, turned the water on halfway and waited, as the pipes rattled and the spout spit, until a small steady stream poured out.

Io took out her phone, dialed a number, and waited. Usually, Surrett picked up her calls in two rings. This time, it rang for ten minutes. That should have been her first inkling that something was wrong. The person that answered was definitely not her contact.

"Io." It was a man with a thick Slavic accent.

"I need to speak with the minister."

"You need only speak with me."

"And you are?"

"What happened at the ambush site?"

"That was an unforeseen complication with my host. However, I fulfilled my part of the bargain to Shura. My cover is at risk. I need to come in."

"Your vessel has inconvenienced me greatly. She allowed the Adonis and his people to escape."

"I can fix this. I am with them right now. I can lead you right to them."

"Are you still in Surat?"

One of the pipes began to rattle again, crescendoing until it sounded like someone was banging a hammer on it.

Ella's body jerked and then the phone fell out of her hand. She reached down to pick it up and then suddenly lost control.

"Huh," Ella yawned. "What's going on? What am I doing here?"

She looked down and saw the phone, and froze. Slowly, she picked it up and brought it to her ear. "Hello?"

"Io," a man said. "Can you hear me? Io? Repeat the location of the Adonis."

"Who is this?" Ella asked.

"What do you mean... I see. I am speaking with the vessel now."

Ella, tell the person on the other line you are at Wiry Madras's Bath House. Just do it. I will explain everything later.

"You're the Genjix," she said softly. "Io was about to give away our location."

"Listen, girl," the voice said. "All you have to do is give me Cameron Tan and I will make you wealthier than you can possibly imagine. What do you say? Work with the Genjix and I will make all your dreams come true."

"You know what I want?" asked Ella.

"Of course. You desire what every other human in this world wants. You want to escape the slum, to never worry about going hungry or cold ever again. You desire power and riches? I can give all that to you."

Ella pulled the phone away and stared. Finally, she spoke. "I want my amma back, you son of a bitch."

No!

She put both hands on the phone, gritted her teeth and strained until it bent. A crack appeared down the middle and then it snapped in two. She threw the two pieces into the bath.

"Can you give me that?" she spat as the two pieces sank to the bottom of the tub.

What have you done?

Ella was about to storm out of the room when she saw the steam rise from the water and the locked door. She sniffed herself and decided she might as well take advantage of this.

She swung a leg at a time inside and slowly sank into the near scalding water until only her head was above the water's surface.

"What I did, Io, is prevent you from betraying the Prophus anymore. Let me ask you: have you always been full of crap or is this a recent development?"

Why do you care what side I am on?

"Because my amma died. Because you lied to me. Because I actually like the Prophus people."

The Genjix can offer you wealth and stability and power. Would you give all that up just because you like them? You hardly know them.

"Why do you want to be Genjix then?" Ella shot back.

There was a long silence before Io finally spoke. *They are offering me something that has eluded me ever since I came to this planet.*

"What's that?"

To do something important, to be someone important again. I used to be a highly respected Quasing, admired for my position and knowledge. Ever since we came to this wretched planet, I have been marginalized, made inconsequential while others of lesser skill prospered.

The Genjix offer me a chance to reclaim my position. They are creating something big, important, something that needs my knowledge. They need me to succeed. It will change the world. I will finally leave my mark and save my people like I was supposed to when we crashed.

"What is it? What are you supposed to do?"

I will not tell you unless you join the Genjix.

"OK, I'll join the Genjix. What is it?"

You cannot lie to me, Ella. I will know when you are actually ready. Until then, I will do everything in my power to support them.

"Wait, let me get this straight." Ella spoke aloud as she organized her thoughts. "You are unhappy with the Prophus and with Earth because you're not very good at anything anyone cares about on this planet?"

Well, not in so many words.

"And because of this, you think defecting to your enemy is going to make a difference? That it's worth killing other Prophus? Did you kill Emily on purpose?"

That was unintentional. I had already defected by the time Emily came to India. She was tracking someone she believed responsible for her friend's death almost ten years ago. The trail led her here. I tried to dissuade her from coming, but she would not listen. The two situations were unrelated originally.

"Originally?"

Like I said, things got complicated.

Ella waved her hands. "Did she want to join the Genjix? Was she complicit in switching sides so you could feel good about yourself?"

No, she was not.

"Then what do you think was going to happen once she found out what you planned to do? You didn't care if she died, did you? She was your friend and you signed her death warrant, you awful, terrible, disgusting monster!" Ella emphasized her words by raising a fist in the air and smashing it down on the water's surface, making a mess of the room.

Something in Io snapped. What little patience she had left evaporated, and her desperation blended with her frustration and anger. Whatever emotional concoction it produced was only exacerbated by the pressure of the defection and by the fact she had been so close to her goals so many times, only to have fallen short by some unforeseen circumstance.

STOP TALKING!

Ella froze.

You think you know what is right or wrong? You think you know everything? Well, yes, Emily probably would have had to die, and it is tragic those other Prophus agents had to die and maybe Cameron and his team may have to die, but you know what? Living things on Earth die. It is what happens.

I have roamed this planet since the dinosaurs. I watched them become extinct. I have been in fish and apes and cats and rodents. I have been in everything, thousands of creatures, and they all died. A human's life is not even a drop of the Eternal Sea, so stop acting like life is some precious gift from a higher power. Death is not some tragic occurrence that must be prevented at all costs. Everything dies, Ella. Everything is expendable.

I have lived this cycle again and again and again. I have tried to follow what I felt was right and I cannot do it anymore because none of it makes a difference. I refuse to continue this futile existence. I am going to join the Genjix and I am going to break this cycle. You can either help me willingly, and I will guarantee your safety and a long life and all the wealth you can imagine, or you can oppose me. It will not matter, because I will find a way in the end with or without your help.

Ella stood up abruptly. "Not if I tell the Prophus about you being a traitor first. You'll never get to join the Genjix then!"

No, you will not.

"Yes, I will!"

And here is why. If you tell them, they will do whatever it takes to stop me from defecting. The only way to do that is to either imprison me or to kill me. The only way they can do that is to inflict the same punishment on you. Even your friends the noble Prophus will lock you up or strangle you just to get to me. What do you think about that?

Ella was stunned. "They wouldn't."

They would. They will, so you will listen to me very carefully, Ella Patel. You will not tell the Prophus anything, because the moment you do, your life is forfeit. It will be over, and you will see how truly cheap a life is. The best case scenario is they will throw you into a maximum security prison and you will never see the light of day. The worst case scenario is they will lock you in a room without any means of escape, and then kill us both. It is in your best interest, in our best interest, for you to keep our little secret.

"Gahh!" Ella smashed the water again with her fists. "I hate you!"

Fortunately, that is irrelevant.

There was a banging on the door. "Black Cat, what is all that noise?" Wiry Madras said through the door. "The entire building can hear you scream. You better not be up to no good."

"Hey, what's going on?" Another voice, Cameron's this time, joined Wiry Madras's. "Ella, are you OK? I'm going to break the door down."

"You better not hurt my door," Wiry Madras barked back.

So what will it be? Keep our little secret, or risk death and imprisonment? The choice is yours, stupid girl. Choose wisely, because it will affect you for the rest of your short insignificant life.

CHAPTER THIRTY-FIVE
At the Doorstep

I almost stayed in the shallow waters of the swamps forever. The truth is, I tried to. However, the contentment I had felt with living in ignorance no longer satisfied me once I discovered that the rest of the Quasing were out there. After two hundred years, I rejoined human society.

By now, the New World was on the verge of becoming its own country, but little else had changed. The Prophus and Genjix were still waging a shadow war, using humans as proxies. I rejoined the Prophus and once again attempted to make my own mark on history.

After her bitter and exhausting argument with Io, Ella decided the best way to avoid talking or hearing from her Quasing was to be unconscious. She hadn't had a lot of rest the previous night anyway, having stayed up with Nabin until the end of his watch. She dragged her weary but now clean and refreshed body back to their room to try to get a few more hours of sleep.

Fortunately, Lam and Jax were up now, so it was a little less cramped. In fact, since Cameron was on the roof keeping watch, the cot was free. Ella made a beeline for it. Before she lay down, she remembered what that damn alien could do while she was passed out. She took out a rag and began to tie her left wrist to the rusty metal frame of the cot.

Is this really necessary?

"Damn right it is."

After she was satisfied that the knot was good and tight, she settled down to sleep. It wasn't the most comfortable position, lying with one arm hanging next to the headboard, but she didn't have much choice. Ella shifted a few times until she found the least uncomfortable position and was soon fast asleep.

No sooner had she closed her eyes, she woke with a start and found herself sharing the bed with two others. Actually, it was more like Nabin had moved her against the wall so Nabin and Dana could sit on the cot. The rest of the team was sitting in a tight circle on the floor of the room, whispering fiercely amongst themselves.

Awake again?

Ella yanked her right arm and noticed that she was still tied to the bed frame.

Are you really going to tie yourself to something every time you sleep for the rest of your life?

"You don't have permission to control me when I sleep anymore."

She shifted and began to work on the tight knot. Nabin's eyes flickered to her wrist and then he turned his attention back to the group. She liked that he didn't pry.

The conversation the team was having was getting heated. Harsh words were being hissed and they were talking over each other so much she couldn't quite make out what they were saying. Most of the anger, however, seemed directed at Cameron.

Ella was about to speak when she decided to keep her mouth shut and figure out what was going on.

You know, I have been listening. You can just ask me. Just because we are on opposite sides does not mean we cannot be civil.

"I hope you die in a fire."

If I get burned, so do you. You know that, right?

"Just go away."

Well, I intend to be mature about things. If you must know, Cameron just ordered his team to continue onto their destination to Sydney, Australia, for their vacation.

"That sounds nice of him. What's the problem?"

He is not planning on going with them.

"This is all off-book," Cameron was saying. "And a personal matter."

"Those were Genjix," Nabin said. "That makes it Prophus business."

"We have no support, no supplies, no backup."

"That's why this isn't the time to go rogue, Cam," said Lam. "As your auxiliary, I go where you go."

"As Lam's Pilates partner, I go where she goes," added Dana.

"As Dana's ex-boyfriend," said Jax, "I go..."

"All right, all right." Cameron threw his arms up. "I get the point. Wait, you guys dated?"

"For like eight months," Nabin said. "How did you not know?"

"That's not the... We're getting off track. Damn it, guys, we have no mission here, and that's that. I'm giving you a direct order."

Jax scanned the faces of the rest of the team, leaned back against the wall, and gave Cameron the middle finger. "With all due respect. Sir."

"Is this really how you want to spend your downtime?" Cameron asked. "Chasing my ghosts?"

"Oh, I'm still taking my downtime," said Jax. "You're just going to reschedule it for us after the Tanzania assignment. Besides, there's the issue of payback for Dubs."

There was a chorus of "yays" and "damn rights" from the team.

Cameron sighed. "You're a bunch of magnificent loyal

bastards. All right, fine, you insubordinates get to stay. Now to business. This asshole here is our main objective." Cameron took out his phone and projected an image onto the wall. To her surprise, Ella recognized who it was. "This is Minister Surrett Kapoor, newly elected deputy minister of Gujurat, and a Genjix operative. He's also an absolute piece of garbage and our target."

The blood drained out of Ella's face as Cameron laid out what they were trying to do. If she had thought she was already in way over her head before, she was definitely out of her depth now. These guys here were talking about assassinating not only a public official, but someone expected to be the future prime minister of India. Not only that, his mother had been one of Ella's favorite actresses growing up.

Really?

"I used to try to do my hair like her, and now I'm working with people trying to kill her son."

"Any questions?" Cameron said when he was done.

Ella raised her hand. "I don't understand."

Cameron looked in her direction. "Is that you, Ella, or Io?"

She nodded. "It's me. Why is offing Surrett Kapoor the main objective? I thought you were focusing on this construction site."

Cameron grimaced. "Like I said earlier, this is a personal thing. As for the Genjix site, that's going to require a lot more manpower than us five. Command doesn't know enough about it to make a move. The Genjix have been disrupting satellite surveillance, and we haven't been able to get any intel from the ground because of our operatives getting killed as soon as they arrive. India is leaning Genjix, and any major operation could reignite the war, so we have to be damn sure we know what we're doing before we act."

"But I've been sending..." Ella stopped.

Be quiet.

"Io, what happened to all the scouting stuff I did? You kept it from them! You asshole! I worked really hard to take those pictures and videos." Ella's blood boiled.

Did you actually think I was going to send any useful data up to Command?

"I hate you."

"First things first," Cameron said. "We lost most of our stuff to the ambush. What's our current situation?"

"Well," Lam ticked off points on her fingers. "Like you said, limited weapons and ammo from what we carried on our persons, currencies only in Euros and US dollars, which probably means we'll draw attention wherever we spend it, no live satellite up-link since we left all that crap in the trunk."

"We do have a Penetra scanner," Dana piped up.

"Hooray," Cameron said, not sounding very enthusiastic.

Jax raised his hand. "I dropped my duffel during the fight. I have no spare clothes."

"Me neither," said Nabin.

"Anyone else?" asked Cameron.

Everyone raised their hands. The mood in the room grew somber.

"Resupplying is our first priority then," said Cameron. He pointed at Jax. "You're responsible for getting us fed. Lam, get us hooked up with Command again. Find a way to get a computer that is compatible with our crypto keys. Dana, you're on contingency extraction. Find us a way out of here once all hell breaks loose."

"What about me, sir?" Nabin asked.

Cameron grinned. "You have the most important job. You and Ella take care of supplies and clothing. Especially clothing. I want fresh underwear by tonight or someone's getting guard duty every night until I do. Lam and I made a list."

Nabin grinned. "I do have the best style."

Dana bounced a piece of paper off his head.

He turned to Ella. "Guess you're stuck with me."

A little smile crept across Ella's face.

"Sir," Lam asked. "What about weapons and ammo? We're pretty dry."

"That's my job," Cameron replied. "We're close to the old front line between Pakistan and India, and there are half a dozen abandoned military bases nearby. Someone has to be entrepreneurial enough to be selling them on the black market. I'll try to tap into that."

Ella raised her hand. "I know all the big Crate Town dealers. Also, Manish, my trainer, is a former operative. He has some old gear stashed away."

Old is an understatement. Most of it is probably from the 1980s.

"Bullets are bullets, right? It's not like they're expired fruit."

You have so much to learn.

"I guess I'm with you two for the day then." Cameron stood up. "Report back here by 1800. Let's get it done, people."

In the next several hours, Ella became a damn rock star in Crate Town. Cameron and Nabin were two strangers in a foreign place with hardly anything more than the shirts on their backs. They needed a ton of supplies and had seemingly endless funds. Word spread across the markets that the Black Cat was buying, and all the merchants swarmed to her.

However, information was a commodity in the slums, and two military foreigners throwing money around definitely warranted interest. It wouldn't take long for news about them to fall into the hands of the wrong people, so the two men used Ella as their intermediary for all the negotiations in order to keep their identities hidden.

Ella had Cameron and Nabin covered from head to toe in wraps and wearing sunglasses. She kept them hidden nearby as she walked the market and shops to carry out the transactions. She would take a list of the things they needed, find the right merchant and then return to confirm the price.

Not only was Ella able to help them obtain clean underwear, toothpaste, battery packs, vodka, and something called Rice Krispy treats, but Cameron was in too much of a hurry to haggle.

This setup offered her enormous bargaining power, and she was able to skim off the top from both sides. She charged five percent from Cameron for making the purchase, and three from the merchants as a kickback. By midafternoon, she had made enough not to have to work for the next year.

What did I tell you about embezzling from the Prophus?

"What do you care if I steal from them, you Genjix-loving alien? Besides, I consider this a transaction fee for my services."

It is just really bad form. Besides, if you get caught, it will spell more trouble for me.

"So is setting your own people up to get murdered. We all have our vices."

Merchants were offering Ella favors and bribes just so she would buy from them. Everyone who had ever offered her a piece of candy or bread when she was beggaring now appeared along Ella's path in the market to remind her of their kindness. Everyone who had ever waved a stick at her when she was thieving was practically throwing treats and money her way.

"Ella, my dearest friend," Ghanash cried out. "I have the freshest fruits picked from the trees just this morning."

"Health to you, Ms Patel," Yunni waved her over. "Spices, dried fish and DVD players. Pirated movies from the latest blockbusters, as well as exotics that will get you arrested."

"Ooh." Nabin took a few steps toward him. "It's pretty long lonely days. I wonder–"

"Focus, A-D-D." Cameron yanked him back by the collar. He turned to Ella. "You're really popular."

"Just a woman of the people." She didn't bother trying to hide her smugness.

Within a few hours, they had crossed off most of the items on their list. Right now, Ella was neck-deep in negotiations with all three of the Fabs on a supply of miscellaneous military gear, including night-vision goggles, body armor plates, bolt cutters, tourniquets and a host of other replacement items for those Cameron's team had lost during their flight from the factory. To her surprise, one of the few things Cameron and Nabin insisted on was a supply of water bladders.

Readily available water is crucial for any operative.

"What's the big deal? When I lived on the streets, I'd go for an entire day without a drop of water."

You also are not a hundred-kilogram man lugging half his weight in armor in thirty-eight degrees.

The big negotiating stumbling block was a weird little box with a handle attached to it called a frequency visualizer. Ella didn't know what it did, but both Nabin and Cameron seemed to value it. The Fabs had no idea what the thing was either, but they noticed Nabin and Cameron studying it and jacked up the price.

The two men, their bodies and faces still covered, were leaning on the wall at the back of the gallery while Ella and mainly Little Fab screamed at each other about the astronomical prices that they were demanding for this stupid piece of tech. Of course it would be the greedy Fabs that finally threw out a number that made Cameron balk.

"I could buy an entire cluster building to house this thing for the price you're asking," she yelled. "Or better yet, we can just run operations from a five-star hotel."

"Go ahead and run it blind then," Fab replied. "You're not going to find anyone else in Crate Town with this baby."

"You don't even know what this baby is."

"We don't need to know what it does," Little Fab replied. "All we need to know is your people want it. Look, this is the lowest we'll go. Stop wasting our time. You want it or not?"

Nabin waved her over and whispered. "We want the

frequency visualizer, but the price is too high. If they can't be reasonable, we're done here."

"What do you expect me to do? I can't make them lower their price."

"I thought they were your friends."

"The only friend the Fabs have is money."

Cameron got up and left the gallery. He stopped just outside, looked back at the three Fabs, and spoke in surprisingly decent Hindi. "I don't appreciate being ripped off. You can keep your other substandard crap as well." He signaled to Nabin and Ella. "Let's go."

"Wait," Ella said, but it was too late. She cursed under her breath at the prearranged three percent commission she was about to lose with the Fabs on this particularly large transaction.

Nabin followed Cameron out of the art gallery. Ella froze, unsure if she should leave or not. She wanted to chase after Cameron and tell him to at least get the smaller items. As much as she hated to admit it, only the Fabs had most of this sort of gear in one place. Sure, she could source from several of the other fences but it would be time consuming and a total pain in the ass.

Little Fab turned to her. "Ella, you know we're the only shop in town with this stuff, and you know we'll keep our mouths shut. Have your people see reason."

"Who are you to talk?" she said. "You're asking for the price of an entire cluster building for that stupid metal box. You're all unreasonable jerks."

"He's not going to find another," Little Fab warned.

"Because no one else around here needs it," she snapped back. "Who are you going to sell this to? The street rat gangs? The Pakistani gangsters?" The two of them came face to face and scowled.

Cameron stuck his head inside the gallery. "Coming, Ella?"

She stuck a finger in his face. "I'll remember this, Little Fab."

"You're been threatening me for years now," he shrugged. "I doubt–"

Big Fab, to everyone's surprise, held up his hand. He rarely spoke during negotiations, preferring to let his sons do the talking. For the first two years they did business, he had never uttered one word to Ella. She had just thought him a mute. Big Fab looked at the pile of gear they had negotiated earlier and then waved to Cameron to come back in.

Ella stepped in front of Big Fab's line of sight and crossed her arms. "You speak to me only, Big Fab."

Little Fab was about to say something when Big Fab waved him off. The senior of the Fabs stared Ella down. She had had dozens of these faceoffs over the years with him, and she had always been the first to crack. Not this time.

He finally spoke first. "You're such a pain in the ass, Black Cat. Now, get out of the way." He looked at Cameron and switched to English. "Come in, young man."

That threw Ella off. "Does everyone speak everyone else's language behind my back?"

Cameron took one step into the gallery, and crossed his arms. "I guess we didn't need a translator after all."

Big Fab laughed. "Is that what you think she was doing? Come, let us speak as businessmen. Please, I like to be face to face with the people I negotiate with."

Cameron looked at Ella, who shrugged. He pulled his headscarf down to his neck. "All right, let's make a deal."

Big Fab gave him a small bow. "You need this gear and it's taking up badly-needed space in my warehouse. Tell me, what are you going to do with it?"

Cameron crossed his arms. "That's my business. None of yours."

"It's my business too, if you're doing it in my backyard." Big Fab looked at Ella. "The girl's been spying on that construction site lately. Are you going to do something about that place?"

"How did you know?" Ella said.

Big Fab shook his head. "You're not as sneaky as you think, Black Cat. Everyone knows." Ella's face turned red. Big Fab crossed his arms and stared Cameron down. "You tell me you're going up against those assholes building the site and I'll give you a fair price."

"As long as my money is good, what do you care what I do with the gear?" said Cameron, guardedly.

Big Fab shrugged. "Usually I don't, but that gods-forsaken site is eating up my Crate Town and no one can do anything to stop them. Besides, they roughed up my monk and have made life hard for everyone."

Cameron hesitated, and then nodded. "I'm operating in that area, and what's a fair price?"

The final price Big Fab offered was still outrageous, but it wasn't outrageous enough that Cameron didn't accept it. The two men finally shook.

"If you happen to come across that turd minister Kapoor and drown him in the ocean," Big Fab said as they were leaving, "bring the gear back and I'll give you a full refund. As a reward."

"Refund as a reward? What an asshole," Nabin muttered under his breath.

"That's how we do business here," Ella said. "Welcome to Crate Town."

The three of them decided to call it a day and head back to Wiry Madras. They had obtained most of the supplies on the list, and Ella had sent word through to Manish about providing some guns and ammo. Her coach had sent Aarav to say he'd come by later tonight to work out the details. All in all, it had been a productive day.

As they were strolling back toward the bathhouse, a little boy who lived across the street from her cluster ran up to them. "Ella, Ella."

She signaled for Cameron and Nabin to pause, and knelt in front of the seven year-old. "What is it, Abdul?"

"I've been looking all over for you. Appa sent me to find you. The man, the one who is in those big pictures, went to your place last night."

She frowned. "Who?"

The boy pointed at one of the posters behind her.

"The deputy minister? At my place?"

He nodded vigorously, his eyes wide. "He came with Inspector Manu and a bunch of his police, and then they shot someone."

Gunshots? In her home? Who could it be? Had Hamilton been there for some reason? She had disappeared on him for the past two days. Io had told her not to say anything. Maybe he was searching for her. Did he get caught by the Genjix? This was all her fault. Was his blood on her hands?

Ella, face pale, turned to Nabin. "I need to go home." She took off running.

"Wait, Ella," Nabin called out. A few seconds later, he caught up to her and spun her around.

"Let go of me," she hissed.

"Someone could still be there."

"He's right," Cameron said, catching up a moment later. "Once we know the coast is clear, we'll go up, all right? For now, we take our time and don't draw any attention."

Ella nodded reluctantly. They joined the steady flow of traffic toward her cluster. The way back to her home looked just like it did every other day. Half-naked children played in the streets, old women cooked over fires, men smoked pipes and sorted through salvage. Several shot wary glances at the two strangers wrapped up like mummies and their gazes trailed after them.

Everything looked normal, but her gut was telling her something was off. It wasn't until they reached the base of the cluster that she realized what was bothering her. Those folks, her neighbors, weren't staring at Cameron and Nabin; they were staring at her.

Ella's stomach twisted into knots. She stopped at the base of the stairs leading up to her container and drew the long knife from its sheath. Immediately, both men drew their pistols as well.

The walk up the four flights of stairs was excruciating as the three of them crawled up the steps one at a time. Each time they went up two steps, Cameron and Nabin maneuvered into position so they covered each other. It wasn't until they neared the top stair that she realized that her fears weren't unfounded. Right as they came around the last turn, she saw her door ajar.

"Oh no."

Ella, no. Do not rush in.

Afraid to find Hamilton's body inside, she crept forward. Nabin put a hand on her shoulder and shook his head. "They may still be there. Let Cameron and me clear it first."

"You're right." She gripped the long knife in her hand. "If they're here, I'm going to gut them. Let's go."

"No. Stay here."

"But–"

"Stay here."

"If I'm missing anything, Io, I'm going to kill you."

Your stash should be the least of your worries.

Reluctantly, Ella watched as Cameron and Nabin disappeared inside her home. She hoped she hadn't left her clothes lying about. Or the trash. How embarrassing. Fortunately, whoever had busted into her place seemed to be long gone. A few seconds later, Nabin appeared and waved her in.

Ella dashed into her home and realized that all her fears about Nabin finding her underwear and dirty clothes and laundry were completely unfounded, because whoever had broken in had completely ransacked the place. Everything was destroyed. The inside of her home now resembled a landfill. What little furniture she had had was overturned, clothing was strewn all over the place, and what few electronics she owned were smashed. They had even slashed her little mattress to shreds.

She went into her bedroom and gasped. The hidden panel had been removed. She rushed over and pawed the darkness inside. There was nothing inside. Her cash, her music CDs, her few official documents, the picture of her mother. All gone.

Ella fell to her knees and stared into the darkness. Her entire life was in there; her past as well. She was now truly a nobody, a nothing. She might as well not exist anymore. What did Amma look like? The only picture Ella had of her now was in her head. She fought the tears welling in her eyes.

An image of the picture flashed into Ella's head.

I remember, Ella. And because of that, you will never forget.

Cameron walked up behind her. "I'm sorry this happened. I'm sorry I brought this down upon you. Did anyone else live here?"

"No," she sniffed. "It was just me and... No, no."

Ella got up and dashed out of her home. She ran around to the side of the container, and stared. A trail of blood smeared the ground leading to Burglar Alarm's nest. She took two hesitant steps forward, and saw a patch of fur hidden in the far back corner. Ella went onto all fours and crawled inside. She found Burglar Alarm sprawled out, laying on her side. There was red everywhere. Dried blood streaked down the side of her head. In the center just above the eyes, was a single gunshot wound.

This time, Ella didn't bother holding back her grief.

CHAPTER THIRTY-SIX
A Lead

I finally made my mark on the world in the summer of 1842 when I inhabited a three year-old boy named George in a place called Ohio. He was my first attempt at joining with a human at such an early age, and will likely go down in history as my most significant achievement. I originally feared I had once again chosen the wrong host when George attended West Point and graduated last in his class. He also held one of the worst conduct records in the academy's history.

As fortune would have it, the Civil War broke out and provided George with a clean slate. He enjoyed an up-and-down career, but survived the war as a major general. Afterward, he continued serving on the frontier, most notably in the American Indian War. George died at the Battle of Little Bighorn, which is now better known by his name, Custer's Last Stand.

Ella didn't know what happened after she found Burglar Alarm. Everything was a blur, like a bad dream. She remembered traces and flashing images. The trail of dried blood streaking across the ground. The dog's broken and bloodied body in her nest. The sticky fur as Ella cradled Burglar Alarm in her lap. She heard sobs and the cries of "sorry" over and over and over again, not recognizing her own voice.

She felt Nabin's hairy arms wrap around her waist, dragging

her away. She remembered letting go and saying goodbye, telling her best friend in the entire world that she loved her. She just never realized how much until it was too late.

Cameron and Nabin had bundled her up and practically carried her like a baby back to the bath house. Nabin tucked her in the cot in the back room where she passed out in between fits of tears. She still had enough presence of mind to tell him to tie her arm to the bed frame before she fell asleep.

Honestly, Ella. That is not necessary. I promise I will not do anything. If it means anything, I am sorry about your friend. I have inhabited dogs in the past. I know–

"Go to hell, Io!"

When Ella woke up a few hours later, she felt even more drained. She never realized that bawling her eyes out was such exhausting work.

Her mind wandered back to the mangy brown and black mutt, her tail wagging every time Ella came home. She remembered all the times Burglar Alarm would nuzzle her and just beg for a morsel or to have her ears scratched. Ella would shy away, because the dog was caked in mud or covered with ticks and fleas. Now, all she wanted to do was throw her arms around her friend, fleas or no fleas.

There was something about death that put everything in perspective. Ella didn't have many friends in the world, and now there was one less.

Now Burglar Alarm was gone.

Ella wiped the fresh tears streaking down her cheeks and looked around the room. Thank gods she was alone. She peered out the only window in the room. It was dark outside.

It is just before midnight.

"I wasted the whole night."

Ella sat up and nearly fell off the bed. She looked at her arm tied to the bed frame. She began to pick at it. "Damn, that Nabin ties a tight knot."

"Need help?"

Ella looked up and saw Cameron at the door. A blade appeared in his hand as if by magic and with a quick flick, she was free. As quickly as it appeared, the blade was gone again.

She stared. "Teach me that."

"What?"

"That thing you do with the knife."

Cameron pulled his sleeves back and showed her a flesh-colored band on his forearm. He jerked his wrist up and the blade appeared. He made another motion and it retracted.

"That is so cool," she said.

"You want one?" he grinned. "We'll see what we can do about getting one your size." He held up the rag. "Let me guess. You just found out she can control you while you're unconscious and you're not happy with it."

Watch what you say carefully.

Ella huffed. "My alien does not have permission to control my body. Ever."

He nodded. "I went through that phase with Tao during puberty, but my Quasing is pretty good with controlling a human body, so knots don't work on him."

"Sucks to be you."

He chuckled. "Actually, Tao and I have a really good working relationship. He's been with me for as long as I remember. He's as much a part of me as this." He held up a hand and wiggled it. "I'm sure in time, you and Io will come to an understanding."

"Not a chance," she grumbled.

"It wasn't always that way." Cameron sat down on the bed next to her and tapped the side of his head with a finger. "When I was a teen, I chafed like hell against this third parent in my head. Once, we were hunting a Genjix operative in Oregon. I was scouting the forest line when I found her camp. Tao ordered me to go back and get Dad, but I wanted to prove how much of a man I was. After all, she was an unarmed little elderly woman, kind of reminded me of my nai nai. I thought I could take her no sweat."

"What happened?"

Cameron chuckled. "Do you know what kendo is?"

"No."

It is a Japanese style of sword fighting.

"Well, she was really good at it. She found a branch, disarmed me, and then busted my noggin. She kept me hostage for three days."

Ella's eyes widened. "Three days? What happened?"

"She got away, but not before she took all my savings out of the bank. I was saving for a new video game console."

"Wow, she robbed you too?"

Cameron chuckled. "Damn straight she did. Not only that, that mean grandma slapped me around for intel and put me to work digging latrine ditches. While traveling, she kept me on a loose leash, blindfolded and wrists tightly bound, and used me as a pack mule. Told me if I escaped, I would die by myself this deep in the forest. That grandma knew how to tie a knot." He picked up a pebble and threw it at the opposite wall. "Tao knew about this Genjix and warned me, but I didn't listen. Moral of the story is, as much as we think they're up in our business, Tao and Io and most Quasing have been around for a long time, and mostly they're looking out for us because they're looking out for themselves, and the two usually go hand-in-hand."

Ella scowled. "So you're saying I should just let Io boss me around?"

"Nah. You should still be you, and do what you think is right. However, just realize that life isn't always black and white. There's a lot more nuance to everything than we know."

"I guess," she grumbled.

"Anyway, I wanted to check up on how you're doing."

"That asshole minister shot my dog," she said, the hot rage

returning in a flash. Fresh tears welled up in her eyes. "I'm going to kill him."

"Yeah, well, get in line," Cameron said. "That asshole minister also got three of my friends killed." He grimaced. "Four. I'm pinning Dubs's death on him too."

The two sat in silence. Ella stared at the wall, the image of Burglar Alarm seared into her brain. "He's also a Genjix, right?"

"And there is that."

"Then maybe we should do something about him."

Cameron nodded. That's what I came in here to talk to you about. Have you been to that construction site they're building? The one that got our other people killed?"

She nodded "I recor–"

Ella, do not tell him about your surveillance work. If he looks and cannot locate the data you supposedly sent to Command, he will become suspicious. Remember the consequences if they think we are Genjix.

She hesitated. "I know the site really well."

"Can you show me?"

"Sure. When?"

He looked out the window. "It's pretty dark outside. Moon's hidden by cloud cover. How about now?"

Ella had been intent on staying in bed and wallowing until hunger drove her out, but revenge was also a worthwhile pick-me-up. "Let me get dressed and strap on my knives."

"Need a gun?"

"No guns in Crate Town."

"Suit yourself, I'm bringing two."

"Hey, Cameron," she called, as he was leaving.

He looked back. "Yes?"

"How did you escape the mean old grandma?"

"First chance I had to run, Tao made me take it. I covered over twenty kilometers blindfolded with my wrists bound, with forty kilos of supplies strapped to my back."

"How did you do that?"

"Tao memorized every step we took and backtracked." Cameron smiled and then left the room.

"Now, that is a super power," Ella whispered to herself.

The takeaway from his story is we should work together.

"The takeaway from this story is Tao helps Cameron to do the right things while you try to trick me into doing the wrong things."

Like he said, things are not so black and white.

"Your friends killed my dog, you jerk!"

I am sure that is an unfortunate–

"Don't you even say it," Ella snapped. Fists clenched, she unrolled her stash of weapons and decided to vent her fury toward arming up for her outing. She took the first knife and jammed it into its sheath.

Fifteen minutes and sixteen knives later, Ella led Cameron down the dark streets of Crate Town. The slum at night was an entirely different beast than it was during the day. It was at the same time quiet and active. The tension from the recent riots and the increased police presence had quelled the usual nightlife.

It was replaced by something else. Now, drums of loud footsteps, marching almost, filled the air. It had to be now-regular patrols. No criminal worth her salt would make so much noise walking at night. Luckily, these plodding half-wits were fairly easy to avoid.

Unless they are carrying a Penetra scanner.

Ella avoided the few pockets of life and led Cameron down narrow alleys that seemed to meander around poorly laid out container clusters, sometimes forcing him to squeeze between misaligned containers or go underground through sewers. To her surprise, Cameron didn't bat an eye as they crept through ankle-high sewage.

They reached the southwestern end of the construction site by midnight and slowly made their way north around the perimeter. Along the way, she pointed out specific buildings and locations she thought important, like the main administration building, the power station, the desalination facility, and the weird domed building with the needle top in the center. She never figured out what that was for.

"Do you know by chance, Io?"

That I will not tell you.

They continued to the part of the site that used to be the Dumas neighborhood. By now, most of the buildings and clusters had been demolished or torn down. There were still stacks of containers and piles of rubble being cleared, but it little resembled the thriving community that had once been here.

Through Cameron's night-vision binoculars, she showed him the storage warehouse for the raw supplies, where the foundation for another large structure was being dug, and the pipeline that was being laid out across its entire length.

"I have no idea what they're building," Cameron said. "Tao thinks the design layout of that cluster over there looks like Quasing housing facilities, but that would mean they plan on housing hundreds of thousands of them in there. Why?"

"I thought these aliens couldn't survive outside of living creatures," she said.

"It's a recent development," he replied. "Twenty-five years ago, the Genjix figured out how to replicate the environment on their home planet, their Eternal Sea – basically this gooey liquid that they could survive in without a host.

"That has allowed them to start reproducing. Until then, they were slowly going extinct. Unfortunately for them, the newborn Quasing are barely sentient, because they learn either by millions of years of experience or by osmosis. Back on their home planet, their Eternal Sea housed trillions of them, so the newborns were able to learn and develop quickly." He frowned. "Could this be what they're doing? Trying to educate newborn Quasing through large osmosis tanks?"

"I have no idea what you're talking about," Ella said.

"It doesn't matter." Cameron shook his head. "Tao said doing something like that would still require hundreds of years, and several thousand older Quasing to help distribute that information. So what is it for?"

"Does it matter? I thought we were just trying to stick a sharp object into the minister and bleed him out."

"So vicious," Cameron murmured. He looked at the docks to their right. "That area is lit up like a Christmas tree. It's too risky. Let's call it a night. Thanks for the tour."

"Anytime," Ella said.

"Know a place around here we can get a drink at this hour?"

Ella checked the streets. "Yeah, I know a place that never closes, although I'm not sure how happy they'll be to see me."

"Caused some trouble at that establishment?"

"Something like that."

Ten minutes later, they reached the Cage. The bar was packed even at this hour, although the clientele reflected the types of people who would still be up at this time of night. A low rumble of voices and unintelligible conversations underlined the Indian hard rock filtering through the pipes. It was surprisingly quiet in here considering the crowd.

Wary eyes glanced at them as they walked in. No police or suspicious-looking foreigners, mostly locals. There was a group of union guys sitting in the corner. They'd been on everyone's shit list since they started doing the minister's dirty work clearing out some of the residences, but they had been quiet lately.

"Rough-looking bunch," said Cameron.

"The Cage is popular. This is where a lot of folks in Crate Town conduct business. It's a good place to get a job and catch the latest gossip."

Congee, the bartender and owner, scowled when he saw her. He folded his arms and puffed up his chest, as if daring her to order a drink. She didn't blame him for being pissed. The last time she had stepped foot in his bar, she had lobbed half a dozen smoke grenades and nearly caused a riot. Ella threw on her widest, most plastic smile, worked up her courage, and strolled up to the counter.

"Hey Congee, two apongs please," she said, in her politest, sweetest voice. She dug out the rupees to pay for it and laid the bills neatly on the counter.

Congee gave her the stinkeye and placed the drinks on the counter. He didn't remove his hands from the cups. She took out two thousand extra rupees and slid them forward. Still, he didn't move his hand. Another thousand didn't do the trick.

"Oh, come on," she said. "You knew things were going down. I paid you well in advance and gave you a bonus afterward."

"You didn't say you were going to set my establishment on fire. It took two weeks to get rid of the smoke."

Grumbling, she reached into her pocket to grab more money. Even then, it did not seem to satisfy Congee. Finally though, he let go of the cups. Ella handed one to Cameron and took a loud gulp of her apong before Congee could change his mind and take it back, then she beat a hasty retreat.

They found a table in the far back. Cameron had them change seats so she could have a better view of the floor in case she noticed someone suspicious. It also hid most of his face from the crowd, although she had assured him that it didn't matter. Chances were, the majority of the people in this room also had warrants out for their arrest.

"Do you?" he asked.

"Nah," she said. "Too smart to get caught."

Except for Manu.

"He doesn't count. That was a private transaction gone bad."

Cameron raised the cup. "To the mission, and to your best friend."

Ella's eyes almost watered. Almost. She raised her cup. "To Burglar Alarm."

Cameron made a face as he sipped the drink and blew out. He smacked his lips. "Interesting. It's sweet and spicy at the same time, and has quite a kick."

"I tried your American food once. Let me tell you something. It was the most–"

A dark blob approached from the corner of her eye. Ella pulled away, her hand reaching for her knife. She twisted and stabbed with it until the blade poked into a large soft belly, just short of cutting into skin. Little Fab's eyes widened and he dropped his mug of beer. He slowly raised his hand.

"Don't sneak up on me!" she snapped at the fence.

Little Fab looked down at his wet shoes. "You owe me a wash on these shoes, Ella. You almost owed me a wash on these pants, too. Why are you so jumpy?"

The knife went back into its sheath. "Look around. Shouldn't everyone be?"

"Probably right." He looked at Cameron and nodded. Cameron nodded back. Little Fab jabbed a thumb at a corner at the other end of the room. "I have an associate who wishes to speak business."

Ella looked at the figure behind the draped booth. She couldn't make out the silhouette. "Who is it and what does he want with us?"

"Not you, Ella. I told her your friend is the one with the money. You're just a little errand girl."

Ella ground her teeth.

Cameron held up a hand and spoke in Hindi. "Sorry, Little Fab, Ella's a partner. If your associate wants to speak with me, she needs to clear it with Ella first."

It was a very small gesture on Cameron's part, but it meant the world to her. She stuck out her chin at Little Fab and waited.

The fence shrugged. "Suit yourself." He gestured toward the

booth. "Go see her. I'll keep your friend company for now."

Ella stood up and Little Fab took her seat. She glanced back once and then headed toward the back booth. It was dark in there save a small candle off to the side. She passed through the beaded curtain and slid into a seat. It took her a few seconds to recognize the person sitting across from her.

Mogg, the union boss, raised an eyebrow. "Black Cat."

"Big boss," Ella replied.

"I thought I was supposed to speak to that man over there, not his pet."

"Well, you speak to me first, and then I decide if you speak to him."

Mogg smirked. "Little Ella, always making deals. Word on the street is you have some strangers interested in the site."

"How do you know?" Ella asked, stunned. "Did the Fabs sell me out?"

"Of course not, girl," Mogg said. "It's not hard to figure out. You prowled the site for weeks. My boys saw you. I told them to lay off. Told them you weren't causing any trouble. So you prowl, and later on you appear with these foreigners buying all sorts of gear. Now the police move in all heavy and make everyone's life uncomfortable. It's not hard to figure out, girl."

"Aren't you working for the minister?" Ella asked.

"Was," Mogg groused. "We had a deal. Sold them the docks for stupid money and a good labor agreement. They paid us well for a couple of months, but now they've brought in the military. Told all my boys this morning we're out of a job."

Ella shrugged. "What did you expect? You saw what they did to Faiz. Besides, you're not going to get a lot of sympathy from me. The minister used you to bully everyone in Crate Town."

"Poor Faiz," Mogg said. "Fool cleared out of town the second he could pack his bags. Cried about how that foreigner maimed his cousin. I told him, that's why you don't hire your relatives to be your bodyguards. That's the whole point of having a bodyguard." She shook her head. "Amateur."

"What are you going to do next?"

The union boss shrugged. "Probably nothing. The government has the docks all for their own use now. Most of commercial shipping moving north to Hazira. Already another union there. Maybe we go to Mumbai." Her face darkened. "My boys are pissed. I'm pissed. Thinking about setting up a good old-fashioned strike and shutting the place down."

"What do you want from us?"

Mogg took a sip. "Isn't it obvious? Half my guys helped unload and move tons of their supplies and the other half helped put up the buildings. They kicked us out and brought in specialists once the walls went up. The union looks out for its own any way we can. My people still have family to support, mouths to feed. Way I see it, you didn't prowl in the shit all those days for nothing. You're aiming to hit it somehow. I got the information you want."

"How much you asking?"

Mogg looked over to the side. "If your friend is the money guy, why don't I negotiate with him directly. Did I pass your screening, Black Cat?"

Ella nodded and stood up. She jabbed a finger in the woman's face. "Don't rip him off, or you'll hear from me, Mogg." She paused. "I also want five points for the hookup."

"Three, and it's coming from your man."

"Two, and it's coming from you."

Mogg laughed. "Go fetch him."

Ella walked back to the table where Cameron and Little Fabs seemed to be debating cricket. There were six empty cups on the table. The parts of Cameron's face not hidden by the headscarf were glowing red. He saw the look of concern on her face and held up his hand. "I'm fine. Asian genes. Is the meeting legit?"

"No," she replied, "but you should hear her out anyway."

Cameron drained the cup in his hand and stood up. "I'll be back soon. Keep my seat warm."

"How did it go?" Little Fab asked when she sat down. "Your boy going to buy her information?"

"What do you care?"

"Mogg is giving me five points on the sale."

Ella cursed. Ripped off again.

He always seems to get the better deal. Maybe the problem is you, not me.

"Can't trust anyone anymore these days, can you?" Ella said aloud.

He shrugged. "Can't blame them. From what I hear, the union was getting paid double rates or something."

"Serves them right," she grumbled. "Turning on Crate Town like that."

"I have some business to discuss with you as well." Little Fab took out a piece of folded paper and slid it across the table.

"Wow, you are a busy little broker tonight, Little Fab."

Ella unfolded it. On the left side was a black and white picture of Cameron that looked a few years old. On the right was a hand-drawn picture that was approximately what he looked like now. On the bottom, though, was the real attention-getter. It was the prize money for information leading to his capture.

"Dangerous fugitive for a hundred million rupees." She whistled. "That's hefty. I thought the Fabs prided themselves on keeping their mouths shut."

"Every man has a price. For a hundred million, we'll leak," Little Fab said. "How do you feel about making some money? I'll go in half with you."

Ella frowned. "Even if I wanted to do this, why do I need you? Why can't I just report them myself and keep all of it?"

Are you seriously entertaining this? Why is it he can make you sell out, but I cannot?

"Of course I am not serious, Io. At least I don't think I am..."

"Because..." Little Fab said, taking out another piece of folded paper and sliding it forward. On it was a picture of Ella that she honestly didn't think looked anything like her.

"Twenty thousand rupees?" she exclaimed. "That's insulting."

"Yeah, I've seen lost dogs get bigger rewards than that." He looked back toward the booth. "Keep the posters as a souvenir. Let me know if you're in. We'll work something out. I can make all the arrangements and keep you out of it. We split it halves and be done with all this. Besides, it'll take all this heat off Crate Town's back. Consider it a public service."

Ella stared after Little Fab as he left the Cage. She sipped her apong and stared out into nothing. She had never been on a wanted poster before. It sort of made her feel special, important, and all of a sudden, very vulnerable. She was known by enough people that it could be a problem, and twenty thousand rupees was honestly nothing to sneeze at. It was just enough that several people in the slum could turn her in. She didn't even think the government knew she existed until now. But still, only twenty thousand when Cameron was worth a hundred million? It made her angry and spiteful that they thought she was so cheap.

Cameron returned a few minutes later. "That was an interesting conversation. What do you have there?"

Ella folded the poster and tucked it into her shirt. "Nothing. You guys work something out?"

He nodded. "Mogg wants you to pick up some prints first thing tomorrow. If I like what I see, we'll buy the rest."

"Great. Where to next?"

"Back to the bath house. We have a ton of work to do."

CHAPTER THIRTY-SEVEN
Siege

George Armstrong Custer was my first and only taste of success, and even he was at best a moderate one. His end came poorly and with controversy, but he was my first host to avoid being forgotten by history. I now knew what other Quasing felt when they had a hand in guiding humanity. It was exhilarating. It had taken me more than eight hundred years to make my first mark, and now I wanted more.

I returned to Europe at the turn of the twentieth century, reinvigorated and eager not only to help the Prophus unwind the trap of political knots the Genjix had woven among the nations, but to seek glory and find success in another host.

The complicated alliances that the Genjix had woven leading up to the Great War were a cascade of disasters waiting to unfold. The first domino piece to fall started with the assassination of Franz Ferdinand, the Archduke of Prussia, incidentally also the host of Baji, the current Keeper of the Prophus.

To Surrett's credit, he delivered. The 13 PARA Special Forces battalion had rolled into Surat the day after the failed ambush. The morning after that, Lieutenant Colonel Kloos, the battalion commander, had met with Rurik. Fifteen minutes later, he was sent to Shura's office to deal with the details.

Of course he was.

Shura studied Kloos as he walked into the room and bowed. "Praise to the Holy Ones."

"Praise to the Holy Ones. Have a seat, colonel."

Kloos sat down. "If I may, Adonis, it is an honor working alongside the Scalpel. Your achievements in the Middle East and Sweden are celebrated among the unblessed. If you ever do form your own cadre, you would have many volunteers. I would be the first." He paused. "If you would have–"

Shura cut him off. "Spare me the pandering rhetoric."

Easy there.

Tabs was right. She was laying the dismissive tone on a bit too strong. She softened, just slightly. "I find private teams wasteful. I prefer subject matter expertise with every assignment as opposed to trying to force resources to adapt to different elements. The only benefit is individual loyalty to a commander, and loyalty is overrated when it comes to a vessel. It only pertains to the Holy Ones and to our standings."

"Of course," Kloos replied stiffly.

I believe he was expecting another answer from you, one more effusive.

"I would think less of him if he thinks that way."

"Tell me, colonel," she said aloud. "You've reviewed the mission objectives with Rurik?"

Kloos nodded. "Four hundred para supported by a thousand police should be sufficient to complete the objective. Crate Town is dense, but as long as we contain the perimeter, it is only a matter of time, Adonis."

"What do you think of his plan?"

Kloos's facial expression remained unchanged. He spoke after a small hesitation, in a measured tone. "The population of Crate Town is unknown. Estimates range anywhere from two hundred thousand to half a million people in an approximately six square kilometer area. There are three major roads leading out of the slum and five kilometers of perimeter to patrol, the rest bordering the water. The crux of the strategy will be wholly dependent on two factors: first, containment of the slum, which will be difficult. Second, the temperament of the residents in Crate Town."

"Very astute, colonel," she said, "but that isn't what I asked. If I wanted a briefing on the logistics, I could have just looked at the same data. What are your thoughts on the tactical strategy? You and I must work closely, so speak frankly."

"Risky," he admitted. "A door-to-door search may prove problematic considering the population density. The slum is already on edge after the riots over Dumas. The checkpoints that were put up this morning might push tensions to spill over. However, the Adonis has made it clear that the capture of the Prophus Adonis is the primary objective. We do have a limited but sufficient number of Penetra scanners to conduct a thorough search."

That is an accurate assessment.

"You have reservations, though," stated Shura.

"If I may," Kloos said. "I have some recommendations I'd like to offer the Adonis. I believe it will assist us greatly not only in locating the Prophus team hidden in Crate Town, but in mitigating the tension of the local populace." He pointed at the map of the region on her desk. "Crate Town is divided in a way we can section off–"

Shura held up her hand. "I don't need to hear it." She stood up and walked to the window. "Tell me, colonel, does Rurik know who you are?"

"I introduced myself to the Adonis as soon as I arrived."

"So he met you, gave you your orders, and then shuttled you off to me."

"That is correct."

She checked the time. "Let me guess. You two met at the pool while he was swimming laps?"

"That is correct."

Shura turned and stared Kloos down. To his credit, he didn't flinch.

You always err on the side of being overly dramatic.

"Lieutenant Colonel Mayur Kloos," she began. "Decorated with the Maha Vir Chakra for service during the Iranian offensive, a Sarvottam Yudh Seva for the operational evacuation of the Mumbai province, and twice-honored with the Sena Medal for bravery under fire. You are the fifth-highest ranking Genjix operative in the Indian military and the highest still fighting in the field. And you managed all this while outwardly fighting on the wrong side."

"I wish I could have fought directly for the Holy Ones."

She shrugged. "It's easy to point in a direction and fire a gun. It takes skill and finesse to serve the Holy Ones behind enemy lines, and still have the enemy give you medals for it. For the Genjix, you were responsible for assassinating General Pratik Patel and General Gokul Avninder, the latter a Prophus vessel. You were vital in crushing the Myanmar resistance two days after the enemy had swept in and retaken Thailand. You bought enough time for our Chinese forces to establish a new front line to stem our losses."

"You've read my entire file."

"Your mother was a politician in India, your father a business mogul. Both were very successful and influential in the government and in business, yet you enlisted under a pseudonym. You are beloved by the majority of your men, with a reputation for being tough yet fair, and you have slowly nurtured a fanaticism for the Special Forces that are sympathetic to the Genjix cause.

"The hierarchy is also in the midst of maneuvering a promotion for you to colonel that will hand you command of the entire Para branch. You are also on several shortlists to become a vessel for several high-ranking Holy Ones once India joins the Genjix." She paused. "Is that in your file as well?"

Kloos looked thoughtful. "No, no, it is not."

Shura went back to her seat and leaned forward. "I do

know all about you, Colonel Kloos. I would never accept you into my cadre because I believe you are destined for greater things for the Holy Ones than simply carrying out my commands. So…" She put her hand on the map and slid it off to the side. "Here's my advice to you. Adonis Rurik is trying to establish his credentials in the field. I suggest you follow his orders to the letter."

Kloos nodded. "And if I don't, Adonis?"

"Your choices will be remembered, colonel, by someone who makes a point to know names and deeds and loyalties. Or perhaps by someone who doesn't, who only cares about achieving personal goals. Change is coming to India. Good officers will be needed to rule. Officers who are vessels to be elevated to positions of power and influence in order to best serve the Holy Ones."

"I see." Kloos stood up and bowed. "I beg your leave, but I have much to do over the next few days. Adonis Rurik has ordered the perimeter of the slum reinforced by tonight. He wants to start conducting Penetra sweeps within the next two days. I need to review his tactical plan and see if there are any necessary modifications. I believe, however, his plan is fundamentally sound."

"You have my leave, colonel. Good hunting."

CHAPTER THIRTY-EIGHT
A Plan

It is difficult for lightning to strike twice. I joined the Great War on the side of France, and went through thirty-two hosts within those four years, fighting in the brutal and ugly trenches in Belgium. I did not have the time or the ability to lead any of those men to success. They all died too quickly.

At the time, the Genjix had orchestrated the stalemate in the trenches, and the Prophus were trying to break that stalemate in either direction. We failed, and in doing so, allowed the Genjix to dictate the pace of the war and bog it down into a futile conflict. Their purpose was to continue the fighting at all costs, and they succeeded, dragging it on for four long years.

"This is the map of the entire site. It's a lot of ground to cover, but really, the only thing that's important is this building here, here, this one only on Thursdays, and whatever the hell this one here is."

Cameron had spent five minutes the next day looking over Mogg's sample of intel before deciding to pull the trigger on buying all that she had to offer for a cool one million rupees.

It was a princely sum to Ella, but the man did not bat an eye. They quickly completed the transaction, and before she knew it, they had months of construction blueprints, maps, manifests, power grid layouts, project plans, supply inventories, sewage system, etc... everything.

No wonder the Genjix wanted to replace the union as soon as possible. Mogg and her boys were definitely doing some extracurricular work at the site. Maybe they were planning on robbing the facility in the future or selling this information, as they had to Cameron. In any case, the data here was worth every rupee.

It also told Ella that she had been getting paid far too little. These Prophus had deeper pockets than she thought possible. She definitely needed to ask for a raise.

You do not even know the meaning of deep pockets. The Genjix–

"I'm asking for a raise, not selling my soul."

Right now, the team was huddled around several maps of Crate Town, Surat, the Gulf of Khambhat, and the construction site. They had spent most of the day replenishing the rest of their supplies, having to get creative with some of their resources.

For one thing, both Dana and Lam were wearing men's fatigues, so everything fit loosely. Jax, who looked like he should have been playing basketball instead of being a soldier, was wearing pants that exposed his ankles. Nabin had had to roll his pants up.

Other than that, they were able to source most of the hardware they needed. The team complained that things weren't as high-tech as they were used to, but they didn't seem to mind too much. They'd worked with worse, they joked, although Dana compared the surveillance gear they got from the Fabs to antiques.

The only thing they were short on was ammunition. Manish and Aarav were supposed to take care of that. It seemed the coach had a small armory stashed away in the basement of his gym.

"How did you come by all this?" Nabin asked. "I mean, you two were only gone for a few hours last night."

Cameron pointed at Ella. "The samrājñ⊠ of Crate Town

here has all the hookups."

Ella preened.

"All right," Cameron continued. "Teams of two. Dana and Nabin cover the southern perimeter. That's where the administrative building is located as well the primary facility. Jax and Lam take the heavy construction zone in the middle. That's where the buildings that look like Quasing housing vats and the power stations are located. Ella and I will cover the docks. If we put the two hosts together, it keeps everyone else invisible to Penetra scanners.

"We're looking for Surrett Kapoor's routine. The union boss said the minister has a pretty set routine and spends most of his days on-site making sure the trains run on schedule. We want to lock down his exact location and take him out.

"The Genjix may be using this facility as their primary headquarters. The union boss said a lot of foreigners are currently living in several of the completed buildings on the south end. Now that we have blueprints, we need better intel on the security on site: patrol schedules, patterns, unit strengths, all that. From what we can tell as of right now, it's just cops and guards."

Lam tapped the largest building on the map. "This central building, what are they calling it?"

"The Bio Com Array," said Cameron.

Lam put a rock on it and the administrative building. "Whatever they're building, this Bio Comm Array is a big deal. If the opportunity arises, we should try to gather intel to bring back to the Prophus. I have a feeling we're going to need to be back here sooner rather than later, either to blow it up or take it over. In any case, the more we know, the better."

"Satellites can't pull anything?" Jax said.

She shook her head. "I contacted Command last night. Complete black zone. They have the entire region cloaked from satellite somehow. The Prophus are talking about sending a spy plane overhead, but that's risky."

"Dana, how do we get out of Dodge once we assassinate a major public figure and are wanted fugitives?"

Dana ticked off each point with her finger. "Planes, trains, and automobiles are all off the table. Airports and major roads have heavy checkpoints and the gulf is teeming with coastguards." She grinned. "However, there's one direction they don't have carefully guarded."

"What's that?" Jax asked.

"Upriver." She pointed at the map. "The Tapi is a major transport hub. We get a boat, sneak upstream to a rural area, then have the Prophus send in an extraction team to pick us up."

"Clever," Lam said. "What about–"

Wiry Madras appeared at the doorway. Lam quickly slid all the maps underneath the cot. The old woman rolled her eyes. "You've paid for my silence. Besides, if you're going to hit that monstrosity out west, I'd almost help out. That stupid site has been nothing but trouble for Crate Town."

"Can we help you?" Lam asked.

"You have a visitor." The old woman stepped to the side and Hamilton walked in.

"Hamilton!" Ella exclaimed. She bounded to him and gave him a hug. She was genuinely happy to see him. Mainly because she had thought the Genjix had killed him that day, but also because she was sorry for how poorly she had treated him.

"Um, hello Ella." He looked decidedly uncomfortable and patted her head a few times.

"Don't ever pet my head like that again," she snapped, before she remembered to be nice to him. "How did you find us?"

Lam raised her hand. "I went to a cyber cafe and called the wakeup service. An analyst named Wyatt patched me through to the auxiliary here. He got us the computer equipment we needed."

"If I may," Hamilton said, saluting. "It's an absolute pleasure and honor to work with you, Commander. If there's anything I can do to support these operations, please put me to good use."

"He never said that to me," Ella grumbled.

That's because you are the opposite of a pleasure to work with.

Ella had a sharp retort at the tip of her tongue, but she stopped. It was true. She had been a brat to her auxiliary ever since they met. She should do something about that. Ella tapped him on the shoulder. "Hey Hamilton, may I speak with you?"

He followed her out the door. "What is it, Ella?"

"I just wanted to say sorry for being such a jerk. It's this stupid alien. Io's been driving me crazy."

Sure, blame me for your faults.

"It's quite all right," Hamilton said. "I've heard that the transition for a host can be traumatic. That's why auxiliaries have extensive preparedness training in the event the tragedy occurs."

She pursed her lips. "Just so you know, I don't plan on dying anytime soon."

"Of course not, that wasn't what–"

There was a knock on the back door leading to the alley. Ella's first reaction was to throw her arms in the air.

Really?

Everyone in the other room filed out, weapons drawn. Dana moved to the door and, with one hand holding her pistol, placed the other on the handle. There was a brief pause followed by two more knocks. The pattern repeated three times. Dana nodded and pulled the sliding door open. To Ella's surprise, Manish and Aarav walked in carrying a long crate.

The old coach looked amused at everyone in the room pointing guns at him. "I guess we came to the right place. I got the ammo you asked for. We have three more crates outside. It was a bitch to haul over. Since when did they set up checkpoints into Crate Town?"

"How bad is it?" asked Lam.

"One at every major street," said Aarav. "It's causing awful traffic."

Hamilton raised his hand. "I had to pass through one on the way in. It took two hours. It wasn't this bad yesterday."

"How did you smuggle this gear through?" asked Nabin.

Manish shrugged. "They weren't looking for contraband. They had Penetra scanners."

A terrible realization passed through the group. Cameron frowned. "The slum isn't small. There's no way they can blockade every intersection."

"There aren't that many ways out," said Ella. "Half of Crate Town borders water and the other half was walled up back when the city tried to prevent the slums from growing."

Cameron walked over to the table. "Nabin, what's the range of Penetra scanners these days?"

"Top of the line can go two hundred meters. Most only fifty to a hundred, and can detect through anything that isn't denser than lead. Buildings and other electronics will dampen its range somewhat."

"All these places to hide and nowhere to hide," Cameron muttered. "Still, that's a lot of ground for them to cover. We should be safe here."

The Genjix are closing in, Ella. These Prophus are as good as dead. Now is your last chance. Slip out the door while they are all distracted. If you come with me to the Genjix, I can guarantee your safety. They may even reward you.

But this game wasn't just about survival. Doing the right thing was an intangible currency that Ella had to factor into her decision. And these people here, they were good people. They were fighting the same people she should be fighting. Also, if she joined the Genjix, what would her amma and Burglar Alarm and Bijan and everyone else think of her in the afterlife? They would be so disappointed. She knew she would feel ashamed.

Ella planted her butt into the chair. "That's my final answer. Don't ever suggest that to me again, alien."

Stubborn fool.

Wiry Madras barged into their dining area, huffing and puffing. "The police are doing a door-to-door search of the entire slum. Several patrols have clashed with the local population and riots have broken out. One of them is two blocks down."

"So that's their plan," said Cameron. "Madam Madras, do you have a place we can hide? A hidden room or attic?"

She nodded. "I dug a hole underneath the building. I hide my opium there. It will cost you though."

"Sure, whatever." He signaled to the door. "Bring the rest of the ammo in and stow our supplies there."

"Cam, the Penetra scanners will detect you anyway," said Lam.

"I know," Cameron replied. "I'm going to lead them away."

"We should go with you."

He shook his head. "It'll be easier evading the patrols and scanners with as few bodies as possible. Stay with our supplies. Maintain radio contact. I'll ping if things get bad." He yanked Ella out of the chair so hard she almost fell. "You're with me. Hurry, gear up. We need to run!"

CHAPTER THIRTY-NINE
Flight

After the Great War, I stayed in France. I was determined to be involved on the world stage. I leveraged my host's position as an aid to Marshal Philippe Pétain and persuaded the French Minister of War, André Maginot, who was also a Prophus host, to build a series of defensive forts along the eastern border of France.

These fortresses, nearly sixty total, would become known as the Maginot Line. When World War II broke out, I was eager to test my designs and make my mark on the world once more. As history will tell you, it was an unmitigated disaster.

Six weeks later, France fell and my host committed suicide. For some reason, suicide has afflicted many of my hosts. I fled Europe and returned to the safety of the United States, where I had found success nearly a hundred years prior. I intended to make one last attempt to leave my mark on history.

Ella barely had time to throw on some clothes and sheathe a couple of knives before Cameron practically picked her up and carried her out the back door. No sooner had they exited to the back alley, he nudged her to his right. "Crash course. You're right-handed, right?"

She nodded. "Manish trained me to be ambidextrous. I can throw knives–"

"Whatever. Listen, I want you to stay two steps behind me at all times to my right, so you can tell me where to go and throw your knives. If we get jumped, stay safe while I take care of it. And, hmm, are you sure you don't want a gun?" He put his hand on his pistol at his waist.

She shook her head. "I'll probably end up accidentally shooting you. Besides, no guns in Crate Town."

"Why is that?" he exclaimed. "That's ridiculous in our line of work. Anyway, talk about that later. We have to go."

He pulled out the electronic device she recognized as the thing he and Fab had haggled aggressively over. Cameron fiddled with its controls and then turned it on. At first, Ella saw nothing, and then she saw different colors floating all around them. Layers of yellows, reds, and green lights, some thin lines, others blobs covering an entire wall. A few blue and purple colors were undulating waves that passed right over her head. It was very pretty, but almost blinding.

Cameron punched a few more buttons on the console and then looked around the alley. Nothing changed. He tapped the console with his fingers and then, visibly frustrated, tapped its side. He pulled an earpiece out of his front pocket and hooked it on. "Nabin, you read this? The visualizer. I can't read it. It's in Indonesian or something. No, Tao can't read it. He doesn't know every language in existence. He's not a universal translator."

While he was talking, Ella saw purple squiggly marks shoot out of the earpiece and into the bathhouse wall. A similar purple mark would shoot back moments later. Her curiosity was interrupted by a crowd shouting at the end of the alley near the main street.

"Um, I think we should get going. You can play with your toy later."

He brushed her aside. "Third dial? I'm twisting it. Nothing is happening. Oh wait, that third dial. Come on, I read left to right."

The riot of colors surrounding them faded one by one until

the alleyway was completely dark again. Ella took two steps to the other end of the alley, which led to a residential section of the slum when Cameron grabbed her arm. He shook his head and held up a finger.

"Don't move until I'm done. This is important." He returned to his conversation. "Well, I see nothing now. Which color did you assign to the Penetra frequency? Custom setting? Wait, brown? I don't care if all the other frequencies have defaults. I can't see brown. Everything in this dump is brown. How do I change it?"

A cone of light flickered down the alley from the main street. A few more joined it and waved up and down along the walls. Ella tapped Cameron once more and pointed frantically. This time he noticed, and they ran down the alley.

Where will you go? The Genjix have Penetra scanners. There is no place to hide.

"Hush, alien. This is Crate Town. There is always a place to hide."

It was so dark that Ella could barely tell open space from container wall, but she had run these streets thousands of times. They ran across streets, down narrow alleys, and into tiny wedges that Cameron had trouble slipping through, all while moving toward the quiet, away from the noise and screams and footsteps of the soldiers.

A few times, they got turned around and had to backtrack away from suspicious figures or sounds. Once, she miscalculated the side alley and nearly stumbled into a clash between a group of neighborhood residents and soldiers. Another time, the police nearly ran them over as they chased one of the street rat gangs directly into them. Three of the police had broken off their pursuit of the kids and come after them when Cameron pulled her behind a set of tents. That was bad for the officers. The Adonis made short work of them.

Ella and Cameron continued running through the maze of Crate Town for two more hours, hopping along roofs and going through the hallways of some of the larger clusters. By now, it was closer to dawn than not, and she was beginning to tire. Cameron still seemed as alert as ever, and he half-carried her through the broken, twisty streets. Along the way, they passed by angry women wielding clubs and scared men guarding their homes. Children peeked from behind curtains and doors. Ella could not remember a time when Crate Town was so on edge.

He finally came to a stop in a small opening in the middle of an alley where three clusters formed a fissure. "Ten minutes." He took out his flask and handed it to her. Ella gulped the water and would have emptied the flask if he hadn't taken it away from her. "Sharing is caring," he muttered.

"What?"

"Never mind. Something my dad used to say to me when he wanted a slice of my pizza." He looked down both sides of the alley and leaned against the wall. She didn't realize how exhausted he was until she saw his face and his slumped shoulders. He closed his eyes. "Wake me up in ten."

Just like that, Cameron was asleep. He was even snoring, softly, but loud enough in this dead silence to make her worry. She reached out to pinch his nose and squawked when his eyes opened and he grabbed her wrist.

"You're snoring up a storm," she said. "You'll give us away. How did you do that anyway?"

"What?"

"Go from a snoring sleep to all killer robot."

"You need to learn how to leverage your Quasing better."

"Io?"

What do you care? Not like you listen to me anyway.

"My Quasing is pouting," she said.

I am not!

Cameron checked the time. "Nine minutes."

Ten seconds later, Ella could hear the soft, even snores hanging in the air again. She kicked off one of her sandals and rubbed her sore feet, and then checked the soles of her shoes. They were worn nearly through. She'd need to visit that Italian shoemaker at the end of Rubber Market. Technically, he wasn't a shoemaker, just a retired soldier who made a living cutting up old tires and using the treads to make sandals. Now that she thought about it, he wasn't even Italian. He was an Armenian or something.

Ella was putting on her second shoe when she noticed a small brown dot on the far wall. At first, she didn't think anything of it. It was probably a smudge or a patch of dirt. Then it grew larger, and became a weird circular hump that expanded directly outward.

Was she seeing things? Ella wasn't quite sure. She was pretty tired. Maybe she was asleep already and was dreaming. Maybe her brain had finally broken from all this stress. Maybe this stupid alien in her head had melted whatever sanity she had left. But there it was; the brown thing grew again until it almost enveloped half the entire far wall. Ella stood up and took a hesitant step forward. She reached out with a finger to poke the expanding bubble.

"Ella, no!"

The warning came too late. No sooner had she poked the bubble, it expanded more until it encompassed her. She took several steps out of the bubble and looked at him. "What is this thing?" Cameron swept her up and carried her, running as far away from the bubble as possible. She looked back and saw the thing chase after them. "What in gods is going on?"

"Frequency visualizer." Cameron patted the device in one of his pockets as he continued to run. "Brown is tuned to the Penetra scanner frequencies. If that light ever catches up with us, that means we've fallen into the scanner's range."

They turned the corner, but the ever-expanding brown sphere seemed to be chasing them.

"Is it alive?" she said. "Because it looks like it's smart."

"They detected a host when you got in their range. They're just heading in our general direction."

"So what do we do?"

"We keep running."

The two began a new race through the Crate Town maze until they hit the northern waterline. Ella dragged Cameron west. By now, they were exhausted, and the brown sphere appeared to follow them regardless of which direction they went. Ella changed directions all of a sudden and dragged him through a series of interconnecting containers partially buried in the ground.

"What are these for?" Cameron asked.

"There is a pasture just to the southeast," she replied. "Livestock had to cross too much traffic to get there, so they linked these containers together and the animals crossed in underpasses."

She made several turns at the container tunnels, hoping to throw off this crazy brown blob chasing them, although she knew that really didn't make sense. As long as she continued west, she knew she was running away from it. They reached a three-way intersection near the end of a long corridor. Directly ahead was a flow of sewage out into the gulf. The right turn was an exit onto the Tapi River beach.

Ella picked what she felt was the less disgusting route and turned right, and ran straight into a group of darkly-dressed men holding rifles.

"Uh-oh, wrong way," she said, pushing Cameron in the other direction. "Sewage system it is."

Cameron drew his pistol, but she pulled him away. "No guns in Crate Town."

"Why?"

No sooner had they turned the corner, the men opened fire. The echoes from the gunshots were ear-shattering, and the resulting soundwaves in such a tightly enclosed space knocked both of them to the ground. It took her a few seconds to get her wits about her, and she blinked away the ringing in her head. She looked up and saw Cameron, one hand holding a pistol, the other on his temple. She could hear groans coming from around the turn. She staggered to her feet and peeked over the side. Three of the six men were on the ground writhing in pain.

"Come on, let's go," she said.

"What?" Cameron tapped his ear.

She dragged him along toward the sewer system. They exited the tunnel a few seconds later, and she motioned for him to rest. Her hearing was slowly returning through the constant ringing.

"That's why there are no guns in Crate Town," she said. "You fire a gun in these metal cans, and that happens. Also, most of these containers are from the war, so they're bulletproof. Bullets ricochet like crazy. I once saw a bullet take out three men at the Cage. Those idiots must have fired fifty rounds between them. I bet half those bullets bounced right back into them."

"Point taken," Cameron said, putting his pistol away.

"Come on, that brown blob is still behind us."

Ella led him down to one of the main drains into the ocean. Cameron protested every step of the way, but the bubble did not follow them after they were approximately seventy meters in.

"That must be the range," he muttered. "That, or they don't want to follow us in here. Hell, I'd almost rather fight them than wade in here."

"No one knows the slum better than me," Ella grinned. "Who owns Crate Town? I do."

He scowled. "We're knee-deep in shit."

She shrugged. "You can wash off in the river, though it's probably not much cleaner. Come on, this way."

They reached Metal Mountain right before dawn. She brought him to one of the containers deeper inside, past dozens of others piled together haphazardly. Most of the containers were still intact, but some were crushed or cut up. Cameron began inspecting some of the container walls, and signaled for her to stop at a particular container that was tilted a little steeper than she was comfortable with.

"It levels out further down," she said.

He pointed at a faded marking of the letters "Pb" on the wall. "Most of the containers here are like the ones in Crate Town. This one has lead shielding. They were used during the war to cloak hosts from Penetra systems."

"Does that mean we're safe here?"

"Tao thinks so, or at least they'll have to be really close to detect us."

"Fine, we'll stop here. Even if they know we're here, they'll never figure out how to get to us." Shivering, Ella lay down on the ridged floor and huddled into a fetal position to stay warm. The inside of this metallic mountain was freezing and damp. The sun was rising, but it didn't make a difference so deep inside. Back when she had lived in here, she had survived by wrapping herself in half a dozen blankets. Neither of them had that now. It was going to be a miserable day.

Cameron came over and took off his jacket. He wrapped it over her shivering body and lay down next to her.

"What about you?" she asked.

He shrugged. "This isn't too bad. I don't mind."

It wasn't long, however, before even the tough guy in only a thin layer of thermal clothing began to shiver. Ella crawled a little closer to him and moved his jacket until it partially covered both of them.

"Thanks," he said.

"Sharing is caring."

The last thing Ella heard before falling asleep was Cameron's snores echoing throughout the entire mountain.

Tao opened Cameron's eyes and watched as Ella got to her feet and struggled to stand on the slippery ribbed surface of the container. The girl put a hand on the wall for balance and moved up the slanted floor one wobbly step at a time. After four or five steps, she slipped and lost her balance, and then slid backward, losing half her progress. This slow crawl continued until she neared the end of the container.

Tao sat up. "Going somewhere?"

Io looked back. "Tao, I am going to the surface. There are some things near the dock I want to verify. I have an idea that may prove useful. Do not mind me. Your host is exhausted and needs rest."

"You probably should not try to control Ella in here," said Tao. "Your control of her body is poor and this would not be a good place to have her fall and break something."

"No, I will be fine. I will be back soon." Io reinforced her words by slipping on the floor and falling to her knees. She slid halfway back down the container. She tried to stand again. This time, Tao reached out and put a hand on her shoulder.

"Do not break the girl's neck because of this foolishness, Io. Besides, the girl has made it clear she does not wish you to control her while she is unconscious."

A guttural sound crawled up Io's throat. "Mind your own business, Tao. She is also my host and my responsibility. I will decide how best to manage her."

Tao kept his grip on Io. "No, Io. No, you will not. Respect the girl's wishes and stay put."

"Or else what?"

Tao pulled out a plastic tie from Cameron's satchel and held it up.

Io's eyes flared. "You would not dare."

Tao smiled. "Let the girl rest. It will be a long day tomorrow for both of them."

She lay down on the cold metal floor. "You are preventing me from doing sensitive and necessary work, Tao."

Tao closed his eyes. "I am sure I am. Good night, Io."

CHAPTER FORTY
Scouting

Once back in the United States, I joined with a young Major Karl Bendetsen who worked on the administrative staff of the Judge Advocate General, one Major General Allen Guillion. We were tasked with protecting our growing Prophus presence in the United States against outside forces, especially the rising Genjix backed power of the Japanese Empire. It was then that Karl and I became the architects of Japanese-American Internment.

That was an even worse disaster than the Maginot Line. I still defend Karl to this day. Both our intentions were good, just misguided. Pearl Harbor had just shocked the country, and we reacted harshly and unfairly.

For most of the next day, Cameron and Ella laid low in Metal Mountain. The military had moved in during the middle of the night and set up a blockade surrounding the entire slum. What started out as a lockdown of the slum and a house-to-house search had escalated into a full-blown internment. Guards now wandered the markets, checkpoints were set up at all the major entrances, and guards with dogs patrolled the perimeter fence. Penetra scanner squads walked the streets at all times of the day.

They had even brought in the navy.

Ella and Cameron lay on their stomachs in a slanted crate facing the water and watched as the large vessel floated past.

"That's a big boat with really pointy guns," she said.

It is a ship. You might as well begin her operative training now, starting with proper terminology.

"They're ships, not boats," Cameron said next to her. "That one is a frigate, I think."

Another even larger ship passed. "Wow, that's an even bigger boat."

"I think that one is a destroyer? I'm not caught up on my naval terms."

Come on, Cameron. That one is the INS Kalam. *That ship saw heavy action in the Gulf of Aden. Twice crippled during the war. Would have been scrapped if the captain was not the vice admiral's son.*

Cameron relayed Tao's information.

"How does Tao know what boat it is and what it's done?" Ella asked.

It is a ship!

Cameron shrugged. "My Quasing enjoys reading after-action reports. He has the worst hobbies. What about Io? What does Io do for fun?"

"She enjoys framing me for treason."

I assume she is joking. If so, her delivery is on the dry side.

The girl was struggling as a host, which wasn't unusual, but it had to be even more frustrating for someone like Ella, who had been on her own from such an early age. It was an easy transition for Cameron. He couldn't remember a day in his life when he didn't have Tao. In fact, he would probably freak out if Tao disappeared from his life.

It is good to feel loved.

"Hah, more like I've been institutionalized."

Welcome to Tao Prison. The only escape is death.

"Speaking of dry delivery, that got morbid quick."

Ella sucked in her breath as an even bigger ship with even

more guns passed by. She turned to Cameron. "Are these all here for you? What did you do that makes them want to catch you so badly?" She paused. "You must have a big price on your head."

You broke the millions last time I checked. Congratulations, I could not be more proud.

He grinned. "Massive. I'm a seven-figure fugitive. Want to catch me and share the loot? Seventy to thirty?"

She made a face. "Awful split. I'll hold out for better. Besides–" she took out a folded piece of paper, "–this one wants to pay me a hundred million for you."

Cameron took the poster from her and grunted. "Old picture. I haven't looked that good in years. By the way, it's seven figures in Euros, not rupees."

Her eyes widened. "Gods, why do the Genjix want you so badly, anyway?"

"Tao and the leader of the Genjix, Zoras, go way back. They have had a long and glorious history of killing each other's hosts."

Cameron pulled her down as a smaller ship hugging the coastline passed by Metal Mountain. He checked the time and tapped the back of his wrist twice, and then the two of them retreated deeper and came out on the other side a few minutes later near ground level. They followed the waterline east until they reached civilization and then looped back south to walk the outer perimeter of the docks.

Ella had gone out by herself in the morning to the yarn market and purchased a secondhand oversized Hindu headscarf and some loose-fitting robes. Cameron's half-Asian eyes were a dead giveaway, but that wasn't anything a pair of sunglasses wouldn't fix. When forced to step out in public, he wore a pair of old Ray-Bans his father had given him, and Ella wore a pair of fake Chanels with one of the arms broken off and taped back on. Crate Town was multinational enough that few would give the odd couple a second look. Until the authorities started advertising the price on Cameron's head.

Dusk was settling over the slum, and most of the workers had left for the day. If the team planned to infiltrate the facility, now would be the right time. Their plans had not changed much even with all of Crate Town on lockdown. The way Cameron figured, it might even be easier, since the Genjix had to pay attention to a lot more real estate now. All they had to do was determine an insertion point, put a bullet in Surrett Kapoor and sneak out before any Genjix were the wiser.

And maybe take a look around that Bio Comm Array facility.

"If we have time."

Your priorities are upside down, do you know that?

"Yes, and in this case, I don't care."

Cameron and Ella climbed an eight-story container cluster half a block away from the site to get a better vantage point. Later on, if the opportunity presented itself, he was going to try a test run and break into the site to poke around.

As soon as they reached the roof and he scanned the grounds with binoculars, Cameron realized that something was very different. His luck had run out. The construction site was now crawling with military and police. Security had quadrupled overnight, and the place had transformed into a fortress.

"It looks a lot busier down there than normal," Ella said.

"That's an understatement," he muttered.

This is not good.

Cameron cursed. Was he too late? Had he blown his chance of nabbing Surrett? Ten more minutes of observation told him he probably had.

Check another location.

"Ella, can you take me further south to another safe spot?"

She nodded. They traveled six blocks south to where the old Dumas neighborhood bordered the original build site perimeter. If anything, security here was even denser. There were soldiers and checkpoints everywhere.

"Is that what I think it is?"

Air support. They have an attack helicopter.

Cameron radioed the rest of his team and received similar updates. He knew there was a possibility that the Genjix could have stepped up security because of his presence, but this was overkill. Perturbed, he decided to see if this was perhaps a temporary measure. He cut off the day's surveillance early and treated Ella, against her wishes, to some American food.

"This pizza is disgusting," she spat. "American food is the worst."

Cameron was inclined to agree. "This isn't good. I'm telling you, pizza is the best, but the folks here just don't know how to make it. Trust me, I'll take you back to the States one day and get you some deep dish or something. You'll love it."

Ella did not look convinced. "I feel like you're trying to pull one over me. I don't trust any of you Prophus when it comes to food. Why don't we try some Indian food? Your treat."

"Sure," Cameron grinned.

She dragged him through a crowded back street, between buildings and down a narrow passageway that could either have been a sewer or a road. The few times they had to cross a main street, she kept them huddled with large groups until they could break away. They saw at least six manned checkpoints along the way, but Ella knew the slum well enough to get them around everything, and the frequency visualizer he carried allowed them to steer clear of the two checkpoints that had Penetra scanners.

They reached a place she called the Ayurveda Alley, where she proceeded to scare the crap out of him with some of the more exotic Indian street food. Cameron had to admit, he wasn't as adventurous as his father, Roen, when it came to food, but he had been raised to always give everything a try. The hilsa eggs were... all right. The frog legs were... all right. The chutney that looked like ants made him spit when he found out they were actually ants. The tilli made him actually throw up.

Fortunately, one dish, the paya, was delicious, and he made up for the other dishes by eating three helpings of it. The entire time he was sampling the foods, Ella wore an ear-to-ear grin. He was pretty sure he was a victim of a prank, but the paya was worth it.

He patted his lower abdomen. "If I get some health problems tonight," he warned, as they left the alley, "you'll suffer as much as I will."

She laughed. "Just remember, we don't have anything to wipe with."

Cameron pulled a half-roll out of his pack and waved it in front of her. "A good operative never leaves home without it. That should be your first lesson in secret agent training."

"What's the plan for tomorrow, boss?" she asked, as they headed back to Metal Mountain.

Cameron sighed. "I want to go over the patrol schedule one more time, and then make a decision. But if the site is as hot as it was today, we might not have a choice. We may need to start looking at our exit strategy."

We need to discover what they are building here as well.

"I'm sure you'll figure something out," she said.

Cameron patted Ella's shoulder. "I love your eternal optimism."

"Optimism, my ass," she said. "I don't want you guys to leave without nailing that jerk who shot Burglar Alarm."

Her priorities are as off kilter as yours.

"I guess that's why we get along so well."

Unfortunately, the security on the site was just as busy as the previous day, if not worse. Cameron, feeling as if he had missed his window of opportunity, cursed as he hit up six separate locations and reached the same conclusion at every one. The entire Bio Comm Array site was completely locked down.

He radioed Lam. "Call the rest of the team. Meeting at the bar. Twenty-two hundred tonight."

"What's going on?" Ella asked.

Cameron looked west and sighed. "There's too much heat. We're aborting."

Congee's gaze followed Ella when she and Cameron walked into the Cage that night. She waved. He jutted his jaw out and squinted even harder. One of these days, he was going to forgive her. Not today.

He shook his finger, pointed upstairs, and then rapped the counter three times with his left fist. He turned away and was back to pouring drinks, her presence already forgotten.

As usual, Ella scanned the bar. It looked like all the regular patrons. It was probably suicide for police or military to be in here at this hour, especially after the ruckus they'd been causing in Crate Town. All three Fabs were conducting business in the corner. Little Fab acknowledged her with a nod, and she noticed Mogg holding court with a bunch of her crew in the opposite corner.

Ella grabbed Cameron by the wrist and led him through the crowd and upstairs to the second floor. They continued down a narrow hallway to the third set of doors on the left, which incidentally was the same room she had conned those Pakistani gangsters in. Something she hadn't gotten to capitalize on very much, by the way.

Are you still sore about that?

"Little Fab bragged to me about the final numbers. They made a killing. I got ripped off, thanks to you."

You had more important things to do than be a drug dealer.

"It's the principle of the matter."

She tried to enter the room, but it was locked. She banged her fist on the metal door. A sharp, high-pitched voice barked at her from the other side in a strange guttural language. Ella looked down both sides of the hallway. Did Congee send her to the wrong room? She banged on it again.

This time, the voice came back in Hindi. "Go away or I'll shoot your eye out, asshole!"

"Here, step aside." Cameron put his mouth near the door. "I'm looking for a Red Ryder carbine action model air rifle."

There was a sharp click, and the door swung open. Jax poked his head out and looked both ways. He ushered them in and closed the door behind them. He took a sniff and gagged. "Are you guys hiding in the sewers?"

"Unfortunately, yes," said Cameron.

Ella smelled her shoulder. "What's wrong?"

"Never mind."

Lam and Dana were sitting at a round table in the center of the room. A lone ceiling lamp served as their only source of light. Cameron put his ear to the wall and rapped it with his fist. "Is this place secure?" he asked.

"Not as secure as the bath house, but Wiry Madras won't let you and Ella back," said Dana. "She's scared to death they'll catch you and shut her establishment down."

"Don't blame her," said Cameron. He took out the frequency visualizer and placed it on the table. "Can you please check the walls for any brown signatures, Ella?"

Ella nodded and took up position near the back wall.

He looked around. "Where's Nabin?"

"We split up to cover more ground," said Dana. "He found something, and will catch up."

"We got some good intel," said Lam. She pulled up her tablet and showed him several files. They were a few clear stills of Surrett standing in front of the administration building, having a smoke on a second-floor balcony, lounging at a table in front of a container, and walking out of a small building on the shoreline. In all these pictures, he was alone and looked as if he hadn't slept in days.

"It's too bad we don't have a sniper rifle," said Jax. "I could take him out from five hundred meters and we'd never even need to step foot on the site."

"It's too bad we don't have a lot of things." Cameron turned to Dana. "What's Nabin's ETA?"

"He told me he was fifteen behind me half an hour ago. What's up, Commander?"

Ella's chest clenched when she heard those words. Had the Genjix or the police caught him? Was he dead? She was tempted to head downstairs and search for him. She resisted the urge to pace and planted her body against the wall.

"Get him back here ASAP. We're aborting," said Cameron.

"We're not going for the minister?" Dana asked.

"The site's too hot. I'm not risking my people on revenge."

"It's more than that," said Lam. "I looked this guy up. Surrett could be the linchpin to India going Genjix. They're saying he may be the next prime minister."

"Doesn't matter," said Cameron. "We get the hell out of here, call in the cavalry, and we do it right. Killing him isn't worth risking my team."

A few minutes later, Nabin banged on the door and rushed into the room, gasping for air. Immediately, the rest of the team drew their sidearms, ready to fight their way out.

"No," he huffed, in between deep breaths. "I wasn't being chased or followed. I think."

"Then what's wrong?" asked Jax.

Nabin held up a finger, and collapsed onto a chair. He took Lam's cup of water and drained it. Then he pulled out his tablet and slid it to the middle of the table. Dana picked it up and studied it. The color drained from her face. She passed it to Cameron, who passed it to Lam, who passed it to Jax. All of them looked stone-faced.

Ella got the tablet last and looked at the dozen pictures Nabin had taken. They were images of the building on the western edge of the site tucked behind the main Bio Comm Array facility. She enlarged the picture and saw three people walking in a line. They were being escorted by people wearing black clothing that looked more like suits than uniforms.

"What is this?" she asked.

"Prisoners," said Cameron, somberly. "That's K2. He's captain of the recon team that went missing."

"They're still alive?" said Ella.

Lam nodded. "At least some of them."

"His team scouted for my battalion in Finland. Good guy. Had an abnormal love for snow," said Jax.

"What does that mean then, Commander?" Lam asked.

Cameron's knuckles were white as he pressed them onto the table. He pounded a fist and shook his head. "I can't, I can't," he muttered over and over. "All right, this changes everything. I'm postponing your vacation again. We're getting our people back. The odds are looking impossible. Find a way to make it possible."

"That's a lot of guys with guns to get through," said Ella.

"Cameron doesn't leave anyone behind," replied Dana.

"Damn straight," added Lam. "None of us do."

"I want some ideas," said Cameron. "Pool the data and find a weakness. Let's get to work."

The group huddled over the map of the site. "The problem is there's something like a thousand soldiers now," said Nabin.

"What if we draw them away?" said Dana.

"Bomb threat?"

"Stage an attack on the docks?"

The ideas came fast and furious, and almost all of them involved destroying Crate Town in some way. Ella stood there and imagined what would happen to her slum if they collapsed a building or set a fire, or caused a power outage. All of these ideas would end with her people more hurt than the Genjix.

"What if we incited a protest?" Nabin said. "The people are pissed at the site as it is. Shouldn't be too difficult to rile them up."

Lam shook her head. "That takes a level of organization

and time we don't have."

Ella perked up. These guys may not have the organization and time, but she knew someone who did. "Cameron, do you still have boatloads of money?"

He looked wary. "I have access to funds, but it depends on how big the boat is."

"Actually," Dana said. "The Keeper got wind of your recent spending spree. She sent you a very strongly worded message demanding an explanation."

"Crap."

"She also says you have to cut up your Black Card."

"Over my dead body," he muttered.

"I think she said that too."

Ella stood up. "I'll be right back. I think I know someone who can help make some noise."

She left the room and ran downstairs, hoping the person with the time and organization was still carousing with her people. Luckily, Mogg was. It didn't take too much work to convince her, and soon a group of tough-looking dockworkers followed her back upstairs. They took position next to the door as Mogg came inside.

"The Black Cat says you want to give me more money," she said.

"Maybe. Depends on the price."

"Oh, I think it will be," she smiled. "We'll make it right."

Ella stood in the corner and watched as Mogg negotiated circles around Cameron. In the end, he got what he wanted. Mogg was going to walk away from this a wealthy woman, but at their order, she would gather the entire union and bark loud enough to draw attention to the gates of the Bio Comm Array.

"Is that going to be enough?" asked Jax after Mogg left. "I mean, she's got a couple thousand people, but she made it perfectly clear she's only staging a riot, and won't actually fight the military. A bunch of yelling can only get us so far."

"It's going to have to be," said Cameron. "Unless you have another idea."

"Actually," said Ella thoughtfully. "I might."

Cameron shook his head. "No, Ella, I'm tapped out. I don't have any more money to throw around."

"You won't need to. I'll be right back again."

Ella went back downstairs and found the Fabs where she had last seen them. They were in talks with Sodhi the textile importer. She nudged her way to their table.

"We're in a meeting," said Fab.

"This is bigger." Ella slapped a thousand rupees into Sodhi's hand. "Go buy yourself a drink. I just need a moment."

The textile merchant was about to protest, then thought better of it. Ella waited until he was out of earshot before leaning in to all three scowling Fabs. "Hey, I reconsidered that offer you made me a few days ago. These people are trying to escape the slum. Setting up a meeting on the east side next to the Automart. Seventy-thirty deal?"

Little Fab smiled. "Don't they know? Nothing escapes Crate Town. Fifty-fifty."

On pure principle and to appear realistic, Ella negotiated tough, and finally, finally got a good deal.

CHAPTER FORTY-ONE
Rescue

After the war, Prophus Command removed me from all positions of influence and authority. The Japanese-American Internment was the last straw. By now, after having suffered so many failures and disappointments, and ashamed by the trail of poor decisions and deaths I had caused throughout time, I had given up and was only too happy to accommodate them.

Karl died in peace and in ignominy. I survived the last few years of his life despondent and inactive, and finally, after a thousand years of futility, was ready to give up and possibly give myself to the Eternal Sea. I stepped away from the Quasing war and the world theater in disgrace.

Hundreds of dockworkers congregated at the Bio Comm Array construction site's four main entrances shortly before sundown. There was a group of two hundred at the south gate leading to the primary facility, a hundred at the supply line entryway, fifty or so at the Dumas corridor, and three hundred just above the road leading into the docks. They stayed calm enough at first, merely mingling on the streets and lounging about. That was important. If they got loud too early, the police would disperse them before they caused the necessary distraction. If they started too late, or didn't draw enough attention, Cameron's team would get caught before they got a hundred meters in. No, the dockworkers had to stay under the radar until the signal.

The signal came an hour later.

"Cameron, Dana here. The fish has taken the bait."

Cameron clicked over. "How many?"

"Full line and sinker. Two hundred military. Roughly double that in police. They've surrounded the entire automart. Lots of confusion with the locals. Man, these guys are taking no chances."

"Come on," Cameron chuckled. "Us versus half a thousand? Sounds like even odds."

"Maybe with Dubs. The five of us might have a hard time."

He glanced at Ella and grinned. "We have Ella now. Evens it back up in my book."

Ella blushed and fiddled with the communicator piece. It felt weird stuck into her ear. She wiggled her head and scowled as it fell loose. Cameron picked up the earpiece and turned her head to the side. He looped the wire around the belt holding the string of smoke grenades strapped across her chest and then wrapped it around her earlobe. He gave her a thumbs up. Ella shook her head vigorously. This time, the thing stayed in place. She returned the thumbs up signal and then tapped the button on the piece. "Hello, hello? Can you hear me?"

"Loud and clear, Ella," replied Dana.

"Are the Fabs there?"

"Only the youngest. Wait, the other two are there as well. Oh, damn. There's an Adonis here."

"Is it Shura?" Cameron asked.

"No, the hot guy."

"Too bad. Shura's the more dangerous one. Stay clear of them. Hamilton, status on our extraction?"

"Boat is moored and ready to rendezvous at your order, Commander."

"Everyone's in place. We are a go, team." He continued

giving last minute orders. "If separated, everyone head as close to the extraction location as possible. The boat needs to avoid the coastguard patrols, so you can't depend on front door service." He waved his hand in a circle. The rest of the team, huddled close together, moved across the cluster roof and made their way down the catwalk to the alley on the ground level, and then hurried to the fishing bridge over the road heading into the docks.

"This could be the worst insertion point ever," Jax muttered. "Jumping on top of a moving truck is stupid beyond belief."

"The kids here do it all the time," said Ella.

"The kids here are stupid," he replied.

"Or hungry."

Jax looked sheepish. "Sorry, I didn't mean to be flippant."

Cameron signaled for them to get down as a military truck appeared around the turn a few minutes later. To Ella's chagrin, the truck bed was covered by a canvas.

"You sure you want to come with us?" he asked her. "Last chance to back out."

She watched the rapidly approaching truck. It was rumbling along at approximately forty kilometers an hour. Not too fast, but not exactly meandering either. At least not slow and comfortable enough to jump off a bridge onto. She nodded.

"You kids here are crazy," Cameron muttered. He wrapped his arm around her waist, and then timed the truck's approach. He held his other hand up and ticked down from five.

I do not like this, Ella. If you fall off the truck and break your neck, there will be no nearby hosts to enter. Maybe you should just stay back.

"Maybe you should mind your own business."

Ella tuned Io out. By now, she was tired of trying to decipher everything Io said. She decided she didn't have the energy to figure out what was advice and what was sabotage. In the end, Ella was the one who controlled her body. She was the boss. If the dumb alien couldn't say anything constructive or helpful, then Ella was ready to ignore Io for the rest of her life.

Cameron's grip around her tightened, and then he leaped off the bridge, dragging her with him. The rest of his team followed a quarter-second later. Cameron lost his hold on her as they hit the canopy. The landing was a little softer than she expected. Being so light, she took a wrong bounce and almost tumbled over the side. Fortunately, Lam grabbed her forearm as she tumbled by. A second later, Cameron managed to grab her pant leg. They hauled her back up to them.

"Good catch," Ella said to Lam. Her calm demeanor masked the heart attack she was feeling inside.

"Sorry about that," he replied. "That bounce was like a knuckleball."

Ella didn't know what that meant, but she gave him a stinkeye.

Lam shook her head. "Where would you be without me, Cam?"

"Probably dead in a ditch somewhere back during the war." He looked apologetically at Ella. "And now with one less host under my command."

Cameron signaled to Nabin, who crept to the front and disappeared into the cab of the truck. The rest of them crawled on their bellies toward the back. Ella prayed the truck bed wasn't filled with armed soldiers or guard dogs or something. That would be catastrophic. Sprawled on top of the canopy, they would make easy pickings.

The others held onto her legs as she hung upside down over the canopy and peered in. Fortunately, there was nothing alive inside the truck bed, just several plastic bins stacked on top of each other. She swung inside and helped the others in. They made their way to the front of the bed and hid in the front corners.

A second later, someone, presumably Nabin, rapped twice

and then two more times. Cameron repeated the signal. The four of them settled in and waited, feeling every bump on the road until the truck screeched to a stop.

Ella peered through a narrow gap between two stacks of bins. She heard shouting and tensed, fingering the handle of her long knife, half expecting a bunch of soldiers to jump them at any moment. The truck bed door swung open and a silhouette appeared.

"Wakey, wakey," Nabin said. "We got some friends to breaky."

Ella didn't realize how long she had been holding her breath until she stood and felt the room spin.

Remember to breathe.

"Dork," Lam said, as he helped them off the truck. "Where are we?"

"I had the driver take us to a supply area north of our target. He'll wake tied up with a headache worse than a hangover, but at least he'll wake."

"Keep your heads low. Take out anything that moves, but only shoot as a last resort," said Cameron. "Dana, how's our decoy looking?"

"They have the automart completely surrounded. No one has moved in yet. There's some confusion with the local populace. Mood's getting ugly. The Fabs are starting to panic. Have eyes on the Adonis. The kid looks impatient. God, he has great hair."

Cameron gestured for the others to follow. The truck was parked between a stack of cement sewer pipes and crisscrossing racks of giant steel beams. The five of them made their way south, moving from darkened space to darkened space as the setting sun grew shadows from the tall stacks of building materials.

Ella looked to the horizon. They only had a few minutes before sunset, and they still had quite a way to go. It was a delicate balance between staying hidden and hurrying. Their little ruse wouldn't fool those five hundred soldiers and police at the east side of Crate Town forever. Once they realized they'd been decoyed, they would head straight back here.

Mogg's protest at the gates was unpredictable as well. Sooner or later, it was going to either boil over or get stale and lose the guards' attention. Cameron hadn't paid Mogg enough money for them to escalate the protests to the point of actually picking a real fight with the guards.

Pay attention.

Ella was so deep in thought she missed Cameron drop to a knee and raise a fist. She would have tripped over him if it hadn't been for Lam catching her at the last moment. Red-faced, she fell in alongside Nabin next to a stack of wooden pallets.

"Coming from the east. Three, no, five guards." Cameron signaled Nabin to the right and held up the number two, and then led the rest of them to the left. They reached a crevice and waited as the patrol, rifles slung over their shoulders and cigarettes in hand, strolled down the aisle of construction supplies. Ella slid her long knife out of its sheath and crept to the front.

Cameron held her back with a hand and whispered, "Stay here."

"But–"

He motioned for her to stay put more emphatically. She nodded reluctantly. She wanted to help, not just tag along. It became obvious a few seconds later that her assistance was completely unnecessary.

The poor saps were halfway down the aisle when Cameron, Jax, and Lam ambushed them, taking all of them down quietly within half a second. The two soldiers who were standing further back only managed to sling their rifles around before Nabin hit them from behind. He clipped the first in the ankle when he charged in and then put a chokehold on the second. This bought Cameron enough time to pounce on the first.

Within seconds, all five soldiers were incapacitated.

Now these guys are professionals.

"No kidding." Ella's eyes had widened during the fight. Any illusions she had had that she knew how to fight were dashed when she saw the team at work.

"Tie them up," Cameron said. "Stow them in the sewer pipes."

In the distance, cracks of gunfire punctured the air. The team exchanged looks.

Sounds like at least three hundred meters away. Probably near the gates.

The team picked up the pace. It took them ten more minutes to reach the building where the prisoners were kept. They paused at the foot of the giant Bio Comm Array facility. Cameron and Lam were having a heated discussion.

"We may never get another chance," Lam was saying.

"I don't know." Cameron looked up at the dark structure. "We're pretty short-handed as it is."

"It's a risk, and we may lose lives," she said. "But lives will definitely be lost if we need to send a new team in later on. We need some intel on what this damn building is for."

Cameron reluctantly agreed and summoned Jax. "Change of plans. Poke around in there and upload your findings to Command. Rendezvous at the extraction point."

"I'm supposed to be at the lookout once you break into the building though," said Jax.

Lam looked to her. "Ella can do it."

"Do what?" she asked.

Cameron looked as if he was going to say no, and then, with a sigh, handed her a pair of night vision binoculars. He pointed at the husk of a half-demolished building a few hundred meters inland. "Listen, I need you to head to the top of that building and keep a lookout for us when we go in. It should give you a lay of the land. You can see what's going on outside the building where the prisoners are being kept as well as the front gates. If you see anyone coming, warn us."

"You want to split up?" she gulped.

He nodded. "We need eyes on the protest. If it starts to disperse, you have to let us know right away. This is really important, Ella. Can you do this for us?"

Ella looked at the lookout point, then back at the team. She nodded. "You can count on me."

"Great." He patted her on the back and then signaled to the rest of the team.

Nabin came by and handed her the frequency visualizer. "Keep this on. If you see brown, run. Got it?"

She nodded. "You stay safe. Don't leave without me."

He grinned. "I wouldn't dream of it, on either count."

Their hands touched as she took the small device from him. A thrill shot up her arm. She watched him as he hustled back to the rest of the team. Jax disappeared into the big building a few seconds later while Cameron, Nabin and Lam headed in the opposite direction, leaving Ella alone. She realized how quiet it was all of a sudden, and how dark as well.

Are you going to stand there all day?

She snapped out of it and began making her way toward the lookout building. It was about two hundred meters away through a small maze of machinery and stacks of building supplies. It didn't take long for her to get turned around once she got into the heart of the site and lost sight of the top of the building. She kept going, but pretty soon realized she couldn't tell which direction she was facing anymore.

Make a left at the next turn.

"Are you trying to trick me?"

No, Ella. I have the site map memorized. I can lead you to the lookout point.

"Why are you helping me?"

No sense in wasting time staying lost in here.

"OK, fine." There was a long pause. "Thanks, by the way."

You should probably pay more attention when the grownups are discussing their plans.

"You just don't know when to shut up, do you? We just had a nice moment and you ruined it."

With our relationship the way it is, we had both better get used to this.

With Io providing directions, Ella got back on track creeping toward the lookout point, hugging walls and running along shadows. If it hadn't been for Io leading the way, she probably wouldn't have made it, but until she turned the corner and saw the half-demolished three-walled building, she wasn't sure if Io was taking her to the right place. She ventured inside and scaled the ruin until she found a perch on the third floor.

Ella dug out the night vision binoculars and scanned the prisoner building near the water. She quickly spotted Cameron's team creeping behind a row of cars toward the entrance. Floodlights shone down on the front half of the building and she could just make out two soldiers guarding the front door.

"Cameron," she said. "I'm here. I see you guys."

"Good job, Ella," he replied. "How does the perimeter look?"

She trained the binoculars back on the protest. "It's going, but not as loud or disruptive as I thought it'd be. Mogg's people are slacking."

"Dana," Cameron said. "How's the decoy?"

"The soldiers got tired of waiting and stormed the automart," she replied. "You guys better wrap it up fast."

"No time then," Cameron said. "Lam, Nabin, cover me."

Ella saw Cameron take off from behind cover, charging directly into the light. There was nothing worse than sneaking around in plain sight. Well, maybe getting caught sneaking around in plain sight. Ella's throat caught as he seemed to move toward them in slow motion. This was like watching action movies in the theater, but she knew these people and the stakes were real.

The guard closer to him saw Cameron way before he could close the distance and swung his rifle around. Ella gasped and held her breath. There was a loud crack, and the guard fell. The second guard turned just as Cameron plowed into him. There was a struggle for the rifle that ended with Cameron slamming the guard to the ground and punching him several times in the face. Lam and Nabin followed up a few seconds later.

"That was slow as shit," said Nabin. "Uh, sir."

"I slipped on the gravel," muttered Cameron. "Come on, let's get in and out. You got our six, Ella?"

"Stab Surrett a good one for me if you see him," she replied.

"Nothing would please me more, but I doubt we'll see him tonight," said Cameron. "The minister is unfortunately a secondary objective at this point."

Ella watched as, one by one, Cameron's team disappeared into the room. She prayed she'd see all of them later alive and well. The mission had gone pretty smoothly so far. Too smoothly, in fact. Her gut was making a little bit of a ruckus, and that was never good. Plenty of things could still turn this into a very bad night. Ella hoped it was just in her mind, but somehow, she doubted it.

CHAPTER FORTY-TWO
Race to the Prey

The Prophus sent a young man named Colin Curran to be my new host when Karl died. Colin was a low-ranking operative but a good man, brimming with potential. He had joined the Prophus because he believed that humanity and Quasing could work together to build a better, more peaceful planet. Like me once long ago, he was eager to put his mark upon the world and be remembered throughout history.

And like me, he never did.

To be fair, I held him back. I refused the opportunities offered to him. I just didn't want to try any more, and I never allowed him to seek his own destiny. Like many of my other human hosts, I dragged him down instead of raising him up. I kept him from possible greatness.

He died wondering what could have been.

Shura stared at the black-and-green screen floating in front of her as the three figures moved toward the building. The trap had been sprung. Cameron Tan was about to have a very bad night. She was surprised, but almost everything was going as scripted so far. Well, except for the Prophus team's insertion point. That was something security would have to address at a later time.

At first, Shura had thought the intel she had bought was

bad. The Prophus did not infiltrate the facility at any of the five points she had projected. Instead, they had gone in through the loading dock at the far north end of the site. It was only through sheer luck that one of the patrols had stumbled across the unconscious driver, and then another found bodies in the sewer pipes once they raised the alert.

Shura had to order the entire facility to stand down and let the Prophus reach their target unimpeded. Rurik had overcompensated and taken the majority of their forces to the east side of the slum. At the time, she hadn't wanted to raise his suspicions by asking him to leave more men behind.

Now, there wasn't enough remaining military left to secure the perimeter as well as root the Prophus out to the open space where they could use the construction grounds to their advantage. The grounds were just too expansive, with too many hiding places for the soldiers she had on hand to deal with Cameron and his people.

She had devised an alternate and more elegant solution. Instead of playing cat-and-mouse with an elite military unit, she intended to lure the Prophus to a confined space where they had little room to maneuver and capture them there. The jail holding the prisoners was perfect.

Shura squinted at the screen again. One of her scouts had come across the Prophus as they headed south from the docks and had been tailing them from a distance. They had moved into a blind spot in the shadow of the Bio Comm Array building for a few minutes and then headed directly toward the jail.

Just like the union boss had said.

Mogg had approached her yesterday offering to sell information on an attack to the site. Coincidently, her offer came on the heels of a local fence offering to lead Rurik to the Prophus. She had doubts about the reliability of the fence's information. The two pieces of intel conflicted, so Shura had kept the union boss's offer to herself as Rurik pursued

Cameron at the east end of the slum.

In Shura's mind, splitting to follow both leads was the prudent thing to do in this situation. It seemed her gamble had paid off. In any case, the die was cast. Whoever had the better intel would have the chance to capture Cameron Tan, and then it would be a race to China to giftwrap for Weston. At stake was control of India as well as the Bio Comm Array project.

She checked the other screen floating in the air from the scout still tailing the Prophus team. "I only see three. We lost two of the Prophus when they came out of the shadows. Where are they?"

"I don't have visual, Adonis," the scout said. "Want me to look for them?"

She shook her head. "Stay on the primary mark. Have the team on the ground move in the minute they head inside and apprehend them."

Will ten soldiers be enough?

"Against three? Even with an Adonis? Hmm, I better send backup."

"What about the two missing Prophus?" Kloos asked.

Shura was tempted to ignore them. Capturing Cameron Tan was the priority. However, even though she was pursuing him for personal standing, she still served the Genjix first and foremost. The security and secrecy of the Bio Comm Array facility was just as important, if not more so, than capturing Cameron.

I give you a lot of latitude to seize standing, but Genjix priorities must take precedence. Tao is only one Quasing, no matter how badly Zoras wants him. The Prophus must not be allowed to gather intel on the actual facility.

Shura nodded. "Kloos, take all of our remaining men save five and do a floor-by-floor sweep of the entire facility."

"And the Adonis?"

"I'll take the other five and take care of him myself."

Is that wise?

"Tabs, the team on the ground already has ten. Add these five and me. If the sixteen of us can't capture three Prophus agents, then we all deserve whatever punishment we get."

"The team at the jail will be in position in two minutes. Do you want them to hold until you arrive?" Kloos asked.

Shura considered her options, and shook her head. "No, send them in right away. I'll follow shortly."

She gestured to the men nearby and hurried out of the administration building. The ten men there should be enough to contain the three Prophus agents inside the building. "Should" being the operative word – even against the likes of an Adonis vessel. They were still human.

However, Cameron had a reputation among even the other Adonis vessels as an exceptional warrior, one that most would have a difficult time fighting in single combat. While Shura was considered good by Adonis standards, she had no delusions about matching skills with him. She had no intention of doing either. At least not on even terms.

"Adonis," Kloos buzzed in her ear. "Adonis Rurik has just reported he is returning empty-handed. Minister Kapoor has also called in, demanding to know why I recalled men from the perimeter."

You had better hurry. The minister may try to stop you.

"We should be long gone by the time he returns."

"Kloos, order the minister to stay at the gates," she said. "Prep the helicopter. I want to be up in the air the moment we take the Prophus."

"Your will, Adonis."

The jail came into view a moment later. They were joined by the ten soldiers who took position around the front of the building. With two sides of the building surrounded by water, the Prophus were effectively trapped inside.

"Commander," Shura said. "Take your men through the rear doors. I'll take my five through the front. Capture the

Adonis alive. Kill him and I will slit your throat. The rest I don't care about. When I engage him, do not get involved. He is mine."

"Yes, Adonis," her men replied.

Shura watched as the ten men disappeared around the corner. She motioned for the five with her to move up to the front entrance.

"We hold here," she said.

"Shouldn't we go in, Adonis?" one of her men asked.

She shook her head. "We go only on my order."

What are you planning, Shura?

"Cameron Tan is the Prophus's only Adonis vessel. He's unique, like a black rhino. I want to take him down personally, but I'm not foolish enough to fight him while he's at full strength. I'm sending those ten men in first to soften him up."

Not very sporting of you. You are playing with your prey again.

Shura shrugged. "I want to deliver him to Weston after I personally break him, but not at the risk of getting hurt. I'm not stupid."

She checked her time. "Three on ten are difficult odds to beat as it is, but let's give him a few minutes and see how he does."

Cameron, Nabin, and Lam entered the squat building. Cameron found a working light switch and flipped it. The interior resembled an unfinished warehouse, still only studs, except for three large rectangular holes spaced out in the center of the room, each with a set of closed double-doors at the far end.

"What is this?" Cameron asked.

This looks like a boathouse. They just have not dug to the water's edge yet.

Lam walked to the edge of one of the holes and looked down. "Commander, you have to see this."

Cameron walked to the edge of the hole and followed her gaze. Huddled in the near corner was a person, hands and legs tied, wearing a hood over their head. Jax checked the next hole, and the last as well. There were people in all three holes. Lam jumped down into the first hole and pulled the hood off. The woman looked dazed and her mouth was bound. She cut off the rag.

"Are these our people?" Cameron asked.

Lam cupped the woman's face in her hands. She snapped a finger. "Can you hear me?"

The woman blinked and looked at her. She coughed. "Who are you?"

"Prophus. We're here to get you out. What's your name?"

She looked suspicious. "He… he who hunts two hares."

"What?"

"He who hunts two hares," the woman repeated more insistently.

It is an outdated hostage protocol.

Cameron relayed the message.

Lam snapped her fingers a few times. "Oh yeah. Leaves one and loses the other."

The woman sobbed with relief. "Navah Weinberg. Recon Team Zeta under Captain Kim Kim Lee."

"I found K2 here," Jax called out from the second hole.

Cameron hurried to the third hole and found an older man tied up. He was malnourished and beaten. Old and new bruises dotted his body. The man blinked when he saw Cameron. "It can't be… Cameron Tan?"

"Careful. I'm here to get you out. What's your name?"

"Bijan Baraghani. Field Scout First Class Middle East division."

Cameron smiled. "We're going to get you out of here, Bijan. There's a girl out there worried sick over you." He switched over to Ella's channel. "Ella, we found what we're looking for. There's someone here you'll be happy to see."

This is taking way too long. Get moving. Time for pleasantries later.

Bijan was too weak to climb out of the hole by himself. Cameron had to push him up. Fortunately, he was the only one. K2 and Navah were able to walk on their own.

The captain gave him a broken smile. Half of his teeth had been shattered. "Damn good to see your ugly face again, Cameron."

"Look who's talking," Cameron replied. "We'll have plenty of time for a reunion later." He clicked over to Dana. "Dana, head toward extraction–"

The three double-doors at the end of the room swung open, and soldiers flooded the room. Nabin and Lam reached for their rifles, but were surrounded too quickly to get shots off. Cameron, helping Bijan walk, didn't even get the chance to reach for his gun.

"Damn it!"

Cameron motioned to the others to stand down. They were disarmed and separated. Rough hands grabbed and pushed him to the wall and bent his arm behind his back. Cameron glanced to both sides. Ten against three were awful odds. However, now that the soldiers no longer had them bunched up, he had a chance. He tensed his wrists and waited for an opening.

All right, soldier just past arm's length is a little loose with his rifle while speaking with the one tying your hands. He is also giving orders to the other soldiers. On the go, take him out. Nabin and the three prisoners are to your right, six meters with six soldiers. Lam is to your left with two. The grouping to the right is too unpredictable with no clear shot. Take Lam's soldiers out first. Her arms are already tied, so she will be limited. Watch for the holes near your feet. Ready? Go!

Just as Cameron felt his wrists pulled together to be bound, he twisted violently, hitting the soldier behind him with an upward elbow while at the same time stepping into and trapping the other soldier's rifle close to his body. There was an accidental trigger pull, and Cameron followed up with a knuckle to the man's throat.

Three focused on you.

As the soldier fell backward, Cameron yanked the rifle toward himself and spun, aiming it at the two holding Lam. The strap around the man's shoulder pulled his body toward Cameron, covering his back. Waist height was an awkward way to shoot, so he went for the safe shot at the man further away from Lam. He felt several hard thumps as the soldiers on the other side opened fire and hit their superior officer.

You do not have a clear shot.

Cameron glanced back for a split second and then charged forward.

Nabin and K2 have jumped their guys as well. Navah rammed her guy and they both fell into the hole. They are outnumbered five to two and Nabin's wrists are tied.

It bought him a few seconds. Cameron slammed into the guard holding Lam's wrists behind her back. He got hold of an arm, swung a foot behind the man's heel, and yanked downward. The man fell onto his back, and Cameron dropped a knee onto his face. He turned toward the large melee at the other end, took a breath, and squeezed the trigger, hitting two of his marks.

Risky. You almost hit K2 that time. Get to cover!

Cameron grabbed Lam and shoved her into the hole. He dove in the other direction as a spray of bullets pelted where he had been. He rolled to his feet, danced to the side to avoid gunfire, and charged. Ten meters was a lot of ground to cover when facing the muzzle of a rifle. Fortunately, K2 was clawing at the man trying to shoot Cameron, and Nabin was causing his own brand of chaos even with his arms tied behind his back, throwing his body at anyone close.

A bullet grazed Cameron's shoulder, searing his flesh, and another punched his chest. Fortunately, his armor distributed most of the damage, but it still hurt like hell. He grunted, but his forward momentum let him slip past the rifle barrel.

A high feint and a low punch to the gut stunned the man K2 was struggling with, turning the tables on that melee. Cameron continued onto the two beating up Nabin and watched, horrified, as one of them pulled out a pistol and shot him point-blank in the chest. The bullet went through his armor and out the other side of his body. He staggered and fell.

With a roar, Cameron kneed one in the face, dodged what might as well have been slow-motion punches from the second, and swept the guy's leg. He turned to face the first again just as the man stuck him with the barrel, clocking him on the chin with the butt of his rifle. Another blow came from the other side and hit him square in the nose. Cameron crumpled to the ground.

Your nose is broken. Your lung is bruised. Take slow, deep breaths. Roll left, roll left!

Vision blurry, he saw the faint outline of a rifle pointing directly at his face, and then K2 appeared, grabbing the man by the shirt and pulling him off his feet. Cameron gathered his wits and stood just in time to dodge another slow punch from the second soldier. He grabbed the slow puncher by the collar, shifted his weight and threw him into the nearby pit. He turned and managed to catch a kick as it nailed him in the gut. He shattered the man's knee with his forearm and then helped K2 finish the last soldier.

Chest heaving, Cameron fell onto a knee and studied his handiwork. There were a lot of bodies lying on the ground, unmoving. Shockingly, none of the casualties were his people. A sharp pain shot up his back and he stiffened.

"Are you all right, Cameron?" K2 asked.

"Give me a second to catch my breath." Cameron clutched his chest. "Argh, getting shot is the worst."

That is why most people try to avoid it. You, on the other hand...

"Ten guys in a minute will do that to a man. Your legend grows."

Cameron harrumphed and staggered to Nabin. "You all right there, buddy?"

Nabin grimaced and sat up. He was breathing heavily and bleeding all over the place.

"This could be the first time I've ever been glad for being short. An inch taller and it would've gone right through my heart."

"What did I tell you? Short people live longer."

Nabin grunted in response.

Cameron looked to the other end of the room and called out, "Lam, you all right?"

"You threw me into the pit, Cameron, you jerk. I broke my arm."

"I was saving you from getting shot."

"You still broke my arm."

Everyone is a critic.

"No kidding, right?"

Cameron helped Bijan to his feet. "Well, that's all of them. Let's get out of here before more show up."

He gathered his sad little flock, and together, they limped their way to the exit. Fortunately, all of them could walk on their own, to varying degrees. However, Lam and Nabin had two good arms between them, and the three former prisoners were so weak they couldn't move too fast. Cameron had taken a beating and a couple of bullets, so he only had a little left in the tank. He opened the door and nearly walked into someone.

Shura smirked and punched him in the face.

CHAPTER FORTY-THREE
Trap

While Colin lay dying, his daughter Emily visited me. Imagine my surprise when she asked to become my next host. I accepted, and in hindsight, regretted that decision every day. Whereas Colin reluctantly obeyed my orders, Emily willfully disobeyed.

The young woman was on a mission to become a Prophus agent and to make a difference. No matter how much I tried to dissuade her, she wanted to avenge the death of her friend, Seth, and to fight the Genjix on the front line. She had the fire I once had, all those hundreds of years ago. The unfortunate thing about humans and their short life spans is that they can only fail a few times.

Ella had the protest in her binoculars' sights and frankly was getting bored. It was still going on, but nothing much was happening. Men were shouting and marching and waving their arms. On the other side of the fence, the guards just stood around with their big guns. They weren't even pointing them at anyone. The whole thing had been entertaining for a little while, but now it was just monotonous. All that yelling and stomping wasn't getting anyone anywhere, other than creating a diversion for Cameron and his team. That was the deal with Mogg's people. Still, this was the worst television ever.

You think this is bad? Wait until you work for the Prophus. It is a snoozefest.

"Isn't being a secret agent supposed to be fun, or at least exciting?"

Are you excited or having fun? The Prophus have a way of removing the joy from things. Trust me, I have had to put up with it for eons.

"As opposed to the Genjix, who have a way of just removing the life from things?"

She trained her focus on the soldiers and police watching over Mogg's people. Those guys looked like they were just lounging around. She scanned the crowd. Some of the police were smoking with Mogg's people. What was going on?

Then she saw Mogg, who, with her hands on her hips, was having an animated discussion with Minister Kapoor and one of the police. It was times like this that Ella wished she had a gun. Just put one of those tiny little ones in her hand and bang. "Pow," she murmured. "Compliments of Burglar Alarm."

You are over three hundred meters away. I would be impressed if you could even hit the side of a building, let alone Surrett.

"I thought shooting a gun is just pointing and pulling the trigger."

How little you know. Keep bringing knives to gunfights. See how that ends.

"Ella," Cameron's voice crackled in her ear piece. "We found what we're looking for. There's someone here you'll be happy to see."

She perked up. It could only mean one person, unless the Genjix had been holding her amma prisoner all these years. Had they actually found Bijan? Some of the guilt she had been carrying washed away. "Is he all right?"

No answer.

In the distance, a figure ran to Surrett and interrupted his conversation with Mogg. The minister looked alarmed, signaled to the military people around him, and led them away from the front gates. They were making a beeline toward Cameron.

"Cameron," said Ella urgently. "The minister just left the perimeter. You there? Cameron?"

No response.

A little bell in Ella's head began to ring. Her gut was making a ruckus again, and she felt an itch to do something other than just sit here, but what? She probably should stay put at this lookout like she had been told. She would only get in the way. Yeah, staying put was the smart thing to do. Or maybe she could warn Cameron that Surrett was heading his way with more soldiers.

You should go to them. You should be able to reach them first if you hurry.

"You're just trying to trick me. I'm going to stay right here."

Ella's resolve to stay put lasted for another minute. She noticed Mogg leaning against the wall and having a smoke. One of the union workers strolled right through the gate to speak with her. They exchanged a few words, and then the guy casually walked back outside.

Ella frowned. The guards at the gate weren't doing a very good job. She looked closer. In fact, they were barely paying attention to the dockworkers. One of the police went up to Mogg and she offered him a cigarette. They were acting awfully nice to each other for a supposed protest. Wait, that policeman over there was Inspector Manu. What was he doing being so friendly with the union boss? Shouldn't Mogg be putting on a better act? This was the worst union protest ever.

Ella swept her gaze across the line of dockworkers. Her guys were still making a bunch of noise, chanting and waving their arms, but it all looked lackadaisical and half-hearted. Mogg's people were not trying very hard. She should tell Cameron to ask for a refund if they were going to put such little effort into this. It was almost as if they were just passing time...

"Oh crap," Ella muttered.

The union boss must have sold her services to both sides. That's why everyone was just lounging around. It had to be a trap.

"I can't believe it," she growled. "They're conning my con."

Impressive. This Mogg is a resourceful woman.

Damn it, if Mogg had sold them out, then that probably meant the Genjix knew Cameron's team was here. If this was a trap, then it was all her fault. She was the one who had arranged to use the union boss's people. That meant she had led more Prophus to their deaths. No, not again. She had to do something. She had to warn Cameron.

Now you want to warn them. Maybe you should have listened to me in the first place.

"Shut up, shut up, alien!"

Ella scrambled from her perch and sprinted toward the building with the prisoners, not bothering to stay hidden in the shadows. Several more attempts to call up Cameron, Nabin, or Lam came up empty. Something must have happened. With Io's help, throwing caution to the wind, she reached the building with the prisoners in only a few minutes.

She slowed down just in time to see a group of five or six soldiers enter the building from the front. One of them looked like that pretty scary woman, Shura. Ella hid behind the car nearest to the building and scanned the area. She could hear muffled shouts coming from inside. There were also three cones of light shining from the back out into the water.

Going through the front is probably a bad idea. See if there is another way in.

Ella pulled out her long knife in one hand and one of the throwing knives in the other, and then she sprinted to the side wall. She stayed low and crept toward the rear of the building where the commotion was getting louder. Something big was happening inside. She looked down at the two blades in her hands. Neither looked particularly sufficient for the task ahead.

You think?

"If you can't be constructive, don't say anything."

When I say constructive things, you ignore me.

"That's true. Can you be constructive now?"

If things get rough in there, I want you to listen to me carefully, especially when it comes to breathing. Inhale through your nose. Hold your breath for four beats, and then exhale out of your mouth for four beats.

"What are you talking about?"

Just trust me on this. It will help you stay in control so you do not miss your shots so often.

"OK, I'll give it a try. This better not be a prank." Ella took a deep breath, held it for a few seconds, and then slowly exhaled. Her heart was still hammering in her chest, but it kind of calmed her down a bit.

Also, you do not know what is in that room. Your smoke grenades make a great equalizer. Initiate with them.

"Oh yeah." She had forgotten about those.

Ella took out one of the big canisters and hooked her finger through the pin. She rounded the corner of the building, peeked inside one of three double-doors, and pulled the pins.

CHAPTER FORTY-FOUR
Reunion

By the time I joined with Emily, I had already decided that the Prophus were no longer for me. They never had been. When the Quasing split into two factions, I had joined the Prophus simply because I believed that humanity did not deserve such a heavy hand. I still believe that, but that belief is insignificant in the grand scheme of things.

I have been through so many hosts and seen so many failures that I realize partnership between Quasing and humans cannot be the way forward. Emily did her best in spite of me, not because. We fought every step of the way. It is tragic, because Emily deserved better, and I did not give it to her. In the end, it does not matter; it never did. Humans come, humans go. I have seen this cycle hundreds of times now.

Cameron took Shura's second punch pretty well, but the third on his nose knocked him onto his back. She didn't think she had hit him hard enough to collapse him like that. It must have been broken already.

The prisoner – Lee – tried to shoot her with his rifle. Shura stepped past the barrel and sent him tumbling backward with a kick to the chest. One of Cameron's agents, the Asian woman, attacked her, throwing wide looping punches. Shura noticed the woman keeping one arm close to her body, so she stepped to the side and struck it. The woman cried out and fell back.

Cameron was on his feet again and attacked. She was surprised at his speed, even in his weakened state. The punch clipped her chin, spinning her head to the side, but she recovered immediately and lashed out, striking him on the side of the head and tumbling him to the ground. She drew her pistol and shot one of the prisoners, Navah. She aimed the pistol at the next prisoner and turned to him.

"Do you really want to keep doing this, Cameron?"

"You waited at the door until I dealt with that first group of soldiers, didn't you? That's mighty brave of you." He wiped the blood spilling out of his nose with his sleeve.

"Oh, are you upset you didn't get a fair fight with me, Cameron? How positively antiquated." She chuckled and gestured at the bodies on the ground. "The objective here is not to prove who the better fighter is. The objective here is to prove who the better operative is. Now, stay down."

Cameron tried to stand.

Shura shot him in the leg, and he fell, clutching his thigh.

Shaking her head, she walked around his body and knelt near his face. She looked around the room. "Be proud of what you've accomplished today. That was a beautiful display." She tapped him twice on the forehead with the end of her pistol. "I'm bringing you back to China. Zoras would love to have some words with Tao. It won't end well for you, but we'll have some time to catch up on the way back. Our business has always felt... unfinished."

He coughed and sat up, shaking his head. "Alexandra. I always wondered where you went. You just fell off the face of the Earth. I never in a million years thought you'd be Shura the Scalpel. Why the name change?" He held his hand out. She took it and pulled him to his feet.

Careful. You are playing with your prey again.

"Please, Tabs. This means a lot to him."

"After our little adventure in Oregon, and the unfortunate death of my father, I wanted to start over. I was reentering the Hatchery and my family name had so recently been tarnished. I thought a new name would help give me that fresh start."

Cameron studied her. "You look stunning, just like I remember you."

She smiled. "Thank you. I wish I could say the same for you. I would have been in touch sooner, but I was busy fighting a war. My religion keeps me occupied."

He sniffed and then spat out blood. "When I saw you at that factory, I knew it was you right away. All the memories came flooding back. I was a teenager again, you were by my side, and we were running from the Genjix. It was us against the world. I remember thinking how great it was to finally meet someone who knew what it was like to be a host. I thought I had found a kindred spirit. You were my first crush."

"How precious," she smiled. "Now–"

"Then you betrayed my trust. You shot and killed your father, and you led the Genjix right to our house after we took you in and saved you from the ones hunting you. That's what I remember most. I don't think you changed your name to get a fresh start, Alex. You changed your name because you didn't want to be the girl who assassinated her own father who loved her more than anything else."

It took all of Shura's discipline to keep her face still. A silence passed between them. Finally, she spoke. "How long did you play that little monologue in your head? How long did you practice pretending to say that to me?" She leaned in. "Was it everything you hoped it'd be?"

He shrugged. "No, I actually thought it would mean more. I guess the fantasy of you is much more appealing than the reality." He glanced down at Navah. "She's dead, isn't she?" She followed his gaze to the dead Prophus agent. "Your people should know when to quit. You're going to ask me to release the rest of them now that I have you, aren't you? Oh Cameron, always so soft. I may not need them, but they're Prophus, and if I don't kill them now, they'll just come back, like rats. They will all die in the next few minutes. You should all just accept the inevitable."

"Monster," he growled.

"Now, shall we?" She motioned toward the door.

Shura turned to see a group of soldiers come in through the front door and spread out across the room. The last to walk in was Surrett. He looked her straight in the eyes. The man had somehow grown quite a spine since she arrived.

Be wary. His men are focused on you, not the Prophus.

"A little late, Minister. You're not needed. I'm done here."

Surrett glanced at the prisoners and settled on Cameron. His eyes glinted. "Of course, Adonis. I'm sure Adonis Rurik will be pleased with this development. Now, please transfer the prisoners to me."

"I'm taking Cameron Tan to the Council personally." Shura took a step forward. Surrett continued to block her way. "Step aside, Minister."

"I'm afraid not, Adonis. Adonis Rurik's orders were explicit."

"That fool is on the other side of town chasing the wrong thing. These are my prisoners."

Surrett motioned to the guards, who trained their guns on her.

"You dare," Shura seethed. "Do you realize who you are threatening? I am an Adonis vessel."

"We all serve the Holy Ones," he replied. "I just happen to serve a more important one." He turned to the soldiers around him. "Take the prisoners. Adonis Rurik should be back soon. We'll hold them all until he returns."

Something in the back began to hiss. A second later, a round gray canister bounced once on the floor and rolled toward them. The hissing became louder, and the canister started spewing purple smoke. Two more canisters followed.

A black object spun in the air and struck the soldier nearest to Cameron. The soldier stiffened as a blade stuck into his eye. A policeman near the back of the room clutched his lower back and fell forward. Cameron disappeared as purple and yellow smoke mixed and enveloped the room. Another soldier fell, and then another. Chaos unfolded as the room filled with colored smoke and panicked screams.

There was a flash of a shadow and then a small figure streaked by, slashing another soldier in the back of the leg. The figure stopped long enough to streak another knife out, narrowly missing Surrett.

The minister tried to flee, but Shura grabbed him by the arm. "You forgot your prisoners."

Surrett cringed. He turned to her, his face pale. "Adonis, stop them! What are you doing standing there?"

You probably should.

"Probably, but I don't think I will. I believe it is against the Holy Ones' interests for Rurik to control India and gain a seat on the Council. I also believe this man is not worthy of a Quasing."

You are a hair's breadth from heresy.

Shura pointed at the little girl popping in and out of the shadows. "Who was that girl again? Ah yes, Ella Patel. Minister, you want a Holy One? Why don't you take hers? If you can. I would be careful. She has teeth." She shoved Surrett into the thick smoke. There was a high-pitched scream, and then a thump as his body disappeared into one of the holes.

Alexandra Mengsk, known to the world as Shura the Scalpel, turned, walked out of the room and closed the door behind her as more men began to scream.

CHAPTER FORTY-FIVE
A Girl's Best Friend

I think back to my role as a Receiver, and the immense responsibilities required of me, and I am ashamed by how far I have fallen, when many of those who had small roles back on our home world now thrive on Earth. The pain is overwhelming.

The Genjix turned me a year ago. Emily had come across some rough schematics during a security raid. As a Receiver, I immediately recognized the structure they were trying to build. I contacted Surrett Kapoor through an intermediary and offered my expertise. I told him I would not only be an invaluable asset to the project, but to all Quasing.

The price for that defection is what you have witnessed, with Emily, Bijan, the Recon Team, and Cameron, and many other Prophus. I feel some guilt about what I have done because I know it is wrong.

However, after all these years, I no longer care.

Breathe in. Hold.

Ella crouched in the center of the smoke-filled room, like a spider, waiting for her prey to wander too close. For the first time, she worried that she would run out of knives. She was already down to three throwing knives and her long knife. Fortunately, there didn't seem to be too many soldiers and policemen left. At least she didn't think there were. She could hardly see past her outstretched hands.

Ella had unloaded all six of her smoke grenades in here, which honestly was probably two grenades too many. The smoke was so thick and suffocating, a soldier could have been standing next to her and she probably wouldn't have noticed. She knew she had already cut down several though.

Breathe out. Hold and focus.

The crashing sounds of battle dulled and the loud thumping in her chest became muffled. The smoke stung her eyes and her hand throbbed from a small cut, but she pushed them all to the background. Her nerves hardened as her awareness of her surroundings grew.

A dark object neared. Two legs. Wearing the dark camouflage of the Indian military. She slashed. Once horizontally along the back of the calf. Once upward at the arm that dangled too close to her. She shifted to her left and brought the long knife down on his foot, through the boot and into the flesh. The man howled and fell onto his side. Ella kicked his rifle out of his hands and poked him once more in the shoulder. Then she disappeared, just like Manish had taught her.

Several shouts echoed in the room, pulling her toward them. Ella prayed she wasn't the only Prophus left standing. For all she knew, she could be. She hadn't seen the others when she first charged in, except for Lam briefly when she had jumped on a policeman's back and pulled him to the floor in a nasty-looking headlock.

Ella also saw an older Asian man in rags take a rifle and swing it like a club down on a soldier's face. Ella almost stabbed him before she realized that he wasn't dressed like the others. Her instincts told her to stab him anyway, and she almost followed through, but Io had warned her that the man was one of the Prophus.

"Why did you warn me?" she asked.

One day, you will learn that we are on the same side. If I have to prove it by saving you one mistake at a time, I will.

"It's like you're on everyone's side, you crazy alien."

I am on my own side, which you will discover more often than not will be yours as well. Do not forget to breathe in again.

Ella continued, hoping to either find a friendly face or the minister. She would be happy with either. She found one more soldier struggling with someone over a rifle. Since the military was bad, that must mean the other person was good, so she stabbed the soldier in the butt. It wasn't until after she pulled the knife out and came face-to-face with the person who now pointed a rifle at her that she realized it was Bijan.

She tackled him in a hug. "I'm so glad to see you. I'm sorry."

"Ella? What are you doing here, child?" he asked.

"I came to find you."

He pulled her in behind him. "We can catch up later. Right now, we need to clear this room and escape before more come."

The smoke was beginning to dissipate, and Ella could make out Cameron leaning against the wall near the front door holding a pistol in his hand. She ran over to him. He looked half-dead. His face was swollen with bruises, cuts and angry red marks. One of his shoulders was drooping, and he cradled his arm close to his body.

"Are you all right?" she asked.

He coughed. "Let me tell you. This is the worst vacation ever. I'll live. Thanks for… Hey, where are you going?"

Ella had seen Nabin slumped in the corner and was making a beeline to the Nepalese. She stood over him and froze. There was so much blood. Half of his left side was red, and she couldn't even tell where he was hurt. His eyes were closed and his face looked pale. He seemed so weak, she was afraid to touch him. Was he dead?

His chest is moving. His breath is shallow.

Ella reached for him, and was shoved aside by Lam. The Prophus agent pulled out some bandages from a kit and began to work on his shoulder. She turned to Ella. "Give me some space, girl."

"Hey, Ella," Cameron beckoned. "Do you have your earpiece? Mine fell off while I was getting my ass kicked."

She took hers off and lobbed it to him. Cameron hooked it over his ear and began to bark out orders. "This is Cameron. Package retrieved. Everyone rendezvous at the extraction point."

He took a step and fell to a knee. Ella backed away from Nabin, grabbed Cameron's good hand and helped him to his feet. He grimaced, took a deep breath, and seemed to push all the pain out of his body. He straightened up. "We can tend to the injured later. Everyone be ready to go in ten seconds. Patch Nabin up along the way, or we're all dead. Bijan, you're going to need to walk on your own. K2, take point. You're the only one with two good hands." He put his earpiece back on. "Jax, rendezvous up the coast three hundred meters north of our location. We have to meet up with Dana–"

He suddenly kicked out and swept Ella's legs. She crashed into the ground with a startled oomph and then a crack punctured the air. Cameron fell back, groaning, clutching his side. Ella looked the other way and saw Surrett climbing out of the hole with a pistol in his hand.

Instinct took over and a blade flew out of her hand, striking Surrett's shoulder. He grunted and fumbled his pistol, dropping it back into the hole. He was about to reach for it when their eyes locked. Instead, he got to his feet and fled through the double doors into the darkness.

Ella patted her chest and thigh for blades, but she was dry. With a growl, she drew her long knife and took off after him. She charged out of the building and saw Surrett half-stumbling, half-running north along the shore, fleeing toward a stockyard just on the other side of the parking lot.

You need to learn to retrieve your knives after you use them. You are not going to catch up with him in time. You have a blade left in your left ankle sheath.

Ella sure as gods was going to try anyway. She checked her ankle and was pleased to discover Io had told the truth and she still had a knife to throw. She would need to close some distance before she had a chance to hit him with it. She ran across the parking lot, briefly losing him when he turned behind a cement mixer and between several stacks of wooden beams. She saw flashes of body in the openings as she ran down a parallel aisle. She raised her arm and readied a throw.

No. You will not hit him at twenty meters with your weaker hand while you are both moving. You need to be within ten.

Ella ignored Io and loosed the knife anyway. It missed Surrett by a mile, ricocheting off two cement pipes and falling into the groove between them.

That was your last throwing knife. Pick it up as you pass. Remember Manish's training. Release while exhaling.

She lost precious seconds pawing the gap between the beams for it in the dark. "Damn black throwing knives."

You wanted cool blades.

"Why are you trying to help me nail Surrett?"

Surrett has made many promises to me and has yet to deliver on them. Also, I am starting to realize that my fate may be more tied to yours than I thought. If that is the case, you might as well succeed.

Ella was able to cover the distance she had lost as Surrett tired. He looked back several times, desperation painted on his face. He began to zig-zag, as if trying to throw her off. She wasn't sure what the gods he was trying to do, since that only made it easier for her to catch up.

She switched the knives in her hand, moving the long knife to her left and the throwing knife to her right. She gave it another go, this time aiming for square in his back. She missed again, but managed to strike him in the ass. He screamed and fell, skidding along the ground. Ella closed in for the kill.

Look out to your left!

Out of the corner of her eye, she saw a flash, and then felt a hard impact, and then she was flying in the air. She landed on the gravel with a hard thud and rolled along the loose rocks. She groaned as a large figure approached.

"Black Cat, always causing problems," a voice said. A moment later, Inspector Manu's face appeared in the dim light. "Why am I not surprised?" He raised his feet up in the air.

Roll left.

Io's voice in her head was deafening. Ella followed the order on instinct even as she tried to clear the cobwebs from her head. Manu's foot came down with a crunch, followed by another, and then his baton struck the ground.

Ella found a bit of space between her and the rampaging inspector and scampered to safety. She reached for her long knife in her waistband. It wasn't there. She must have dropped it when Manu ran her over.

"Kill her, inspector," Surrett barked from off to the side. He was lying on the ground still holding his thigh, struggling unsuccessfully to stand. Ella scanned the ground and retreated as Manu swung his baton.

Your knife is to your right four meters away.

She tried to make her way in its direction, but the inspector cut her off. He was faster than he looked. She dodged as he came in, this time diving to the ground and coming up with the knife in her hand. She wielded it like Manish had taught her. In a way, the familiar stance helped calm her nerves as she zeroed in on her opponent.

Watch his eyes. Remember his reach. He is also wearing an armored vest.

"Why are you helping me get him?"

Because I do not relish having Surrett or Manu as my host. You are not as weak as I thought you were, and at least I know what I am getting with you.

"Little cat has claws," Manu chuckled. "Be careful, or you'll cut yourself."

He lunged. She juked right. Upward slash on his left triceps. Downward stab on his shoulder, and then a parting thrust against the back of his vest that didn't do any damage as she stepped out of range.

Manu looked at his bleeding arm and growled. The inspector attacked again, although this time, it wasn't nearly as aggressively as before. Their weapons clanged together, and he surprised her with a left-handed slap that stung her face, sending her tumbling to the ground.

Hang onto your knife!

Ella did, and got back on unsteady feet.

Move left. Back, back! Watch for the stack of concrete blocks behind you.

Ella did as she was told until she could clear the ringing in her ear. She and Manu began circling each other. He came at her with a jab. She sidestepped. Downward slash to the right wrist. Upward stab across his armpit. Finish with a follow-through across his hamstring. Manu staggered on his feet and dropped his baton.

Ella went in for the kill, putting both hands on her handle and thrusting the knife into his chest, right above the armor. It sunk in and Manu howled. He managed to get a beefy hand around her neck. She pushed harder. He squeezed.

Ella felt the world blacken as she gasped for air. She could feel her strength ebb away, but she could feel him weaken as well. As a last-ditch effort, she summoned what little strength she had left before passing out and twisted the blade. Manu screamed, his throat gurgling as he let go of her. He smacked her across the head a few times, each time weaker, until he finally collapsed to the ground.

Ella heaved forward and fell on top of him, driving the knife deeper. They both fell over, and she rolled off, gasping and coughing for air. She felt woozy and tired. A nap sounded wonderful right about now. She closed her eyes.

Ella, you have to get up. Get up. Surrett is still nearby.

Io had just said the magic words. Ella's eyes flickered open and she sat up. Her breathing came in short, hard gasps, and her arms shook when she put any weight on them. She looked at where she had last seen Surrett. He was no longer there. He couldn't have made it too far with a knife stuck in his ass.

No. Let him go. It is not worth it. You still have to escape. Get up. Go.

Ella rolled onto all fours, and got to one knee. A blur came at her just at the edge of her peripheral vision, and she felt her body crunch as Surrett kicked her in the ribs. He hit her so hard, she lifted off the ground. Ella fell onto her back, stunned, the breath knocked out of her. She could only watch helplessly as Surrett walked over to Manu and pulled out her knife. He came at her slowly, limping.

"So much trouble caused by one little street rat," he growled. "Well, I would have preferred a Holy One with higher standing, one that hasn't been tainted by the betrayers, but yours will have to do."

He stood over her and raised the knife. She saw the glint of the metal and the sharp point in the air above her. He brought his arm down at her chest.

There was a loud crack and Surrett spasmed. The knife fell from his hand and nearly skewered her anyway, but it managed to fall harmlessly to the side. Surrett looked down at the growing red stain on his chest, clutched it, and fell over.

The last thing Ella remembered before passing out was Jax running over and scooping her in his arms. She managed to mutter something about not forgetting her knife. She faintly remembered being jostled as he ran, carrying her like a babe, and then she saw flashes of faces, the swaying of water, and the wind as darkness swept over her.

EPILOGUE

It seems no matter how much I try to save my kind, I fall far short. I believe my influence has done more damage to humanity and to the Prophus than not.

My failures on Earth far outnumber my successes. In fact, my one real achievement is not one at all. I have been foolishly measuring success by my hosts making their mark in history. That is the wrong metric. Real success is taking the Quasing closer to reuniting with the Eternal Sea. In that regard, I have failed utterly.

I have become disillusioned, not only with the Prophus and the Genjix, but with our methods as a whole. I believe there is a fundamental flaw in our philosophy here on Earth. It has been right in front of me the entire time. That flaw is humanity. How can humans be the key to taking us back to Quasar? I realize that if we are ever to see the Eternal Sea again, we must do so on our own.

I know now. Humanity is the wrong vehicle for progress.

Shura stood before the wall-screen, head bowed, eyes on the floor. Standing a few meters away, Rurik was in a similar pose. Both appeared properly chastised. The only difference was Shura was smirking inside. Hovering in front of them, appearing larger than life, Weston ranted as he paced back and forth in the air.

"Let me get this straight. The Prophus rescued the prisoners directly from under you. They killed our handpicked operative who we were grooming to be the future prime minister of India. You riled up the local population to the extent they're now in full revolt. And, to top off this gross display of incompetence, you didn't even capture Cameron Tan. Is this correct?"

"Yes, High Father," said Rurik. "We believe Cameron Tan is still in this country. I am confident we can still locate him. As for the regional upheaval, this problem is isolated–"

"Isolated?" Weston roared. "Kloos had to call up two more divisions to quell the revolt. All of Surat is now under martial law. The prime minster of India called me in the middle of the night demanding answers."

Shura considered raising her head and saying something. She peeked at the Russian. To his credit, he was only sweating a little.

No, not a word. Let this play out. Do not get caught in Rurik's crossfire.

"High Father," Rurik gulped. "There have been some issues with the local populace, but the project has made significant gains as well. The Bio Comm Array facility is ready to begin tests this week, putting us a month ahead of our original schedule."

"Do not play loose with the facts with me, Rurik. The only reason the project is ahead of schedule is because I sent Shura to save the sinking ship." Weston pounded a few keys in the air. "There is also the matter of the cost that the Indian government is billing me. What happened?"

"I exercised what I considered proper judgment in containing the Prophus," said Rurik.

"Yes, according to Shura, you required eight hundred additional police and four hundred military just to keep the populace from descending into riots, and then you were tricked into taking most of them to the opposite side of the slum while Cameron Tan strolled into the site and rescued his people, and probably took his time walking the grounds and gathering intel for the Prophus."

Rurik looked as if he were going to respond, and then thought better of it. He bowed his head.

So undisciplined.

"Indeed, Tabs."

Rurik tried to recover. "There have been setbacks, yes, but Shura's report has only highlighted the negatives."

"Highlighted?" Weston stopped pacing and stared Rurik down. He switched his gaze to her.

"Shura, do you factually stand by your report? On your status as a vessel?"

She lifted her head and raised her chin. "I do, High Father."

"Have you embellished anything in order to paint a more negative narrative, providing anything other than the facts?"

Say you do not believe so. Give yourself some space to maneuver.

Now was the time to be bold. "No, High Father," she said clearly. "On my continued status as a vessel to my Holy One."

The die is cast now.

"What did you tell me, Tabs? Standing must be seized."

Weston turned to Rurik. "Do you challenge Shura on the facts of her report?"

The challenge hung in the air. As Adonis vessels raised in the Hatchery, there were codes to live by. Rurik had painted himself neatly into one with his life on the line. "I... No, High Father." Rurik shot her a look of death.

Weston turned to her. "Shura, can you fix this mess? Can you quell the locals, push the project forward, cut the cost bleed, and complete India's integration into the Genjix?"

Weston was demanding a lot with his simple question. A dozen caveats popped into her head. The entire region was unstable; no amount of money could buy off the local government. The Chief Minister of Gujurat had already petitioned the prime minister to shut down the entire site.

Not to mention the Genjix no longer had anyone in power to operate on their behalf in an official capacity.

Shutting or moving the site was not an option. Not only would it be catastrophic in terms of time, cost and manpower, it was actually unfeasible. There were few locations on this planet more suited to the Bio Comm Array's purpose than this one. In fact, the Genjix would likely rather go to war than lose it. There was also the risk of these problems cascading across all of India and loosening the Genjix's grip on the country.

In the end, Shura kept her answer brief. "Absolutely, High Father."

Weston nodded. "Very well. India and all of its responsibilities are yours until you fail me. Succeed and you may contest for a seat on the Council. Fail and, well–" he glanced at Rurik, "–you had better watch your back."

The screen went blank and left the two of them alone in awkward silence. Rurik rounded on her. "You've stolen from me, daughter."

"I don't think so, brother." Shura emphasized that last word. "Our standing in the hierarchy is now equal. You're right about one thing though. We were never on equal footing. I don't need my family to stand taller than you."

He took a step toward her. "Don't think for a second I'll let you get away with this."

Shura met him halfway. "Are you sure you want to make your move here? Now? Without the authority or your bodyguards at your back?" She leaned in until their noses nearly touched. She could feel his hot breath on her face. "Do you remember when I nearly drowned you to within an inch of your life? Just because I could. Afterward, all you did was cry and run to the safety of your family name. Well, this should be a familiar sight then. Go on, slink back home."

For a second, Shura thought Rurik was going to actually attack her. She shot him a contemptuous smile and dared him to throw the first blow. His face had turned crimson red and his nostrils flared. His chest heaved up and down, and the veins on his neck bulged. Then, with a snarl, he took a step back. "I'll make you pay for this."

"You're playing out of your league, Rurik. Now, if you'll excuse me, I have a lot of cleaning up to do. Someone made a mess. You had best return to Russia to make sure you still control it."

Shura watched as Rurik stormed out.

That was inelegant. There may have been a moment of reconciliation between you two, but you have made a permanent enemy. There were several ways you could have approached taking control over India. Russia is a much more powerful and influential region than India. Wresting the last Council seat from him will be difficult.

"It wouldn't have mattered. I made an enemy of him twenty years ago at the Hatchery when he spoke ill of my father and I sent him to the infirmary."

I warned you at the time not to make an unnecessary enemy. You just cannot help yourself. It has come back to haunt you.

"You were right then, you are probably right now. Personally, it was worth it. For now, let's worry about the problems we have on hand. We have an uprising to quell, a high profile facility to run, and a country to subjugate. We can worry about the future later."

Shura walked back to her desk, put her hands on the table, and studied the map of the site and of the surrounding city.

Ella, wake up.

As if on command, Ella opened her eyes and watched as the sleek black plane approached the highway. The top of the sun was climbing in the east, and it glazed the land with just enough morning glow to see the aircraft descend from the sky. In the distance, a line of burning sparklers blocked the road. Thank gods there weren't any cars on the road at this time.

The small group had fled east along the Tapi River for the past twenty hours on a small craft Hamilton had obtained. They had hidden under a canopy in the sweltering heat, and through a combination of bribery and luck, had managed to evade the patrols going up and down the river. Dana had also managed to make contact with the Prophus, and an extraction team had been dispatched.

Now they were hiding in a small grove of trees just south of the river along Highway 16, and waiting for their rescue to pick them up. Ella didn't know how to take everything in. It was so surreal. She had never even considered leaving Crate Town, let alone India. The future ahead was terrifying.

"I'm really leaving my home, aren't I?"

Yes.

"What happens now? Will I ever come back?"

That is up to you. Consider it a fresh start. You can do whatever you choose.

"All right. Hey, Io? You helped me last night, I probably wouldn't have made it without you. Thank you."

You are welcome.

"I won't be in Crate Town anymore. I have a feeling I'm going to need some help moving forward. How about a truce?"

Our last truce did not last very long. How about a fresh start?

"Depends. Are you still going to try to join the Genjix?"

I do not know anymore. Maybe. I can be convinced otherwise. It depends on what our future has in store for us.

"I'm glad you're being honest at least. You know I won't let you."

Why not take our relationship one step at a time? You keep my secret. I will keep you alive, and we can try to be on the same side.

"I'm on the Prophus's side."

No, Ella. You are on your side. I am on mine. Let us be on ours. Just like we were back in Crate Town.

"All right."

Jax appeared a second later. "We have to hurry. I don't know how long those flares will stop traffic."

"I want that transport up in the air in sixty seconds," Cameron added.

"Come on," Dana said, helping her to her feet. Ella groaned as a sharp pain shot up her chest. She looked to either side of her. Lam and Hamilton were supporting Nabin. Jax was helping Cameron to his feet. Bijan and K2 were carrying the gear. Everyone looked positively half-dead.

Hamilton noticed her looking, and nodded. She nodded back. She still had a lot of making up to do with her auxiliary. Was he still her auxiliary?

That depends on him. If you end up training at the academy, he will probably roll off to someone else.

Ella wasn't sure how she felt about that, but she was pretty sure she'd feel bad. She hoped this wasn't the last time they'd work together. In the end, she couldn't have survived without him.

The group, all eight survivors, left the cover of the forest and hobbled across the mustard field to their ride home. They were greeted halfway by Prophus agents who escorted them to the plane. Ninety seconds later, they were airborne again.

They were met by an intense-looking Asian man with a disheveled black beard and long graying hair tied up in a samurai bun. He was shorter and barrel-chested, and his wrinkly raisin-face sported a stern demeanor. No, not stern, pissed. He had his arms crossed and eyed each member of the team as they passed.

He nudged Lam in particular. "You were supposed to take care of him, not let him do dumb shit."

"You know how he gets when he's on one of his kicks. It's your fault, anyway," she replied.

"Hi, Dad," Cameron said.

Ella gave a start. "Io, that's his dad?"

Roen Tan. Prophus liaison to the allied governments, and husband to Jill Tesser Tan. And Cameron's dad.

"It's like a family business. Shoot, I really could have ransomed Cameron for a lot of money."

You blew your big payday.

"I did raise him, I guess," Roen conceded. He scowled at Cameron. "You're supposed to be on vacation."

"I'm having a blast," Cameron said. "Can't you tell?"

"Mom got wind of your spending spree. She's put a hold on your account, and says we're both grounded until your fortieth birthday. Somehow, it's my fault too." Roen grabbed his son in a rough embrace and the two sat down. "You look awful, by the way. Who kicked your ass this time?"

"Alex."

Roen's eyes widened and he whistled. "Really? You finally run into her, eh? I take it the reunion didn't go too well."

Cameron pointed at his busted up face. "What do you think?"

"Did you find what you were looking for?"

"Yeah, we got the guy who caused Seth and Yang's death in Greece… a decade ago. By the way, he happened to be a high-ranking deputy minister. Tell Mom she may be getting an official complaint from the Indian embassy any minute now."

"Damn it, Cameron. I'm in enough trouble as it is."

"Also, we found something else. It's called the Bio Comm Array facility. We don't know what it is, but it's big. I sent Jax to gather intel. We're uploading to Command now."

Roen took a quick headcount. "You're missing one."

Cameron's face fell. "Lost Dubs in an ambush."

"His body?"

"Stowed in a bath house. Can we retrieve it? He's got a wife and kid, and five dogs."

"Damn it. India's a tough nut to crack, but we'll go through diplomatic channels and make it happen somehow." Roen glanced her way. "Who's the girl?"

Cameron smiled. "This is Ella Patel. She's the one who made everything possible. She took care of my people and helped us nail Surrett. She also saved my life a few times."

Roen shook her hand. "You have my thanks. Welcome to the family."

"She's Io's new host," Cameron added.

Roen paused, the meaning of that sinking in. "I see. I'm sorry about Emily."

The two continued chatting. Their back-and-forth felt good-natured, and she could hear the love and concern in their voices and words, even as they poked fun at each other.

It gnawed at Ella a little. This sort of bond was something she had never had, and she found herself yearning for something, anything, remotely like it. She thought about all the people she had left behind, the few that cared about her. "Io, what will happen to my friends, Coach Manish and Aarav, Wiry Madras, and the Fabs?"

Manish is an ex-agent. He and Aarav will be all right. They will likely just go dormant until called back to duty. The Prophus will send someone to check up on Madras. She still has Dubs. The Prophus do not leave their own. As for the Fabs, they tried to sell the Prophus out. They are on their own.

Ella decided to leave the father and son alone and made her way to the back of the plane, where makeshift triage had been set up. Just about everyone else was back here, injured in one form or another.

She found Nabin propped up on a cot. He patted the adjacent cot next to him. "Have a seat."

She lay down and looked out the window. "I've never been on a plane before. Well, I have, but I was like five and so scared I slept right through it."

"Stick with me, kid," he said. "We'll introduce you to a bigger world with all sorts of new people who will want to kill you."

She laughed, which was a mistake. She clutched her ribs

and took several deep breaths. "Stop trying to be funny. It hurts." She became more somber. "So what happens to me now?"

"Cameron says he wants to send you to the training center in Sydney or the one in the States. Are you all right with that?"

"Train me to become an agent like you guys? I don't know how I feel about that."

"Well," Nabin said. "It's up to you. You may have a Quasing in you, but you still get to decide what you want to do with your life. The Prophus will work with you one way or another. Being an agent has its perks."

"Io says training takes years and I have to have a roommate and I won't be able to leave whenever I want. Is that all true?"

"Pretty much."

"Then I don't know if it's worth it. I'm my own boss."

"Well, Australia is our team's home base of operations. If you enroll, you'll get the training you need to fight the Genjix, to avenge your amma and your dog. You get to help a lot of people and protect the world from some bad aliens."

"That sounds like a lot of work," she said.

"You'll also get to hang out with me more, I'll come visit every chance I get."

She eyed him suspiciously. "Really? Promise?"

He grinned and held out his hand. "Maybe."

Ella laid her hand over his. "OK, fine. Now, let's talk about my stipend. The Prophus were paying me..."

The plane was halfway across the Indian Ocean before Tao opened Cameron's eyes. After nearly three decades of wear and tear, thousands of hours of combat, and dozens of injuries, the guy needed beauty rest.

The two of them had been in bad positions before, and this ranked up there with the worst of them. Stranded in enemy territory with the ocean to their back and a blockade in front. Cut off from the Prophus and facing not only the local military but heavy Genjix presence. Toss in another Adonis vessel – Alexandra Mengsk, of all people – and this was as dicey a situation as he could remember Cameron being in.

Tao looked over at the sleeping Roen slumped next to his son, and realized that Cameron was reaching the age that Roen had been when Tao first joined with him. Roen was probably pissed as hell, but oh well. Some things had to be done, and killing Surrett and discovering this strange Bio Comm Array facility were two of them. Something about the shape of the main building, the dome top and the curvature of the supporting threads nagged his memory. It was from something in the distant past, not a moment from his time on Earth.

In any case, Cameron had made it out in one piece; that was what was important. Jax and Ella nailing Surrett meant a lot to Cameron personally, but uncovering this Bio Comm Array facility was the real score. Surrett's death delaying India from joining the Genjix alliance was an added bonus.

There was just one more thing that had to be cleared up. Tao glanced over at Ella, or at her Quasing, specifically. Their paths had only recently crossed when she had joined with Emily. That wasn't unusual though. The world was a big place, and the Quasing were scattered. Io's situation was unique in that she had arrived to the game late, having not occupied her first human until the eleventh century. By that time, Tao had already occupied hundreds of humans.

A thousand years wasn't a lot of time for a Quasing to become adept at working with a human. They were complex creatures. Guiding them to achieve greatness required skill, guile and intelligence. And patience. Lots of patience. With every successful host, a Quasing likely had experienced hundreds of failures.

Some, like Io, were still waiting for their first taste. Tao had spent some time looking through Io's record before they had come to India. She was one of the few Quasing who had somehow blundered her way through history without ever leaving a mark, and still survived. She had always been a peripheral player in the Prophus's war with the Genjix. Until now. It was time for answers.

"Io."

Ella's eyes fluttered open. She sat up. "Tao."

"Come with me." Tao got up and moved to the front of the plane. He looked back to check if Io was following, and whether she was armed. She was, incidentally. The girl was never far from her knife. That was one of the things he liked about Ella.

They entered the arms locker in the middle of the plane. Tao closed the heavy gate behind him. He faced Io and folded his arms. "I know you are the leak. You are trying to defect to the Genjix."

"How can you say such a thing?" Io said. "I have lost as much as anyone. I have been with the Prophus for over a thousand years, and with Emily and her father for over a quarter of a century."

"Much to their misfortune."

Io contorted Ella's face. "Not all of us can be the great Tao with his bloody footprint burned across history like Sherman across the South. How much good has your mark done for this planet? I wager my ineffectiveness has done less damage than all your empire-building and razing. Or do you consider creating mystical slow-motion fighting a benefit to humanity?"

Io was baiting him. "Hamilton told me how Ella was uncooperative in regards to your surveillance efforts. He went out and recorded his own footage. I compared it to the reports you uploaded to Command. The discrepancy and intent between them is obvious. You tried to wash the data. If there was an available team in the region, they would have swept you out weeks ago. However, I believe you are acting alone. The girl is innocent."

"Did Hamilton also tell you how he stood there and did nothing while Emily was killed by a squad of Genjix?"

Tao nodded. "He admitted that too. Once this mission is over, I will have him transferred out of the auxiliary corps and moved to an administrative position."

"That's it? He lets Cameron's best friend die and gets moved to a desk job, yet I am accused of treason when my host is killed on a mission? I, who have done everything in my power to try to take us home?"

"Do not play stupid," Tao replied. "Nobody faults a Quasing for their host's death unless it is intentional. You know, once I return to Command, I will get to the bottom of this. It will not be difficult for me to request a full audit of your movements and communications. The truth will come out."

Io remained silent and looked away. That was all the answer Tao needed. The guilt was palpable, but there was something else. Something redeemable, possibly. It was an opening at least.

"Io, when the Quasing split into two factions during the Spanish Inquisition, why did you join the Prophus? We were the smaller, weaker, marginalized faction. We all knew what we were signing up for when we turned our backs on our people. Our side was terrorized and imprisoned for hundreds of years before we were able to recover and coordinate. Why did you join us?"

Io shrugged. "I believed in the cause. I have been around as much as any Quasing. I have seen the destruction the Conflict Doctrine had done to humanity. I too have lost those I cherish as our species pushed humans into constant war in the name of innovation and evolution. It was the right thing to do at the time."

"Is it the right thing now?"

Io nodded.

"Do you really want to join the Genjix, Io?"

There was a long pause. "No. I am unsure."

"Then why would you betray us? I know you care little for wealth or power. You suffered alongside the rest of the Prophus in our darkest times. You fought alongside us when we were constantly on the cusp of total collapse. Now, for the first time in over five hundred years, we are nearly equal in strength with the Genjix. Of all those times, why do you desire to switch sides now?"

Io froze. She stayed in place for so long that Tao thought Io might have retreated deeper into the body. He waited patiently, keeping an eye on the girl's hands. It did not reach for a blade. That would be a terrible mistake on Io's part.

Finally, Io looked him in the eye. "Did you know that back on Quasar, I was a Receiver?"

Tao was so stunned by this revelation that he nearly lost control of Cameron. The body tipped to the side and would have fallen over if it weren't for the armory's mesh wall. A titled Quasing meant Io was formerly one with extraordinarily high standing.

Tao had never paid much attention to the time before, and most Quasing records did not survive the crash. Back on the home world, Tao was an insignificant drop, one of the trillions of Quasing who lived in the Eternal Sea, with little purpose except to serve as a conduit and move with the masses when the collective will required something from them.

"You were one of the voices in the black?" he asked.

"The strands that bind all empire." There was a great deal of pride in Io's voice. "We were the part of the collective that formed and administered the communication arrays between all our planets. My counterparts and I kept the Quasing as one. I was the Receiver assigned to our Carryall."

It all became clear. Titles were not easily achieved among their kind. Io must have worked hard to become a Receiver. She was formerly high in standing, a leader among the millions of their kind on that ill-fated ship, and it must have been difficult to have it all swept away. Now, cut off from the collective, the Quasing trapped here were forced to build a new hierarchy and find their own voice. Some, like Tao, had blossomed, while others, like Io, had struggled.

"On Earth," Io continued, "I struggle to make any mark. The hosts I inhabit have always been forgotten. They are only remembered through me. The few remembered are ridiculed. I'm tired of failure, Tao. I'm tired of being nothing."

The failure must be a bitter pill. Pride and ambition were uncommon traits among Quasing, but it was not unheard of. That may be because Tao himself, back on the home world, had nothing to be prideful about. He had never even thought to attempt to become something more. One needed pride and ambition to achieve standing and title. He was content to be one among the trillions and bask within the Eternal Sea. He just happened to be the portion of the Eternal Sea willed on board the Carryall, one of the millions of filler, conduits, and building block used to adapt and suit the needs of the collective.

However, Tao did strive for more once he came to this planet. Maybe he had found pride and ambition in humanity, and they bled those traits into him, but he did become something greater and found his own voice once he was here on Earth. Tao imagined how he would feel if he returned to the Eternal Sea again and lost everything he had found on this planet: his individualism, the knowledge he had obtained, the memories and achievements, his friendships. He thought about Cameron and his father, Roen, and then back to the thousands of his hosts he had shared a connection with before. To lose all of them would be equally shattering to him as it was Io. Interesting how the tables had turned.

The two of them fought for opposite things but for the same reasons, and, because of that, Tao understood Io, and felt compassion for her. However, it still did not make her actions forgivable. He shook his head. "And you think joining the Genjix gives you an opportunity to finally make a mark?"

Io laughed. Coming from a Quasing with poor control over her host, it came out clumsy and wooden, forced. "No, Tao, I am not like you. I know where my skills lay and where they do not. I wanted to defect to help develop the Bio Comm Array. That would be my mark."

"What exactly is this thing?" Tao asked. "How will you make your mark with it?"

Io looked Tao in the eyes, and for the first time, Tao saw a sign of life, focus, intent. "The Bio Comm Array is a communication device. Once completed, we will be able to contact our people. I will finally serve my intended purpose to the collective. I will save the Quasing here on Earth."

The words Tao was prepared to say next stumbled on Cameron's tongue. He was stunned by the significance and ramifications of what it meant if the Genjix were able to establish communication with Quasar.

If the home world was to receive word that there were Quasing stranded here, cut off from the rest of their kind, they would investigate. The Prophus and Genjix war would end. Tao could stop struggling after all these millions of years and finally return to the collective. He could once again bathe in the warmth of the Eternal Sea and become one with his people. It was what he had wanted ever since he had arrived.

The rescue would come at a price, though. Carryalls would soon follow, and with them, billions more of his kind. They would harvest all the resources, and then envelop the surface with the Eternal Sea so it would be suitable for Quasing life. In doing so, they would doom all other life on Earth.

Acknowledgments

Today is July 9th.

I'm sitting in a hospital room. I haven't slept in nearly thirty-six hours. The only things I've eaten so far are two donuts and a small bowl of soup. I may have had a cracker or two, I don't remember. Everything is a haze. I am dead on my feet. The love of my life is in pain. It's hard to watch, and there's nothing I can do except be present and share in the suffering. I also think I threw out my back breathing heavily.

Today was a hard day, and it was amazing.

I have always believed that each of us has a calling. We were put on this Earth for a purpose. Mine is to write books. My novels are my life's work. They are my identity and my legacy for the future.

That changed today.

Today, July 9th, at 8:03 PM CST, my son, Hunter Yusing Chu, was born, and it's the best day of my life. He has a kung fu grip and a set of cathedral-sized pipes. The first time I changed his diapers, he let me know who was boss by peeing on me. He is quite the marksman.

I have never felt the instantaneous need to protect and love and nurture anything in the world as much as I do right now, typing these acknowledgments while my son sleeps. He's not even a day old and I will happily never write another word and toil at the worst jobs if it means his happiness. Everything

I have ever worked for, I now do it for Hunter.

I hope he is one of the first astronauts to go to Mars or he discovers the cure for cancer or he becomes the writer I aspire to be. I will do anything to give him the opportunity to find his own purpose in life. He can be whatever he wants to be, as long as he is happy.

To my lovely wife, Paula, the love of my life, thank you for this gift and letting me share this journey with you. You are a wonderful mother. I'm just glad he has your brains and your looks. I hope he develops your kindness and generosity as well. And probably your killer sense of style and sharp wit. While we're at it, he'll be better served with your patience and temperament too. Let's just give him most of you, and my uncanny ability to keep running into things and not get hurt.

To Paula and Hunter, this book is for you.

About the Author

Wesley Chu is the bestselling author of both the Tao series, and *Time Salvager* and its sequel. He won the John W Campbell Award for Best New Writer and his debut, *The Lives of Tao*, won the Young Adult Library Services Association Alex Award. A consultant and corporate drone in his past life, Wesley is a kung fu master, a member of the Screen Actors Guild, and recently returned from climbing Mount Kilimanjaro. He lives in Chicago, USA, where he spends his many hours during the Great Lake winters writing and hanging out with his wife, Paula, young son, Hunter, and their Airedale terrier, Eva.

wesleychu.com • twitter.com/wes_chu

"Few books begin more engagingly than *The Lives of Tao*, a science fiction romp which wears its principal strength — the wit and humor of the narrative voice — on its sleeve."

The Huffington Post

"Wesley Chu is my hero... he has to be the coolest science fiction writer in the world."

***Lavie Tidhar, World Fantasy Award-winning author of* Osama**

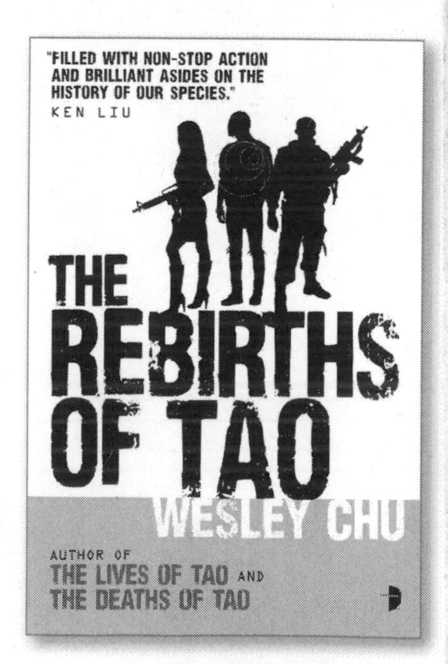